SHARPSHOOTER

WAR MAGES

Arron Owen

Cover Illustrations Copyright © 2024 Arron Owen
Cover design by Ken Dawson, Creative Covers Ltd
Editing by Sarah Dronfield
Proofreading, Line and Copyedit by Magic Pencil

War Mages:
SHARPSHOOTER

(This First Edition)

A Ricasso Independent Press Publication

ISBN: 9798385842612
Paperback
ISBN: 9798385843770
Hardback

To all who put themselves between us and War's desolation.

To Absent Friends.

Miracles do not, in fact, break the laws of nature.

C. S. LEWIS

CONTENTS

PROLOGUE:

MONDAY, 11th AUGUST, 1919. 0303Hrs

Alarm bells rang out across Antwerp's fortified containment wall, spurring the Imperial German Army to man their positions. A network of crenellated battlements, machinegun emplacements, field phones, searchlights and anti-aircraft cannon awaited any intruders. Dozens of highly trained men, armed with the finest weapons and equipment, spilled forth onto the wall, only to stand there gawping and powerless.

A zeppelin, enwreathed in flames, was on a collision course with the remnants of Antwerp Cathedral. Losing altitude rapidly, it dived towards the containment walls, ready to collapse on itself at any second, back broken. Landing lines snagged momentarily on the parapets, but any attempt to grasp the cables dangling from the balloon was as pointless as it was suicidal, as the cables whip-cracked free.

Rotor engines growled, protesting against fate, the remaining crew fighting to prevent hellfire raining onto those below as the massive envelope was consumed. The airship fell inexorably into the heart of the Antwerp Exclusion Zone, illuminating the last vestiges of stained glass in Cathedral, before brutally crashing in a screech of metal and a thump of air. The beached, blazing whale, crumpled before rolling to starboard.

A dragon's throat roared, belching dark red fire and choking black clouds as the canvas torpedo exploded, marking the pre-dawn in the prison city.

1:

The constant downpour would kill him if the enemy didn't. To prevent either, Daniel Archer wiggled his toes in his boots, forcing life into feet aching with cramp. The mud was almost solid around his unmoving joints, thanks to the heavy clay in the spoil heap. The trench it was excavated from was below, to his front, and he could hear the large drops of rain pattering onto the steel helmets of the sentries from the Canadian 4th Division.

Careful scanning of the enemy parapets revealed several trench loophole plates the Germans used, the distinctive shapes marking their jagged line. Unlike the British or Commonwealth trenches, with sandbags regimented and squared off, the enemy positions were deliberately uneven and untidy. It allowed plenty of places to snoop or shoot from that a casual glance would miss.

The mud fought him as he carefully panned his weapon across the kill zone, body pivoting by increments, the weight in the rough hessian smocking his rifle and telescopic sight increased through sheer damp. The glass itself was a Hensoldt, one of the best, taken from a prisoner of war who shared Archer's trade of calculated, efficient slaughter.

He mentally checked the loopholes against the sketched map he'd drawn over the past three days of observation. All carefully prepared and properly sited, but none had been used during his deployment, yet the solitary Mauser bullets had still whistled overhead. The Canadians called Third Army HQ for help with this very capable German sniper, but here he was on day four, still with nothing to show for it.

Desperation had driven him to crawl from the trench early in the morning, using an Allied artillery barrage for cover. Archer was certain the bulk of the loopholes were decoys, because the enemy weren't idiots, but if he was wrong someone would end up with their head blown off – and it might even be him. The wind shifted the rain, subtly changing the angle of sickly dawn light where it struck the enemy line.

There. That had to be it.

Covered in mud and rags; the newly observed loophole was adjacent to the mangled remains of a British Mark IV tank. The assault vehicle was destroyed completely, the carcass not worth recovering, just another corpse on the Western Front. It was perfect to both shelter and conceal the metal sniper plate, which lurked four-hundred yards from the Canadian line, rising at an oblique angle, providing a good command of the Allied trench immediately opposite. It was impossible to see from the prepared periscopes or blinds, and any *Tommy* sticking his head up for a peek would have more than a headache.

Professional courtesy stirred Archer's admiration as he prepared to make war. Immediately behind and to his right was a shallow crater filled with stagnant water, and he kept a careful distance from it. It would provide cover if he had to dismount in a hurry. It smelled of old earth and silt, thankfully not rotting corpses.

The smocking sniper robes he wore were sodden, but worth it – this part of the front was a melange of soil, blasted timbers and sandbag parapets. With any luck, his shape would blend into the environment, the canvas smock with sewn on ragged hessian strips hiding his shape, and dyed carefully to fool the eye. Archer peered out through a stained scrap of scrim covering his face, waiting, ignoring the absolute discomfort now the real hunt was on.

Commonwealth soldiers below and to the left of his chosen spot, were oblivious to his presence, save for a couple of their officers who knew by necessity. Generally unimpressed by his patched and scrappy uniform, even they gave him odd looks on arrival, but his scoped rifle; complete with its intricate camouflaged sleeve stalled any questions.

Surprisingly, the rain ceased, and not a minute later, the loophole he was watching gradually opened. The furtive motion sent a buzz through his body, banishing the ache and lethargy. Wondering what had tempted the enemy sniper, a slight tilt of the scope dipped his view to witness three Canadians having a smoke.

The first man had already struck the lighter, and mere seconds separated his comrade from death. Knowing time was short, Archer let his rifle come back up with a slight shift of his body. He re-sighted, slipping the safety off, keeping his finger well out of the trigger guard, a round already chambered. He took a deep breath, felt the tension pulling on his left arm from the sling keeping his rifle stable, and expelled the air slowly, steadily. Crosshairs bobbed up and down, the target a boat floating on the rolling swell.

Focusing as taught, the strange power flowed from him, and down into the mechanism of the rifle. Part Lee-Enfield, part magic staff, he felt the energies build until the weapon could hold no more, a bowstring creaking, the waiting bullet like an arrow nocked tight against his ear. A twitch behind the loophole told him the German had chosen a victim. The lighter's flame snapped for a second time. On the third, a fatal shot would follow.

It needed to be his.

Breathing in again, this time he held on the exhale.

When he squeezed the trigger, the *Runebolt* shoved hard into his shoulder, months of practice on the Sniper School ranges, shooting at balloons and Papier-mâché replicas of human heads, told him it was a good shot. A blinding lance of blue witch-light speared towards the enemy sniper, flooding the landscape with a strange azure haze in passing, and the immediate tang of ozone. The beam connected with a thump of displaced air, followed swiftly by the sound of a struck, wrought-iron bell. It echoed across no-man's land, fading quickly into eerie silence.

Watching through the scope after the shot, and giddy from the exertion, Archer released the half-held breath. He ignored the outbreak of panicked calls from the allied lines, men rushing to prepare rifles and mortars to repel an attack, but the threat from the Germans was gone for now.

Blasted skyward, the loophole plate finally landed a hundred yards from where it originally stood, now with a fist-sized hole punched through it, molten edges still glowing orange where the shot went home. A prone body was revealed; the upper torso bifurcated into a flash-fried, smouldering ruin.

Archer dismissed his gruesome handiwork, feeling the sympathetic heat from the wooden stock, warming his hands for the first time for several hours. He felt a stab of guilt that it eased the ache in his fingers. The German snipers would be wary about poking their heads up for a while. He knew any sniper could have done this job with an Elephant gun – but HQ sent him to make an example and cheer up the lads.

Groaning, before he extricated himself from the mud gluing him to the ground, he snapped the safety back on without cycling the action. It kept the dirt out, and prevented accidents. Satisfied he wouldn't shoot himself, he crawled down toward the relative security of the Canadian trench, calling out to prevent nervous men from shooting him.

'Friendly coming in! Captain, are you there?'

'Hold your fire, men! One of ours!' the Canadian officer called, 'Come in Corporal, the kettle's on!'

Slithering to the edge of the trench, Archer dropped inside, close to the would-be smokers. He pulled back his sniper hood, and met their stunned stares. He looked at the man with the lighter. 'That'll kill you one day.'

The soldier's attention strayed to the rifle, lingered on it without saying anything. Ignoring the glance, Archer had nothing but a hot brew on his mind as he turned for the command dugout, but one of the men behind him grunted.

'Bloody murderer.'

'Bloody *Warlock*,' one hawked up and spat.

Phlegm spattered the duckboards near Archer's feet, but didn't fall on him, unlike the common accusations with it. He wondered if they'd add 'freak' as well, but the contempt infesting the taunts rendered it unnecessary. The spitting served two purposes – to slander, and ward off evil.

Gratitude didn't exist in this line of work, or for his kind. To fight was the job of a soldier, taking life in the heat of battle, but a sniper picked a man, and killed him in cold blood. Seen as quite unsporting, it set him apart. Being an Arcanist doubled his damnation. He levelled a stare over his shoulder, past the muzzle cap of the *Runebolt*. He would never find out who'd said it, but the glare would forestall further incident. Soldiers were a superstitious lot, and a meaningful glance was enough.

The immediate disquiet was smartly punctured. 'Corporal Archer?'

Turning, he found himself staring at a man decked out in a thick flying jacket over his officer's uniform. Sturdy goggles rested on the brow of a lined leather cap, thin face dirty from the cheekbones down, brushed with soot and cinders. Archer didn't salute. An airman was a prime target, even if the sneaky bastards opposite minding their own business after a good zapping, there was no reason to risk it. The pilot smiled, knowing, steady brown eyes too old for his youthful face.

'Sir?'

'Flight Lieutenant Jackson. Get all your kit and follow me.'

'I'm standing in it, sir. Where are we going?'

'Oh, you're a lucky lad. Third Army, Corps HQ, urgent.' Jackson grinned.

The sun rose to his right as the Bristol F2 biplane lifted off. The golden rays were warm, but as the aircraft popped and sputtered its way aloft, Archer's damp clothes were instantly chilled by the rushing air. He eyed the soggy mess of his camouflaged outfit, glad he'd stripped the robes off, but not looking forward to cleaning them.

A borrowed scarf and flying helmet at least warmed his head and neck, the fleece cap muffling as he crouched awkwardly in the observer seat. His kit was trapped between his knees in a vain effort to stop it smashing his legs, and a safety belt tugged at his waist. With white-knuckles, Archer clamped his hands onto the mounted Lewis gun, and anywhere else that felt sturdy enough as the pilot sawed them around the sky.

'Keep an eye out for Fritz!' Jackson called.

'Why? Have you stolen his fare?'

Flight Lieutenant Jackson laughed at the poor joke, working the controls of the aircraft.

Combating his growing nausea, Archer scanned the skies, mainly to keep his eyes off the rapidly shrinking landmarks. Trained in a different kind of observation, it was all the same underneath; spot the odd shapes, movement, or any slip of light from a man-made flat surface. The clouds had settled into spun gauze, ribbon thin and weightless, as the aeroplane levelled off.

He cast his gaze out, over the lines of trenches stretching away into the distance, a giant zip, or maybe a scar, cut into the flesh of the Earth. Stretching all the way from Switzerland up to the French coast, it was an incredible feat of engineering and misery. He spotted what he took to be a vulture, circling the battlefield he'd just left, until it powered against the wind, and the sun betrayed the length of wing only an aircraft possessed.

'Ware behind!' Archer yelled, straining against the harness to shake the shoulder of the pilot.

Jackson's head swivelled briefly. 'Good eyes! Be a dear, and man the Lewis?'

The output of the engine moved up a gear, increasing the strange noise that accompanied a propeller under strain.

The aircraft pitched right, going up in a hard turn to evade the raptor streaking down to tear them apart. Archer's *Runebolt* was next to useless here; weight of fire was the order of the day. He seized the Lewis gun.

Not even qualified on the infantry version, with its distinctive cylindrical cooling jacket and shoulder stock, this thing was an amalgam of tubes and rivets, with what appeared to be spade handles bolted to it. The difference was stark, and finding the cocking handle took a moment. Seizing it, he charged the gun, giving the bulky pan magazine a brief glance as it chugged round, settling the first .303 cartridge into the breach.

With only heartbeats before their opponent was on them, he wrenched on the Scarff mount, surprised at how easy it was to manipulate, before pointing the automatic gun in the direction of the enemy aircraft. The Bristol Fighter pitched and thrashed as they fought for altitude, the stink of engine fumes caught at the back of Archer's throat, the *pap-pap-pap-pap* of linked enemy machineguns reached his ears a moment after the snap-crack of bullets they spat.

Jackson's desperate dodging meant the attack missed anything vital, especially the vulnerable flesh of the crew. The bright red plane flew by them, searching for a better angle of attack. The colour and markings hadn't escaped the pilot. 'It's Manfred!' he shouted. 'Give the Baron some breakfast!'

Heart sinking, Archer didn't need telling twice. He allowed the swooping crimson plane a generous lead with the light machinegun as the Flight Lieutenant took further evasive action. A chattering stream of red tracer fire sliced harmlessly into the blue sky, the bullets tumbling short of the enemy plane. His first dogfight was going to be a lethal learning curve.

If Archer could ride, he suspected this was what a runaway horse was like; the beast cantering across uneven ground, just wanting to be free of the rider. It certainly didn't resemble the illusion of considered, artful acrobatics he observed from the trenches when there was an air battle.

He deemed the chief quality of being a pilot was a cast-iron stomach.

Displacing the fear of falling by shooting at the Red Baron, the brilliant crimson Fokker biplane painted a superb target against the infinite backdrop. Yet despite changing elevation, or point of aim by desperately flailing the Lewis like a fly-swatter, hitting was proving frustrating. He cursed himself first, then the gun; despite the lively recoil, it was a dead thing in his hands, so unlike his own rifle. In mockery, the German Ace once again filled the air around Archer's head with bullets.

The spank and snap of rounds perforating the fuselage, scant feet from Archer's position gave him little warning, sparks fizzing as the sizzling incendiary gunfire careened off the Lewis gun, ripping large holes in the ammunition pan. Archer threw the weapon up, shying away when the dinner-plate sized magazine detonated in a bright flash, wrenching the mount and gun loose as shrapnel cut the bungee cables. Black smoke began to billow from the fuselage where it burned.

'I think we're done, old boy,' Jackson said.

Yet he didn't give up, gallantly pitching left and then banking right, presenting a hard target for the opposing pilot. The engine sputtered and groaned as though it had been gassed in a chemical attack, choking on the fuel that kept it alive. The rattling was uneven, the ripping noise of the propeller rising and falling in pitch as the airman postponed the inevitable.

Archer watched the Red Baron come back around, positioning to counter anything the brave airman tried. No longer wanting to empty his guts, the sniper was exceptionally annoyed at the easy, almost smug, dismissive manner of the German's manoeuvres.

'Can you get him to line up right over our tail again, sir?'

'Are you mad?'

Archer managed to grab the *Runebolt*, hands tight

so not to drop it in the maddening yawing of the plane, showing the weapon up close. Now unwrapped from the clinging hessian, the rifle's differences were apparent to the uninitiated.

Jackson gave a startling whoop of appreciation. 'An Arcanist, eh? I'm game if you are! Alright old man, give it your best shot!'

The smoke was a problem at first, but the Bristol slid slightly to the right, and the trail was perfect. Archer's determination to reward the pilot's willingness grounded him. He gauged the distance, feeling the change of wind on his face, trapping the rifle against him by slipping his arm through the sling and taking up tension. He focused hard, the rifle alive in his hands, absorbing the rushed power greedily, until the markings and embellishments on the bolt-action and body were glowing warmly. The agile red gnat behind them buzzed into his iron sights, the scope safely away in his rucksack.

He squeezed the trigger even as the biplane shuddered beneath him, trying to stay aloft under the damage wrought. It dipped again from the pressure of the shot discharging. The beam screamed into the sky, punching a perfect hole through smoke and clouds. The ozone set his teeth on edge for a second time that morning, before being whipped away by the wind. He expected to see a fireball tumbling to the ground, the great Von Richthofen dying in a blaze of Arcane glory.

Archer's finest, greatest kill.

Except the bastard *wasn't* dead, because the plane had *dodged*.

'Bloody hell! Did you get him?'

'Not yet, sir,' Archer growled, dismissing both the incredible feat of piloting and sheer improbability of what he'd just witnessed in favour of pure survival. Gripping the bolt handle between finger and thumb to let it pivot smoothly, he jerked it back and forth for another shot. One way or another, he vowed to bring the Baron down to earth.

Richthofen approached from starboard, drawing

parallel with the stricken Bristol Fighter. He levelled out, flying into close formation, crimson wings two yards from those of the British plane. Archer could see the port side of the Fokker carried a long slash of burned and blistered paint, running along the fuselage. So then, he hadn't *quite* escaped. Grey smoke fluttered thinly from the tail.

Waving and shouting to indicate a ceasefire, Richthofen pulled his goggles up to expose a face printed on a thousand newspapers and posters. Despite the dirt and powder smoke staining his face, he grinned at them both.

'You fly beautifully, Englishman, but the victory is mine!' His voice carried smoothly and confidently over the churning of propellers. He informally saluted Jackson, offering another to Archer. *'Herr Kriegsmagier*, maybe next time!'

Banking away to starboard, he was gone into the distance, rapidly dwindling to a speck as quickly as he'd attacked. The Bristol began to protest at the suffering imposed on it, clanging and banging out a death rattle of machinery. The stop-start noises became almost continuous.

'Better land while I can,' Jackson shouted over the sputtering engine. 'Hold on!'

The aircraft's propeller cut out shortly after; Archer heard the flutter of the wing canvas, and recalled bed sheets snapping on a washing line. His momentary dislocation was abandoned as the green fields below rushed up at him. The pilot yanked back on the stick at the last second, the nose flaring, and a heartbeat of silence was broken by thunder as the undercarriage bumped and rolled across the ground. Clods of torn grass thudded into the wings and body, undercarriage ploughing ruts in their wake.

When the Bristol stopped, Jackson vaulted free with practiced ease, but Archer's legs were leaden. Fouled by the tangled equipment around his legs, he fell out, landing with all the grace of a sodden sandbag. He wiggled his fingers and toes, thankful to be down and alive. Even though the engine was off, the droning from the propellers carried on inside his head, drowning his relief in beehive noise.

With effort, he picked himself up, arranged his gear over his shoulder and stumbled after the Flight Lieutenant, who shielded his eyes to get his bearings, before checking his revolver. He doffed his flying helmet and goggles, before tossing floppy brown hair loose with fingers still wrapped in thick leather gloves. He clumsily fought for a compass and map, getting his bearings, before pointing. 'Manfred put us off course, but our lines are that way.'

'Yes, sir.'

Archer followed the outstretched hand, rolling hills and trees fading into the distant farmland. The sun was shining, birds chirruped and the late morning dropped into somnolent silence. The march would dry out his clothes at least, and he set off without thinking, feeling the loneliness that came from being an Arcanist. His dark mien, and the pastoral scene, was interrupted by the thud of distant artillery.

Jackson let out a long, low whistle. 'Anyone would think there's a war on. I say old man; wait for me – Fritz is about!'

2:

Once they'd found the communications trenches on the right flank of the New Zealand Division – and hadn't been shot as deserters or spies – Third Army HQ dugout was a brisk march over well-trodden duckboards, and the Flight Lieutenant took the lead. They passed through shallow trenches cut into the chalky soil of the reserve area, up into the sturdily built battle zone, and the heavily fortified command bunker.

A brace of Brigade officers sheltered within, red collar tabs bright at their throats. Even in the poor light from storm lanterns, Archer could detect the strain in them. Younger faces carried dark rings around their eyes, idle fidgeting betraying tension. The handful of older men in the clutch moved with weariness, and false vivacity in retelling well-worn jokes. He was thankfully too far away to hear them, but knew the polite smiles all too well.

Large, mismatched chess pieces carved from wood, stained in both red and black were holding down the map corners and bits of paper that held old orders, handwritten lines hastily scored out. Ruddy coloured pawns strung along the Western Front made Archer think they were stained with blood instead of dye.

All the way to the dugout, Jackson babbled either about aircraft, using his hands to demonstrate daring aerial manoeuvres, or where he'd been drunk in France. Archer let him talk, finding him surprisingly personable for an officer with the equivalent rank of an Army Captain; but here, apart from a friendly nod, the pilot's enthusiasm was stilled to silence.

In the din and bustle, the newly arrived pair went

almost unnoticed. Like all soldiers forced to wait for inspection, Archer took the opportunity to tidy his battle order. Listening with half an ear, he absently felt for the stock of his *Runebolt* – or at least that was his name for it. Slung over his right shoulder, the solid presence of the rifle was reassuring, an old friend. Without him, it was useless. Without it, he had no purpose.

Commissioned by the Royal Small Arms Factory at their Arcanist Works, he imagined the carpenters spending long hours carving the unfinished stock of the rifle with hand tools, each cut made to conform to a careful diagram before Ministry certified Magesmiths pressed ensorcelled metallic inlays into wood. Each was matched to his magical Discipline to manifest his gift into this magic wand, this...*focus*. Once handed over to the Holland & Holland gunsmiths, they chose the best components for the deadly assembly, finished the weapon and tested it. Finally, it received a magical Runic proof-mark, to certify it was ready.

It was a masterwork of technology and art, of skill and soul.

One of the staff officers moved out of the way, startling him from the daydream, and he recognised General Sir Julian Byng. They'd met twice before, but Archer doubted he would be remembered, he was just one face in a sea of muddy khaki. His sniper smock was rolled up tightly, trussed to the bottom of his pack, so to casual eyes he was just a regular *Tommy*.

Their gaze met, and a broad, but lopsided grin broke out from under a thick, well-maintained moustache. Byng came towards them and the Flight Lieutenant, now once again with his boyish locks trussed under his flight helmet, got his arm up in salute. The General returned it, but transformed his down stroke into a smart open palm, which the pilot took after a moment.

'Have a good flight, Jackie?'

'It was rather exciting, actually.'

'Oh?' Byng's eyebrows convulsed.

'We got caught by the Baron, in his new Fokker.'

The pilot relayed what happened in close detail. The officers eavesdropped, at first pretending to shuffle papers, then just listening in rapt silence. The conclusion of the tale caused them to look at each other, the final details eliciting a long sigh from the General.

'Good show, my boy,' Byng reassured the airman, 'get some rest. You can leave 'Curtains' with me.'

'Sir.' After exchanging salutes, Jackson shrugged and departed immediately.

Archer groaned inwardly when the General used his acquired moniker – in his experience, upper echelon bonhomie meant trouble. Perhaps Byng was being nice now, because he was saving up to be nasty later. He tried to puncture his cynical misgiving by saluting and offering his best bark.

'Corporal Archer, reporting as ordered, sir.'

Byng returned the salute just as briskly, looked him up and down. It would have been impossible to miss the dried mud and chalk stains from crawling around on the Western Front before the crack of dawn, but he ignored it. 'Have you eaten, lad?'

'Not recently, sir.'

The General took him by the elbow and steered him to a table with plates of sandwiches roughly cut into triangles, but in defiance of commonly held trench belief, the crusts were still on. Mugs of congealed tea stood on parade at the end of the table. Someone handed Archer a plate, and he duly loaded the picnic fodder onto it, trying to ignore the fact there wasn't much bounce in the bread, and the scent of bully beef betrayed the rudimentary cuisine. Byng patted him on the shoulder encouragingly as he gobbled, seizing one of the cups in turn, and jamming it under his moustache for a slurp. He instantly spat it out, face twisted in disgust.

'Good Lord! Who made this?'

'ADC Astor, sir.' An amused Public School voice replied from the back of the dugout.

'Hmm, Haig's cousin,' Byng mused, swirling the cup, staring at it. He drank again, with a genteel, but hesitant swallow. He couldn't hide the grimace. 'Did he brew it from old socks and axle grease?'

'Don't know, sir.'

'You're a Staff Officer, Corky. You should.'

A good-natured sigh prefaced the response. 'I shall enquire, sir.'

'We could shell Fritz with this, and end the war. What do you say, Curtains?'

Archer said nothing, chewing and polite nodding let him sidestep the game. If he was a condemned man, he was having breakfast first. He was already on his fourth sandwich. Manners seemingly suspended for the luncheon, he attacked another.

The General was stalling, and it wasn't just the taste of a bad brew in his mouth, or to let Archer get a bellyful of beef. Seeing he was getting nowhere, Byng allowed the sniper to finish before offering a rueful smile. 'Alright lad, no need to eat us out of house and home. Step through here.'

He led Archer through a short tunnel and into another chamber of the underground lair. This was dominated by a huge map pinned to boards on the wall, attended by a Major. Archer caught the rank tabs at the cuff, following the arm up to the shoulder flashes for the Artists Rifles. On a small table in the corner, the peaked cap displayed a badge with twin heads of Mars and Minerva – the Roman God and Goddess of War.

Eccentricity warred with starched regulation in the rest of the man's uniform. In handmade brown riding boots and tailored, slender jodhpurs, the man stood squarely facing the map. Hands clasped behind his straight back, trapping a crumpled letter in his left fist. An issue Webley was holstered at the officer's hip, the lanyard a loop around his right shoulder.

The Major rocked from heel to toe in a gentle sway, abruptly stopping as the two men entered, twisting around to look Archer up and down. His gaze struck the stock of the *Runebolt* before moving on. The lamps in the side chamber guttered, making the room gloomier and more oppressive than the first. The earthy smell of spade-cut soil and burned lamp-wick were a familiar mix in the enclosed space.

Byng tugged a blanket curtain shut, separating the two halves of the dugout.

'This is Intelligence Officer Garfield,' he introduced them, 'Garfield, this is 'Curtains', he had a run-in with Richthofen today.' His voice lost some of its presence as it was absorbed by the tomb-like walls.

'Interesting...' Garfield replied, pursing his lips. 'Did you kill him?'

'Maybe next time.'

The Major half turned, frowning; Archer found himself staring into a face that probably didn't frequent the warm climes of humour often. He'd never heard of the man either, another bad omen, since he knew most of the Intelligence Officers active along the front. Snipers were wont to move between sectors, and established faces were a routine sight; this was an HQ man, a signature on warrants that sanctioned executions the same way it ordered stationery.

'What do you know about the Antwerp Exclusion Zone?' Garfield snatched a tack from the edge of the map and stabbed it firmly into the body of roads and rivers that formed the walled city of the Belgian port town.

Archer licked his lips, momentarily wrong-footed. His interaction with Intelligence officers, plus the news-rags from England only gave him some of the picture. 'Not much, apart from rumours, of course.'

'Which are?' Garfield demanded.

'It's a prison for deserters, free to do as they please.'

'Almost,' Garfield replied, a curl growing across his clean-shaven lips. 'It's a German Reprisal Camp for POW's and wayward Arcanists – like you.'

A reply was expected, but Archer didn't bite.

Major Garfield lifted an eyebrow at the truculent silence, but didn't comment. 'Early this morning, an airship was shot down over Antwerp by the Imperial German Air Service. A handful of Americans are now trapped inside. We believe the Ambassador to France is one of them.'

'You believe?' Archer blurted. 'Who reported this?'

'Reliable agents within German command, civilian observers in Belgium.'

'Not the Americans?'

'Not directly. They released a statement which all but confirmed it.' Garfield nodded, pivoting to regard the map again. 'Your job is to rescue the Ambassador, his aide if possible, and the documents they carried.'

'What the hell were they doing flying over the AEZ?'

The staff officers shared a glance.

'Nobody is saying,' Garfield replied, tight-lipped.

To Archer it was more admission than evasion, the man probably didn't know. He continued probing. 'Have the Americans asked us for help?'

'No,' Byng said. 'However, doing so puts the United States in our debt. A significant favour owed, perhaps.'

'More War Bonds?' Archer asked, but their faces showed it didn't ring true. He tried again. 'An expeditionary force?'

Garfield met Byng's eyes. 'Not just a blank file. Good.'

The way the Intelligence Officer said it gave Archer a sinking feeling, the same as when he stalked through craters in no-man's land. The mud was treacherous and the water deceptively deep. This was a quagmire waiting to take him under, so he thrashed for a branch to pull free.

'Sir, even if the passengers are still alive, how am I supposed to get in? The AEZ is miles beyond our lines, surrounded by a German Heavy Siege Corps. It's suicide.'

Garfield slowly span on his heel so he was face-on; drew up to his full height – a good four inches on Archer. He pocketed his battered letter carefully, drawing out the theatre. 'Are you refusing?' His voice was dangerously soft. 'You've got

Special Dispensation to be out here, haven't you?'

Archer glowered, knew where *this* was going. As an Arcanist, the law provided a choice: live in the purpose-built facility on Rannoch Moor for the safety of the public, or use his talents against Britain's enemies. He'd signed up in 1915; desperate to get away from constant tests and studies, the painful isolation of whitewashed prison walls, incarcerated for an accident of birth. His parents passed on more than good cheekbones and sharp eyes.

'You'd have to be replaced, of course. Your younger brother, maybe even your sister, under Paragraph seventeen. They're rated Third Class by the Manville Codex, but still.'

The Dispensation was another reason Archer was out here. As the strongest and eldest, he'd chosen the lesser evil to keep his siblings safe from War Ministry clutches, and their bloody *Codex*. Compiled by the English Doctor Frederick Manville in 1875, it identified and assessed an Arcanist's power, and streamlined their abilities into broad brushstrokes of the *Disciplines*. It was a cornerstone of how the British Establishment treated Archer's kind.

How he hated that book.

Despite hands curling into fists, his temper held. These threats weren't the usual Army browbeating; Garfield was laying it on thick because Archer would be far from the beady eyes the Army kept on Arcanists, and they badly needed his compliance for something utterly vital. As the notion dawned, Archer relaxed, realising it was a chance he couldn't afford to miss.

'No need for that, Charles,' Byng warned, 'Curtains knows the score.'

'If you say so, sir,' Garfield tipped his left wrist, pulling the cuff back to examine his watch. 'Any questions?'

'Not so much a question, General,' Archer said, carefully. He deliberately drew Byng into it as he broached the idea. 'This sounds like a big show. I'd like something in return, for services rendered: a guarantee.'

'You're in no position to negotiate, *Corporal*.' Garfield sneered. 'It's an order!'

'I can decline suicidal orders, *Major*. Paragraph ten.'

Garfield's eyes narrowed. 'Fancy a dawn firing squad, eh? It can be arranged.'

'Enough,' the General said. He didn't raise his voice, but authority in it filled the tight quarters. Silence parted the angry men, and Byng let it draw out painfully, carefully watching them.

'Sorry, sir,' Archer said, staring at the floor, admonished. The General's almost paternal demeanour spurred the sudden absence of his father. He half-expected a large, calloused hand to ruffle his hair in forgiveness.

'Your pardon, sir,' Garfield grunted, coldly.

Perhaps sensing it all, Byng swept his moustache left and right with a practiced finger and thumb. 'It has been a trying morning, gentlemen. Speak freely, Daniel.'

'I'd like amnesty, for my family.'

'But you'll stay?'

'The Dispensation ends when the war does.'

'And that might be sooner, rather than later?'

Archer allowed a wintry smile.

The General's steady gaze filled with appreciation. His jaw worked side-to-side as he considered the appeal, the freshly groomed lip-fuzz contorted, a pet seeking a place to sleep. 'That's...not outrageous, given the circumstances. The Field Marshal has the final say officially, but...alright, agreed.'

Without thinking, Archer put his hand out to shake on it. Byng looked at him, and he was suddenly aware of the social disparity between them, but the General grinned, grasping the hand gamely, pumping his arm with a vigorous tug. He felt the weight on his shoulders increase as he realised he needed to push the suggestion to more than a gentleman's agreement. 'I'd...like it in writing, sir. If you don't mind?'

Byng let out a bullish, braying laugh. 'In the King's own hand presumably! Listen lad, just do it right. Field Marshal

Haig will hand it over – once you've done the job.'

There was nothing comforting in that statement. Maybe that was the point.

'Go to Harley Street. Wait until I send for you,' Garfield told him.

Archer saluted both officers and got out, heading for the largest dressing station in the rear zone, the final line of battle before the landscape spilled into uncut green fields, and the illusion of peace.

Byng sighed, pushing into his pockets to produce a cigar case and gilded lighter. He lowered himself to a small wooden seat next to the table in the corner, pushing Garfield's cap out of the way as he withdrew and fired one of the expensive cigars. Wisps of smoke and rich aroma blossomed into the dugout whilst Byng stared at the map on the wall, measuring Antwerp with the gaze of an experienced campaigner sizing up his battlefield. Garfield had no doubt the General could see the city in his mind's eye.

'No need to be so hard on the lad, Charles. Especially not one I like.'

Garfield clasped his hands behind his back, rocking on his heels once more. Byng hadn't been playing a part; the sobriety of the dressing down in front of the Arcanist sniper was unexpected. 'I'm doing my duty, sir.'

'I appreciate that, but there's no need to be a prat-arse about it. Vinegar and honey, man.'

'I doubt Archer prefers either, but I must protest.'

'Oh? That's unlike you.'

Garfield ignored the sarcasm. 'Giving amnesty robs us of a singular resource. If word gets out, well, they'll all want it.'

'*They* are people, Charles, not *things*. By God, Vimy Ridge taught me that the hard way. Thankfully I'm in charge here, not the bunglers at the War Ministry!' Byng flexed his shoulders, tugging the hem of his uniform blouse to straighten it. Calm order restored, he continued. 'Besides, the motivation of our agreement will push young Daniel on.'

'And you'll honour it?'

Byng dismissively blew a stream of smoke, gestured with the cigar. 'Eton was good to us both, but you forget yourself. Do you think your ruffians can really do it?'

Garfield didn't answer immediately. Archer just one player in the team he was assembling, with the most to lose. If the General was right about the amnesty, Archer would see to the success of the mission one way or another, and hopefully pull off a coup to persuade the Americans to enter the war. Maybe then they could all go home. He patted the letter in his left breast pocket for luck.

'Yes, sir.'

'Let's hope to God you're right,' Byng said.

Garfield came to attention, saluted. 'With the General's permission?'

A sharp nod dismissed him, and he left the earthy tomb, heading for his next appointment.

3:

Garfield waited until the documents were checked, grateful he was sitting down in the back of the staff car. His driver and *Aide-de-camp*, William Schofield, passed the papers through the half-rolled down window of the driver's door. Frowns greeted the sheaf of credentials, aided and abetted by pointing and reading.

'Perhaps you should call *Commandant* Delacroix?' Garfield tried in French.

The men in their odd grey-blue uniforms looked up, before the Day Officer nodded, retreating to the guardhouse. Garfield took the chance to admire the architecture of the building. Before the war, it was the mouldering residence of a Duke, located in the town of Abbeville on the river Somme, then served as the retreat for wounded Commonwealth soldiers, before finally becoming a prison.

Despite the veneer of intransigence granted by entrenched stalemate, things changed quickly in this war –

he remembered working with officers from the Australian 3rd Division who fortified the town, replaced in turn by the New Zealanders. He hoped that through clever feints, underhanded schemes, and as Haig called them, 'Bungo's Dirty Tricks Department' that the bloody battles along the French river would not be repeated.

He could live in hope.

The Day Officer returned, waved the barrier up, and the car lurched forward, pulling forward into a cobbled courtyard where another man waited. Back ramrod straight, his uniform was immaculately pressed and looped with golden braid and frogging. Campaign ribbons decorated his breast and throat, rank insignia announcing a Colonel of the Land Army of France. Garfield smiled through the window as the car drew up, and he let himself out, pleased the Commandant came in person.

'Major, this is very irregular,' warned Delacroix in excellent English.

Garfield saluted, given their difference in rank. 'It's good to see you well.'

The rigid discipline gave way to a grin under the tight confines of a fashionably trimmed moustache, before protocol was destroyed completely as Delacroix embraced him, kissing him on both cheeks in greeting. Even though the gesture was complete, the Frenchman continued to clasp Garfield's shoulders.

'Charles, it has been too long.'

'It has, sir.'

'So formal! I am your Godfather, not your commander!'

'*Pardon, Jean-Baptiste.*'

'Better! My Lieutenant says you want our special guests?'

'Just the one.' Garfield smiled.

'We'll talk over breakfast.' Delacroix released him, the morning sunlight bounced from the silver facings of his *Légion d'honneur*. He turned and led up the steps.

Breakfast consisted of freshly toasted bread, preserves, cheese, eggs and crispy bacon. Whilst the Colonel ate, Garfield pushed the remains of his own feast away, studying the glass cases on the wall. Expedition ribbons, pennants and flags were framed, honouring the Siege of Peking nineteen years before, where Delacroix and Garfield's father first met. Usually, Jean-Baptiste would have lapsed into the tale, but he was absorbed by another.

The Commandant leafed through the papers, a thoughtful wrinkle occupying his brow. *Pince-nez* hovered in gilded semicircles on the bridge of his nose as he studied.

Finally, Delacroix pulled the glasses free and laid them on the white tablecloth, before allowing a sigh. He stuffed the papers back into the leather satchel and closed it. 'This is madness, Charles. The Americans won't thank you for interfering.'

Garfield ignored the comment, instead tapping on a German communiqué the *Commandant* had left loose on the table from his own French Army dispatches bundle. 'You have this man here?'

'We do.'

'Is he difficult?'

'Apart from a wild sense of humour he's a model prisoner. Should I fetch him?'

'Considering this is *your* copy of the order, I think you've got him waiting in the corridor.'

Delacroix had the grace to smile, he dabbed at his chin as he reclined in the high-backed chair. He beckoned to the sentry lurking at the end of the room. 'Admit the prisoner.'

When the door opened, a uniformed German stamped into the room, with exacting precision. Halting two yards from the Colonel, he smartly saluted both officers.

'*Unteroffizier* Kurt Eisner. Storm Battalion Six.'

'A soldier from Bavaria,' Garfield said. He resisted General Byng's earlier advice on humanity, and adopted his usual cold mien when dealing with Arcanists. He found it kept the dealings straightforward. He could be nice to them after the war, if it ever ended.

Eisner said nothing.

'Read this.' Garfield pushed the letter he'd been tapping across the table; watching it skim the polished oak, the crest of the *Abwehr*, the Imperial German Army Intelligence Service at the top. Eisner's green eyes were wide, and Garfield suppressed his pleasure. It was a remarkable symbol to see, especially here. Eisner picked the letter up, carefully searching their faces. Reassured, the German studied the letter closely.

'It appears genuine,' he concluded.

'Indeed.' Garfield's brow arched as he took the letter

back. The letter *was* real, yet whatever cipher secretly dwelled within, remained unbroken. More examples would crack it, but for now there was a bigger fish to catch, so he had to trust that Eisner's superiors hadn't ordered the German to scuttle the operation. He moved to the task at hand. 'You agree to undertake this mission?'

'I will be released afterwards?'

'Repatriated to Germany,' Garfield said.

'Think about this carefully, Kurt,' Delacroix warned, shooting Garfield a shrewd look. 'Antwerp is not a forgiving place; you go from a frying pan into a fire.'

'The Fatherland *and* the British have need of me.' Eisner shrugged, grinning. 'Who could refuse?'

Annunziata Corvalho angrily plucked thick balls of cotton from her ears as she trotted through the boatyard workshop. Being called away from the installation of the control stick chafed, her input was required for the proper tuning. Pulling thick leather gloves off, she caught sight of two figures in silhouette at the entrance to the workshop.

One was smaller than the other, a stores overcoat masking most of his shape, but she knew her uncle's frame, yet the briefcase and well-fitted suit of the other man hinted at trouble. Closing on them at a rate of knots, her instinct proved undimmed by the long hours spent with axle grease and monkey-wrenches as they turned into the light and she recognised the Italian Defence Minister.

Yes...definitely trouble.

'Miss Corvalho.' The suited man nodded amiably.

She allowed him to take her hand and bow over it. He held a good reputation amongst the people for his courage during the retreat of the Italian Army at Isonzo. She studied him as he recovered from the greeting, his dark hair running to silver.

'We should talk inside, Nunzia,' her uncle said.

'Why is that?'

Their voices were raised over the bang and thump of hammers driving rivets.

'Discretion. Your country needs you.' The Minister offered a benign smile.

Taking the hint, she didn't reciprocate, but nodded and followed his directions to the car to take them home to a mansion built on the profits of shipbuilding. Many hulls were laid down at *La Spezia* in order to bring the family out of their small townhouse. Large grounds allowed experiments with vessel designs like her uncle's, which began as a pet project until the Italian Navy realised the potential, and the value of her investiture as pilot and captain.

Nunzia's talents helped to stem the calls for disbarment from the fighting forces. A female Captain in the Royal Italian Navy! A woman in charge of a boat! Scandalous! They shut up after the *Orca's* trial run. The submarine was not without drawbacks, true, but it proved the concept. Underwater scouting, a frogman delivery vehicle, torpedo carrier; her boat was capable of all – and equipped with the undeniable advantage of War Mage artifice.

When they arrived, her uncle led the group into the morning room, the fireplace set and lit by the servants to take the chill from the house. The Minister opened his case and removed lots of papers carrying ink-stamps of the flags of the Allied Powers.

'The British are meddling in American affairs,' the minister began, 'but they need our help to pull it off.'

'Our help?'

'Yours specifically, Miss Corvalho.'

'Me?' Her surprise was genuine; she knew her reputation as a square peg, even allowing that the Europeans were more accepting of their War Mages. Her uncle and the War Minister knew her talents, and her *vendetta*, her little war. She assumed they were happy to let her paddle in the pool in order to keep her uncle on board.

'It's an opportunity, child,' her uncle said.

'For who, exactly?' Nunzia realised they had discussed this without her. Bristling, she tugged her dark mane of hair free from where it was bound up at her nape.

Her uncle knew the signs, intervened. 'Please listen, Nunzia. For me.'

She glared at him; smouldered as the Minister continued.

'An American airship crashed in Antwerp, a diplomat is in mortal danger.'

'My God.'

'Indeed. In return for the government meeting the cost of *Orca*'s refit, we want you to bring the diplomat safely back to Italy.' The Minister glanced at her uncle. 'You will work with a British rescue team. It would be beneficial however, if they were lost at sea on the return voyage, if you understand.'

Nunzia lips twisted in disgust at the suggestion. Not only was it sordid, but the Allied servicemen would likely have as much reason to hate the Germans as she did. Patriotism warred with decency, but the former did not absolve her of the latter. 'I'm not an assassin. I'm a sailor.'

'You are the *Sea Witch*. How many corpses have floated in the ocean thanks to our indulgence of you?' the Minister fired back. 'Besides, we have already committed to it. Refusal will shame our nation, and there may be repercussions elsewhere.'

'Nunzia, they will throw you out of the navy. The scandal...you will never take a ship out again. Our financial partners will abandon us.' He waved his hands at the walls and ceiling. 'Our home will be repossessed, the disgrace!'

She sighed, defeated by the spectres, the insufferable clamour in the halls of power to humble the family. They knew how to bend her, how to saddle the horse. So be it. She would agree now, and hopefully think of something to throw them off later. If not, what was a bit more dirt under the fingernails?

'When do I sail?'

Boots smashed in time along the corridor, a trample of men marching in line. Checking his watch, Garfield didn't expect this to take long. When a man was offered a reprieve from death, only a lunatic would refuse. He found he was drumming his fingers to the tattoo of the march. Either side of him were Canadian officers, making up a hastily convened panel, a hard-faced Major on his left, and Captain Edmond Carter to his right. Carter was an intelligence officer, Garfield's opposite number in the Canadian Corps.

The doors of the tiny room burst open, and the Royal Military Policemen escorting the prisoner quick-timed into the room, forming a guard either side of a giant with copper hair. His shoulders were broad and he was tall, every inch a bruiser who Garfield wanted nothing more than to aim at Fritz. The prisoner's eyes bored a hole into each wall in turn, then the ceiling. He ignored the panel, eyes flicking, repeating the pattern over and over. Far from defiant, to Garfield, the prisoner looked unsure. He reasoned it fitting, because the documents on the table were damning.

Harold Ross, Sapper, 1st Canadian Divisional Engineers, had been sentenced to death a week before, and it was sheer fortune that his name dropped across Garfield's desk as part of general dispatches. As an intelligence officer, the mundane military circulars carried stories between the taut lines, stories he could use to the army's advantage to prevent squandering precious resources for the war effort.

Since he was in charge, Garfield drew the silence out – one of his greatest weapons in attrition to get his own way, to let the mind of his opponent do all the work for him, to envision the terrible consequences of refusal. It seemed as though he didn't have to do much. Ross was looking queasier by each tick of the clock on the wall, a metronomic torture. Finally, after three long minutes, Garfield broke the tension by introducing himself.

The prisoner licked his lips. 'Just say your piece and let me go.'

'*Sir*,' Captain Carter insisted.

'Quite. You'll stay until I am finished, Ross,' Garfield said, letting the impudence slide off him. 'Do you want to die a coward, Private?'

The Canadian soldier was sweating, eyes almost feverish. He erupted, seizing the table with a roar, but Garfield was already up and moving, spine screaming from the sudden exertion. Finding the Webley revolver on his belt, he stopped when he realised the tight quarters would brutally punish a missed shot. Besides, he saw the look of sheer panic on Ross' face. *He's terrified, but not of us.* 'Don't be a fool, man! Listen to me!'

The RMP Corporals tried to stop the burly prisoner, but Ross shrugged them off, using the table as a shield and battering ram, driving them back, fighting his way to the door. The room was a whirlwind of scattering papers and violence, Carter going for his own pistol, ready to execute the death sentence there and then, to bring down the rampant moose in their midst.

'Stop!' Garfield barked, shoving Carter's hand.

Too late.

A shot banged out; loud as cannon fire in the confined room, the bullet screamed along the brickwork, burying an inch from a Military policeman's head in a spurt of dust and brick shards. In the gap, the table broke as Ross pinned the other RMP man to the wall, the wood splintering under the assault. Another three Military Policemen burst into the room from outside, cramping it further, brandishing batons and blowing whistles. They collided with Ross, battering him about the shoulders, kidneys and ribs. They finally took him to the ground and got him under control.

'Enough!' Garfield snarled, angry at everyone *but* the prisoner. 'Get him up for God's sake.'

They hauled Ross upright, damage to his face and limbs

already done, but the wild panic had been exorcised into dull, glowering resentment by the beating.

'Can you hear me, Private?'

The Canadian soldier spat out blood, nodded.

'I'll keep this short so we can leave,' Garfield said, as calmly as possible, ears still ringing. He saw the sudden interest, knew he'd reached the man. 'I am here to commute your sentence; on the condition you serve His Majesty on a critical mission. You're trained on the Lewis, and the best Sapper in the Division. A clean slate and a ticket home...to open skies, empty fields.' He fed Ross a meaningful stare.

'Where am I going?'

'Does it matter, Harold?'

Ross' eyes narrowed at the unexpected familiarity. He carefully stood to full height, testing for aches and pains on the way. He swayed a little after the battering, but fought it off with a shudder of his large frame. His heavy boots crashed to attention, leaving him directly facing Garfield, and him alone.

'No. No, *sir*.'

4:

The staging area for the operation was the French coastal town of Dunkirk. In the distance, behind the buildings and shop fronts, was the beach, and beyond it the English Channel. It lay as a ribbon of molten gold with the sun waning into dusk. Held by the determined French Army, Archer counted the toll it paid for defiance.

Teams of workmen gathered in the streets, sweeping up the grit and rubble amongst the soot–blackened remains of buildings. The slew of debris emptied from wheelbarrows into craters stirred up great clouds of dust so that the men had taken on the appearance of living statues, freed from smashed frescoes and shattered plinths only to clean up their destruction.

Ignoring the years of fear and devastation, the city square and streets were just like any other close to the front lines, peppered with uniforms. Peering from the back of the truck as they passed, Archer could see soldiers mostly in French blue-grey, greatcoats pinned back from the knees, rifles at low carry in the Foreign Legion manner. Here and there, knots of British Khaki moved amongst them, just as numb to the ruin as the populace.

Garfield insisted on going mufti, but despite the subterfuge of civilian clothes, Archer was sure anyone with half a brain could guess their profession. He examined the Intelligence Officer sitting on the opposite bench, arms folded and eyes closed, not a care in the world. In contrast, Archer was laden with bags and packs of all description, carrying notebooks, maps and clothes, and hoping he hadn't forgotten anything.

When they reached a bend in the road, the truck slowed to a crawl. Garfield suddenly opened his eyes, glanced outside, gesturing sharply to get out. He dropped from the back of the wagon without further warning. Cursing, Archer grabbed for the bags and followed him. The lorry continued to trundle down the French avenue, blithely ignorant of the escape. He shrugged; his burden jostling from the movement, striving to keep pace behind the Major, who meandered across the cobbled streets as though he owned them. After a short tour of cafes and restaurants, the once jaunty coloured shop signs and awnings beaten into faded submission, he turned, and headed in the direction of the docks.

'Keep up,' Garfield barked over his shoulder.

Archer stemmed brewing annoyance over the 'British Officer Abroad' by taking in the scents of fresh bread, the pungent aroma of French coffee. He kept quiet as the gulls and sharp horns of fishing vessels coming into dock grew louder, along with the static-like rush of the sea against harbour walls. The Major led him down to a storehouse, which was set apart from its quayside companions by several yards.

Only lightly scathed by the bombardment, it was a broad building with thick stone walls, tall wooden eaves painted red. Upper windows carried solid wooden shutters in the same colour, cut with Jerusalem Crosses, minus the crosslets. Archer peered at the angles of the designs and appreciated the coverage of the street and surrounding buildings should they be used as loopholes. This was a redoubt dressed up as a townhouse. He wondered who peered from the slots at the two British soldiers approaching.

As they got closer, he relaxed as he slipped below the decorated murder-holes and closed with the protection of heavy, stone walls. A plain wooden door was the only way in, the board heavy and dark, hung on strong hinges. Mounted above the entrance was a simple coat of arms, of a sort. The seal set into the stonework, a circular plate depicting what appeared to be a river or ocean, with a small boat crewed by two men. He couldn't place it.

Garfield knocked, almost immediately answered by a shutter in the door cracking open an inch. Archer could just make out the scarred barrel of a pistol nudging from behind the gap. He subtly shifted out of the immediate line of fire, leaving the implacable Major staring down the barrel.

'I have a delivery for the merchant,' Garfield said, very deliberately.

'He is at the library,' a man replied in accented English.

'I am returning his book.'

'The one with naked dancing girls?' A lusty chuckle spilled into the alley.

Garfield rolled his eyes. 'Open up.'

With a snap, the shutter closed and the sturdy door was jerked open to reveal a man still pointing his revolver, albeit in the general direction of the visitors. He was a short barrel of a man, with a thick, unkempt moustache. His large spectacles and balding pate caught light from outside and the lamps within. Despite his jovial responses, hard eyes studied the two British men, and the battered revolver in his right fist dispelled Archer's initial impression of a shopkeeper. He gestured for the two soldiers to enter.

When the door was forced shut behind them, Archer found himself in a small room with tiled floor and sturdy wooden furniture. Plates and cups, smeared by oil and greasy fingers, cluttered one of the two tables. A fireplace gently crackled warmth from coals. Behind a door on the other side of the room, he could hear the sound of metal ringing on metal, accompanied by shouting in a foreign language. Above his head, the boards betrayed another person by creaking under heavy footsteps.

His eyes followed where the noise led, to a staircase at the back of the kitchen, just in time to see a figure hurriedly descending. Stocky and short, with close-cropped brown hair, there was no mistaking the newcomer for anything other than a soldier. Hooded green eyes showed experience of fighting, of fatigue ingrained in the lines around them, and a scar ran from chin to cheekbone on the left side of his face. Shallow trenches in his skin marked a life lived in dugouts and shellfire. Even though innocence was missing, a certain type of mischief added youth.

Despite the man sporting some civilian clothes, Archer recognised the boots and trousers. Reinforced at the knees with leather patches, they matched what he'd seen through crosshairs a hundred times. At the man's left hip sat an exquisitely worked black leather sheath, trapping the head of an axe, the wooden haft inlaid with slivers of gold and silver. Germanic proofing Runes were embossed into the metal, etched into the wood.

He ventured a small smile. 'Hallo *Tommy.*'

Impulse drove Archer up, to square off with the German, but Garfield was between them in a smart step across the tiled floor. 'Control yourselves, gentlemen. Corporal Archer, This is Kurt Eisner, *Sturmpioneer.*'

Eisner bowed, but didn't click his heels in the Prussian style.

'What is he doing here?' Archer demanded.

The German's face hardened. 'I am a friend of Mr Garfield.'

'I doubt he's got any.'

The surly reply didn't bother the German. A grin shattered his momentary stern demeanour. 'I like you, *Tommy.* We will work well together.'

'I don't think so.'

The awkwardness was punctured by the doorman. 'You have come for the lady?'

'Of course,' Garfield replied.

That was where Archer's understanding was abandoned, because the two men conversed in lively, if hushed, French. Whilst he could make out some of the words, what little he gleaned consisted of difficulty and coarse language. He supposed the gist. With them being at the docks, the idea of using a boat to get into Antwerp made sense. The spectacled man glanced his way often as Garfield babbled on, but rather than just stand there like a fool, Archer took the opportunity to regain his seat.

The exchange ended with Garfield approached the table, lips pursed, frustrated. 'We're going to have to wait. We can't get the boat out now.'

'The tide is out?' Eisner asked.

'No. The boat is being repaired. Engine trouble, apparently.'

'This is the "Lady", I take it?' Archer tried.

For the first time, Garfield offered a genuine, but thin smile, and beckoned for the two men to follow through the heavy door, shoving it hard with his shoulder. Sturdy hinges scraped and squealed open, admitting the scent of diesel and old oil on the draught. The door was actually only timbered on the inside, Archer noticed; the back of it was a solid iron affair, the body crushed together by thick rivets ages old, the shape and style found on medieval buildings.

The hammering had stopped, but there were men in Royal Navy working uniforms along with other sailors he didn't recognise. Broken English and laughter at a language barrier were going back and forth. It wasn't French, but even if indecipherable, the banter was familiar, comfortable.

'*Mein Gott! U-boot!*'

At the simple expression, they all looked just in time to see the whole vessel denuded of a protective tarpaulin. The hull was carried by five cradles, all affixed to heavy block-and-tackle pulleys. Bulbous and pug-nosed, it carried an array of fins, blisters and pipes as though a large steel cigar had been used as a pincushion.

Archer studied the machine from stem to stern. The tower at the front was truncated, stubby and carried the all important deck mounts for heavy binoculars and an array of wide tubes, the function of which escaped him. He marvelled at the metal whale, noticing concave channels in the hull. He didn't need to imagine what those were for – bulky torpedoes, clamped snugly to the body, similar to those that *almost* sank the Lusitania. His gaze fixed on the golden-coloured cap which braced the propeller in place, set squarely into a frame on the rear. Flight Lieutenant Jackson described the rudders of aircraft, and instinctively he knew this was a similar contraption.

The vessel and hiding spot were ingenious and Archer appreciated that on a professional level. The stone walls of the warehouse stretched out over the water, a private quay built for the previous owners. The slipway raced down into the dark waters.

'It's a bit small,' Archer thought aloud. A clout on his shoulder brought him round, instinct readying defences, until he realised his assailant was a woman, albeit with a large wrench balanced across a small shoulder.

'Don't be rude about my boat, English,' she said.

'Your boat?'

'*Si*,' she flicked a plaited rope of oil black hair from her shoulder, smearing her face with grease and grit from a heavy leather work glove. 'I am the Captain, no? So be nice.'

Disarmed by the introduction and warning both, he offered an awkward shrug. 'Sorry...Captain. I just thought submarines were bigger.'

'Mostly true,' she allowed, 'but this is special, called the *'Orca'*.' She spread her arms in a grand sweep. 'On loan, from my country.'

'Your country?'

'*Italia.*'

'And we are grateful, Miss Corvalho,' Garfield told her with a small, courtly bow.

Eisner fired a narrow glare at the woman. 'I know that name. *Die Meerhexe.*'

She laughed, fixed the German with a bitter smile, thumping the heels of her heavy work boots together, in mockery of the Prussian greeting. She plodded away, cradling the wrench, making for a large motor others were already working on.

'The Sea Witch,' Garfield translated.

'Oh, of course,' Archer said. He'd never heard of her.

He glanced from face to face; doubtful being famous among enemies was a good thing. Being famous to allies carried enough of a burden.

Several hours into the evening, two visitors arrived at the secret submarine bay. A Captain escorted a large colleague obviously from the rank and file. The officer was introduced as Carter, a Canadian version of Garfield, a mote more charming, but his frequent smiles were the equal of a card sharp. His companion, looking quite worse for wear, was called Harold Ross, a hunter and miner from Ontario.

Broadly set, cropped red hair was a shock across his scalp, and his broken nose and bruised face spoke of a temper that recently settled a quarrel with fists. His ample shoulders, poorly concealed by his tight civilian clothes, told Archer of the power to make those arguments short. His eyes furtively searched the room, gauging the size. He patted the stone, visibly relaxing as he left his minder, and ambled towards Archer.

'Daniel.' Archer extended his hand.

'Call me Hal,' Ross said, hesitating briefly before he shook.

Regardless, Archer was glad to have someone other than the German and the two Intelligence agents to share his company with. He hadn't seen anything of the submarine Captain. He imagined her up to her elbows in grease, swarf and oil, haranguing the sailors and her crew. Whilst the officers conversed in hushed tones in the corner, the three soldiers shared glances.

'Who's this?' Ross pointed to Eisner.

Archer sat down astride the chair and picked small crumbs of cheese from a plate that served sandwiches to the growling stomachs in the house. The German was not without guts, and Archer watched as the man introduced himself coolly.

'Met some of the *Kameraden* up at Vimy Ridge,' Ross said, carefully.

'Thiepval Ridge.' Archer stretched his arms, fighting a yawn.

'Tannenberg,' Eisner added to the battle roll, his face still open and pleasant in the face of the simmering hostility. 'Eastern Front.'

'Hmm.' Ross sat next to Archer, shrugging dismissively. 'Cards?'

'I don't gamble,' Archer replied, by reflex.

'Me neither,' Ross replied a little too quickly, brightening with a sly grin on his face. 'We can play Rummy if you like?'

Archer didn't know the game, only heard it mentioned at the Sniping and Observation School, but was otherwise ignorant, and didn't want to be fleeced.

Ross noticed his disquiet. 'I can teach you if you want.'

'I know the game,' Eisner said from across the room, looking hopeful.

'Alright,' Archer moaned, 'but you have to tell us about the Sea Witch.'

It was Ross' turn to be ignorant, but Eisner sat down and gently taking the deck of cards from the table, shuffled expertly.

'She is a beauty, my friends, but a most dangerous sea creature.' He warmed up to his tale whilst dealing. 'She hunts German ships like Captain Nemo and his Nautilus.'

'I'd rather know more about this job,' Ross muttered.

Garfield interrupted the Rummy lesson, pointing upstairs. 'Let's get you briefed, gentlemen,' he told them, glowering when they failed to move immediately. 'At your convenience, of course.'

Reaching the head of the stairs, they were greeted by a

short man of very slim build, smartly turned out in a Royal Navy officer's uniform, complete with holstered pistol. The upper room had the same dimensions as the kitchen, the stone walls stretching up, with small windows facing the street, letting in the final rays of the day. Across the back of the room lay heaped equipment and firearms. The sailor caught Archer's eye and smiled knowingly at the hardware. *An armourer.*

The soldiers were startled by Captain Carter noisily unfurling charts. 'Alright,' he said, adjusting his tunic. 'Take a seat. You can grab your toys after.'

Garfield pinned a map of Antwerp to the wall, jabbing at it with a wooden pointer. The city was a sprawling conurbation, hemmed in by huge walls between ten and thirty yards tall, and in places four or five yards thick. The walls were unbroken save for water inlets at the base, which filled tidal channels under the city to help with flooding. The system provided constant water for the forts along the wall. Three road bridges connected to the outer town that had gradually built up over the centuries by virtue of being next to the vital port. The same town now reduced to a battered husk by German siege guns.

Antwerp's main entrances were the many river quays and loading docks that abutted the Scheldt River, the waterways and canals guarded by two fortresses upriver of the city, forming a lock-gate of sorts against Spanish attack in the 1600's. Checkpoints dotted the roads, with the main tributaries also overlooked by blockhouses. Outside the towers and battlements of the walled fortress, were a ring of satellite bastions, meant to hamper the advance of any invading force.

It hadn't even slowed the Germans down. The siege of Antwerp was a bitter blow to the Allies, and especially the Royal Navy, the allies being shelled by super-heavy artillery and plagued by infantry assaults in September 1914, until the British and French were forced to withdraw. When the Garrison surrendered, it was replaced with an entire German Division, slowly scaled back to a containment Battalion with responsibility for the perimeter.

'Ever since, things there have been…difficult,' Garfield advised, taking his pointer in both hands. 'Refugees have escaped to inform us of the conditions.'

'The Imperial German Air Service drops food and medical supplies every five days.' Eisner folded his arms.

'We know, but there isn't quite enough to go round. Plus, you corralled the indigenous families with criminals, deserters, Arcanists, and other people you call *undesirable*,' Garfield said.

'And I am here to correct that as per our agreement,' Eisner replied, pointedly.

Garfield nodded, conceding. 'Indeed. The party will leave the submarine, and—'

Captain Carter began to tack aerial photographs of the AEZ to the map, specifically the area around the cathedral at the heart of the city. Garfield's pointer rapped them in turn.

'—you will scout this area. Intelligence reports this is the crash site. You will pick up the trail of the American Ambassador and his aide, providing an escort back to the submarine. Miss Corvalho can only wait for forty-eight hours.'

'Why only two days?' Eisner's interest picked up.

'The craft will remain submerged in shallow water, using a snorkel for air and the engines during the night. During the day they will be forced to employ battery power to remain undetected.'

'Undetected?' Archer asked.

Garfield looked at him steadily, saw the question was genuine. He boiled the answer down to basics, explaining since the submarine had an engine, it therefore vented exhaust, causing bubbles. Not only that, but there were some prototype sound devices that could hear the submarine engines under the water, so it would have to run on batteries, to be quiet.

'Moreover, this is a scouting vessel, not designed for long-range, like a battleship. Fuel consumption for the return trip must also be considered,' he concluded.

'So even if it isn't discovered, any extra time waiting for us means we might not get home?' Ross asked.

'Precisely,' Garfield replied.

'Can't the navy loan us a tanker?' Archer probed.

'And provide a tempting target for German torpedoes?' Garfield responded, icily.

Archer nodded at the riposte, understood. Sitting still, doing nothing to attract attention, the submarine would float, playing dead until it was forced to leave through necessity or mission success.

They would be on their own.

Nothing new there.

'So where do we all fit in?' he asked.

'*Herr* Eisner will get you into the city and translate occupation forces communiqués,' the Major continued, 'Private Ross speaks French, and as an Earth Arcanist, is an expert sapper. He will demolish obstacles and strongpoints.'

Archer took a breath, but Garfield fired a warning glare and, almost imperceptibly, shook his head. 'Corporal Archer is the team's tracker and scouting expert. He is also in charge.'

There were groans, which Archer ignored, quietly fuming at the imposition. Besides, despite the clever team composition, Archer wasn't satisfied – not by a long shot. Garfield's blunt intervention unsettled him, so he kept his peace, feigning indifference, but unable to immediately pin down his misgivings.

He suspected he'd find out more on the ground.

Meanwhile, he gave his companions a sidelong glance to see how they were absorbing it. Eisner was the enemy, but he was no defector – Archer's instinct was sure. The German's arms and knees were folded up defensively, which was understandable, since they were talking about back-stabbing a few of his countrymen. Hal Ross on the other hand, continued to take it all in, with a relaxed slump in his chair.

Archer wondered what bargains or spurs drove them into this, which pushed his thoughts towards the Italian submarine Captain. Whilst she wasn't present, the reason *why* she was included was brutally clear. *How* she came to be involved was another matter entirely, and Archer suspected a web of favours was being brokered in the shadows, or even some stripe of war bond payments to the Italian government.

He didn't particularly like either suggestion.

'We'll provide maps, false travel documents and identity cards,' Garfield said, pushing papers into a leather satchel. He brought the briefing to a close with a snap of the lid hasp. 'Get your equipment.'

An array of webbing pouches, holsters, belts and slings confronted them. Not all of it was British; French and captured German equipment sprawled in the tangled pile. Likewise, an eclectic variety of pistols, submachineguns and rifles were arranged by size and manufacturer. A narrow ammunition crate caught Archer's eye. Apart from the explosives hazard warnings and iron banding, a label across the side proclaimed:

.303 INCH AMMUNITION IN CHARGERS.

The words 'Volatile, IX' were stencilled in large, bold red print over the label, identifying the cartridge type. He gently, and carefully, patted the crate filled with Spitzer-Brice ammunition for his rifle. There would only be a few 5-round charger clips in there – the rest of the space taken up with packing straw and thick cotton wadding. He would carefully prise the rounds loose from the clips later, using them singly, since firing them in salvo would certainly destroy the weapon, possibly end the world, and definitely bankrupt the War Effort at the same time.

On another table there was a pile of clothes that would not have disgraced a Women's Institute jumble sale. A *snap-clack* drew Archer's attention, to find Eisner handling one of the machine carbines. The German brandished the weapon, now fitted with a magazine. The muzzle went back and forth across the room, albeit pointing at the ceiling.

'To think, I could save the Fatherland much trouble by killing you all.'

'If these things were loaded, I'd be worried,' Ross replied, drily.

'*Achtung!*' Eisner bellowed.

Ross and Archer dropped to the floor, trying to get as flat as possible against the stale-smelling boards, grasping for helmets which weren't there. In a heartbeat, they realised that Eisner was making machinegun noises with his mouth, bellowing and chattering whilst jerking the gun around.

Eisner stopped and began to laugh. 'Ha! Look at the brave allies!'

'That wasn't funny, Fritz!' Ross bellowed.

Anger blossomed; living wire-tight on the front line had conditioned them both to taking cover. Archer identified the shout itself as the culprit, then a lesser evil delivered by the stupid noise. Loud and constant, the chattering burps of a German machinegun forced a triumph of instinct over sense. Death came in many forms on the Western Front, the whistle of a whizz-bang, the fizz of a grenade fuse, or the strange chug of gas projector. The unknown was dangerous, and certainty meant hugging the earth.

Looking across at the Canadian, it was clear they shared resentment at being had. Ross held the look, flicked his eyes at the Intelligence officers and the Navy armourer, all of whom stood there looking confused. In that contrast, Archer began grinning, and suddenly burst into a belly laugh. It was infectious and spread amongst the soldiers, an outpouring of relief, mostly at the expense of po-faced Garfield and his colleagues.

'And *alles gut* – all is well!' Eisner beamed.

'Is that what passes for friendly fire?' Ross tried.

Eisner's face changed, shadowed, haunted. His humour evaporated.

'Boys will be boys, no?'

The soft feminine voice from the landing embarrassed them from their play-acting, and rushing to his feet, Archer was certain he wasn't the only one looking a little sheepish and red-faced. Eisner's smirk returned, blue eyes alight with mischief. Whatever shroud had eclipsed it, passed.

'Miss Corvalho?' Garfield remained unmoved.

'We sail in one hour, *Bambini*. Don't be late,' she vanished downstairs, the fleeting ghost of amusement tugging her lips before she was out of sight.

'Bambini?' Archer asked.

'*Children*,' Garfield answered. 'A handsome assessment.'

The team got down to business, with Archer seizing a Webley automatic for close-range, lots of ammunition for his rifle, two Mills bombs, a marching compass and Orilux trench torch. He adjusted the leather Pattern '14 pouches and canteen to sit no further forward than his hips, turning a small box respirator out of its bag to fill with goodies. His battle order wouldn't pass inspection, but this wasn't the place to enforce regulations.

For their parts, Eisner clutched the German machine carbine like an old friend, Ross, shoulders and biceps flexing, took a Lewis Gun which was so heavily modified, it was reminiscent of the gun on Jackson's plane, but this had a rudimentary shoulder stock, and grips for the hands. The amount of firepower on display was incredible. The sapper affixed a holster to his webbing for good measure, and filled it with a revolver.

All banter was replaced with the sound of weapons being checked, magazines tested, ammunition packets rattling as they went into pockets and rucksacks. The simple routine let Archer speculate over Garfield's brief. He wondered what he wasn't seeing.

'Archer?'

'Major?' He realised it was the second time he'd been addressed.

'Do you want to make up your sniper robes now?'

He took a second to understand Garfield meant the special, handcrafted camouflage vestments used to blend in with the terrain. He would need canvas, plus plenty of jute and burlap to cut up and apply as he wished, with cans of dye and paint for staining it all into a messy shape that looked anything other than a human being.

All the materials were placed at the back of the room in neat stacks.

He made a face – of course they were.

5:

When the team left the arming room, they found the submarine had been lowered into position. Walking down the quay, a sailor directed them to stand back as the war machine was placed into the water. Under the surface, shapes broken by ripples, Archer could make out a wheeled trolley of some kind, linked to a long chain he followed back to one of the capstans.

The ventral hull of *Orca* was slapped by the swell, a playful tap under the tummy of the iron beast, telling of the rising tide. It may have been shallow water, but it was just the cupped hand of a mighty ocean, and thinking about it made Archer wince. He'd already been tossed about in the air, but he relished the idea of being crammed into a bully beef can under the water even less, especially if the Germans were on the prowl.

Given a choice, he'd rather be hip deep in mud.

Finally the boat settled, displaced water rushing up around it. The Italian crew boarded smartly, having done it a thousand times. It was meant to inspire confidence, but they would be going two men short of their complement in order to squeeze the soldiers and their esoteric equipment into the tub. Nine people trapped in a cigar case, breathing each other's scent. Or at least when they eventually submerged.

'What do you know about the plan?' Archer asked Captain Corvalho.

'Little,' she replied firmly, 'and that's the way I want it, English.'

'You're not coming in with us?'

'Hopefully not. Taking a boatload of *Bambini* to the beach and back is enough, no? *Ciao* Charles!' she waved to

Garfield, who merely scowled.

'Antwerp isn't a holiday resort,' Archer protested.

She shrugged dismissively, clambering onto the deck, quickly swarming up the short ladder of the conning tower, beckoning them to follow. Eisner grinned and stepped off, mistiming his step against the slight rocking of the deck in the cradle beneath the submarine. Archer grabbed him, pulled him upright at the last second. The German nodded his thanks and climbed on, followed by a cautious Ross.

Archer took one last look at the storehouse, wondering if he'd ever see it again. The Italian Captain told him it used to belong to a trading group called the Hanseatic League, a society of merchantmen and sailors from the 17th Century. The lamps all along the dock were at full light, casting a strange glow over the dark vessel and the deep black of the sea outside. The moon would be the only companion to their voyage.

Eeriness clung to him, making everything surreal. This morning he was in the mud and blood-soaked earth of Flanders, but now he was about to board an Italian pocket submarine on a mission to raid a German prison fortress. Shaking his head free of the useless clutter, he judged the distance between the quayside and the hull, stepping across. A gust in the gap snatched at him, provoking a sharp cry of warning from one of the crew, but his boot thumped down onto steel, and he promptly hid his smile.

Recovering, he spotted Major Garfield staring at him. Not the boat, nor the lamps, nor even the moon beyond, but him. The man nodded once, something terribly tired about it, before he strode back through the bulkhead door and was gone.

'*Signor*?' The worried crewman called, positioned ready to close the hatch.

Offering an apologetic shrug, Archer hurried to climb down into the metal killer whale, catching a short snap of static from the ladder rungs. The whole submarine was a possible friction hazard. He'd have to be careful.

Garfield was cautious in observing the launch. Mostly concealed by the heavy door lintel, he watched the submarine slip into the embrace of the North Sea. He didn't pretend to know the tides and currents; they were merely numbers in charts. Still mindful of the presence of the English and Italian sailors, he relaxed only a little, unwilling to humour the deep consternation brewing in his chest.

The noise of wrenches and mallets knocking out pins from the heavy block and tackle pulleys was a rhythmic clamour in the background, long chains piling up in metallic ring and clash. With the grunt and grind filling the makeshift dock a background for his thoughts, he spied the fireplace, reached for a poker and stirred the coals. Opening the briefcase, he carefully pushed the documents piecemeal into the coaxed flames.

He allowed the briefest shake of his head at Eisner's horseplay. He hoped the range of idiosyncrasies and sympathies were the best alloy of talents he'd sourced. Even so, there were hidden agendas, impurities in the metal so to speak. The Italians hadn't loaned the submarine out of altruism; he suspected they knew more than he did, and personal circumstances aside, the Germans had their own reasons for supplying one of their elite soldiers. Even the Americans were being deliberately obtuse. He realised his hand was fussing at his letter pocket, and stopped before he drew it and stupidly burnt it.

Everything confidential destroyed, he stood up, dusting himself down.

The operation was a huge gamble, and maybe the outcome of the war rode upon it. With the Americans making noises about joining the Allies-but-not-yet, the British hand was quietly forced. Significantly outnumbered by the Germans ever since the Russians made peace in order to continue fighting a protracted civil war, Haig needed a miracle, be that either military or political.

Garfield's shoulders carried hopes of both. He glanced at Captain Carter, the rudimentary launch bay now abandoned and still. The only evidence of occupation was the occasional scuff where machinery had gouged the stonework, or an oil stain here and there. The efficiency and industry of the Navy engineers in dismantling the submersible's cradle was impressive.

'That went well, all things considered.' The Canadian sniffed.

'We're risking a lot,' Garfield chided, betraying his thoughts.

'A sideshow menagerie composed of cowards and freaks, sir?' Carter scoffed with a cruel chuckle. 'Surprised you didn't call up Chaplin!'

There was no real reply to that.

'Good riddance to the lot, I say. Come on, back to the real war.'

They headed for the front door and the sunny French street beyond. Emitting a long, slow sigh, Garfield stared into the English Channel a moment, his gaze trying to fathom the depths hiding the submarine. Outside a horn peeped, signalling the driver's impatience to be away. He motioned to the few remaining Royal Navy personnel, and they grabbed the last tool bags and rigging, ferrying it down and hauling it through the narrow door at the front of the house. Garfield envied their strong backs when his own spine ached in sympathy.

Weary, he reached for the pouch of Sovereigns kept in his hip pocket, jangling them in front of the doorman. He dropped them into the expectant, outstretched palm, grubby fingers clasping them over, manipulating the pouch to try and gauge how many were inside. Garfield headed out, a rueful sigh at the unwelcome return to Third Army HQ in a rattling old lorry, rammed full of the equipment they'd brought.

Inside the submarine was cramped, as Archer expected. A jumble of pipes, tubes and telegraph instruments, along with gauges and levers he didn't even pretend to understand. Each station was served by a man shouting numbers, reporting to a rapid-fire series of questions from the female Captain as electric valves lit and sparked.

The three soldiers remained close to the conning tower ladder. It was the place with the most headroom, and kept them out of the way of busy sailors. Thunder sounded, and the stink of diesel engines flooded the compartment before vanishing through air vents dotted along the inside of the hull, to escape from a tube in the roof. Even with everything shaking, Archer could feel the slipway cradle moving under the submersible's ribs, the propeller biting into the water, chopping it with a steady *thrum-thrum-thrum* of noise. The deck rattled in sympathy under his feet.

'We will travel for two miles submerged before surfacing in open water,' Captain Corvalho told her trio of passengers.

'As long as we don't sink,' replied Ross, but only Archer heard him. The man had his eyes shut and was murmuring under his breath.

He leaned in to the Canadian's ear. 'It's meant to sink, it's a submarine.'

Ross looked ready to swing a punch, but his hands were clamped, white-knuckled, on the ladder.

'What's the matter Hal? Is it the water?'

Ross reddened, no doubt expecting the incessant baiting common in some parts of the army, but cooled when he saw Archer was sincere. 'It's too tight in here, Daniel. It's just too tight! And... there's nothing I can do about it.'

Archer gripped a burly shoulder. 'We'll be back on deck soon. It won't be long.'

Crimson frustration drained to pasty white in the electric lamps of the submarine. Ross nodded, uncertain, going back inside himself to fight his own battle. Fear of enclosed spaces was common enough for Archer to understand. He never suffered from it, but it could make men do very odd things. He'd seen a soldier so scared to enter a dugout he would only take shelter in an open one, consisting of just a thin roof of corrugated iron and a few sandbags to keep the shrapnel off, or not at all. Later he'd found out the soldier had endured being buried alive after a bombardment.

It was a simple panic, and dangerously infectious.

The engines cut out as they slid into Neptune's grip. Unlike the troopship crossing the channel, or his flight in the Bristol Fighter, slipping through the sea was far smoother. The turn and tilt of the boat was odd until Archer realised that the submarine was actually countering currents. The size would affect that, he realised, the swell experienced by a coracle was not the same to a troopship. He tried not to let himself get carried away by his great revelation; the sea was not his medium after all.

'Is everything alright, English?'

Archer twisted his head at the comment near his ear, finding the Captain's unflinching gaze ripe with challenge. 'Quite alright, thank you.'

'Is your friend ill?' Her bright blue eyes softened, flicked to Ross, then back.

'Seasick. My name is Daniel, by the way.'

'Like in the lion's den, yes?'

He'd never thought about it that way. Maybe she had a point.

'Annunziata,' she said, tapped the base of her throat. 'Nunzia. It is *Bella*? Pretty?'

Archer suspected a trap, answered honestly. 'I don't know.'

'Truth suits you, English lion. Come with me.'

She stepped past him, grabbing onto latches and the corners of machinery casings to keep from tipping over in the companionway. He left his gear and the two of them headed towards the front of the submarine – *the bow* – he reminded himself. He saw a man seated, with his eyes roving several instruments. He kept his hands firmly on what looked to be a control stick pulled straight from an aeroplane, but it was as foreign again in design.

The long metal stave was embellished with glyphs and sigils, decorated in gold and silver relief, just like the *Runebolt*. He knew that other types of Focus existed, specifically made for machines, but he'd never seen one before. He tried not to gawp whilst Nunzia removed one of her gloves, flexed her fingers, ready to take control. She said something in rapid Italian, and the man gave up his seat to her.

As soon as her bare hand took the articulated lever, the submarine trembled around them. She reached across to her right, finding the broad handle of a ratchet, and cranked it clockwise. Metal panels slid back to reveal a thick glass dome, three feet across, jutting from the nose of the boat, allowing a panoramic view of what lay ahead.

'We cannot go very deep with the iris open,' she told him, 'but I like to see.'

'The glass is so clear,' he said, surprised.

'*Si*, it is crafted by the Murano artisans.'

Only having experience of either the distorted images through jam jar-like windows at the sanatorium or the razor sharp focus telescopic sight glasses, the name didn't ring any bells. He covered his ignorance by peering outside. The keel of the submarine put out a slight glow, the intensity matched by her Captain's face, as she concentrated.

The vessel responded promptly at her urging, and they slipped near to the bottom of the channel. Darting fish caught the light on the descent, as Nunzia closed her eyes, corrected course, dropping to the seabed. Large shells and strands of grass waved at them, flatfish shuffling across the sand, small bubbles streaming from the skittish movement of tiny silver shoals. A golden, dinner-plate sized starfish was decorated with dappled light, two of its arms twitching as it lazed on a rock.

'This might help your friend as well?'

Archer smiled, appreciating her insight. 'I'll get him.'

Ross was like a small boy looking through a sweet shop window, nose almost pressed to the glazed dome. 'It's amazing,' he whispered.

Nunzia's pleased smile flashed in reflection from the glasswork as the vessel continued to roam close to the sloping contours where two worlds collided.

An hour passed before they surfaced; the speed of the *Orca* restricted by the shipping lane traffic of the English Channel and French coastal waters. Gripping a sturdier seaborne equivalent to the flimsy trench periscopes Archer was used to, Nunzia barked orders, which her crewmen repeated. The boat lifted steadily, the engines bursting into life. *Orca* quickly accelerated, and the boat lashed through the water at a steady clip.

Nunzia closed the handles on the spotting device; the cylinder vanishing into an alcove above her, before she vaulted from her throne, to the ladder at the base of *Orca's* conning tower. One of her crew turned a long handle through ninety degrees, provoking a loud hiss of air lasting several seconds. When it finished, she wrenched the wheel on the hatch, turned her face away from the bucketful of water that spilled down, and went up.

Fresh breeze spilled down into the cabin, bringing with it the promise of an escape from sweat and tight walls. Archer let Ross go up first, following close behind. The night above was cool and clear; Archer could admire the stars and the large silver coin hanging in the sky, its light turning the water into a shimmering carpet. Ross went to the far end of the deck, staring out across the seemingly endless vista, taking the air calmly. Eisner, on the other hand, elected to stay below and read.

Holding onto the rail above the truncated conning

tower, Archer listened to the engine puttering and the sea's wash and rush, noticing Nunzia was barefoot, her uniform rolled up to above her knees. When the brine tossed over her toes to form puddles, she shut her eyes and the water ran up her legs, forming small horse's heads, before tumbling back down in a foamy wash.

'I'm impressed,' Archer said.

'You surprise me,' she mocked, 'you've never seen an *Acquamago* before?'

Quickly thanking the heavens for the Latin root, he kept his experiences with the Water Mages in Rannoch sanatorium private, unwilling to spoil the moment. She didn't need to be regaled with the pranks involving shower heads, or taps soaking anyone and everyone, or that one occasion of an exploding lavatory pan. Sometimes he suspected the doctors encouraged it.

Unbidden, he was assailed by memories of a Christmas Eve, when one of the girls made the ornamental fountain in the gardens sprout a tree composed of water, and one of the older air mage boys froze it with a gale, the baubles glistening on boughs made of diamonds. The catering staff put lamps around it, and the fire mages lit a small bonfire to keep everyone warm. No matter how accustomed with everyday miracles the internees at Rannoch Moor were, that one moment in December 1914, with the adults singing carols or roasting chestnuts, bordered on the divine. He fought back to the present with effort.

That was another part of him, for another time.

'Where were you?' Nunzia asked gently.

Embarrassed, he shook his head and offered a smile. 'The past. This boat is your magic broom?'

He got a confused glance, but then her mind caught up. 'Ah, the Sea Witch has to be special,' she batted her eyelashes, her face lit with moonlight. 'Do you have a special name?'

It was Archer's turn to catch up. 'They call me 'Curtains''

'*Tendaggio?*' She laughed, clapping her hands, before rolling the English word around in her mouth. 'Curtains – is not very threatening, no?'

He grinned in the moon and starlight. 'Maybe it's because I like going to bed?'

Nunzia chuckled softly, watching him very closely. 'If you are trying to woo me, English, you'll have to do better.' She kicked her foot to splash him, and a rolling wave sprawled across his feet against the tide, topped by miniature horses racing the wake. Each little pony was perfectly detailed. Their manes tossed where they thrashed in a mad canter across the deck towards him. 'But don't stop.'

He didn't know what to say.

The horses dissolved into the sloshing water.

Silence lingered between them, in which he admired her. She was striking without being a terrific beauty. He sensed a dangerous shift within, the lowering of defences. Attachment was a mistake, it was enough to leave his family, but losing friends made it worse, because they chose him. How many spotters or old pals in the grave now? The deck shuddered and bobbed contentedly, and he knew he had to break the comfortable quiet in the hum of engines and rush of waves, had to drop the portcullis. He could trust no-one and himself even less.

'How long to Antwerp?' he asked.

'We are making twelve knots. We should be there in a few hours with a good current and my hand on the tiller,' she shrugged, but her head was cocked, listening to something he couldn't hear. The water ceased tickling her toes, draining away in a sudden flush. Her face changed, wrenched into alarm. 'We must dive. *Now!*'

They hurried below, Ross's face tight. The slap of Nunzia's bare feet against the steel panels was obliterated amid emergency bells, the submarine nose-diving into the water faster than Archer appreciated, heavy hatch slamming the light out, *Orca* vanishing beneath splashing waves, entombing

Archer and his comrades once more in the deep, deceptive stillness.

6:

Orca was a rush of activity, with Nunzia at the eye of the storm. She leapt through the companionway to the helm, slipping between machinery and transoms with familiar grace. The moment her backside landed in the control chair, she grasped the Focus control stick, barking orders. The submersible turned slowly in the plunge, the crew going silent; the steel coffin muffled inside by the cold murk and danger without.

Nunzia kept the boat moving, creeping forward, but the engines were cut, a trembling heartbeat severed. Archer couldn't feel the deck vibrating; only hear the ribs of the vessel creak occasionally when the sea gave them a squeeze. Sweat broke out on all of them when they saw it, a large shadow passing overhead. Archer couldn't gauge the distance, the water and glass throwing off his perception.

'A German destroyer,' she whispered.

Eisner was there, standing as a member of the group. His eyes met Archer's, but he didn't speak. His axe was still safely trussed at his side. The thump of the enemy warship's engines came through the hull, the heart of the giant beast above them.

'Did they see us?' Archer asked the question at large, voice tiny.

'Possible,' Nunzia replied.

'How do you know it's Fritz?'

She spared him a glance. 'I just do.'

Everyone hushed; the veteran Italian crewmen froze in place, looking up. The atmosphere in the boat became increasingly muggy, choking the short reprieve granted by surfacing. Small shadows skipped along in the wake of the vessel above, bouncing on the choppy surf before slowly sinking; although Archer thought he could make them out as oil barrels in the sparse moonlight. Bubbles fluttered up from small cracks in the steel drums as they got closer. It spoke of something fizzing away inside, the ugly barrels now made strangely graceful by tumbling in slow motion. The impression was shattered as he imagined a stick handle on an oversized grenade, and froze, feeling as powerless as Ross. The Captain gritted her teeth, sinuously wrapping half-bare legs around the metal feet of her chair where it bolted to the hull. That wasn't a good sign either, he decided.

'For what we are about to receive...' Archer muttered.

Nunzia rattled away in Italian, translated for her passengers. 'Brace for impact!'

Only a moment later, the submarine was tossed sideways. Archer flailed for a railing, gripping onto it with as much strength as he could muster. Head swimming, the effect was as though he'd been walloped in the temple after too many beers, the world lurching with a sickening violence, threatening to capsize him. When *Orca* groaned under the buffeting, Nunzia cursed, clinging desperately to her perch. Another thunderous belch outside tossed the little boat so hard that the cries of sailors accompanied it, as they fell into panels, bounced from pipes and machinery.

Fighting the ocean, the Sea Witch struggled to turn the boat into the roiling current generated by the bombs, finally pulling out of their reach, the propeller bravely chugging out of the tormented water as more explosions smashed the waves behind them. After several minutes of dodging the deadly barrels, Nunzia took *Orca* down, the water becoming still, but dark. Somewhere above them, the German ship prowled, waiting to get a glimpse of them maybe, or see their bloated, water-swollen bodies float to the surface with skin like turgid, pale rubber. The Western Front was no stranger to that.

Shaking his head free of craters filled with corpse-stink, Archer glanced at Ross.

Cowering, clinging to a stanchion, the Canadian's eyes were mad with fright. The noise on the hull, the violent motion, it was so easy to understand. He abandoned his anchor point to begin slapping the walls, then banging on them. 'We must get out! We have to get out!'

'Stop, they'll hear us!' one of the crew hissed.

Without asking how that was possible, Archer moved, grabbing the Canadian and pulling him down to the cold metal and oil-stained deck. It only mattered that the sailors knew something he didn't, so he kept his voice down. 'Hal! Hal!'

'We—'

'It's a long way to Tipperary, come on Hal, how does it go?'

'Goodbye, Leicester Square!'

'Shh!' Archer warned. 'A lullaby, Hal!'

The decibels lowered. '...But my heart's right there...'

Archer grinned at him. 'Again, mate.'

The Canadian rallied, armed now with a weapon to fight the fear, he gripped Archer's hand and whispered the words, over and over. The order didn't matter, or any kind of tune, it was just important to fill Ross' mind. Clarity returned as the noise stopped.

'Well,' Archer advised, assessing Ross' performance with a tipping hand, 'it won't bring the house down, but it'll do.'

Ross smiled weakly, but gratitude filled his stare.

'Now what?' Eisner mumbled.

Strain on their faces was a map to their suffering. Everyone had been at their wits' end; Ross had merely been the one to voice it. Archer hadn't thought about anything but his comrade, and so the German's question lingered, barbed. Nunzia bared her teeth at the implication.

'They had their chance and failed. Now it is my turn,' she growled.

'They only do their duty, *Meerhexe*!'

'Would you have thought that, choking on freezing

ocean water?' she sneered. 'They are sailors, and this is the sea. We all know the game here! How many ships have your U-Boats sunk?'

Eisner said nothing, caught between truth and duty, his face liking neither.

Nunzia was unfazed as she sharply guided her crew into attack position.

The submarine swung around purposefully, banking in the water sharply, the vessel fuelled by the hot Italian blood of its mistress. The glow was radiant, and Archer had to shield his eyes as the War Mage poured her power through the vessel, charging it to unleash destruction. The slow whale of the destroyer was a blob of shadow in the moonlight.

'*Lanciare!*'

Orca listed sharply left and right, a *clunk* from either side of the hull, and long cylinders darted out in front of the boat, one slightly behind the other. Racing on midget propellers, the metal fish left a string of bubbles in their wake, illuminated by the energised submarine. Inexorably, they rushed onward towards the ship.

'I cannot watch this.' Eisner turned away.

Archer didn't blame him.

A terrific blossom of water followed the muted rumble of detonation. A strange groan of tortured metal wrenched through the water in distorted echoes. In moments a slick of black oil slapped across the viewing bubble of *Orca*, only to slide away like rinsed blood. The chum of a warship carcass began to clot the water around them, and Nunzia barked in triumph. She steered the vessel around the prey, circling shark-like and dangerous, before commanding the crew to bring them up.

Through the nose cap, Archer watched the vessel burning, desperate men pitching over the side, on fire. He couldn't hear the screams over the noise or distance, but his mind scourged him with the sounds he knew to be there. The German ship, her black and white dazzle paint blistering from the raging inferno, rocked as secondary explosions cooked off ammunition in a shower of fireworks, temporary magazines blasting several holes in the hull. A flare went up to call for help, illuminating the German Ensign fluttering madly in the gusts of heat. He could only hope someone came, because the submarine could do nothing.

'Take us to Antwerp,' he told Nunzia, surprised at how flat his voice was.

He pulled Ross up from the deck and with Eisner in tow; they made for the back of the boat, and the hammocks that awaited them, the submarine listing to starboard told him they were already coming to the new heading. He had a feeling they would need every moment of rest from now on.

Half an hour later, whilst the others were sleeping to the gentle rhythm of the engines, he felt a hand on his chest.

'Are you awake, English?'

He pretended not, at first, but her gentle whisper fell over him, waves lapping the rocks on a moonlit beach. He opened his eyes to find her watching him. She was mere inches away, blue eyes catching the light, searching his face. Her proximity lent the moment a maddening intimacy. He wondered if it was just a by-product of living in an oversized sardine tin. 'Do not judge me. I have seen your magic gun.'

'So?'

'I know you are a killer too.'

'Yes, but I don't enjoy it. I don't hate them. Why do you?'

Her hand vanished, and retreating into the dark cabin, she was gone.

Marching back to take the stick, the deck told Nunzia the story of everything that happened aboard. She could feel every tremor and nuanced vibration in it. She tapped her helmsman on the shoulder, and he rose from her seat with a grim smile, shuffling out of her way. Flexing her fingers, she sat without further word, the solid grip and sway of the steering column resisting the sea through clever levers and gears linked to the control planes.

The work and strain of engineering soothed her, as did the rush of the sea against her senses, stretching out via her own magic wand, touching the ocean world separated from her flesh by a fragile metal skin. Forcing outwards, she detected the myriad currents, and the even greater variety of creatures on them. Prickling resentment prevented her latching onto anything, so she just piloted to headings called out by the navigation officer behind her. Her irritation pushed *Orca* to full speed.

Damn English. She'd made water ponies for him as well – and that made her feel foolish, the attempt at connection. She looked down and found her left hand had strayed to her stomach. Her anger vanished then, washed away in the sweep of waves rolling over her boat. She focused ahead, a practiced slap striking the lever to crank the metal dome cover over the glass iris to protect it.

Nunzia pushed the stick forward. The words of her uncle, and the Defence Minister floated to the top of her mind. What was all this trouble for one diplomat? Her questions had been deflected, unsatisfied. She would have to leave the boat and find out – and if she did, what then? *An accident at sea.*

She frowned, attachment to the British soldier was a mistake, and if it was a choice between disgrace and a handful of strangers, it would...complicate things. Her thoughts spiralled. Maybe she was just trying to find a reason to disobey her despicable orders. Maybe she just liked Archer's honesty amid the stink of intrigue and engine grease under her nails.

She forced the propeller onward.

Down they went into the darkness.

The River Scheldt wended its way through the soil of Belgium, cutting little channels and islands through centuries of erosion and pot luck of elevation. *Orca* slid into the waterways, unerringly avoiding the myriad fishing boats, German river monitors and forewarned Royal Navy blockade ships as she did so. Archer saw that Nunzia hadn't slept that much. Her dark-ringed eyes were different, distant and almost haunted as she steered the boat, cannily avoiding things even as simple as fishing lines from the numerous jetties. The submarine proved its nimble worth, coasting gently to a stop in the early light.

'We still have plenty of cover,' Eisner said, as the men geared up.

They looked like vagabonds. To be fair, the clothes weren't new to begin with, but carefully fretted, looked worse than they actually were. Each outfit was a hodgepodge of dull greys, similar to the German field uniform, but patch-stained unequally with black and brown dyes. Apart from keeping them warm, the baggy clothes would break up their outlines at any distance.

As always, when not actively on the stalk, Archer had his sniper robes bundled up, the tattered burlap and sackcloth matching his clothes in colour, except for additional patches of green to simulate moss or plants. If there was any real foliage, he would add it to his ensemble as required. With the *Runebolt* coddled in hessian rags, he tucked the brass butt under his right armpit; muzzle capped and padded to form a crutch foot, there was enough room to send a bullet through it without blowing up. It wasn't chambered – for safety – but just in case, his pistol certainly was.

Hunching over, with an affected limp, he felt every inch the old, wounded soldier.

'Here we go,' Nunzia said.

The weird bobbing sensation of shifting buoyancy told them they'd surfaced and the hatch was clear. One of the Italian sailors went outside, looked around, signalled. Eisner went up, his German language the best weapon to confuse and delay the enemy. Ross followed, satchels across his back and waist carrying ammunition for the Lewis light machinegun, the weapon concealed inside a large duffel bag. The Canadian sprang up the ladder like a dying man escaping the clutches of Hell, and when his boots cleared the topmost rung, Archer followed.

On deck, he marvelled at how close Nunzia had brought them, the wooden dock was a step away, which he made easily, hopping forward across the boards, and quickly affecting his limp. Before he knew it, the Italian Captain was behind him, a look on her face that didn't seem to enjoy being on land. Her belt held a pistol, several pouches for tools, first aid, and a flare gun. Her garb matched the landing party. She packed her long black tresses under a cloth cap.

'What are you doing?' he asked.

'You'll need this to signal,' she told him, tidying a stray lock of hair from her face, handing him flare cartridges.

'Thank you,' Archer said. He looked up as harsh challenges came from the sentry, but the German words were too quick, leaving him bereft.

'He wants to know who we are,' Eisner muttered. 'I will handle it. Do not kill anyone this side of the wall!'

'What about inside?' Ross asked.

'Fair game,' the Sturmpioneer replied.

The others shared a glance as a uniformed man approached. Beyond him loomed the containment wall, over one-hundred feet in height for most of its circumference, it was lowest here. Only *ten* yards to fall, Archer thought, quickly gauging it, examining the rough brickwork meant to keep the ne'er-do-wells at bay. He grudgingly admired Garfield; it was a decent entry spot.

Nunzia spoke in a whispered rush to her crewman, and he grunted before dropping down into the sub. A rush of hissing bubbles announced their departure as Eisner intercepted the sentry, striding confidently with his arms out in greeting, barring him from seeing the submarine's exit with a swift sidestep.

'*Ah, Kamerad! Alles gut?*' Eisner beamed at the man, brandishing a leather wallet and some printed credentials. It looked like some form of warrant card, probably one of Garfield's 'funny papers', provided for the purpose.

A second man joined him at a jog, his guard dog straining at the leash, jerking its handler forward and barking furiously at the strangers. Angry spittle flew from the dog's maw and Archer hoped the bark was worse than the bite. The guards were wary, although fixed on the impromptu appearance of the group on the dock, it seemed *how* they got there was a bigger source of consternation.

This was evidenced by the flurry of pointing up and down the quay, and Eisner waving his arm vaguely to the East. The dog handler awkwardly clutched a machine pistol, the stock trapped under his arm, where his companion had the chance to slowly pull the slung rifle off his shoulder, eyeing the axe-haft on the Sturmpioneer's belt, the precious metal inlays gleaming in the lamplight.

Calm words were exchanged along with tobacco. Whenever the guards looked at them, Archer at least tried to prove a sullen demeanour, avoiding the gaze. Antwerp was full of prisoners; it would do to act the part. The time seemed to stretch for tortuous minutes, question followed by answer, with the occasional laugh. The longer the challenge went on, the more the barking dog began to fray his nerves. The beast somehow knew everything was wrong, Archer was sure, but the handler wasn't listening. He was ignoring the warnings, either confused, or hopefully taken in by Eisner's bluff.

Yet another sentry joined them, this time a junior officer in a soft cap strode into their midst, adjusting his pistol holster for easy reach. He seemed to grasp what Eisner was feeding him very quickly – a little too readily for Archer's liking – dividing his attention between the sentries, and the gaggle of unkempt tramps cluttering up his dock.

Finally, all three clumsily saluted Eisner by coming to attention, and the dog handler yanked the dog onto his haunches by a tight chain before finally departing. Slowly, the Sturmpioneer's left hand came out his pocket, filled with a Luger pistol. He holstered it, letting out an audible, long slow breath as he rejoined the group.

'And that, my friends, is why I am here.'

Now there was just the small problem of physically getting over the wall.

'You should return to the submarine, Captain,' Archer whispered.

Nunzia shrugged in the continental manner, an infuriating insouciance. 'I cannot. They have gone under to wait for us.'

Archer shook his head slowly, suspicion nagging at him that she'd deliberately missed the boat, and that bothered him for the wrong reasons. Instinct suggested it wasn't down to his enduring charm. Their brief exchange in the cramped and gloomy cabin aside, he suspected he was being hoodwinked, the flirting a decoy, reinforcing his earlier misgivings. Well, two could play that game.

Approaching the wall, Ross insisted on going first. He pulled off his gloves, placing his hands to the brick and mortar, hesitating. Just as Archer thought he'd frozen again, the Canadian nodded firmly, starting to climb, deliberately placing his hands and feet so they could make out his careful route.

Nunzia went next, letting out a yelp as Eisner got both hands under her backside to boost her up. She looked down at him from her tenuous grasp of the broken plaster and brickwork to hit him with a murderous glare, before Ross' powerful arms pulled her up and over. The German followed, Archer keeping watch at the base of the obstacle. Crouched, his ears yearned for the words to start the climb and get over to safety from the guards, but his heart didn't want to leave the ground.

The scrape of boots against bricks seemed terribly loud, despite the backdrop of creaking dock timbers, the river caressing the walls and banks and the odd clang of buoy bells as the water tipped the floating markers. Eventually the hiss came, and Archer slung the rifle-crutch across his back, strap over his sternum, and began the ascent.

Clambering to the top wasn't easy. The foot and

handholds were just where Ross indicated, and Archer tried not to deviate. His fingers ground on the grainy purchase, and although he jammed his feet well into the gaps, the sense of falling backwards was almost a weight around his guts, the clutch of gravity pulling at him. He froze in place, willing himself to stay aloft, determined not to look down, but compelled to do so.

'Don't think about it too much.'

Not even realising he'd closed his eyes; Archer popped them open at the voice, looking up to find Ross peering down, complete understanding written on his face.

'Just let your body do the work, Daniel,' the Canadian said, reaching down. 'It's just a ladder. Come on, over the top.'

Training took over, but sweating and blowing all the way, he got to Ross, pulled onto the wall to straddle the top like a prize pigeon waiting to be shot any second. He controlled the dizzying sensation of being too high up for his own good by trying to keep a look out. He nodded thanks to Ross, who smiled and let himself off the wall, dropping down to the others. The Canadian recovered from the plummet with a practiced bounce, tugging his gloves back on and readied his Lewis gun, discarding the cloth covering and snapping the weapon together with a steady hand.

Archer took a breath, swung his leg over the drop, shortening the distance by lowering from fingertips, then surrendering to the pull of the Earth, falling into the walled prison of Antwerp.

7:

The first thing to hit them was the smell. It was a mix of dirty, impoverished humanity, pulverised buildings and ingrained propellant. This was followed by the staggering visual spectacle of the ruination inflicted on the city. The group made their way through an old house, smashed to splinters by artillery fire. The remains of a child's cot lay broken in the corner of the destroyed home, a plaster bust of a dog stared out at them with a split face.

The thick wall they'd just vaulted was a difficult climb, but not insurmountable. Looking at it from this side wasn't so rosy. Archer saw it was a mess of scorched and pock-marked brick. At the base, buttressed with thick footings, stark pieces of bone were strewn amongst the assorted debris. A cracked, jawless skull leered up at him from the weeds. He threw his hand up to get the attention of his fellows.

'Halt! Nobody move!'

The soldiers froze instantly, Nunzia following their lead. She turned from the smashed cot to watch him, and he was sure she'd been elsewhere, to a nameless place without a map.

'What is it?' Eisner's expression was a mix of frustration and concern; he scanned the buildings ahead for anyone watching.

With the group dangerously exposed, Ross menaced the dark windows with the Lewis. Archer bent down very slowly, pointing to the head of stick grenade, the pin half pulled by a taut wire going under a plank. It was interesting Ross hadn't detected it, but then again, he was in boots and gloved hands, his senses prevented from perceiving the threat.

'Ah.' Eisner licked his lips, offered a hollow smile.

Thin, gossamer wire traced back to another bomb. It was foolish to have expected less. They were in a kill zone of booby traps and it was a miracle they hadn't been blown to bits already. It was keeping the reprobates from swarming the walls to freedom. Like the copious amounts of concertina wire, that men were spitted on, and slashed open by, this was a crude form of what the Army called 'area denial'. The Germans likely didn't need to refresh the traps, since the blackened timbers, bone fragments and dark stains decorating the ruins would be warning enough.

Fresh shrubs were sparse, growing low to the ground, trained by the unskilled pruning of fire and shrapnel. It was a lethal walled garden none of the intruders wanted to see bloom. It certainly wouldn't take first place at any Royal Horticultural Society flower show. Archer brought that train of thought into a siding; memories of his mother weeding and planting in the small window boxes were a distraction which would kill him fast in Antwerp.

'We should have come in by airship,' Ross ventured, grinning. The paralysing malaise which gripped him aboard the submarine was gone, confidence and attitude returned. He tugged a glove free by gripping the fingertips in his teeth. He placed his palm onto the ground.

'The Americans already tried that,' Archer replied drily. He declined to share his dislike of heights, hoping the Canadian wouldn't mention it.

'Well, I'm safe up to here,' Ross said, chewing his gauntlet. He was the furthest forward, having the best cover from the buildings overlooking the devilish allotment. He paused, trapped in deep thought. 'I've got it. I know the safe route out.'

'Everyone retrace your steps, follow Hal's path – you know what to do,' this last he said to the man in question, who grunted and gave a curt nod. Suddenly, there was the distinctive *twang* of a snagged wire. Archer braced, waiting for the explosion, but it didn't come.

'*Mein Gott.*'

Deathly stillness stole over that small part of Antwerp, the illusion of freedom in a huge city beyond contracted to only a few square yards of reality. Eisner's appeal to heaven was reverential, unlike the imprecation torn from him at seeing the submarine. He balanced awkwardly on loose boards, and Archer could see why. He'd strummed a line tied to a German mortar-bomb used in trench attacks. The Sturmpioneer would be very well acquainted with them, albeit he would likely be on the throwing end, as opposed to the where the fun happened.

If the bomb went off, big ragged chunks of Eisner, and anyone nearby, would instantly follow. The detonation and screams would alert the natives and the guards close enough to respond. The callous temptation to leave the German here now he'd served his purpose went through Archer's mind. He refused the nasty temptation to use Eisner's plight as a distraction for the locals. Instead, another idea presented itself.

'Hal, Nunzia, keep going, get safe on the other side.'

'I'm not just going to—'

'Do it, Ross.' The Corporal in him gave the order firmly, but without any heat. He watched them go, then very carefully shifting his weight, picked his way over to the stricken German. No further words were exchanged until Archer settled down next to Eisner, satisfied he wasn't inadvertently hatching an explosive egg.

'I thought you would leave me, *Tommy.*'

'The thought occurred to me.' Archer looked under Eisner's boot; saw how the cross-wired trap was woven under the plank he'd stepped on. 'Jesus...'

'Hopefully not yet,' Eisner muttered.

Patting his pockets, Archer found the clippers used to snip thin wire, and carefully prised up the end of the rotten timber. It broke off his grasp, shedding wriggling woodlice of all sizes. Ignoring the harmless, scuttling creatures, he pulled again, making more room for the snips. He could see the network of wires properly now, a naughty little web. He held up three fingers where Eisner could see.

'Why are you really here?'

Sweat rolled down the German's upper lip, he licked it away. 'Just cut, *ja*?'

'One cut per answer.'

'*Himmel!* My government want the war finished, yes? The Fatherland is in ruins, our crops are rotting. This will help to end it.'

Snip.

'Why work with the British?'

'It was the best way. If anything goes wrong, we blame you. You pull it off, we deny involvement. Win and win. I was also offered a deal by Major Garfield.'

Now that, Archer could believe.

Snip.

'Last one: what did you *really* tell those guards at the dock?'

'An officer escorting a work party inside.' Eisner was fairly sweating now.

'Bollocks.' Archer pretended to pack up, making to stand. 'I know a few words, Fritz. I've heard enough of them.'

'Alright! I told them I was going in, and they should not interfere.'

'Why would they listen?'

'That's four questions, *Tommy*.'

'You're gobby for a bloke stood on a mine.'

'But Garfield's documents–'

'Aren't *that* good!' Archer cut him off.

The interrogation was interrupted by a sharp hiss from Ross. He jerked his hand down the street, at figures darting from building to building. It was obviously a reception committee. Archer gave the Canadian a thumb-up. Whatever secrets Eisner was hiding would have to wait.

Snip.

'*Danke, Kamerad—*'

'I'm not your comrade. We'll pick this up later, now move.'

There were definitely more than a few of the inhabitants stirred up by their presence. Archer could count at least ten, maybe eleven ragged shapes in the early dawn. Light or movement were the biggest signals to a trained observer, and the different, flitting silhouettes told him everything. A ragged mob was forming, and nothing good ever came of those. He could hear the banging of metal on metal, a signal to others. The sound echoed in the broken streets, ripples spreading through a puddle.

'We need to leave!' Ross hissed.

Archer pulled out his map, quickly orientated himself and dabbed his nail into their current position, making a dent. He looked at the flat lines and contours of the paper, translating them into the streets, rapidly adjusting for a landscape disfigured by war.

'We go left here, through the houses. It will put us on line for the crash site.' After which, he reckoned, they could just follow the giant plume of smoke now discernible in the waxing dawn light.

Abruptly, the sound ceased, and a motley gang of what Archer took to be locals broke cover to run across the street. They were in very poor condition, barefoot and filthy; they carried clubs and cudgels made from a variety of pipes, table legs or just lumps of broken masonry. Archer had seen enough trench clubs in his time to know how easily each could brain a man. He strapped his *Runebolt* to his back and drew his pistol. The Navy officer had demonstrated how to use the blocky automatic sidearm, and Archer chose it for the rapid firepower it delivered in close quarters. The mob was thirty yards away, and closing fast.

'Warning shots first – this will make a lot of noise!'

The Lewis spat a short clatter of rounds shy of the

running feet, causing ricochets that careened off the cobbles and broken brick, catching a few in the arm or leg. It didn't slow them. Eisner rattled a burst from his machine pistol; which narrowly went over their heads. The mob continued their pell-mell charge, unimpressed.

'Did you load it this time?' Ross chuckled.

'I should not have bothered!' Eisner spat as they kept coming.

'Rapid fire! Shoot them down!' Archer called.

'Wait!' Ross, reached for his entrenching tool with his still bare hand. He ripped the sturdy implement from a canvas sheath at his spine and rammed the ornate blade onto the ground, lodging the tip into a crack in the road surface. The strange and intricate knots and laurels on the metal head began to brighten, and Ross gritted his teeth until his face turned beetroot. There was a strange rumbling in the ground, as though a nest of ants all heaved at once, and the loose rubble began to topple from the shattered buildings around them.

'Look!' Nunzia cried.

A trench, three feet wide and twenty-four feet long, cut quickly in front of the sheltering team. An invisible ploughshare cleaved grit, soil, and shucked cobblestones yards into the air. A plume of dust and dirt rolled across the charging mob, blinding and choking them. Those at the head of the pack saw the danger too late. They were too close to avoid falling, although they desperately tried, but pushed on by those behind, they tumbled into the pit with shocked cries, their fellows piling onto them in a crush.

'They'll live,' Archer said, finding his voice. 'Let's go while we can.'

Ross was reeling, tired from the exertion of his power and the fatigue of journey catching up to him, adrenaline wearing off. As a team, they picked him up under the shoulders, Nunzia bringing the modified Lewis gun, the extra grips and lighter parts making it noticeably easier to handle. Even so, watching her wrestle with it tickled him.

A motley circus troupe, they stumbled and staggered across the road, into the shelter of houses with better walls. It was only to be expected someone would come out to play, the natural instinct of a beast against unwelcome intruders. Archer kept his pistol hand free, finger resting on the trigger guard in anticipation, but there was no pursuit. Despite Eisner's assurances, he couldn't rule out the guards reacting to gunfire, but if they did it would at least cause a distraction, letting the team slip away into the city.

Archer wondered how many more surprises it had for them.

The team climbed through rubble and patches of wilderness which were once gardens, going street to street in the ruined city. Ross gradually recovered his strength during the measured march beneath tattered buildings, all gloomy and imposing. They kept heading in the direction of the city centre, alight with a crucible glow. The hulks of buildings that stood witness to centuries of history were now just sparse, jagged bones, thrust up from the rotting corpse of the earth.

Leading the group through a tight alley Archer paused between two ruined townhouses, a lethal defile anywhere else; here it provided the most cover. Light from flames up ahead gave enough light to see by in the otherwise pitch shadow. They moved forward again, reaching the mouth of the alley, which opened into the main plaza, onto a sea of rubble and orange light.

They'd found the zeppelin.

The crashed air vessel was mostly gone, consumed by a riot of flame. A leviathan carcass; just reduced to bones and scraps of canvas, each doped with solution to make the panels weatherproof, the material would have been devoured at a startling rate. Archer thought of whale hulks, the mighty creatures of the depths cast up on the sands, just bone ribcages and hard cartilage jaws, bleaching in the sun.

'Look at that,' Nunzia whispered.

Through sheer scale, and the horrific grandeur of the scene, Archer had forgotten the others were there. The sight before him had stolen his senses completely. The heat from the conflagration consuming the city capitol building was fierce, even at two hundred yards. Burning for over a day, the fire still gorged itself on the hulk, stealing breath, all the air taken by the flames. He reasoned that if Hell came to Earth, it wouldn't be far from this.

It took him a moment to catalogue the different dangers the team were exposed to. 'We have to search for survivors.'

'Survivors?'

Archer looked over his shoulder, fixed Ross with a look. 'Around it, I mean. They may have kept close to the fire.'

'It would keep them warm,' Ross allowed, 'but...it's better than a flare.'

'That's what worries me.'

Ross' expression shifted to one of nervous agreement, and he clutched his modified Lewis gun a little closer. 'Let's get on with it.'

Grunts of approval followed, but no-one moved. They all stood staring at the burning airship corpse for long moments, entranced by the ghastly sight. Gunfire somewhere ahead and to the left of the crash broke the spell. Tucking the stock of the *Runebolt* into his shoulder, presenting the weapon at low-ready, Archer set off, scanning the windows of the nearest buildings, watching for faces lit by the flames.

8:

A sharp snap jarred Garfield to sudden wakefulness. A mask danced on the other side of the room, and for a second he didn't know where he was, until he realised it was a reflection of his own face in the large mirror over the small fireplace. Another snap betrayed it was merely pine resin popping in the flames, not bullets. A dull hissing noise came from the sideboard, where his gramophone needle treadled dead, scratchy notes.

The smell of the room, old books and stale ink, told him he was in Third British Army Headquarters. He rubbed his eyes with finger and thumb, relieving the stress of waking to dancing shadows. Typically, the countryside around Villers-l'Hôpital got dark early, and dusk pushed weak pink fronds through the poplars along the hill. He stood up, pushing the Louis XIV chair away from the desk with some effort, socks slipping on the old oak flooring. Pain lanced up his spine as he turned and stalked to the gramophone. A deft flick of his wrist prevented any further damage to his nerves or the precious imprint of Schubert's *Death and the Maiden*. It was not a gentle ballad, so to sleep through it was revealing.

He adjusted his standard issue flannel shirt, tucking in the loose tails, shouldering his braces, gazing at the ghostly figures at the end of the room. Ancient suits of French armour smocked beneath long dust sheets, eternal sentinels over the march of time. Garfield wished he could stand up for that long.

Wincing, he stretched to the sound of hushed notes emanating from a banjo being softly strummed. The noise floated into the room through a small open window, which he reached up to close. Despite a firm tug on the latch, it was stuck open, and Garfield was forced to smile, listening to General Sir Julian Byng burning the night oil with some light 'musical' practice.

Music Hall Theatre.

It was a good job the General loved that kind of thing.

Garfield looked out over the fields, the town church topped with its spire, off to his right. It framed a glorious display untainted by the bright flashes of high-explosive bombardment, at least for tonight. The church bells struck *Eight, Pip.Emma* – eight p.m. in civilian money, followed by a swift, smart knock at the door.

'Come.'

His ADC appeared. Schofield looked for the desk first, before finding him lurking in the half-light by the window. 'Telegram in for you sir, urgent.'

Garfield took the small buff-coloured envelope with an unhurried air, casually noting that it was unopened. The ADC vanished swiftly, leaving the Intelligence Officer alone. Unable to contain himself any longer, Garfield ripped the communiqué open and hurried to the nearest lamp, overturning the screw and sending a huge flicker of flame up the glass chimney, blackening it before he managed to tune it to something he could read by without burning down HQ.

They were in.

A gamut of emotions clamoured for indulgence. All he would allow was a short sigh of relief, a clenched fist. The plan was working, but he daren't hope. Not yet. If this war taught him anything, it was that hope was a dangerous thing. Unerringly, his eyes fixed onto his uniform blouse on the back of his chair, the precious letter in the breast pocket. Dismissing sentiment, Garfield marched towards the fire, roused the embers, and tossed the telegram into the hungry flames.

Stuttering blurts of automatic gunfire contrasted with sharp single-cracks, the tempo of a skirmish escalating in violence. Archer stopped the team short, practiced movements made his hands swift to unbuckle and prepare his camouflaged sniper robes, which he threw over the top of his clothes and belted snugly.

'Is *that* why you are called curtains?' Nunzia tried.

He grinned at her, quickly assessing his options for height and field of fire. They had come through a series of terraces, sticking to the ground floor where possible, but they were now on the corner, adjacent to where the skirmish was brewing in large house opposite. Archer glanced about, assessing. There was a partial second storey and remnants of a flight of stairs. Steps would give him better height, angles to dig into.

'Hold three minutes, then move in. I'll cover you.'

Without waiting for an acknowledgement, he turned and clambered up the stairs, several years' experience helping to quickly discern what could take his weight. A gap in the steps made him leap for the landing, a creak and shift of the board set him wobbling, but he somehow kept his footing, and moved on. The townhouse had an attic, open to the air, and Archer took the stepladder leading to the loft.

The view of the corner and its approaches were perfect, so he settled, fluffing out his robes and attached hessian and burlap, the colour of storm clouds blending with the floor. A small scrap of roof, complete with terracotta tiles gave him enough shade as he brought his compass out and checked he was facing North. He lay down fully, drawing his rifle to him, quickly slotting his telescopic sight into place in line with the barrel, screwing it down before wrapping his left arm in the sling to add tension, firming up the brass-plated butt against his right shoulder. He wriggled forward into position.

Below, he could hear the others advance.

Through the glass, the action in the large house burst into focus. Half the walls blown down, a marble balcony stood proudly overlooking the ground floor, where Archer could see the remains of mosaic decoration. A once proud hall was now just a rubble-strewn killing ground. Like most of Flanders.

A man was moving behind the solid cover provided by a marble block at the top of the balustrade, snapping short bursts from a machine rifle, firing at assailants below. His uniform was an odd green colour Archer didn't recognise, but when the man turned to shoot, three upside-down chevrons clinched it.

They'd discovered the Americans.

Archer prepared to shoot, switching his view to the assailants, a group of men in crudely made black tunics. They fired up at the American with an assortment of rifles, submachineguns and pistols. He was used to the fast style of trench sniping, where a target presented itself for two seconds at best.

He saw a man prepare a stick grenade, and with a practiced flick of the sights and squeeze of the trigger, shot him. Bloody gruel slapped across the wall in a vivid splash. Archer backed off the glass to view the scene, saw the American peer up for a moment, confused, but the crack of the *Runebolt* only stirred more gunfire.

Re-sighting, his view through the crosshairs was limited, only able to see the effects of a shot, or a target diving for cover, but he generally perceived the rest. He wasn't used to working with a larger team, despite supporting massed British infantry attacks at Thiepval Ridge by killing enemy machinegun crews, so his focus split between targets of opportunity and watching for threats. Another victim strayed into his sights, and he fired again. Heart shot. The man flopped down the stairs like Buster Keaton in one of his famous farces, a look of mild surprise on his dead face.

The Lewis gun chattered, knocking over three more assailants, throwing them down onto the mosaic rubble, followed by the rip of Eisner's machine pistol. It was chaos, with the men in black surprised from behind and above. Archer fired again, watched his victim spin away, face ruined, then a heartbeat later shot a man in the back. A fifth bullet found a victim trying to flee the fight; he dropped forward as though pole-axed, gore spurting from the jugular.

And just like that, it was all over.

'You on the balcony,' Ross shouted into sudden silence, 'we're Allies, coming in. Do not shoot!'

'As long as you don't shoot at us, pal.'

Archer snapped his rifle safety on, and went down to meet the neighbours.

Approaching the killing ground, the team stepped over the bodies, checking them as they converged on the Americans position. Piles of masonry and thick stone pillars girded the house, some of the carpet and hanging fabrics opulent enough to suggest this was the mayoral manse. A groan caught Archer's attention, and he vaulted a crashed colonnade, rifle ready, only to find a man struggling to remove his black coat. He was pale, his lower left abdomen a glistening smear across the dark fabric. Without any immediate threat, Archer reached to help the man, hoping to gain some insight.

'Deutsch? Francais?'

The man shook his head. 'English.'

'I'll be damned.'

'We are...in Antwerp,' the man gasped.

He could have been anywhere between nineteen and thirty. The hard life within the walled prison had taken something from him, and he looked up with more than pain.

'Who are you?' Archer asked.

The man grimaced; shock wearing off. 'I could ask the same.'

A shout drew his attention, and Archer left the wounded man, bounding up the battered staircase to go into the room beyond. Once a reception room for an important Burgher, now a charnel house, divots cut from the walls and ceiling by bullets, the pock mark of shrapnel scattered across the walls. Several men lay wounded or dead, corpses covered by their tunics. The few survivors matched the environment, clothes stained and ragged, strips torn from shirts to form bandages.

One of the wounded men sat with his head wrapped, blood across the fabric swathing his eyes. Blinded, he still helped his comrades, groping for a pile of cartridges nearby, then magazines to fill them with. Another man tightened the wrapping around his leg, testing it. Satisfied, he returned to sharpening a bayonet.

Archer could sense the grim determination in them, the solemn mood. He turned to find the man who'd defended the stairs. 'Corporal Archer, British Army.'

'Sergeant Joe Miller, US Marine Corps.'

They shook hands, the grip was firm. It was highly likely that Miller was the one keeping everyone going.

'You're too polite for locals.' Miller allowed a half smile, suspicion warring with the relief breaking through his soot-smeared face. 'What are you doing here?'

'The same as you, I expect. We're looking for an American Diplomat.'

Glances were exchanged and men who lived on their nerves suddenly became taut, hanging on every word. Archer didn't move, sudden gestures could be misconstrued, and he wanted information, needed them to talk.

'Why?'

The challenge came from a man who, until now had his back to the group, bent over a casualty. Unlike the others, he wore no uniform, instead sporting working clothes. He carried a broad satchel with a red cross on a white circle, and as he turned, he stood to full height. He unfolded, his size dwarfing even the tallest Guardsman Archer had seen. That wasn't the only thing to grab attention, the man was dark skinned. Having only seen a handful of men from the Indian Division, this was Archer's first conversation with a black man.

'Who are you?'

'Folks call me Sam. You didn't answer my question.'

Despite his size making it an easy prospect, Sam didn't threaten, but his sincere expression needed an answer. He'd spoken and moved slowly, deliberately, and Archer got that feeling again when someone was trying to fool him. The big man wasn't a dumb brute – Archer could see the way he studied the newcomers, assessing them, the surprise at Nunzia. She nodded at him.

'It doesn't matter why,' Miller said sharply.

Archer couldn't tell if it was a warning to keep his nose out, or to prevent Sam making a slip. Regardless, he slowly reached into his jacket and produced the simple letter Garfield had forced on him, passing it across.

As Miller finished reading, his eyes strayed to Nunzia, passing back the note. 'You're a strange rescue team.'

'You're lucky to survive that crash,' Archer countered, taking a casual half-sidestep left, blocking line of sight to the Italian Captain. He carefully stowed the letter inside his tunic. 'Who are your friends downstairs?'

Miller snorted. 'Not sure, but they've been on us since we crashed. Must have seen the blaze. Moths to a flame.'

Once again, Archer felt the intense heat from the fire still burning outside. He could picture the terrifying flames spilling everywhere, burning men, masonry and metal with equal fury. He didn't need to imagine the appalling stench of sizzling flesh.

'Or they knew who was on board.'

'Impossible.'

The denial was a fast, blunt wall. Archer went around it. 'You didn't get very far.'

Miller paused. 'No. We found a good position, the rest you saw.'

'Is the Ambassador dead?'

More shared glances greeted this, and Miller licked his lips. 'Look, we've been fighting for hours—'

'Is he dead?' Archer pressed.

Miller snapped. 'We don't know, alright? She was taken!'

'She?'

Circumstances came together; reluctance to admit they'd failed to protect their charge, the odd looks at Nunzia, knowledge of what could happen to a woman alone in lawless Antwerp. They'd been fighting for their lives, locked into a siege mentality of guilt. Maybe that, or something else. Ignoring his disquiet, Archer clapped the American on the shoulder. 'Well, one of them is half-alive downstairs. Let's have a chat.'

Miller's eyes re-lit. 'Yeah, let's do that.'

With a quick gesture, Archer beckoned Eisner and Sam to come down with them, the latter clutching his medic bag. The big man looked at the wounds, his patient now feverish with pain. He studiously dressed the injuries, and produced an octagonal bottle containing milky liquid, but Miller stopped him with a gently restraining arm.

'Our boys need the Morphine, Sam. Go see how they're doing.'

'Sure,' Sam replied, making his way back upstairs.

Between them, Miller and Eisner gripped the fallen assailant and propped him up.

'I don't have time for any crap. Who sent you?' Miller demanded.

The man's eyes were focussed, clearer. 'I am with the *Kampfgruppe*,' he muttered, as though it was enough.

The word was pronounced with enough clarity for Eisner to nod, and fill the gap. 'The Fighting group?'

'Yes. We are the strong arm, fist of the Kaiser.'

'A jolly fellow with a big moustache and pointy hat?' Eisner knelt; grinning at this strange Englishman who spoke the German words properly.

A pained, yet scornful glare was the reward.

'Where is the woman from the crash?' Archer asked. He kept his tone level, wanted to see if the middle-ground would work, since the harshness and humour had failed.

'My comrades took her whilst we fought here.'

'Where?' Miller demanded.

The man grinned bloodily, hiding the secret behind his pain.

The Marine put his boot on the injured man's right hand, leaned down hard, grinding; the sound of fingers being mangled was loud in the space. The man resisted as long as he could, but howled, rolling eyes finding Archer, ignoring the American. He gulped air in, tried to speak again, but passed out from the combined agonies he was suffering.

'Great, now what?' Miller stood up, hands on hips.

'Archer?' Ross was standing at the top of the stairs, holding up a tin of bully beef. 'Maybe we should ask the locals?'

As a tool of war, subterfuge was something Archer was familiar with, but this was something else entirely, closer to a hunting expedition. Ross had abandoned his light machinegun, and armed only with pistols, he and Archer laid their trap. On the opposite side of the square, Ross had indicated disturbances, revealing a path across the rubble. The Canadian had picked up threads of clothing, hair and a couple of footprints even Archer couldn't see at first glance.

'I thought I felt someone out here,' Ross mumbled helping to prepare the body of one of the Blackcoats. He placed the tin of food in a jacket pocket, making sure it was obvious, along with an empty pistol in the corpse's hand to add some set dressing.

The body was one Archer shot, so the bullet wound would look like the man was killed at distance, by a rifle, leaving a nice safe corpse to rob. The scent of decay was overpowered by the smell from the smouldering ruins of the town hall, the fire having died out through lack of fuel, but not before gutting several buildings into hulks.

The two men retired to the chosen corner, well off the beaten path Ross had detected, to lie down and wait, shuffling into position. Archer pulled a couple of very pointy bricks from beneath his chest, placing them instead of tossing them away. No sudden or sharp movements. For him, patience was ingrained behaviour from the Sniper School, for Ross, it was from being a hunter.

'I think our American friend is lying,' Archer whispered after an hour of silence, his voice carrying the twelve inches to his left, where Ross was settled.

'About what?'

'We're here to retrieve two people, but Miller only mentioned one.'

'So? Maybe the Diplomatic Aide is dead?'

'I'm not sure. I think I put an idea in his head.'

'This whole thing stinks,' Ross agreed.

'Maybe I'm reading too much into it.'

Instead of replying, Ross hissed and their talk ceased. He gently laid his bare hand on the ground for a few moments, closing his eyes. When he opened them, he held up two fingers, and mimicked walking. Archer nodded, his senses sharpened by the proximity of action, albeit ready to capture as opposed to kill. It was refreshing.

Ross must have sensed the interlopers from a good distance off, because it took ten minutes by Archer's count, until the sounds of two cautious human beings scraped the stonework of the collapsed building. The footsteps were so light Archer had trouble keeping track of them, until the figures came into the shattered room.

Concealed by his ragged sniper robes, he tried not to look at the pair, knowing humans could tell when they were being watched. He hoped Ross was being as careful, peering away from the pair of diminutive wretches, huddled in thick clothes. The trousers were patched and unevenly worn; the hem at the ankle was only roughly caught up. Archer was no seamstress, but even he could darn. The footwear was likewise scuffed and battered, brown leather faded; the dust and hardness of Antwerp beaten into it.

They inspected the body, but didn't speak to one another. There seemed to be some kind of communication in hand signs and body language, but apart from the shrugs, there was no reading it. The larger of the two figures stepped nearer the body, wafting the smell and flies away, before inspecting the pistol half-gripped by a dead hand. The other, smaller in size, went into the pocket and snatched the tin out, holding it aloft and studying it. They moved to turn around and stepped into reach.

Archer erupted from the debris pile in a shower of dust and pebbles, grabbing one of them. Ross helped him, catching up the second. As they grappled, their prisoners squealed sharply in surprise and fear.

'They're bloody kids!' Archer gasped, nearly letting one go.

'*Laisse-moi partir!*' the voice was high-pitched, a girl.

He didn't know what she said, but understanding her thrashing was a different matter. She wanted freedom, and he would oblige her only as necessary. He shifted grip to her arm, pivoting her to face him, pulling free the hat and scarf that hid her features. He ripped the sniper veil from his head, so he looked human. Ross took charge.

'Shh, shh!' he urged. 'We're sorry! *Désolé, désolé!*'

The smallest girl started wailing.

Ross continued speaking in hurried French, explaining and trying to calm both the children – although the older girl was sullen, resentful. Archer could see in her eyes the innocence of childhood gone, the hard realities she lived with all too present. She eyed back just as warily, and it took a lot of back and forth before an understanding was reached.

'They thought we were the madmen.' Ross translated. 'Apparently the ones who attacked us before are either insane, or criminals. They have communes across the city.'

'The lunatics have taken over the asylum?'

Ross nodded. 'I suppose so.'

The older girl stared into middle distance, babbling without really thinking. Archer caught the mood, brain latching onto one word. 'Cannibals?'

The Canadian sapper rattled off a question. When he

got the reply, he cocked his head to Archer. 'Good ears. Yes, cannibals. I told her we will deal with the madmen if they come near us.'

Archer patted his rifle. '*Oui.*'

They got to their feet.

Clutching the tin of beef like it was the most precious thing in her world; the small girl marched close to her companion as the soldiers escorted them to the American holdout. Nunzia scowled at how they'd caught the girls, but Archer whispered in her ear and she nodded.

He decanted water into an upturned Brodie helmet, and she dropped a finger into it, making a small horse stand up out of the liquid. It was perfectly formed, the head swished and nodded, and not only was the child fascinated, the Americans were too. Even though he'd seen it before, Archer was still caught in the moment.

Impervious to the charm, the teenager stood unimpressed, arms folded, huffing. The younger girl found the living toy irresistible, happily splashing the small pony. Not to be outdone, the creature responded, stamping its tiny hooves to make droplets catch the girl. The sound of her delight was reflected in the faces of the survivors, and reluctant smiles began to take hold.

The story became clearer. The small girl was Marie, one of a large group of refugees living in the city after the initial fighting for Antwerp. Others were displaced when their families were killed by savages or the warring gangs, fighting for land and the food drops the German guards put in.

Some older boys witnessed the fighting between the Americans and the 'Blackcoats' during the morning when foraging for food, and told the girls about it. Archer shared glances with Ross, now understanding who he'd detected.

'When the fighting stopped, we thought you'd left,' Marie told them, via Ross.

'And you thought you might find something useful?' Archer asked.

'*Oui.*'

'I am very sorry we scared you. We didn't know,' he continued.

'It's alright.'

'Who are these men in black coats?' Nunzia asked, her tiny horse continuing to trot around the helmet.

Marie shuddered. 'They are the Kaiser's men. He will be angry.'

'They took someone important. Do you know where?'

The girl hesitated, and bit her lip before looking to her surrogate sibling.

'The boys told us,' the teenager replied, 'a woman with long blonde hair.'

'Yes – that's her,' Miller blurted. 'Where?'

'They took her to the Armoury.'

'Can you show us where it is?' Nunzia asked.

'I can,' the older girl replied, pretending not to look at the water pony. She jerked her head at the beef. 'For a tin or two?'

9:

Resupplied with weapons and ammunition from dead Blackcoats, the Americans elected to remain with their wounded. An illusion of choice; they were in a poor state, and took advantage of the excuse. Handily, it also kept the Marines out of Archer's way. He wasn't satisfied the American Sergeant was telling the full story.

Eisner led off, with the older girl directing him wordlessly. They kept close as a group, hoping that if they were spotted by the lunatics, they would be too formidable a target to try and take on. It was late morning, and Archer was thinking they were a little exposed keeping to the road, but the girls couldn't read the map and it would take too long to teach them, so he just kept updating their position by pushing his thumbnail into the map when they stopped for a break under a stunted tree, sprouting from a mound of bricks. It was all too easy to think of it as a family outing, with the children there, now quietly babbling away to Ross. He listened and translated, all the while looking content.

The rumble of wheels on cobbles, accompanied by loud engine noise dispelled the wholesome daydream, alerting Archer first. The others tensed, hearing it a moment after. The small party hurried down the street – a boarded up row of shops left to rack and ruin, hounded by panic as they searched for a way inside. Archer had visions of fighting door-to-door, a protracted battle which was ultimately futile – until Eisner gestured to a shop front with a deep porch. He battered loose planks with his shoulder, and the group rushed in, Archer the last, sweeping the street with the iron sights of the *Runebolt* to make sure they were still alone.

Dust stirred in the sudden light, the timeless gloom interrupted by their rude entrance. Once inside, Eisner searched the shell of what was likely a small cafe in a previous life, for something to plug the gap they'd torn open. The engines were getting nearer, and in desperation, he gestured to Archer and Ross, and the three men grasped a tall, decrepit sideboard, shoving it to barricade the door. Archer turned and put his fingers to his lips before walking around the cafe ground floor, putting his weight on the sides of his boots, rolling his feet toe to heel.

Quickly and quietly, he found the stairs, hurrying the others up them. Ross, being an experienced hunter, was stealthy and quick, Eisner and Nunzia thumped up the stretchers. In contrast, the girls were exceptionally light on their feet, and smart about where they stepped, veterans of living in a cursed city.

Instinctively, Archer moved to a boarded-up window covering the street, keeping back far enough, avoiding being seen. Thin gaps between the slats narrowed his vision to a few yards of the street, but he could hear the clatter of hard wheels on cobble getting closer, moving in from his right, and suddenly, there they were.

Two trucks of German origin laboured into sight, the narrow engine compartments and tall cabins of Daimlers. Each had five Blackcoats, armed to the teeth with Mauser rifles, MP-18 submachineguns, and *Stielhandgrenaten* the typical stick-bombs of the German Imperial Army. They guarded crates of what Archer reckoned were weapons, more rifles or even heavy Maxim 08/15 belt-fed machineguns.

A loud bang rattled the street, and the trucks stopped ten yards past the broken door where the group was taking shelter, steam pouring from the lead vehicle's bonnet and radiator grille. Eisner shot him a glance, likewise peering out between boards. The German carefully shrugged. Ross leaned back, cradling the Lewis gun. The escorting soldiers got down from the truck, and the drivers also dismounted.

One of them, the tallest man, strode around with a slung machine pistol. He looked up and down the street, but seeing nothing alarming, took a packet of cigarettes from his pocket and as two other men approached, he doled the contents out, lighting up as he went, before taking one himself. It was the habit of old salts in the rank and file, used to hurrying up, only to be forced to wait. A simple enough pastime: A sleep, a smoke, a snack.

Both drivers approached the stricken Daimler, shedding hats and rolling up sleeves. Archer could see one was a woman. She hurried to the back of her lorry as the male driver propped open the bonnet, returning with a small can of oil. Even she was armed, albeit with a holstered pistol. She vanished from sight under the steam clouds.

Glancing to Nunzia, Archer found her watching him. Uncomfortable, he looked back down into the street, heart sinking. Three of the Blackcoats were taking an interest in the barricaded door. It suddenly occurred to Archer that these people might be as intimately familiar with the city as the girls, would have noticed anything different on a section they passed regularly. He knew he would have. After staring at trenches for days, mapping them out meticulously, even small changes were glaring.

It was how he made the kill, usually.

Then the notion struck him that the dresser would be butted up against the doorframe from the *inside*. How many times had he stared at hedges, ruined craters and blasted landscapes, all to make sure the *outside* of his camouflage suit looked like his surroundings? Even down to the direction the grass was growing? Cursing under his breath didn't make him feel better, the deed was done.

Slowly, he stepped back, bringing his rifle up the ready position. Seeing his stance, the others prepared for trouble, and the girls ducked down. His bare palm pressed against the cold metal inlay on the rifle stock, his eyes flicking from one enemy to another, trying not to linger on any of them.

The three Blackcoats stood talking, a mix of French and German, with the odd word of English thrown in. Archer wished he'd taken one of the Americans' shotguns. One man stepped to the doorway, shoved at the dresser, which creaked and rattled, but didn't collapse. Laughter floated up from the street, suddenly interrupted by the metallic slam of the Daimler bonnet going down. The tall man waved the driver and whistled loudly. The Blackcoats quickly extinguished their cigarettes, clambered aboard the trucks, engines already crunching into gear, and they took the supplies onward.

'*Grazie a Dio*,' Nunzia breathed as the noise of the convoy receded.

The small party slumped down onto rickety chairs or just against the wall, and began breathing properly again.

'What did they want?' Ross asked the room at large.

'They thought there might be wine in the cellar,' Eisner replied, dabbing down his face with a scarf. 'Cigars, too.'

'What was in the crates?' Nunzia wondered, still standing watching the road.

Archer looked up. He'd been thinking that himself, especially as he'd seen the port authority stamps on the wood, along with stencils of the Imperial German Army. Whatever it was, it didn't bode well.

He stood up and nodded to his team. 'Let's move.'

The Armoury was a walled compound in the Northwest of the city, and by midday, Archer and his team counted three convoys, each of two trucks. The vehicle registrations were all as different as the loads they carried. The security at the dock wall was lax, but it struck Archer that this was not the way the crates were coming in. These Blackcoats were equipped as a standing army, trained and motivated.

'They are the biggest gangsters in the city,' Therese explained simply.

On the trip through the city, Nunzia prised the name out of the eldest girl, and while she still watched them all warily, she was opening up with each yard travelled. Archer thought about the word she'd used. Calling them gangsters seemed appropriate.

There were obviously ex-soldiers amongst them, since they were deserters. Their discipline was ragged but present, meaning the Kaiser was either exceptionally inspirational, or handed out brutal punishments to keep the thugs in line. He didn't like either option, but he'd heard of enough men shot at dawn that he was ready to prefer anything as an alternative.

When examined closely through the telescopic sight, Archer could see an old sign with a single word, mostly faded and chipped paint, which he suspected was in Flemish. This had been discarded, propped up against the wall sideways. It was replaced by a truncated flagstaff, with a black scrap fluttering from it. He frowned as he stared through the glass, watching the enemy.

There were several thugs, armed with a medley of weapons. Covered balconies gave sentries a good view of the compound within, and the sentry boxes outside that he could see, commanded the road to the heavy gates at the side of the building. Even as he watched, he could see a procession of three people shuffle across the inner courtyard, their wrists and ankles shackled, being poked and prodded by men who were better fed than they. He continued to observe as the wretches were herded down steps and through a gate.

'Therese says it used to be a police station,' Nunzia said.

'There must be proper cells then,' Archer replied, peering through his rifle glass.

'Underground?' she supposed.

'Mhm.'

The wind picked up as they stared out of the church steeple, the belfry undisturbed by the stiff breeze, the iron-wrought bells partially collapsed and rusting from their exposure to the elements when the top of the bell tower was partially shorn off by an artillery shell. Archer looked at the stone and plaster, riddled with corroded shrapnel fragments, before bending his neck and looking back through the glass, fitted with a device he'd made called a sunshade – an extended tube slipped over the end of the sight to prevent glare into the scope. A scrap of scrim netting across the end prevented reflection.

He watched the guards pacing, not exactly regimented patrols, but certainly not deliberately random like at the Front. The latter was counter-sniper by design, here it was accidental. It made them dangerously unpredictable. He counted a dozen of them visible, with at least one officer, and one non-commissioned rank occasionally stepping outside into the bright, warm sunlight. With the troops on the trucks, there were well over a score.

Archer looked across at Nunzia from the corner of his eye, staring at the long jet plait falling from the nape of her neck. He'd asked all of the team to come up and use his spotter glass to get an idea of the compound layout. Both Ross and Eisner had already had a turn, the Canadian now busy below, making sure his Lewis gun kept nosy maniacs away.

Lying in the ruined belfry was a pleasant relief after the climb, even with Ross' previous advice battering through his brain. With most of the stairs destroyed by a fallen bell, Archer was forced to use rope and grapple, the hook lashed together from angle-iron lying around the ruins. He'd made it all the way up with the weight of his robes and *Runebolt*. When he'd signalled for the others to clamber up, he was grateful he'd thought to put the knots in it – his colleagues weren't in their medium, but just as at the wall, none hesitated.

Nunzia shed her gear and was up the rope in a shot.

He blew out a slow, wistful sigh as they lay together, spying on the foe.

'What's on your mind, English?'

'I'm hoping to be home by Christmas,' he replied, unthinking.

Nunzia rolled onto her back, facing the partially destroyed belfry roof, and snorted. 'At least we will kill a lot of

Germans in the attack.' She chewed her bottom lip.

'They might all be Belgians. Or French. Maybe even Italians.'

She whinnied with a desultory note, but said nothing.

'Why do you hate them so?'

'You truly want to know?'

He turned his head, slowly easing back the veil so he could meet her eyes, finding them hard, distant. 'I think so, if it means you'll do something stupid.'

Her face changed, deflecting. 'Because they have done awful things.'

'Everyone has in this bloody war.' He resumed vigil.

'You couldn't understand.' She wriggled across to him, still on her back, until she was tucked up against him so she could whisper. 'I have an idea, one that will save us a lot of trouble if it works.'

He let her slide away from the previous topic, watching through the scope, but without really seeing. The Grand Army of Russia could have marched past; he was so focused on her. 'Go on.'

Her whisper was a hot lance into his ear, her tone deep and heavy, thick with suggestion and passionate promise. 'You need a distraction.'

Refusing to look, Archer fought to control the heat rising in his cheeks, allowing a sly smirk to take his lips. 'Now? Up here?'

Nunzia chuckled softly, pleased, but then just like the sea; her mood changed and became serious. She carefully and quietly explained her idea, and although it didn't result in a passionate clinch, Archer wasn't disappointed.

'Just one suggestion?' he held up his trigger finger. 'Do it after the convoy leaves.'

It was well past noon, and the Flanders heat was making the Blackcoats drowsy. Nothing was happening; the sentries were lolling, drinking wine, the others sitting around, still on guard, but now smoking. The city was quiet, the odd bang of a random, faraway shot, whilst to the east, the thunder of an artillery duel grew to a petulant rumble.

Here in Antwerp, it was relatively peaceful. Archer swigged more water as the baking continental heat warred with the breeze coming in from the North Sea. The birds twittered, the somnolent afternoon making him feel lazy too, but he shook it off, and checked his watch. It was time. Rolling to the *Runebolt*, he flexed his muscles to loosen them, before he slowly assumed his customary sniping posture.

His body at an angle to the target, based on handedness, one knee bent, stabilising his propped-up elbows. All elevation would be done by breathing and toes now – a push would drop the rifle, a pull to bring it up. Everything braced, but nothing too tight. Distance shooting done well was about clearing the mind, relaxing. Deep breathing would oxygenate his lungs and keep his body working when he held his breath. It was dangerous in a real situation, all too easy to drift off to sleep, especially because he would close and open his eyes periodically to check exactly where his crosshairs were resting, and his pulse would slow. When the familiar shape and feel of the stock completed him, he used the flag flying over the head of a sentry to gauge the wind's strength, maintaining alertness with calculations.

Three-hundred yards separated him from the men he was going to kill. He would have moments before the sound of the shot would strike after his first bullet. Even so, there would be confusion. He checked where the others were, finding Eisner and Ross making their way to the back of the compound, which was the only blind spot they identified. The two soldiers were focused on the job, Archer's scope showing grim, determined faces, their body postures geared for violence. He didn't know exactly where Nunzia was, until he heard her distinctive swearing.

Distance robbed the words of some definition, but a vicious stream of what he guessed was hard Italian invective was flowing. Comprehension eluded him, but he was sure Nunzia didn't repeat herself, which earned a smile. Taking a quick break from planning who to murder, he caught the Sea Witch in his crosshairs.

She was a sight of terrible fury; body taut with raw anger, grasping stones from the rubble floor, hurling them at some unseen *'Bastardi'*. Her hair was loose, a wild mane as she leapt through the debris, spitting and cursing. Wisely, she'd retained her boots, and clasped a jacket, but it concealed little, and she carried no other weapon than outrage.

A sharp slap hit the back of his head.

'Ow!'

He swivelled in response to the assault, caught Therese scowling at him. He'd told the girls to come up so he could keep them safe, but only Therese managed the scramble. Marie was happy enough to sit below, playing with a couple of dolls they'd retrieved from the remains of the church. It felt incredibly strange to be babysitting, and even more so when there was a language barrier. He wondered if this was how a parent felt most of the time, weighing it against being responsible for his younger brother and sister. He shrugged; there was an odd familiarity to it. Different, but there.

He risked another peek at Nunzia, and a deft poke hit his upper bicep.

'What?' he protested.

'*Non!*' Therese scolded.

He chuckled, held a hand up in surrender. 'Alright – Accord?'

'*D'accord,*' she replied, although in correction or agreement was unclear.

Chastised for being a peeping Tommy, Archer kept his view on the guards, sweeping the glass back to the compound. A shuffle beside him told him Therese was watching through the spotter glass. He carefully put his hand out, cupping the end of the scope and pushing it down, countered her indignation with a grim stare and a slow shake of his head.

'*Non.*'

A tiny nod and she relented, looked away to watch the view, or maybe keeping an eye out for Nunzia as she made her pell-mell dash to the guarded gate.

It was working. Sentries brought up their weapons in alarm and confusion. He saw their attitude change, followed by the ripples of laughter as almost all of them came to watch the Italian Captain shying stones and hurling abuse.

They whistled and hooted at her, some even clapped, and as she ran on towards them, Archer spied Eisner and Ross clear the wall at the back, and take up firing positions in the courtyard. A low wall made of loosely piled bricks, some oil barrels stuffed with pipes and metal spars, both provided a sturdy redoubt for the Canadian, who set up his machinegun with practiced ease, and the German hugged the cabin of one of the trucks parked nearby. Nunzia was safe from any crossfire, just as Archer planned.

One of the guards, a young sentry more conscientious than the rest, was still watching the yard. He was young, with peach fuzz on his chin and upper lip, and his face registered shock, yanking up his rifle to fire on Ross' flank.

Archer shot the boy in the throat.

Not a signal, but it was certainly a starter gun. The two men behind the Blackcoats opened fire at the same time. With Nunzia having tricked them into lining up on the wall, the murderous crossfire of the Lewis gun and machine pistol gave them no chance. Archer watched men tumble, gory red slick decorating heat-baked stone walls and cobbles where they fell. He added to it, his movements naught but rote: sight, breathe, aim and fire.

Where Blackcoats scrambled into place to threaten any of his comrades, Archer was there, his rifle barking, stealing life. More men spilled from inside, threatening to overwhelm his friends, but he simply sighted on centre mass of the first man out, shot him in the chest and watched him fall, causing his comrades to stumble, and as the men and women behind him pulled free of the collapsed corpse, he'd re-chambered.

He fired until his magazine was empty, sparing a moment for how the old soldiers at Waterloo or even Balaclava would have given anything for a rifle like this, before picking up the carefully positioned loose rounds within reach of his right hand, slotting them in through the open action, making sure the rimmed cartridges were butted up against each other properly so they wouldn't jam. Avoiding 'rim-lock' was a necessary nuisance the Germans didn't have to bother with.

He found Ross, his position covered in discarded brass, the staccato sound of weapon stilled whilst he reloaded. The barrel of the weapon was fairly smoking. He flinched involuntarily as a bullet spanked against one of his ammunition pans, sending it reeling away. Archer looked for the source of the shot, but couldn't see it, no matter how he panned and swept the rifle; he was just at the wrong angle.

Time to dismount.

Signalling Therese, he indicated she should go down, and as the rope creaked and span whilst she descended, he gathered all his equipment, carefully removing his scope and placing it into his rucksack, before he gripped the rope, the fibres soaking the sweat suddenly springing onto his palms. He dared not look down, but the vertigo came anyway as he kept his eyes firmly on the pathetically thin hemp cable he was putting his faith in.

He climbed down methodically, feeling for the knots with his feet, breathing hard with relief with each secure clinch. The rope twisted as his weight shifted, each yard seeming to take longer than the last, but Ross and his comrades needed him, and that thought carried him.

When his feet firmly met the ground, his legs were jelly, but he managed to keep upright. How he'd survived the Sniper School with all the tower and tree climbing, he'd never truly understand. He could feel the coolness of the shaded building, the walls broken in places but a good refuge for anyone in need of shade. The long pews installed to seat the congregation were long gone, likely taken for firewood or even floorboards.

Archer gripped the stock of the *Runebolt,* bringing it from his back into his hands. A stab of guilt at his killing struck, as his attention fell onto the altar. He tried to remember the names he'd learned as a small boy for the places in church, sadness at the desecration, the statues of saints sundered and smashed. It had long been violated, but he felt ashamed at adding to it. It was an old feeling, as once his talent was discovered, the Church was...reticent to have him darken the door. It took a long time to realise that wasn't his fault, and longer to understand it wasn't God's. He took one last look at the altar, and the tall cross which lay toppled across it.

'Forgive them Father, for they know not what they do.'

The words came from somewhere else, a part of him that didn't know he was mired in brimstone. Then he pulled the breech of his rifle open, thumbed a fresh clip of five rounds into the *Runebolt's* internal magazine, topping it off, and ran outside to kill some more.

10:

The two girls tried to keep pace, but he could hear them behind him, panting and scraping across the rubble of Antwerp's northwest quarter. Therese had the bulk of Nunzia's clothes bundled in her arms; Marie carried two dollies and a pistol belt. Up ahead, Archer could see three people grappling, and as he closed the distance with long strides, his hurry was nearly his undoing. He slipped; almost tumbling in a crazed sprawl into a crater filled with brown sludge. His careful navigation and footwork were meaningless against the sight of Nunzia beating at two Blackcoats who were roughly handling her.

Her need drove him on, over the uneven and treacherous slopes of the pulverised terrain, and he increased his pace, heart thumping in desperation. At one-hundred yards from them, the brawling group fell over together, one laughing as he reeled back to his feet, reaching for the front of his trousers. Archer didn't need to guess the intent, nor did he bother with anything fancy. Huffing and puffing he dropped to his knee. Bullets would move faster than he could.

'Nunzia, get down!'

The rifle cracked, shot thumping home into the target, lifting the first man with an invisible horse kick to the jaw. The Italian Captain was too close to risk a second shot, so Archer ran on, charging the second assailant, who fumbled at his belt for a weapon. Despite the lack of bayonet fitted to the muzzle, Archer screamed and lunged, thumping the kneeling Blackcoat in the chest with blunt force, winding and toppling him backwards. In the gap, Archer stomped forward, bringing the butt of the rifle up and down with all his weight. A dull, wet cabbage-crunch, announced he'd done the job right.

Panting, he stood above the corpse, before laboriously tugging off the man's long jacket and tossing it behind him for Nunzia.

'You took your time, English.' She wasn't as breathless as he was.

'Are you alright?'

'*Si*, they need you inside, go!'

Without sneaking a peek at her, he nodded, recovered enough to run onwards, towards the sharp snap of bullets being exchanged. When he reached the compound, he pulled up against the gatepost, made ready, and rounded the corner with the rifle in his shoulder.

Shots screamed at him almost instantly, forcing him to dive to his right, behind a row of packing cases for ammunition. He prayed they were empty; continued crawling, knuckles bruised and aching by breaking the sudden fall. Behind him, shots clipped through the wood, driving splinters down at him. Finally gaining the protection of a wall, he sat to recover, breathing hard. He risked a peek, just in time to see Ross besieged.

Having moved across the courtyard for a better position, now the Canadian was pinned down, finger-sized holes poking through the oil drums he sheltered behind. One found him, a blot of red staining his rough clothing, and invisible fingers plucked at his back.

'Hal!' Archer called.

'It's just a scratch!' Ross reloaded his machinegun, cocked it, but it slipped out of his hand, leaving a ruddy smear on the barrel shroud. 'Oh,' he said, slumping down.

'Kurt, where is the bastard?'

'Above us, to the right – he is in that window on the end.'

Archer looked out, slowly pushing his head around the corner. Bullets drove him back. 'Can you play pigeon, *Mein Herr*?'

Eisner grinned from where he was half-crouched

behind the truck engine, his teeth shocking white in his dirt smeared face. He fearlessly stood up, firing a burst from his machine pistol, bracketing the window with the gunman hidden inside. Archer leaned around the corner – it would be a left-handed shot, but he took his time, lining up squeezing the trigger until it was a hair-break. As Eisner ducked, reloading his weapon with its eccentric snail-like magazine, the gunman pinning them popped up to reply.

Archer fired, redness spilling over a stone windowsill of the police barracks. A long-barrelled pistol fell onto the ground below with a dull *click-clack*. The noise seemed to be the last note of the battle. He stood up, collecting himself before making his way across the horribly open courtyard to see to his wounded friend.

'Just the shoulder,' Ross complained, a few red bubbles appearing on his lips.

A bullet hole through the grey and black tunic was clotted with blood, but the shot had come down from such an angle, Archer suspected it was more than a trifling flesh wound. His thoughts were confirmed when Eisner swapped glances with him, shaking his head almost imperceptibly when the Canadian wasn't looking.

'We need to get him inside.' Archer decided, just as Nunzia and the girls came into the compound.

Holding up his hand to forestall them, Eisner rummaged in a side pouch of his webbing order, extracting a German battle dressing. Tearing the packet open with his teeth, he shoved it underneath Ross' tunic onto his wound. The latter groaned, but no more escaped him as the two men gripped him under the shoulders.

'Nunzia, take Kurt's weapon. Sweep it out, make sure it's safe.'

She nodded, once more dressed in her loose-fitting gear, snatched up the gun and lead to the main door at a stride. The girls moved to pick up the Lewis, but Archer shook his head. 'No, leave it.'

The Italian Captain mule-kicked the door in, jerked the machine pistol left and right, before waving to her companions that the coast was clear. Coming in behind her, Archer watched as she warily manoeuvred down the corridor, lit by the meagre efforts of buzzing electric bulbs overhead. Her footwork careful in the rubble-strewn passageway, Nunzia menaced each doorway, gap and window, until they found an office with a desk. She dropped the weapon onto it and heaved, ramming it against the wall, before grabbing French issue greatcoats from pegs, spreading them on the table and bundling another up for a pillow.

'Put him there,' she instructed, retrieving the machine pistol.

The two men wrestled the tough Canadian onto his makeshift bed. Archer remembered the man's fear in the submarine; so pivoting his rifle, smashed through boards nailed over a shuttered window. The brass butt crashed the timber through, making short work of the planks and spilling good, clean sunlight into the room.

'Enough space, Hal?'

Ross nodded weakly, a thin smile on his pale face.

'Girls, Nunzia,' Archer tore himself from the stricken man, 'stay with him. Kurt, go and get the Lewis.'

'*Jawohl.*'

'I'll try to find the key to the cells,' Archer clasped a hand on Nunzia's shoulder before vanishing. Without further word, they left the room, the German splitting off to get the team's machinegun.

Italian was close enough to the Latin Mass that Nunzia could offer the French girls broken instructions. Between the three of them, she thought they made a decent hospital team. She told Marie to find alcohol, bandages, anything to try and compress the wound. She led by example, pushing down hard, before Therese offered up a bottle of medical spirits and a towel. She took them, and seizing her knife, cut away the uniform matted with blood. Ross groaned as she peeled the German battle dressing off, soaked the towel in the cheap spirit, and hurriedly clamped it down. A discarded pistol belt went around it, and she tightened it up as best she could.

Nunzia watched Ross' eyes roll, and shook him. 'Hal? Hal!'

'Mama?'

'No, Hal. Nunzia. Come on, wake up.'

'It hurts.'

She searched for something to keep him awake, talking. 'Tell me about Canada. Is big, no? Is pretty?'

'Sometimes.'

She changed tack. 'Why are you here Hal, why did you come?'

'Ran away. Coward. Was curtains for me, unless I went on the mission.' He grasped her hand where it pressed against his wound.

'Curtains?' She tried to mask her interest.

'Like the theatre,' Ross mumbled, 'show's over, lights out.'

In the darkness of the police station, Archer slung the *Runebolt* over his shoulder, exchanging it for the self-loading pistol. He was sorely tempted to mount the Orilux trench torch he carried, but the darkness wasn't deep enough to trade the advantage of stealth for the ability to tell what colour the wallpaper was. The torch, like a lighter, was a liability. Slowly, he moved down the hall in the opposite direction to Eisner's flight, following signs to the Commandant's office, and hopefully the keys to the cells below.

Each step was a creak away from getting his head blown off. Even though the ground floor was swept clean, he couldn't be certain the upper rooms were similarly disinfected – and although he had the grenades to make sure, he couldn't discount the possibility of prisoners, innocents or exceptionally combustible materials lurking within.

The lights were pathetic, but at least the gloom would hide him if he needed to dive into a corner. The air was damnably still, the windows closed and shuttered against draughts in this wing. Any kind of breeze would clear the dust, carry scent or sound, but there was nothing except the settling of bricks in summer heat.

Archer paced forward, the boxy Webley low at his waist, his other palm touching the partition walls of offices, storerooms, and a library. When he looked inside, he saw a shaggy shape move, flinch as he suddenly shied back. He nearly fired, but steeled himself to look again, reasoning it could have been a frightened prisoner. They hadn't shot at him, after all. Carefully, he leaned into the doorway, the shape moving with him. He lifted the pistol to fire at the soot-scorched face looming in the darkness, before recognising his own reflection.

'Bloody hell,' he breathed loudly, turning to continue.

At the end of the corridor, a small man suddenly appeared.

'*Mon Dieu!*' He scrambled for his gun, diving back into the office he'd just vacated.

Likewise, Archer sought cover, tumbling into the library, just before two shots clipped the doorsill, the echo of the rapid gunfire ringing down the hall. He cursed, wondering where Eisner or Nunzia were. He got to his knees, hearing the snap and crack of glass under his body, thankful the clothes protected him. He brushed them out of the way, finding he'd landed on the mirror.

Seven years' bad luck. Wonderful.

The impression Archer got of his assailant was tidiness; uniform and web equipment in good order, an officer who sought refuge when the shooting started. Trying to peek again, another shot banged into plaster, right by his head. A good shot, proving the man had a clear line of fire, and little else to shoot at.

The bullet was followed by a demand in a French

accent. 'Still alive, Englishman?'

Smarting from the sting of a near miss, Archer said nothing, no reason to play pigeon. He felt for one of the mirror pieces and tilted it, edging it closer and closer to the doorframe; he could see the man leaning out with a Luger, a bulkhead light casting his silhouette. The glass was blasted from his hand with a crash.

He needed a distraction.

Bang, bang. The rounds came, and Archer could feel the rush from the disturbed air, the tramp of boots as the Frenchman charged, driving him back. By reflex, Archer pressed his hand to the wall, detecting the pulse of a generator pushing power under the plaster. He closed his eyes, latched onto it, hunting. *Find it – there, now follow it. The whole building, lights, switches, everything. The veins.*

He scraped his bayonet free, worked the tip into the plaster, which fell away in clumps to reveal rotten wiring. Bare metal winked, and he tapped the blade to it, felt the jolt as he became part of the circuit. He charged into the flow, a current different from Nunzia's medium, sensing the little glass blisters hanging like ripe fruit. He pulled on the threads, shook the tree.

'I kill you, Englishman!'

Now.

The sharp pops of glass brought him back to the room, a smooth golden glow fading as the Frenchman shrieked in fright, the light bulbs exploding over his head, showering him with fulminate powder and razor-sharp shrapnel. Archer was on his feet; saw the other man wrench away, blinded and bleeding from exploding glass. He lashed out with his right hand, disarming the man, firing twice at point-blank range into his opponent's chest. The Blackcoat reeled, fell, tried to turn over. A gasp left the corpse to sag.

Quickly, Archer ransacked the body, pulling a ring of keys free from a buttoned leather pouch, before walking back to the head of the stairs he knew led down into more darkness.

He would need Kurt. He didn't realise he was breathing hard until confronted by Nunzia, brandishing the machine pistol, guarding Ross and the two girls.

'What happened? Are you alright?'

He half-smiled at her concern, hoping it was genuine. 'I'm fine. Just some light resistance.' Knowing they were on the clock, he called for Eisner to hurry.

Deathly silence accompanied the British Sniper and German Stormtrooper as they descended the steps, reaching a landing. A pipe dripped, water falling in a tap-tap-tap cadence, and nodding in agreement, the soldiers matched it, continuing down into the cells beneath the police station. Strange and unpleasant odours wafted up the stairwell, terminating in a pair of doors wedged open with bricks.

It was much cooler below ground level, yet Archer was sweating, breathing through his mouth to prevent vomiting due to the wretched smell. Blood and ordure filled the air, a bass taint to the sharp clinical tang of iodine and antiseptic. The wretched stink still made him ill. A quick glance at Eisner revealed he was having the same trouble. He considered donning his gas mask, but the light was poor enough without having to blink through distorting glass.

A scuff of boot heel, a clink of chain, told them they were in the right place. Both men made sure their weapons were ready before going any further. The German led down, machine pistol tracking left and right, covering the angles as they emerged from the stairwell, Eisner carefully peeking both ways before motioning Archer to follow. As the sniper entered the adjoining corridor, he could see that to the left was blind end, a collection of buckets in the corner overflowed with ruddy slop. A host of flies attended it, crazily lifting and landing.

The corridor fell away to his right, with six cell doors set into the left side, and another door on the right side, half way along marked with a flag of the Red Cross hanging above it from a couple of nails. At the far end stood a slab of dark metal, pitted with rust, and fitted with large lever handles, it was affixed to the wall by heavy duty hinges. It was likely the original arsenal door. Eisner tapped words painted on the wall, daubed in rough French and repeated in tidier German.

INTERROGATOIRE

VERHÖRRAUM

Archer got the idea. Another rasp of irons reached them, perhaps three doors down. It didn't matter who it was, he vowed not to leave anyone here. He pulled the ring of keys from his belt, and examined them. Each had a scratched Roman numeral in the bare metal fob, and he scanned for the same marks on the doors and lintels of the cells.

The cell doors had a cast-iron grate in the upper half for a window, and a trap at the bottom for food and soil bucket. A quick peek inside the first two cells revealed nothing but bundles of rags, so the soldiers kept stalking forward in their strange rolling walk, until they reached the third in line.

A huddled shape occupied the furthest corner, but Archer couldn't discern anything more. It was certainly a human being, because as he leaned across the grate, he blocked the wan light, and the prisoner recoiled in a rattle of shackles. He recalled the three people taken from the truck and wondered if this was one of them, maybe even a member of the diplomatic staff.

He fumbled the keys in the dim light, holding them up to match the numeral, his efforts prompting the captive to start mewling and trying to fit into the furthest reaches of the cell. The plaintive sounds became more desperate as he opened the door, the rusty lock yielding to the key. The hinges groaned before letting out a squeal that set his teeth on edge.

The prisoner became frantic, slamming against the wall, clawing it, the chains making an awful racket, until finally Archer caught a mumbled string of words. The prisoner was female, speaking English.

'Don't hurt me, please! Don't hurt me, don't hurt me.'

He crouched, thinking best to reduce his height, appear less threatening. It also occurred to him that in the flayed carpet of sniper robes, he possibly resembled a prisoner like her. He kept his distance, made no sudden moves.

'It's alright. My name is Daniel. We won't hurt you. I'm here to help.'

Kneeling down shed light onto her, and the bundle of rags and manacles slowly turned. A crop of matted hair that may have once been long, fine gold, was pulled from a face swollen and grubby from the squalor that surrounded it. Her lips were split, and Archer could see bruised feet and grazed knuckles. Possibly injured escaping from the airship, he suspected more was inflicted by this place.

A metallic clang resounded through the corridor as the huge metal door opened, the vibrations of it rattling through the pipes, bars and grates of the cellblock. Two men emerged, wearing long aprons repeatedly stained with brown blotches. They were red up to the elbows, one of them wiping mess off his hands as he left the sanctuary of the old arsenal. Both carried holstered pistols. They stared at Archer and Eisner, confusion bleeding into deadly understanding. The moment drew out.

One went for his gun.

Eisner was faster.

11:

The machine pistol spat a long burst, the noise horrendous in the confined space, a crash of continuous thunder. The muzzle flare lit the grim corridor with blinding flashes at crazy angles, expended cartridges showering the floor. Through it all, the Eisner's face was stone in the hellish light, his quick humour and gentleness gone. Archer realised that this was the true *Sturmpioneer*.

The stunted silence afterwards was eerie. The German stepped over the bodies, striding purposefully forward, heading for the end room with weapon levelled, ready for whatever grisly scene lurked therein. Archer pushed the woman back into the cell. 'I'll come back. Stay right here!'

'Don't leave me!'

'I won't – it's dangerous – *stay here.*' He hurried to Eisner.

They nodded to each other, and taking a breath, they went through door. It was no longer a clean, ordered storage area for police firearms and seized contraband. Two bodies hung from chains attached to hooks in the ceiling, naked, they had been beaten and tortured, fingers and toes severed. A set of bolt cutters caked in blood shared a table with knives, a hammer, and nails. The floor was ingrained with filth.

Another man was inside, of Archer's height, but Eisner's build. He stepped back from his grisly work, his male victim shuddering and gasping from his attentions. Archer took one look at the hanging man, kicked a low bench across the floor and pointed at the torturer.

'Keep him covered!'

'*Jawohl.*' Eisner spat at the torturer's boots, keeping the machine pistol trained without a tremor, a slow curl lifting the corner of his mouth.

Standing on the wobbly bench, Archer gripped the man hanging like a slab of meat, the prisoner's arms bound so tightly and stretched into rigid bars by his own weight, that it was a simple task to get him off the hook. The man collapsed, and with the burden balanced enough on his shoulder, Archer stepped down.

'I have to get the victims out of here, but I want to question him. Don't do anything until I'm back.'

'You have my word, Daniel.'

He grimaced, hurrying from the chamber, stopping only to find the woman cowering still in the cell. At least one of them was safe. He called out for her to follow him, before getting to the bottom of the stairs. He rested the weight of the victim against the wall a moment.

'Nunzia! *Nunzia!*'

It was a full minute before her long black mane tumbled over the landing rail. 'Are you trying to woo me on my balcony, English – *Mio Dio!*'

The smirk vanished from her face at once, and she swore, rushing down the concrete steps, until she rounded the corner and helped to get the wounded man on her shoulder, blood from the victim smearing her cheeks and hands. Just like Archer, she ignored it as she shared the weight, and they slowly hauled upstairs. 'Who is your girlfriend?'

Blowing hard, Archer was unable to riposte. Hauling the man up to the top had been a challenge, even with Nunzia's help. Finally he replied. 'I don't know. Go downstairs, there's a first aid room or something, might be supplies there – and check in on Kurt.'

'I'm on my way.'

'Wait,' he warned, 'it's horrible.'

She watched him carefully; head cocked, maybe waiting for a joke, but any flippancy was long quashed.

'I will be careful,' she assured. Then, in contradiction,

she smiled, vaulting down the flights, the clatter of boots rapping like shod hooves on cobblestones.

Though the dull-grey concrete was oppressive and imposing, Nunzia didn't hide her approach, trotting with a spring in her step, refusing to be intimidated. Whistling, she descended at pace, the loud approach announcing her well ahead of time. She caught the offal stink emanating from the cells, bracing for whatever insanity Archer had warned her against. The aid station was little more than a small storeroom with a single seat to rest while taking inventory, but she ransacked it for supplies, finding six fresh gauze bandages and a bottle of iodine.

Stuffing her loot into pockets, she carefully approached the large door, peeking round just in time to witness Eisner place down his gun on a bench by his knee, and reach for the case holding his axe. He snapped the rich leather open, gripping the haft. A bright-bladed head slipped free, the light drawn down the rounded cutting edge in a smiling gleam, and the *Sturmpioneer* took the weapon in both hands with practiced ease.

'Having fun, Kurt?' she asked. The noxious odour slithered out into the hall, threatened to make her gag.

'Not yet.'

She could see Eisner staring at a large man, whose burly arms were raised in surrender. A large black coat sat across the back of a wooden chair, the sleeve complete with the insignia for a Sergeant in the Imperial German Army. She didn't speak German, and doubted he could manage Italian, so decided to keep to English. She understood why Archer wanted her to check up on them. Eisner's face was haunted with murderous anger.

Nunzia breathed through her mouth, and stepped into an abattoir. Even the precaution couldn't stop her stomach heaving. She spied the messy bolt cutters, remembered the chains binding the tortured prisoners and picked them up. She whacked the head against the ground a few times to dislodge the gore.

Eisner's voice was hard at her back. 'What are you up to, *Meerhexe*?'

She turned around. 'What does it look like?'

'Not that. You gave the British a U-boat?' His eyes were riveted to the prisoner.

'Loaned, by my government.'

'Hmm. There is something in Antwerp the Italians want,' he shrugged, hefting the axe. 'I do not care what. Do what you must, but do not get in my way.'

Nunzia sneered, ignoring the sullen Blackcoat. 'I should have dunked you like your sailors. It would have improved your manners.'

'You are a fish out of water here, Annunziata. Remember that.'

Frowning, Nunzia swiped at the heavy cutting tool with a rag, before cradling it in her arms. Errand complete, she retreated, leaving Eisner to guard the charnel house, axe in hand.

As soon as Archer came into the room with the tortured man, Therese and Marie knew what to do, making a rough bed for the wounded man, although on the floor. Archer carefully put him down, not noticing that Nunzia had returned, carrying the bolt cutters. Taking them, he nodded grimly, repurposing them from their previous, sordid life, using them to cut away the chains and manacles that trussed the captives.

'Someone owes me answers. I'll be back,' he told the women, before turning and leaving the poor victim to the mercies of the Sea Witch and her impromptu nursing station. Ross was still awake, watching them. He gave Archer a thumb up.

He went back down, walking quietly, because he heard voices coming from up ahead, Eisner was talking to the torturer. Approaching cautiously, Archer could hear Eisner rattling off German as opposed to bullets, but the words were just as pointed. He recognised one as a name: *Abwehr*. He rolled it around in his head before it clicked – German Military Intelligence. The rest was beyond him, but hearing enough, he stepped into the room, Webley pistol held low at his waist. The threat it presented was obvious, but deferred.

'Something to tell me?'

'I told him to spill his guts.' Eisner span his inlaid axe to suggest it wasn't just metaphorical, before the sly grin he wore vanished. 'Is this barbarity what we have bled for all these years? Is this what men have died for?'

The man shrugged. *'Das ist Krieg.'*

That's war. Archer realised the man understood him, had some grasp of English, which somehow made it worse.

Eisner scoffed at the world-weary dismissal with a bitter snort. His face was terrible, outrage bleeding into the room as the life of so many victims had before, the thick walls muffling the screams of the vile crimes perpetrated within.

'The war is at the Front! Not here!' Eisner growled, adding more in vicious German, and taking a pace forward, he brought the axe up.

'Wait, Kurt. Where is the American woman?' Archer kept his eyes on the torturer, keeping his voice steady, authoritative.

The man shook his head, confused. 'No American.'

'From the airship?' Archer pressed.

A vigorous shake of his head in stronger denial greeted that. 'No American – English.'

Archer pointed. *'Alles Engländer?'*

'Ja.' The Blackcoat raised his hands, but in placation or surrender was unclear.

'Lock him up,' Archer offered the recovered keys to Eisner's free hand. 'If he resists, close the door so I don't hear it.'

Eisner spat more of his native language at the Sergeant, contempt thick on the only word Archer knew - *lucky*. The axe flashed as he gestured with it, the silver head making the light dance. The prisoner realised he'd been spared, and complied, moving around the room at Eisner's direction, all the while his gaze fixed on the blade. A grim smile played about Eisner's lips, goading the man to make a costly error.

Archer picked up the machine pistol as his comrade put the torturer in the third cell, before taking a moment to fully appreciate the chamber of horrors around him. He truly wouldn't have been bothered by Eisner's revenge, but instinct warned him a man from the *Abwehr* was worth a little caution. Archer led back upstairs.

Her name was Kate. She told how they used her against the men taken from the airship. They were all gondola crew, serving staff and waiters. The big Sergeant would ask the men a question, and when they didn't give a satisfactory answer, he would drag her into the room and beat her until they did. When it was clear they knew nothing, they forced her to watch as the torturers went to work with all manner of tools.

'The Sergeant said he would…'enjoy' me after they were dead.' She sobbed quietly and Nunzia gently held her around the shoulders.

Eisner's knuckles were white where he gripped pieces of the Lewis gun, busying himself by assembling it under Ross' careful eye. Morphine discovered in a small aid cabinet had returned a spark of the Canadian's colour and he directed the task, a smooth metal clack announced the weapon was ready for service. Ross lay back, pleased.

'What about the American diplomat?' Archer asked Kate, as gently as he could.

They sat in the room amidst the rough breathing of wounded men, motes of old dust stirring in the breeze from the window, the heat of the midday sun now long gone. When it looked like she might not answer, he stood, hands on hips and walked to the window, looking out.

'Diplomat?'

'There were Americans on board, yes?'

'Yes, soldiers, I think, and a large black fellow.'

'Sam?'

Kate nodded.

Archer's heart sank, blood cold, then hot. He noticed everyone was looking at him. 'What were they doing aboard?'

'We don't ask passengers their business,' she replied, simply.

'Did they say anything?'

'Not really, they were angry they had to put their guns in the hold.'

'What does this all mean, English?'

Archer frowned. 'It means I fed the Yanks a line, and they reeled me in.'

'That's not all,' Eisner said from his vantage point, staring out over the courtyard, 'a lot of Blackcoats are coming through the front gate.'

'Make...machinegun noises,' Ross suggested, 'that will...drive them off.'

'And waste ammunition?' Eisner shot back.

Propped up on elbows, Ross chuckled wetly, seized in sudden coughing fit, thick red phlegm sputtering through teeth clenched against the pain. 'You're alright, Kurt.'

The German said nothing, turned his head quickly to view the courtyard.

Nunzia shook her head, black mane twisting with the motion. She gently pushed the injured man back down onto his makeshift cot, a sad smile on her face as she dabbed at his mouth with a handkerchief. 'Boys will be boys, no?'

Ramifications queued up to filter into Archer's mind, displacing the grim urge to laugh. The US Marines guardedly spoke about the airship, and then only in general terms, leaving him to fill in the gaps. Miller picked up on what he said, then fed in just enough misdirection. He sent the annoyance over the subterfuge to the back of his mind, as he and the companions who could fight, crouched by the windowsills overlooking the yard.

Eisner wasn't wrong. It looked like the two trucks had brought not just the complement of people protecting the earlier convoy, but a rabble of other, eager Blackcoats. One of them was heavily bandaged, and Archer recognised his face. Cursing under his breath, his team was being used as a decoy by the US Marines. He should have spotted it, and *that* irked him more.

In all likelihood, it meant his mission was a washout. With the Americans taking their ball and going home, there was nothing he could do about it now, and pressing problems required his focus. He watched the enemy taking up positions in the yard, hugging low walls, crates and barrels. Rifles poked around the same corners Archer had used over an hour before.

Nunzia crouched nearby, the Lewis gun just too heavy; she was instead equipped with a captured Mauser rifle, her pistol belt supplemented by German ammunition cases. She was busy stuffing both the pouches and her pockets full of clips, before getting the weapon ready. She looked up at him. 'I never asked…when I was running – did you see anything you liked?'

'Not much,' he lied, 'Therese slapped me.'

She chuckled softly, pushing the bolt of the Mauser home.

Before he could dig himself a bigger hole, someone shouted from below, calling out for the Commander of the garrison, the soft, rolling language of France echoing from the bullet-ridden walls and corpse-laden yard of the compound.

'Wait,' Archer said quietly.

The man calling out appeared to be an officer, his black coat matched by a black cap. His clothes carried German Imperial insignia, but there the influence ended, because his French wasn't accented. Archer marvelled at the melting pot Antwerp had become – although as a port town it was to be expected, but being walled up exacerbated the process. He was unsure if the men below were deserters from the French Army, or ex-prisoners of war of the Germans. He shrugged, it didn't matter.

'Commandant Faviér!' the officer called again, pistol in hand.

A knot of them were clustered around one of their trucks in the yard, unwilling to expose themselves, and Archer patted one of his pouches, flicking it open. He found the special round by touch alone, could tell them even in the pitch dark of no-man's land, or a trench – because of the feel of the bullet at the nose of the cartridge. Mk IX Spitzer-Brice, lovingly crafted by Holland & Holland, each one worth a Captain's monthly salary. He carefully seated it in the chamber of the *Runebolt*, and concentrated. Power drained from him, making him a touch giddy. The rifle charged up, and he could hear a confused and curious call from below as the weapon began its characteristic glow. He opened his eyes, sighted on the truck, and fired.

12:

The spectacular phosphor-blue thunderbolt and accompanying ozone were replaced with the flat *crump* as the vehicle detonated in two stages. The engine ripped asunder, quickly followed by the fuel tank in an orange-black fireball. Heated air sucked even Archer's breath, pulling everything in to feed its hungry combustion, whilst the blast scattered debris everywhere.

Several Blackcoats were just...gone. In the aftermath, the shouting and moaning of the wounded quickly gave way to angry bullets, chipping the brickwork around the windows where Archer and his comrades sheltered. He noticed Nunzia was stunned. It took her a moment to regain her senses, before she galvanized into action, shooting back at the enemy below.

There were a lot more than he'd thought, but the truck had helped to thin them a little, delay them at least. Even so, they responded aggressively, filling the yard with running men, covered by a torrent of rifle fire. Archer snapped off an opportune killing shot, before being forced to duck back. 'If they get inside, we are dead!'

'Need...a hand?'

Archer looked over his shoulder, saw Ross looming, chest heaving with effort.

Stripped to the waist, bandage straps crossed his torso, the white dressings discoloured with iodine. His wound pads stained with bright and dark redness, the Canadian stumbled forward with grim determination. Archer couldn't move to help, pinned down as he was, but Ross ignored the bullets careening around the room, even though looking likely to topple at any moment.

Ricochets pinging and zapping about him, Ross planted the muzzle of the machinegun on the sill, pushing it out until the weapon took the balance. Even so, his right bicep strained to pull the butt into his shoulder to aim, his left arm hanging limp. Grimacing, he squeezed the trigger and held it down. Barely able to control the recoil, his teeth bloody and gritted, he traversed the muzzle in a practiced swing, an occasional pink bubble sprouting from his lips.

The Lewis was a ferocious, chattering addition to the combat. Spraying bullets everywhere, it tore into the advancing enemy, a scythe threshing wheat, forcing the other Blackcoats to duck back for fear of catching a stray round. Seeing their friends fall ahead of them, the soldiers below took cover behind whatever they could find. Taking his cue, Eisner blasted at the slowest on the uptake with short bursts.

Dropping to his knees, Archer peeked over his parapet, sighting anyone foolish enough to attempt a shot in reply. He fired quickly, taking one man in the eye, another in the throat, the *Runebolt* creaking with the punishment he was putting it through, the stock already warm from the special bullet. He continued searching for targets as he was trained to do, until movement outside the gate caught his attention.

Another truck, face on to his window.

Click-clack, click-clack, bang.

There was a sharp snap of glass, a red smear on the windscreen, and the driver slumped over the wheel, dead.

'This place is a popular tourist attraction!' Nunzia shouted over the din.

'You wanted to come, remember?' Archer called.

She duelled with a man behind a concrete water butt. A bullet snicked a chunk of her hair free, grazing the top of her left ear. It prompted a rushing wave of Italian curses. Archer fancied that if her language was a weapon, she'd flatten half of Antwerp.

Being a gentleman, he killed her tormentor, putting a shot through the corner of the wall, showering the yard with razor shards of brick. The corpse tumbled from behind. A sharp gasp from Nunzia froze him in worry.

'*Mio Dio*,' she breathed, 'do you ever miss?'

'Can't afford to,' he replied, thawing with the rote response, glad she was alright.

Furtive movement drew his attention to a truck in the yard. Stacked up on bricks, it was obviously being slowly repaired by the former garrison, but the man now underneath it wasn't holding a wrench. Wriggling on his back, a clever Blackcoat had found a better angle on Ross than his comrades. *Bang.* The man went limp, eyes closed, his face serene. It looked like he was napping. Taking the chance, Archer reloaded his rifle to maximum capacity.

A sharp shout came from his right, and Ross fell to the floor, his machinegun clattering down with him. A red runnel was torn along the left side of his head, and Eisner was over him in moments, gripping him under the arms and dragging the wounded man back. Archer felt the cold pit in his stomach, but they couldn't afford sentiment, not now. They needed the German's rapid-fire weapon employed.

'Kurt! Get back on the bloody line!'

The German looked angry for a second, but discipline and the keen understanding of the predicament banished it. Having no choice, Archer called out to Kate, still cowering in the room with the other prisoner and the two girls. He couldn't blame them one bit – they demonstrated altogether too much sense. He shouted at her to come out and see to Ross.

Between them, on hands and knees they got the Canadian back into the room.

'Daniel! They are coming!' Eisner tried to repel the attackers by blind firing straight down from his window, and the screams of men and women being shot carried up over the noise. He tore an empty magazine free and ran for the stairs. Once he gained the landing, they heard him bellow his challenge. '*Achtung!*'

Previously in farce, this time the machine pistol rattled

in earnest, just as Eisner promised in the Dunkirk storehouse. The sound continued, the *Sturmpioneer* keeping the trigger down, until finally the shout came up that all was clear. In the courtyard, Archer noticed the officer was still alive, and he was waving to his men to cease firing. Snagging a white handkerchief on a bayonet, the man strode forward.

'Hello?'

'Halt!' Archer demanded. 'One more step, and I'll blow your head off!'

The officer smiled dismissively, accompanying the response with a dismissive shrug at the defiance. '*Monsieur*, you have five minutes to surrender. After that we come in.'

'And die in the attempt.'

The officer laughed. 'It is you who will die, War Mage. A pity, yes?'

Archer offered a pair of raised fingers to reply in rude salute, and the officer and flag of truce both disappeared around the corner, irritatingly out of sight.

Footsteps announced Eisner's return, his face unreadable as he reported in. 'I only have one magazine, but I collected a few grenades.' He shrugged.

Even with the fresh ordnance, it was a losing battle. A futile last stand here would serve no purpose but pride. Archer had to find out what was really happening, why the Americans had gone so far to hide the truth. He groaned to a bent-over crouch, dusting off his knees. Grateful the *Runebolt* was being given a chance to cool, he poked his head out of the window in Ross' room. There was a drop of some twenty feet to the ground, the outside curtain wall four feet away and ten below the window. It would be a tall ask to get anyone out of there, especially himself.

He gathered the others in the room, so everyone could hear him as he explained the situation. 'There's a wire fence at each end of the building, so no-one is behind us – yet.'

'They could be waiting over the wall,' Nunzia bit her lip.

'We will grenade it before we climb over,' Eisner said.

'With Ross?' Nunzia shook her head.

'Forget about me,' The Canadian croaked, surfacing from the stupor induced by having his bell rung, 'I'll keep them busy.'

Blood drooled freely from his mouth, the cumulative trauma taking its inexorable toll. Archer grabbed him, pulled him upright against the wall. Ross groaned, laboured breathing relaxed just enough, but his skin carried a waxen sheen. They shared glances, saying nothing. The shoulder wound was already mortal; the Canadian's bullish fighting had merely finished him off faster – along with a lot of Blackcoats too.

'Leave...the wounded,' Ross gasped, 'you have...job to do.'

Archer gripped his hand, feeling the lingering strength of a hunter hardened to tough stalks and rugged mountains. Eisner stormed from the room, Nunzia's accusing stare following him, until he returned, festooned with weapons. His machine pistol slung over his shoulder, in one hand he held the Lewis Gun, which he promptly deposited on the bed, the trigger in easy reach for Ross' hand. His other fist grasped the entrenching shovel, Ross' Arcanist Focus. Magical in fabrication, a tool by design, in a trench-raid it was as good as an axe. He pressed the handle into the Canadian's bloody fingers.

'My friend, you will need this.'

A shout came from the front of the building.

Ross gave a bloody grin. '*Kameraden.*'

The shooting resumed. Time was up.

Eisner looked at the Canadian for a long moment, a shadow passing over his face before vanishing abruptly as he burst into motion. He went to the window first, holding a stick grenade in his hand, tossing it over the perimeter wall. It went off, casting clods of earth up, but resulting in no panicked screams. Satisfied the way was clear, Eisner followed, landing heavily on the top of the wall, teetering a moment until he caught his balance. He dropped onto his backside, legs astride the wall as anchor, arms out to catch.

'The girls! Hurry!'

Marie looked uncertain, but with frustrated encouragement from Therese, she jumped, squealing. Eisner was there, his burly arms enveloping her in a great hug, before lowering her one-handed, to the other side. Therese followed keenly, the older girl finding the German with staggering ease. Kate was next, but she must have closed her eyes, because she fell only to catch the top of the wall. Eisner was hard pressed to help her stick the landing, but together they forced through it, muted grunts accompanying Kate's swing over, and tumble down. When Nunzia went, she shouted, dodging her catcher altogether, stopping a moment to land on the wall top, before dropping to the other side.

Archer shook his head. Italian bravura.

Bullets and shouting came up the stairs, not far from where Archer stood. The enemy knew the building well, and were tightening the noose. He looked at Ross, his bloody left palm gripping the haft of his entrenching shovel. Vital blood ran freely down the handle, over the head, filling the grooves and reliefs before pooling on the floor.

'I was going to be shot...at dawn,' Ross forced words through a tired smile. 'Cowardice.'

'Not you, Hal. You're the bravest man I know.'

Tears moistened the big man's eyes, all fear and pain dismissed. 'Do me one last favour, my friend?'

'Anything.'

'Bugger off, will you?'

The building began to vibrate as Archer climbed into the windowsill, cracks appearing in the plaster. He flinched as the Lewis gun snarled, spraying the door with a burst. He almost lost his balance and fell, the ground leering up as his vision swam. He felt so very high up, knew he needed impetus to make the leap, but the world was heaving.

'It's a long, long way to Tipperary,' Ross blurted, rasping

at every word. 'It's a long way, I know.'

The building was collapsing, bricks tumbling down in clods, and the room glowed as the Canadian exerted his uncanny power over rock and stone.

'Goodbye...Leicester...Square!'

Roof tiles and joists broke through the ceiling, the Lewis barking sporadically with a stuttering report. Archer could hear panicked voices in German, French and English echoing oddly and he let go of the windowsill, falling, feeling the urge to vomit and knowing he would die. His lungs filled with mouldy plaster dust as he fell, hands tore at his wrists, yanking his shoulders hard, almost wrenching them from their sockets. German cursing assailed his ears, before feeling weightless again. His breath was driven out in a rush as something heavy landed on top of him.

'But...my...heart's *right there!*' Ross yelled, voice breaking above the earthquake.

The house fell down.

13:

The self-titled Kaiser of Antwerp ceased poking and prodding the logs in the open fireplace. Chair leather creaked as he got up, boots swishing on the rug. High up in the Citadel, this was his eyrie, the heart of his own little empire, ignoring the fact there was a real Kaiser, with a true crown, ruling the German Empire beyond the walls of the prison.

'It is outrageous! The rabble dares to attack *my* city!'

Once Captain, now *Hauptmann*, Robert Preston didn't flinch from the outburst, kept his face carefully neutral. Someone, in a fit of suicidal bravery or utter lunacy, chose to hit the armoury in the northwest of the city. Apart from killing a lot of *Kampfgruppe*, they destroyed several crates of weapons, ammunition, and precious vehicles in the process. Reports from the scout groups told of a fortress levelled, a whole sector upended. A press of air presaged a visitor, and he turned as the draught struck his left cheek.

'Herr Hiedler,' a cultured voice cut across the petulance smoothly, boots cutting a stride across bare wood, before falling onto the soft rug. Preston heard the creak and slip of leather gloves being pulled off. 'I heard your displeasure from down the hall.'

Preston knew the man from previous encounters, although never having formally met. He was the Imperial German liaison with the 'official' Antwerp authorities. Major Manfred Von Richthofen, a terror to the Allied Air Forces, a so-called 'Knight of the Sky.'

'If I only had competent men..!' Hiedler complained, patting his breast.

'They are proving themselves even as we speak.'

'Forgive me, Manfred. May I introduce Preston?'

The Baron's step faltered a little. Preston threw a nod of greeting in his direction, suspecting the root of confusion was the uniform he wore. A German flying jacket of the Imperial Air Service, it carried the rank of an Army Captain. It was Preston's preference, since it allowed full movement, was good in a rain shower, and rugged enough to keep the tangled sharpness of Antwerp at bay.

Thankfully, Hiedler indulged it.

A tight slap of leather on the coffee table told Preston the Baron had dropped his gloves, and another object followed it, the sound drum skin taut. Preston smiled – a peaked cap. The attaché accompanying Richthofen carried much less grace, and didn't hide the sneer of reproach. Preston heard it, felt it. They knew who he was, and that they despised him was only grist to the mill. He didn't care, having tolerated all manner of insults and venom hurled at him over the years.

He pushed his sunglasses further up the bridge of his nose, dropped his hands to the pistols fixed to his hip. Preston's palms rested on the broom-handles of the two Mauser automatics, feeling the deep grooves in the wood. He tapped the supple leather of the holsters, a tight metronome designed to attract attention.

'Preston,' Hiedler warned, irritably flapping a hand. 'Look into the matter at the Armoury. Bring me whoever is responsible.'

Preston cheered up, he was off the leash. 'As you say, Kaiser.'

He marched past the Baron and his aide, listening as the most powerful man in Antwerp discussed his favourite pastime of painting. Preston obliterated the nonsense he could still hear by slamming his boot heels down to provide a pleasant echo in the cool stone halls and vaulted entrance approaching the north-facing door of the Citadel.

The tiles were all the same size; but composed of different materials, the sound of his footfall different: flat or sharp depending on his step. It betrayed the fact that the floor was chequered, each panel at least one foot square. It all served to build a well-worn picture in his mind, as he reached for the walls, ran his fingertips against the rough stone. When the grain turned to solid wood, he gripped the large iron ring he knew would be there, the Citadel formally laid out, unchanged in the four years he'd been incarcerated in Antwerp. He broke through the chill of the porch and out into the open air, the sounds and scents of a broken city assailing him. Sunlight and heat swam up around his skin, making him feel more alive.

He slammed the hard oak door leaves shut behind him, the sentries coming to salute with ingrained precision, the slap of hands meeting waxed and oiled Mauser rifle stocks, a pleasant harmony of practiced drill. The sounds bounced around objects near and far, providing orientation.

'At ease,' he advised. He smelled the perfume his driver wore, caught the quick intake of breath as she lurched forward, and he lifted his arm for her to link through.

'Just a moment, sir,' she called. Her height rivalled his own, her voice coming to him at just above his right shoulder. A soft bump of tangling arms followed when her elbow hooked into his, off-hand settling on his forearm firmly. Squeezing gently against her, he signalled he was ready to move, and let her lead off.

'Thank you, Ilsa.' He smiled, followed her directions.

'I've heard rumours. Tell me, what is happening?'

Preston didn't answer immediately, enjoying the sound of gravel crunching under their feet as they walked together to his car. They could have been promenading at Kew. Despite the violent problems, Antwerp was good to him, better than the British Army ever was. He'd learned the languages; put his talents to good use.

'Well my dear, I have to find out who is trying to blow our house down.'

Intelligence work was a house of cards, Garfield thought as

he stared at another telegram, this time from the American officer based in the Paris consulate. They admitted what he suspected, that the diplomat was in fact a renegade Arcanist, and an escaped prisoner. The note almost demanded the British make good on their interference as recompense, dangling the carrot, they would intervene and put the old world out of everyone's misery.

His first urge was to crush the paper, pick up the phone and tell the bloody Yanks there was a war on, and if they didn't want to play, he'd have his Arcanists pick up their ball and go home. They didn't know about a communication that was from German Intelligence to sympathetic comrades in New Mexico. An ace up Garfield's sleeve, the ambassador there, Zimmermann, had been cabling back and forth to secure funds for support and arms in order to start an uprising, a Mexican-American war in the event that the United States gave up being neutral to the German cause.

Garfield reflected that it was a narrow thing. Resumption of unrestricted submarine warfare by the Central Powers certainly played a part in bringing the Rough Riding horses to water, but the only near miss was the Lusitania attack. He felt guilty for hoping that the ship sank, but the Arcanist crewmen below the waterline bore the heroic brunt to save the vessel and thereby unknowingly prolonged the war.

Reluctantly, he returned to the immediate problem. The Zimmermann communications would have to remain secret for now, tying his hands thanks to his German contacts, and now the Americans wanted Garfield to kill the man he was trying to save. He had several birds, and only one stone.

He tore the telegram up.

It didn't make him feel better.

The real difficulty was in getting the new orders to Archer, the only man left in Antwerp that could be relied on. The team were good, elite operatives, but very much a secondary asset to 'Curtains'. He admitted Byng was right – Archer would toe the line with his family's chance at amnesty still on the hook. Furthermore, the sniper knew he was deployed to sectors to deal with problems: a literal trouble-shooter.

In this business, *Faust* was a manual, not just a cautionary tale. In that vein, Archer was his first choice, but he needed a back-up plan, a deal with the Devil which would be a burr under the saddle for the Sharpshooter. Maybe the Royal Air Force or the Navy could oblige with a bomb or two?

It still didn't solve anything. Garfield needed to get the message to Archer, a note that couldn't be intercepted or decoded by the wrong ears. The Germans and Italians smelled blood in the water; were already sniffing. Telegram was impossible, semaphore not only pointless, but ridiculous. He might as well send the RAF to drop a letter!

Pacing up and down on the carpet, his jaw worked and jodhpurs swished as he thought. He strode back and forth, losing track of time working around the problem. He snatched a fountain pen up off the table, flinched from the snap of grounding static.

Static electricity.

He ignored his smarting finger. The world stood still as Garfield's mind raced.

Pivoting, he pulled open his desk drawers, collecting bundles of military papers tied neatly with twine, fervently searching for a single document. It was just one of those oddball details he'd picked up from reading the commonplace dispatches that stuck in his mind. He tugged the papers open, rifled through.

Yes. Here. There was a new department lobbying to help the Army, called the Meteorological Service, and he remembered they had a fascinating machine. His finger stabbed down, and he snatched up the telephone, winding the handle hard enough to feel the ratchets protest. The wait was agonising – the plan needed to be birthed now, along with a dash of luck. The notion was madness, straight out of a Charlie Chaplin reel. Garfield was almost giddy with the silliness. Byng would love it.

'Royal Flying Corps, um, Royal Air Force. Matigny.'

He ignored the slip. Everyone still called the airmen and ground crew by the old RFC moniker, even now several months after the change ratified by the War Ministry. It was sometimes hard to let go. 'Major Garfield here, Intelligence, Byng's Staff.'

'What can we do for you, Major?'

'Is Jackie there – I mean Flight Lieutenant Jackson.'

The man on the other end repaid the earlier grace. 'He is, hold on.'

Garfield could hear a palm going over the receiver, muffling the call before another voice came on, clear and crisp. 'Jackson.'

'Garfield. I need you, a spotter who can Morse, and your kite.'

'When?'

'Ten minutes ago. It's hush-hush. Get to Third Army HQ as soon as possible.'

'I'm on the way, sir.'

The click when the call dropped wasn't sharp, so the pilot was intrigued more than annoyed. Garfield could feel it deep down, the tingle of anticipation. It was going to work. Risking a plane to drop a message into Antwerp was madness, the amount of machineguns, enemy aircraft and maniacs from Richthofen's squadron made the cost too high.

Yet Garfield was keenly aware of Archer's Mage Discipline, and in that understanding, a compromise formed. One which would take daring, skill and the hope the sniper *really* wasn't a blank file. He picked up the phone again. It rang once, which made him smile.

'ADC Schofield.'

'Will, are those fellows from the Meteorological Field Service still about?'

'The Weather mob, sir? Field Marshal Haig sent them all packing.'

Garfield paused, shook his head, annoyed. 'Where, man, where?'

'Hold on,' Schofield sobered, papers shuffled. 'Crecy, sir.'

'Get a car.' He began to laugh. 'We're going to pick up some umbrellas.'

Jackson anxiously wrung his flying helmet whilst watching the Royal Engineers from the Meteorological Field Unit carefully measure up, before taking drills and awls to the bodywork of his new Bristol Fighter. Garfield stood beside him, arms behind his back, waiting for the pilot to say whatever was pushing at his lips. He wondered if Jackson flew his aircraft the way he see-sawed his face.

'You can't be serious, Major,' Jackson complained.

'Deadly.'

Garfield watched as the weathermen unboxed a large contraption: a clock mechanism in a mahogany cabinet. It looked like something a mad Victorian scientist would knock together in his spare time. Seven disks of yellowed Bakelite span freely on a long barrel, with a crank handle on one side and an array of brass bells and rods sprouting from the top. It looked heavy, imposing and exceptionally expensive.

He'd explained the plan to Jackson, and this was the result. The men busied themselves with the work, just as efficient as the Royal Naval team who sent *Orca* on her travels, and just as proud of their efforts. He understood that ethic. One of the Engineers adjusted something called the brushes – a pair of armatures that pressed wire fronds against circles of lead in the disks, building friction against them. It was fascinating.

Snap! A shot of electricity blasted from one brass bell to the other.

'Do you know how much *Archie* is around Antwerp?' Jackson asked, offhand.

'Yes I do, twelve ack-ack guns,' Garfield replied.

'Be with you in a minute!'

Both officers turned to find the new voice, tracing it to a smaller man than either Jackson or Garfield. He crammed a flying helmet on his head, and stuffed maps into a pocket on his trouser leg. The man upended a satchel, spilling out a set of trench armour, a web of ropes with crude metal plates. Donning it, he arranged the harness so one of the slabs covered his backside. Strapped to one of the chest ropes was a large sheath, holding an American Bowie hunting knife, another held a holstered Webley.

'That's my spotter,' Jackson explained. 'Does he know something I don't?'

The Intelligence officer shrugged.

'One crank for dot, two for dash?' the spotter asked.

The Engineer Captain in charge looked the man up and down. 'You can build up a charge and then use this.' He handled a Morse set, twisting the spacing and tension screws before passing it across. 'Only four cranks on that handle, mind.'

'Why?'

'Ever been a lightning rod?'

Jackson turned away in despair. 'How close to Antwerp do we have to get?'

'Within a third of a mile, no further out,' Garfield replied, watching the spotter clamber up the mounting blocks and leap into the rear seat, testing the machinegun mount. The Lewis Gun was still in place, but the Electrical Machine was now fixed to the port side of the aircraft and prevented the gun traversing in that direction. 'Try and keep to the coast in and out, our blockade can cover you.'

Jackson sucked air through his teeth in the manner of an expensive plumber. 'Well old boy, that gives us something to work with.'

'Just bring it back in one piece.'

'I can glide her in if we cop a packet, Major.'

'I meant the weather machine!' Garfield growled.

Jackson grinned, proving he knew what he was provoking, wedged his helmet on and ran for the aircraft, the Engineers proving none too shabby at being impromptu ground crew, hurling the propeller as Jackson indicated, and on the third spin, the engine sputtered into life.

'Contact!'

Electrical mail. Garfield shook his head. It would never catch on.

The throttle opened, pulling the aircraft away. He watched them trundle along; taxiing onto a stretch of road that would give them enough room to take off, which eventually they did, vanishing to a vulture-speck in the sky, leaving a rapidly dwindling buzzing fading into the quiet of the countryside.

Silence. Archer realised it was quiet because he wasn't breathing. It wasn't just a case of his lungs telling him they had no air, his whole chest was tight, unmoving. He couldn't even tell his orientation. In the strange seconds of peace before his body took over for necessary survival, he was floating, and nothing hurt. He remembered the tumble of masonry, clouds of dust and someone shouting in a foreign language. Then light hit his face and he started coughing, raw heaving and dry retching to fight for air.

He couldn't open his eyes, they refused. Pain flared in his back where something battered him, and finally he spit out a cloud of powder, clearing the blockage. His arms were heavy, but he scraped at his face anyway, and his eyes were free. A shadow suddenly cut out the light and warmth of the sun.

'I thought you were dead, *Tommy.*'

By rote and nothing more, Archer got his canteen and drank. He looked at his legs, but there was no blood, and only a few bricks and clumps of mortar over them. He blinked, feeling the ache of lying in entirely the wrong position. He tried to move, but couldn't quite power his body.

'Eisner? How bad is it?'

'You hit your head.'

Archer frowned, regretted it. 'Is it split?'

'No.'

With the help of his comrade, Archer got to his feet, almost stumbling as he turned to look at the compound, surveying the magnitude of what Ross wrought. 'Jesus,' he whispered, and again. 'Jesus.'

The police station was a heap of rubble, and where the detritus hadn't cascaded onto the concrete and cobbles of the yard, the ground was carved with deep runnels. A pall of dust and smoke drifted across the city in a thick cloud.

'We made a mess,' Eisner admitted grimly.

Or a tomb, Archer thought, but held his tongue.

As the wind carried across the scene in an eerie whistle, Archer unlimbered his rifle. He'd been lucky; he'd fallen awkwardly, but saved the *Runebolt* from damage by dint of his ragged, thick sniper robes, and squishy body. He groaned as he stretched, knowing there would be welts down his back, which would form lovely, tender bruises.

Through the miasma, he spotted four dark figures, but recognised Marie and Therese first. The third was Kate, limping and nursing her ribs, Nunzia keeping her upright.

'I think Kate broke her ankle,' she said.

'We need working weapons and as much ammunition as possible.' Archer decided, practical concerns edging out his fears for the small group. He would mourn Ross properly, but later. Now, he mourned the loss of the Lewis gun.

Eisner searched a body, retrieved a Mauser pistol. Once they saw what he was doing, Nunzia followed suit, bringing clips of rifle ammunition from the pockets of those lying in the open, or half-buried. She directed the girls to get the canteens of the fallen Blackcoats. The foraging resulted in piles of French and German guns, a heap of water bottles, and a couple of full bread-bags.

'We need to rest, English.'

They all needed a place to heat food too, he thought, but said nothing. It was the closest thing Archer heard to defeat in Nunzia's voice. Not even during the depth-charging had she sounded so tired. He looked around; spotted the truck still parked outside the limits of the compound, and led them over to it, helping the women to climb into the bed of the vehicle. The girls pulled some rubble from the bench seats, tossed it onto the pile of shapeless, smashed buildings Antwerp was slowly becoming.

'Where are we going?' Kate asked.

'Back to the zeppelin crash site,' Archer replied, 'I want words with Sergeant Miller.'

'Will he still be there?' Nunzia frowned.

The driver's door was badly dented, jamming it shut, so Archer climbed through the passenger seat and pulled at the driver's corpse, heaving the dead man from behind the wheel, discarding the body unceremoniously. 'We'll see, won't we?'

Eisner collected a black jacket to swipe the gory mess from the upholstery, discarding the gruesome rags when he got in behind the wheel, working the pedals and starter to coax the engine to puttering life.

Nobody had the energy to talk.

14:

The manse looked as bad as the police station they'd just left. It was riddled and cratered from heavy fighting, spent brass liberally sprinkled on the ground. In a walled prison city, supposedly cut off, the scarce metal should have been policed for reloading. The dead Blackcoats mixed with the remaining Americans. He stepped over men he'd spoken to a few hours before, but there was no sign of the Sergeant, or Sam.

'Notice anything?' he called over his shoulder.

'All the weapons are gone.' Nunzia's lips pursed.

'What does that mean?' Kate clawed at her matted blonde hair.

She had been doing it on the back of the truck all the way to the crash site, and Archer didn't know if it was some kind of futile attempt to clean up, or one of those weird things that usually happened to soldiers with shell-shock.

'Captured?' Eisner squinted, stepped over a body before squatting next to it. He carefully checked for any nasty surprises before rolling it over. It was the only corpse not wearing a black jacket or uniform.

'No.' Archer rubbed his chin. 'Why didn't the Blackcoats take their dead?'

'Why would they?' Nunzia asked.

'They're old soldiers – they have *some* discipline. I would assume they would care about their fallen too.'

'A big assumption for these brutes.' Nunzia clicked her tongue. 'Would the cannibals take the guns?'

'Maybe,' Archer replied, 'but again, there are no bites or cutting on any of them.'

Nunzia flexed her eyebrows in a pruned shrug.

'Daniel,' Eisner called softly. 'Look.'

The sniper peered past Eisner's fist pulling a bloodied shirt aside, seeing crude tattooing on the chest, an eagle of some sort. 'That's familiar.'

'It should be. He's your ally from the Eastern Front.'

'Russian? What's he doing here?'

'Antwerp *was* a Reprisal Camp. We likely caught him at Tannenberg.'

'Why wasn't he handed over in the 1917 armistice?'

'Farming. We still have a million Russians ploughing in the Fatherland.' Eisner pulled back the left sleeve of the body, and held up the hand, palm exposed. Calluses and rough skin decorated the fingers.

'He tilled the fields so we can shoot each other?'

Eisner nodded and dropped the dead man's arm.

Archer blew out a long sigh as he stood, distracted by hushed French coming from Therese and Marie, but he couldn't make it out, so ignored it. He supposed if there was a problem they would try and get his attention. Lost in thought about the Russian Blackcoat, his heart skipped a bit when he heard Nunzia shout above the sound of running feet.

'English!'

He turned, weapon coming up to defend against a threat, but caught sight of the fleeing girls. Instinct taking over, he jerked the rifle up to prevent a horrific accident, before checking the safety and rushing after them. Nunzia was at his shoulder, the two of them pounding after the runaways.

He cursed himself for making so much noise as the mad scramble continued, the girls gaining ground quickly, disappearing into the ruins where Archer and Ross first met them. By the time the adults got there, the girls had disappeared.

'Do you feel we're going backwards?' he asked, puffing and blowing.

'The tide will turn, English,' she smiled at him, 'It always does.'

They returned to the others, keeping an eye on the windows and doorways of the ruined city as evening steadily fell. When they regrouped, he directed them to clear the floor of corpses, to keep rats at bay. They dumped them on the lower floor, pushing the bodies over the balcony. Once Archer was satisfied they were alone, he took a tour of the surrounding houses, carefully mantling walls to gain height, so he could survey the immediate area with his rifle glass. Divorce from the group would benefit him twice over; firstly to provide privacy and secondly let him relieve himself away from their shelter, since bodily functions attracted animal interest – especially guard dogs.

A gargoyle decorated parapet remained, just out of easy reach, which was ideal for the purpose. He clambered up onto a tiled roof section of the manor house, carefully testing the timbers below to make sure they would take his weight, before forcing himself not to look down, as he clutched a downspout.

Cast iron brackets rusted, but clung stubbornly to the brickwork. Carefully testing everything could take his weight, he leveraged himself and his weapon up onto the small section of roof. Kneeling between the struts of old ironwork, he supposed it had mounted a clock or bell of some kind. He was thankful, as it provided a rest for his arms. He set up the Hensoldt rifle scope, panning left and right. Nothing.

He went to a corner of the building and dropped his trousers, sighing with the relief only a man who'd been eating bully beef and field rations could. In the distance he could hear a gnat buzzing, perhaps an observation aircraft. Cursing that he would be caught in such a vulnerable moment, he hurriedly cleaned up, shrugged on his sniper robes, and hoped he would be virtually impossible to spot against the rubble when he decamped from the site of his dastardly deed. Aerial observers would be hard pressed to find him, unless they were exquisitely familiar with every inch of the city's roofs. He worried they were running daily photography scouts, but dismissed the fear. Who would bother?

Suddenly, there was a painful ache in his teeth. His stomach grumbled in sympathy, but he was certain he hadn't eaten anything rancid. Nerves and simple fatigue maybe. *No,* there it was again. It repeated in a predictable pattern, the buzzing aircraft coming closer, and he could see tiny flashes of light – could feel the static build-up. He quickly searched for the notebook and pencil in his kit, began to write down the intermittent sequence. He had a chance to read it back before the pattern resumed.

*Americans lied / Not diplomat / Dangerous
Arcanist / Mission: Neutralise.*

'What in God's name..?'
Each word was in Garfield's hand, he could even hear them in that clipped, Eton-educated, condescending tone. Archer searched for the plane, found the cross-winged fuselage and adjusted his glass, tilting the front lens to catch the last, meagre rays of the setting summer sun. He interrupted their continuous broadcast with his own, hoping his code was as good as the one sent.

He delivered it twice: *Received/Understood.*
After a healthy pause, the toothache changed:

Deadline stands / Complete job or naval guns will / With shield.

Once more, Archer signalled he'd got the message. Anger coloured his reply, as he realised why the time limit was so tight. It had nothing to do with a submarine's fuel reservoir, reserve battery power, or anything else – Garfield was squeezing the operation in before the Navy flattened the place, and everyone within. No rescues after the deadline.

Archer completed the last line, the adage of the ancient Spartans: *With your shield, or on it.* Byng must have planned it from the start, played them all. Archer's instinct was right; the General had been too nice, all the while saving this nasty little treat for just the right moment.

'What a dirty clutch of bastards,' he whispered, the wind snatching at his robes.

The little plane buzzed along, offered a parting shot: *Received/Good luck.*

It finally banked away, waggling its wings, turning back for the British lines where Garfield was doubtless waiting for the reply. Re-reading the messages, one thing was certain; time was short in Antwerp.

Archer decided he would keep that to himself.

Fatigue was dogging every step, but Archer counselled a move. The manse had been stormed not once, but twice, and it created enough of a disturbance to attract cannibals who might be desperate. The trek was short, moving to a house opposite the manse where they could keep an eye on it if the girls – or other parties – returned.

Nunzia shook her head as she stabbed a chunk of beef out of one of their ration tins and deftly popped it into her mouth. She was using Archer's mess set, the knife and fork actually put to correct purpose, instead of as tools to fix something.

Archer preferred the spoon. Couldn't go wrong with it.

'Why didn't the Blackcoats retrieve their fallen?' Nunzia asked between chews.

'They did not find what they were looking for,' Eisner replied, picking his teeth with a bayonet point. 'Maybe someone told them we had it.'

'What about the Russian?' she countered.

'Wrong place, wrong time perhaps,' Archer replied.

Nunzia bit her lip, disliked the answer. She looked out onto the ruins beyond. 'What if the girls come back?'

Watching her, Archer adjusted the spare pistol in his belt as he sat down, braced against the wall. Eisner glanced between them both, something pushing at his lips, but indecision withholding it. Once Kate had eaten, she spread her greatcoat out on the ground, lay down on it and promptly went to sleep. Archer wondered if it was perhaps the first time in the past twenty-four hours the stewardess had rested properly.

'The girls were doing alright before we came,' he said quietly, so not to disturb the sleeping woman, although he'd seen men in the trenches so exhausted they just lay down and were dead to the world. Even artillery hadn't woken them up, but a light kick to the foot and they were almost instantly perpendicular.

'Things are different, English; we have stirred up the hornets.'

'We don't have time to be careful. We have to track the Americans.'

'We could return to the submarine. Kate has seen everything,' Nunzia persisted. 'She can be called as a witness.'

'To what? As much as I hate it, they'll likely dismiss her account,' Archer replied, knowing how those wheels turned. He thought of Garfield's stiff, disdainful face, and the cold, disinterested bureaucrats of the War Office.

Eisner cleared his throat, leaned forward, hands clasped around the barrel of a borrowed Mauser rifle. 'The Kaiser knows someone has upset the apples. He will be looking for us.'

Archer finished his ration tin, before pouring some water into it and swilling his spoon. He stared into space, the conversation fallen to silence in the wake of Eisner's grim comments, not really knowing what to do. He felt Ross' absence then, his missing voice and keen abilities. It would be getting dark in a while, and there would be no way to track the Americans, and he doubted whoever survived the second battle would return.

There was nothing for it – they had to wait for nightfall anyway, the submarine wouldn't resurface until then, when they would run away, tail between their legs and their mission failed. *His mission failed.* He snorted, drawing a scowl from Nunzia, but she was right, at least they would have Kate to show for it, something pulled from the rubble – a trade of lives to the hunger of the Antwerp Exclusion Zone.

The Americans had lied, but he couldn't blame them for it. He'd have done the same in the circumstances. 'A compromise,' Archer said, finally. 'I'll take first watch. You and Kurt get your head down.'

'Together?' Eisner grinned, wiggled his eyebrows.

'Not in your dreams.' Nunzia pulled her coat off, bundled it for a pillow. 'How long?'

'I'll wake Kurt in an hour, he'll wake you an hour after that, then you wake me.'

The German nodded, slid down the wall with his back to it, taking a good look at everything, committing it to memory. He laid the weapon across his legs, before he let his head sag and his breathing changed, betraying he was asleep. Archer watched them all, but especially Eisner. How many times had his crosshairs swung up and down over the enemy as he breathed in and out, preparing to make it the last?

Whilst imprisoned at Rannoch Moor, such questions scared him. He was taught and brought up to be wary of even his own existence, to be fearful of what he could do unintentionally. Now, out in Flanders' Fields, after the discipline of the Sniper and Observation School, he expected to feel different – and he did. Unfortunately, it was for the worse.

Driving the nagging worry away, he rearranged the pistols again for easy access, tucking one under his arm, so that if he fell asleep it would clatter and wake him up. He was glad there was no fire; the heat would have made him drowsy. Archer listened for unusual sounds, scanned the lined edges of the walls, watching for anything out of place. The relative silence and steady breathing of his comrades did little to help, the relaxing sounds threatened to send him off.

As though to prove it, the pistol slipped, jagging into his ribs as he desperately tried to catch it before it woke up the others. He decided being unsettled was better than being eaten by cannibals, so his thoughts drifted to the prison again, bitterness and anger keeping him in a state of low alert.

Arcanists, they said, are too dangerous.

Governments across the world concurred with the British parliament after the Great Fire of London. It was a handy solution in the middle of a plague, but everyone blamed the Mages. Probative, demonstrable science could not explain the talents of his kind. Some Clerics claimed it was a sign of the Second Coming; fanatics decried the existence of the Arcane Children to be the end of the world, whilst anarchists venerated them. The death penalty was even discussed, but in the end curiosity, common sense, and public outcry won.

In the early days there were only a handful of Arcanists, but numbers grew with time. Ministers saw the benefits to having men like Ross working in mines to cut shafts and reduce cave-ins, of having others who could control fire or water, preventing towns being destroyed in great conflagrations.

The War Ministry wasn't slow to realise the untapped potential either. Archer's forebears marched in many places before him, and when Germany and Austria began their advances into Europe in 1914, they had Arcanists too. Rannoch Moor was emptied of normal prisoners, hurriedly expanded with medical facilities, and converted into a 'Sanatorium for the Gifted'.

Which was an entire rucksack of bollocks.

Two men in khaki brought him the contract to sign when he turned sixteen. Both well-turned out, educated, probably Public School somewhere. Archer recalled that something haunted them, in that sterile room where he sat with his Mentor, reading the words in fine copperplate, declaring him fit for service in His Majesty's Land Forces.

He should have never played darts, showing off for the teachers, 'Go on lad, do it again!' Like a moron he obliged, the bulls-eye, every time.

He didn't even want to think about the light bulb experiments.

Archer checked his watch, seeing he'd been pondering for well over an hour. He peered across to Nunzia's recumbent form, counting the heartbeats between breaths, and decided to take her shift too. It meant the others got an extra hour at his expense, but it didn't matter. He wanted to think.

Tap.

His world froze, and he could feel the strange electric tingle in his body as the adrenaline flooded him. The scuff of boot leather on abraded marble confirmed the plunging sensation in his stomach. Slowly and smoothly, he ran his hands onto his rifle stock, quickly finding the trigger without looking for it. He twisted, felt the pistol under his armpit and cursed. He couldn't shoulder the weapon without dropping it, his anti-sleeping measure a little too effective. He would have to pretend he was incapacitated. A stealthy approach could mean the other party wanted them captured, or quietly murdered.

Nothing wrong with playing into that.

A tall shadow fell into his line of view, broken and jagged by the cracked lumps of stone and scattered brickwork. He could see both hands were empty, but that meant nothing. A weapon could be tucked into a belt or strapped across the back. The cautious steps continued, the shadow advanced until the figure coalesced into a broad chest, with massive shoulders.

A face shiny with the sweat of the considerable effort to make so huge a body so subtle, peered in. The sheen caught the light and it took Archer a second to recognise the face.

'Hello? Anyone here?'

Managing to keep his voice low, despite the sudden elation he felt, Archer replied. 'I'm down here, Sam.'

A wide grin broke across Sam's face, and the big man took off a flat cap that Archer hadn't seen him with before. He continued to be careful, not wanting to wake the others.

'You found the lady,' he muttered, his bulk trying to kneel into an alcove beside the British sniper. He put out a large hand, and Archer gripped it, helping the big man to sit down with his back to the wall. The palms and fingers were roughened from hard work, impossibly strong. 'Did you find the others? They were real nice to me on the airship.'

'I'm sorry, Sam. They didn't make it.' He stopped himself short of going into any detail, but he felt he owed them something. 'They were brave though.'

'Where is your Canadian friend?'

'He died, saving us from the Blackcoats.'

Sam looked troubled, his face closing with a mix of regret and discomfort.

Archer decided to lance it. 'What is it Sam? You can tell me.'

'It's my fault. The Sergeant said we should go, that you'd lead the bad men away.'

'We did,' he allowed, 'but something happened – didn't it?'

'It sure did.'

Sam explained quietly, another attack by the Blackcoats, not many, but enough of them fought their way up the stairs and killed everyone. As he talked, he wrung the cap, and tugged at his medic bag. 'I fought 'em I swear, but there were so many!'

He held up his hands, and showed recently healed knuckles where he'd engaged in fisticuffs. By all rights, they should have been bloody and pulped from his description, in bandages at least, but they were just paler, healthy flesh mending. Archer imagined the pummelling the huge man must have thrown out. He certainly wouldn't want to be on the receiving end.

'How did they get up the stairs?'

'They threw a tin of smoke, but it didn't smell like burning. Brought tears to my eyes, made me feel sick.' The big man looked embarrassed just admitting it.

'Didn't they shoot at you?'

'No sir, they were too busy just beating on me.'

Archer looked away, frowned. It sounded like the attackers had deployed Lachrymal Gas to try and capture the Americans – possibly for interrogation. He'd seen it done in a trench raid in 1918, allowing the raiders to take a prized German Officer, or valuable Senior NCO, prisoner. Meant to be debilitating, the gas was still horrible.

It meant the Blackcoats knew what he suspected, and what Garfield confirmed. The real target was Sam, an escaped Arcanist. The real question was why everyone was so keen to get their hands on him, one way or another. He understood the British motivations, certainly – goodwill, a bargaining chip, that kind of thing. Yet, although Mages were a rare breed, they weren't so rare to cause this much trouble. Rogue magicians and Antwerp went together and no-one had bothered up to now. He dismissed the circular thoughts.

With Sam here, Archer's options had doubled; the original order to extract him still stood, technically not rescinded by Garfield's kill directive. He idly wondered if that was deliberate, it would be typical of the Intelligence Officer, but got back on track.

'Where is Sergeant Miller now?'

'He's hurt bad. He's with friends, the ones who came and saved us.'

'Friends?' Archer remembered the Russian.

'Yeah,' Sam's grin returned, a twinkle matching it in his brown eyes. 'They said to bring you over to where they live – when you were ready.'

15:

The relief column Preston commanded arrived just before dusk, motors chugging as the armoured car in front of his Mercedes 'Knight Touring' vehicle slowed to a stop, turret traversing left and right with a telling metallic groan. *Kampfgruppe* infantrymen spilled from two trucks, out into the dying sunlight, quickly taking up positions, readying for action. Despite the noise of the engines, Preston could make out the slap-smack of bolt handles being worked, machine pistols being cocked.

Beside him, his short-haired Alsatian hound, Max, licked his chops and rose from the seat to peer out of the window. The dog watched the armed men go by, whined in apprehension. Preston patted the animal's flank, scratched his ears and the dog lay back down beside him, panting in the warmth of the car.

At the shout of an officer, the Blackcoats moved in, leaving the Mercedes beyond the perimeter. Preston waited for a skirmish to begin, or some random fire fight with corpse-eaters, but steady silence was the result. He leaned to the window, doping his senses with the smells and sounds hiding in the half-dark.

Dry dust tainted by blood and offal. The flies buzzed, darting away when disturbed, only to land and gorge again moments later. He sniffed, detecting the sharp bite of gunpowder and whiff of ozone. The reports hadn't lied, if anything, they downplayed the battle fought here at the Armoury. Even Preston could see it was a costly one.

'Ilsa,' he said, tapping her on the shoulder.

At the signal, she slipped from behind the wheel, the

car rocking as she got out, and opened his door. Her strong arm was there, for him to lean on. Upright, he was close enough to give her a peck on the cheek.

'Be careful?' she warned.

'I will,' he told her. 'Wait in the car.'

Max barked twice, getting to his feet, ready to follow, but Preston shook his head, speaking to him in English. 'Stay. Defend Ilsa.'

He didn't linger to see if he was obeyed, instead moving into the compound. He kept going, pacing steadily using his swagger stick to test the ground in front of him, but the sweep of craters and broken concrete were telling enough. His toecaps clipped debris and the tinkle of brass skittered away from him. He knelt, fingers dancing over the ground gingerly until he found what he sought. Scooping up three cases, he gently wafted them under his nose.

Propellant residue assaulted him, his palette finding a mixed bouquet of different powder from French and German loads. Not a surprise, this was Antwerp, and different nations all had remnants of munitions storage in the port city. The Royal Navy left behind Japanese rifles and ammunition when they evacuated. War was strange that way.

Preston froze as his thumb and forefinger trapped the end of the final cartridge case, feeling the base, the bold rim brutally obvious. He turned it over, again and again to make sure, vigorous rubbing brought up the brassy smell. No deformities in the case, smooth, tapered and polished. Russian? No, a fraction too long, and the neck was less pronounced than the typical Tsarist ammunition.

He pinched one nostril shut and presented the bottle-neck end of this strange cartridge to the other, inhaling steadily, slowly. The distinctive reek of Cordite hit him instantly. *It couldn't be.* Preston tested another one, but as he sampled it, the air whipped right up into his nose with the snort.

He suffered a coughing fit; the sudden particles

clogging his sinuses stung them painfully, a peppery burning behind his brows. Cuffing the tears from his eyes, he managed to regain equilibrium, desperately grasping the strange cartridge. He dabbed his lips to the neck and blew. When a tinny whistle was the result, a strange stirring in his gut spurred him into action.

'*Leutnant*! Have your men scour this place for brass.'

'Sir?'

'You heard me, I want any they can find, bring it to me.'

The man grinned, the expression carrying in his voice, but there was no mockery. 'There is a lot, *Herr Hauptmann*.'

'Put it all on a table, find me a chair as well, smartly!'

'Sir!'

Preston let him go to his business, heard his orders being relayed, but his mind was elsewhere, to a place that marched in khaki ranks, to green fields and harsh discipline, to the pomp and circumstance of King and Country. He gripped the case, the heat of his palm reflected by the metal .303 Inch case.

The British were here.

Now *that* was a surprise.

The windows were fully open, so Preston listened to the birds chirping as they nested on the parapets on the Citadel roof, smelled fresh bread baking in the kitchen ovens. A batch of supplies for the *Kampfgruppe* was going out. The denizens of Antwerp would be lucky to reap the scraps of an Imperial German airdrop, and it was this, more than anything, that drew them to the black flag.

'This is what you bring me?' Heidler ceased drawing with a sharp pull of a pencil across the plotting device, nudging the brass cartridge cases around so they clinked. The map creased and crinkled as he did so.

'Yes sir,' Preston replied, holding his irritation as the commander of Antwerp failed to grasp the meaning. 'The British are here. I don't know how many, but I have debriefed two sector commanders this morning, and I am convinced.'

'I trust you Preston, you know that,' Hiedler told him, voice directly in front. The Kaiser faced him, and clapped Preston on the left shoulder, meaning it was the right hand, which was a good sign, 'but this stretches belief. The British are many miles away. Tell me more, convince me.'

It was a shame he might spoil the good mood. 'I think it may be to do with the airship, sir,' he suggested. *Keep it light, introduce it slowly. Hold details until the right time.*

There was too much coincidence. From interviewing the previous guard shift at the Armoury, he'd learned that prisoners were recovered from the crash, and a runner said they were headed for the cells under the old police station. It stood to reason they reached it, else why would the British have fought there? *One thing at a time.*

Silence continued, with no-one in the room offering even so much a sigh. The Kaiser scratched at his map some more, perhaps planning troop movements within the city. Preston could have found out by running his fingers over the indentations, but he stood stock still.

'Could the British have landed at the Armoury to destroy it? Are we at risk from a seaborne invasion?' More pencil marks followed, swift and short.

Preston hadn't considered that, but he ran a few details through his head. He'd found Webley .455 automatic cases. The Royal Navy used it in pistols, but if it was an advance shore party, he expected a conventional, methodical assault. The British, as a rule, were not terribly imaginative in attack. His experience of the First Battle of Ypres in 1914, or the Battle of Loos in 1915, where he was captured, proved it. Preston dwelled on it, evaluating, until an irritating rustling noise he couldn't place drew him out of it. He suddenly realised he was fidgeting with his cuff. He stopped.

'Possible, but a routine patrol has failed to return, the search party dispatched to find them hasn't reported in either, and both were sent to the crash site.'

Hiedler removed his glasses, depositing them on the plotting table with a rattle of frames. 'The subhuman locals could be responsible?'

Another voice joined the debate. 'I agree. What could have been on this mysterious airship? Riches and fine wines?'

One of the officers chuckled, and Preston turned slowly to face the sycophant. 'Something that obviously shoots back.'

'Using cartridges without primer capsules?' The man sneered his words.

There was no answer to that. Not yet.

Hiedler laughed, amused no doubt by the bickering. This was the dangerous bit; convincing the leader. Preston needed to tread carefully; use the rope the Kaiser gave him to hang someone else. Thankfully Hiedler was in a good mood, and not one of his dark rages.

'I do not believe in coincidences,' Preston said. 'Let me take my unit, we will be close enough to the wall that the German guard patrols on the other side will protect us. Someone valuable is running loose in Antwerp.'

'You are certain?'

'I am, sir.'

'What if you are wrong?'

'We lose nothing in the exercise, with much to gain if I am right. Besides, sir, it will show the rabble your continued strength.' He hated the play to ego, but grease on the wheel never hurt.

A shift of leather soles on wooden floor, and the grip on Preston's shoulder returned with a reassuring firmness. 'I trust you, Preston. If you are right, bring this intruder to me. I would tell them about our City's glorious future and inevitable victory for the Fatherland.'

'As ordered, sir.'

'I wish you a good hunt regardless.'

Elation warred with caution. Preston swallowed silently as he felt the stir of conviction in his breast; a warm glow rooted in his mind that made him snap heels and bow in Prussian fashion. He wasn't German, nowhere even in the family tree, but Hiedler requested it of his officers, so he obeyed the urge. Released, Preston strode from the room spine ramrod straight, hands resting on his pistol holsters.

He would just have to kick over a few stones, see what came out.

Archer gently kicked Eisner's foot. It was unwise to surprise a slumbering man by shaking his shoulder – especially if he was festooned with loaded weapons. The German's head popped up, hands snatching for the rifle in the deep-seated instinct of the professional soldier. He saw Archer, peered past him to spot Sam, and rubbed his eyes with his knuckles before looking again. He wearily grinned.

'I was wondering where you were, Sam.'

'With some friends.'

Eisner nodded, yawned, checked his watch. He clicked his tongue at the British sniper, but didn't go any further. Kate and Nunzia were woken in the same, foot-tapping manner. They were both surprised to see Sam, but he just smiled amiably at them.

'Where are we going?' Kate asked, blinking away sleep. She massaged her ankle, face creased with the resulting ache.

'Someplace safe,' Sam replied. He stooped down, examined her carefully, with gentle fingers pressing against Kate's leg, foot and ankle.

'I don't think I can walk,' she admitted, voice cracking.

Sam clucked in sympathy. 'I can carry you, miss?'

Kate nodded mutely.

He scooped her up effortlessly in his brawny arms, smiling at the others. 'You folks keep up, now.'

He lurched into a steady jog, long powerful legs easily eating up the distance at a sustainable pace, even loaded down with Kate, her arms clinging around his neck. They continued for over four-hundred yards, until Sam halted them at a crossroads, the junction once abutted by shops and townhouses, but now only debris choked the streets, marking the ghosts of where buildings stood. Weeds and shrubs grew up around the stonework.

Archer saw a fountain, a large plaster bowl supporting a short Roman column at the centre, a statue of a woman in robes atop the plinth. Her hands carried a large ewer, forever frozen in the act of decanting water into the basin beneath her feet. He wondered if it was the depiction of some goddess, but she was past her best, face and upper torso ruined by shell splinters and bullets. The fountain was long dry, the spout which formed the ewer's mouth, chipped and barren.

Sam jerked his chin, up behind the damaged ornament, to a house with a single doorframe standing, the scraped and gouged mahogany door still within it. He led off to the left of the door, revealing a cellar hatch. He knocked three times in uneven cadence, and after a minute or so, the door opened. The man guarding it was a thin adolescent, hardly in the age of manhood, but he brandished a double-barrelled shotgun. He looked narrowly at Archer with icy blue calm.

'Below,' he grunted in heavily accented English.

Sam carried Kate inside, receiving a glance from the young sentry. Archer ushered Nunzia forward first, then Eisner, keeping watch behind them with the *Runebolt* in hand. Finally, he followed, helping the youth pull the cellar doors shut. Large metal bolts were rammed home, before a second metal plate was barricaded across the entrance.

What was waiting for him was more than a surprise. The cellar was lined with tables, piled with crude bandages. Women sat with long shears chopping up curtains, old clothes or tablecloths. Men were counting and boxing ammunition, or rationing supplies into knapsacks. Rifles of all makes were slung on shoulders, including the American guns.

One mystery solved, at least.

Oil lamps dangled from thick nails on the cellar walls, but strings of light bulbs were also crudely strung along a passage leading deeper under what remained of the house above. The air was cool, which Archer found to be a pleasant relief from the late sun, but although men and women milled around clutching coats or blankets to them, the lack of beds told him they couldn't all live in this space. At least the thickness of the walls provided a safe place to work without being observed.

Passing beneath the bulbs, a burly, squat man approached. He was attended by a small group of children, rushing to and fro in the passageway, excitedly babbling in French or the throaty sounds of what Archer took to be Flemish, and the man chuckling happily alongside them.

The chaperone came into the light of the room, peering through circular glasses, the arms repaired with bands of copper wire. His face was partially obscured by a mighty black beard which fell over his barrel chest, sporting a large golden cross on a long chain. He put his hands together prayerfully, showing a battered golden signet ring on his left little finger, and offered a shallow bow of greeting. Behind him, Archer spotted Therese and Marie, and he heard Nunzia's gentle sigh of relief over his left shoulder.

'Greetings,' the stout man rumbled in accented English. 'I am Father Ruslan, of the Eastern Orthodox Church, and Minister to this flock.'

'Corporal Daniel Archer, British Army.' He introduced his comrades.

'Welcome to our Eastern safe-house,' the priest said.

Sam nodded to Ruslan. 'Done what you asked, Father.'

A grin broke the beard, huge bushy black brows lifting in amusement. 'Go and get some rest Sam, well done.'

The American gently set Kate down, and a woman with an apron came to catch her under the shoulder and led her away. One of the children blurted something at Sam and showed him a ball.

'Skittles again?' he asked, grinning.

They tugged at him, forcing him to crouch in the tunnel, but they wouldn't let him go and his chuckling seemed to encourage the group. His head bumped the low ceiling, so he quickly put on his hat, but he accompanied them willingly, holding onto tiny hands. It seemed Sam would have to rest later. The greeting and good spirits lingered. No-one wanted to say anything, and Archer suspected he would have to be the one to do it.

'A strange place to find a priest.'

Ruslan spread his hands with a simple shrug; his dark eyes alight with mirth. 'I go where the Lord wills. I am in the right place Mr Archer, but are you?'

'What do you mean?'

'Follow me.'

Ruslan was unbowed, his stature low enough to avoid the ceiling. Sporting a skullcap in black, he strode along, hands buried in sleeves. His cassock vanished into the shadows at the foot of the passageway, giving the illusion he was floating.

Even stooping awkwardly, Archer saw this was no mere cellar and adjoined storeroom. It was a network of rooms and tunnels leading left and right, with small larders, a dressing station, even a drinking den, complete with rustic benches and all manner of glasses and cups, no doubt salvaged from above.

'Where do you get your electricity?' Eisner wondered aloud.

'From our *Kameraden*, above. They are donating to a good cause.'

Eisner merely laughed.

'And did your congregation do this?' Nunzia asked, running her hands gently along the rough brick and stonework.

'No, daughter. They were the old ammunition stores for the fortress walls and bastions above – sturdy, and extensive.'

Bedrooms and bunkhouses, a children's playroom and schoolhouse, the whole city had simply moved downstairs. Words painted on the wall led to the infirmary or galley, but as they reached a long passage, Archer noticed religious murals, and took the chance to examine the crudely hewn reliefs.

'This is our church,' Ruslan said, gesturing to a door.

'Are you taking me to the altar, English?' Nunzia breathed in his ear. She pulled her hat on, covering her head as convention required.

'We will not be disturbed here.' Ruslan ushered them through the arch, closing the solid oak door behind them.

Inside were stunted pews, all facing a large, plain, timber cross mounted on the wall. A small table was draped with a red velvet curtain and the platter and chalices were modest, made of simple, hand-carved wood. Ruslan noticed Archer admiring them.

'The men made them for us,' he said proudly, his chest inflating a little more.

'Handsome work,' Archer admitted. He gently lifted one, running a finger over the smooth finish before carefully replacing it.

'The Lord was a carpenter,' Ruslan smiled, 'I think it would please Him.'

'You are far from home,' Nunzia remarked, hushed.

Her reverence made Archer realise they hadn't raised their voices at all. He looked over at the cross again, the humble nature of the place unsettling. The early believers would have huddled in places like this – away from those who might come to harm them. Nothing changed.

'True. I was studying in St. Petersburg, until the war came.'

'You were conscripted?' she continued.

'No, I obtained permission to travel with the men as a Chaplain. In my previous life I was a medical student. I was captured at Tannenburg, volunteered for Antwerp.'

'Madness.' Eisner shook his head. 'You chose to come here?'

'As did you, and your companions.'

'That's one way of describing it,' Archer warned, face hardening.

The conversation stilled in the denial, the stout priest

looking at the others for explanation. Finding none, he simply sighed. 'It is the same for many. You are here for the Americans, though. Correct?'

'Not entirely.' Archer closed his hands, clasping his fingers together.

Father Ruslan looked ready to say something, when the doors at the end of the small church banged open, the shotgun toting youth from the door blabbering in excited Russian. The priest was on his feet in a heartbeat, answering all of the sentences fired at him, replying with terse questions of his own before addressing his small congregation.

'My friends, it seems the Kaiser has found one of our outposts. One of our scouts report troops massing outside an old shop we use for refuge.'

'Where?' Eisner stood up, arranging his battle order.

'The Northwest quarter, it is only two miles from the Citadel.'

Archer knew an appeal when he heard it. 'There's a price, Father.'

'There always is, my son.'

16:

Described by the defenders as a safe-house, it better resembled Ruslan's description of a battered shop front. The edifice of the building was apparently the only bit which forgot to fall down when the rest caved in. The ceiling creaked with every breath of wind whistling through the gaps. In the space under the stairs, viciously truncated by the collapsed roof, lay a filthy mattress and small stove for a sentry, or desperate fugitive exhausted from pursuit. Ruslan's refugees added to the protection of the walls with stout boards and metal plates, mimicking trench sniping loopholes. No sandbags draped the windows, but broken bricks were piled to improve the barricades.

By the time Archer got there, the battle had started. Hobnailed boots crunched on the road outside, a casualty on the shop floor mewled, hands clutched to his stomach. Two of his comrades pulled him back, leaving a bloody trail where the wound had leaked and pooled. The injured man was pale, face drawn from pain and the exertion of flight.

'Ruslan?' One of the men demanded.

Archer pointed at the trapdoor he'd come through, supposing the men had been ambushed in the street, or caught thieving from the Kaiser's storehouse. The ruckus outside told of a running battle that forced the refugees into somewhere they could hold, and, in that desperation, led their attackers to the last place they wanted to be found. The wounded man was pulled through the trapdoor by comrades.

Mauser bullets chewed into a wooden panel two feet from Archer's head, driving him to shy away. The abandoned store reeked of stale cigarettes and cigars – a tobacconist's.

With every movement and round, the smell grew stronger, stirred by the activity. Archer always fancied himself a pipe man, but the glow of a bowl was a big invitation to a sniper – *smoking will kill you*, he thought, falling down to crawl forward behind what remained of an interior wall. Apt, since this place appeared to be a death trap.

Blackcoats were swarming, but even though they had more numbers than the paltry defenders, they looked happy enough to sit there taking pot-shots, possibly awaiting reinforcements. It was a mistake. They should have brought their weight to bear in a formal, frontal charge to overwhelm them. Now the defenders had help, the youth with his shotgun, and Archer's team, brought the live bodies to a paltry ten. It was a start.

'English? Anyone?' he tried.

'I speak!' barked a man covering the door.

'Russian?'

'Ha! Polish!'

'What's your name?' Archer asked.

'I am Marek.'

'Translate for Russian, yes?'

'Of course!'

Archer unlimbered the *Runebolt*, checked his pouches for bullets. He had a good supply, but was reluctant to waste any on the rabble outside just yet. A dull tap and clunk announced a grenade, and as it blew, the front of the tobacco store was engulfed by dust and smoke. The teeth-loosening force wrenched plaster and bricks from the walls to fall onto the defenders, but none were hurt.

A second bomb, followed by a third, the enemy moving to remedy their earlier mistake, probably realising more defenders could appear at any second. They made a determined rush at the doorway, which was enough to change Archer's mind about shooting. He aimed at the dark figures in the pale fug as they erupted, firing and cycling the bolt quickly. The first intruder clutched at his chest with a groan, going backwards. Another Blackcoat cried out, spinning into his comrades before falling over and spoiling their charge.

Before he could fire again, the combat was on him. Close and brutal, the Blackcoats struggled with the defenders, Marek lashing out with a length of polished mahogany. A police truncheon in a former life, it was now oil-stained, adorned with a vicious looking arrangement of cogwheels at the top. Archer watched it crunch down onto a Blackcoat's arm, the terrible crack of splintering bone at the shoulder followed immediately with a groin kick. The victim despatched, Marek lunged at another brawler with his rifle, using it as a blunt stave. Trench raids were like this. The brutal nature of a street fight, with none of even those scant rules, each combatant fighting tooth and nail for their existence.

A loud bang nearby drew his attention to Nunzia. She grunted in the aftermath of firing her pistol at close range, slashing a Blackcoat across the eyes with bayonet she'd picked up. A flap of bloody skin blinding him, the man abandoned his weapons to desperately ward off his assailant. In a bizarre moment of Music Hall Slapstick, his bloodied, groping hands gripped her chest, eliciting a cry of shock and outrage. She brought the pistol butt down on his neck, quickly following with Italian curses as the man dropped at her feet, nearly unconscious.

With no room to swing his axe, Eisner was stabbing and stamping, a hunting knife in hand, he employed quite the dirty trick – pinning their feet to stab the blade up into their groin. It was hard to defend against, the German continually moving, the rapid work making a mockery of the flesh it savaged.

One of the assailants tried to grip the knife out of blunt instinct, but Eisner just pulled, ignoring the scream from the sliced palm, before ramming forward into the stomach, taking his opponent went down. A rifle butt from somewhere finished the victim off.

Seizing his self-loading pistol, Archer fired into the

melee. The rapid flash and blast of the gun was violent in the confined space, louder and more piercing than the dull thump of grenades. Bodies crumpled, immediate slack buying a moment from the tumult. More Blackcoats pushed in, trying to force their numbers to an advantage, but they were coming in blind to a fierce resistance. Archer's instinct warned him that the battle had reached a pivotal moment; likewise, the enemy pushed harder, sensing victory was near, on that knife edge.

He filled his lungs.

'Fix bayonets!' His voice cut through the din of men and women battering each other senseless, stunning the Blackcoats for a heartbeat. The look on their faces told Archer everything – and in that understanding, he knew the enemy was lost. Drawing his 1907 pattern bayonet, he slotted nearly two feet of edged steel onto the muzzle cap of the rifle.

Ramming forward, he unleashed all his constrained fears, screaming it at them. He speared into the mass of flesh, finding a throat, the victim dropping in a pained gurgle. The bayonet punctured a leg, a stomach, a groin. The order for close action was centuries old, and Marek redoubled his efforts from the doorway, helping to stem the tide. Bayonet fighting meant death or victory by steel and stinking guts, and this was a battle they desperately needed to win.

He dropped into a trained rhythm, left foot going forward, momentum of the step building in the arms and shoulders, delivering the power from his hip to the rifle stock in a pendulum swing. A pained cry erupted to match his own shrieks, then another step forward, until he was shoulder-to-shoulder with Eisner, who was lunging with his reddened blade, using the gap to cleave the foe with his freshly drawn axe. Together, they closed with the Pole, his cudgel matted and clotted with lumps of hair-covered meat. They pushed forward in unison, an axeman, a swordsman and a maul wielding maniac, bellowing until hoarse, inexorably driving the enemy out into the street.

In four-hundred years of technological advances, of gunpowder and tanks, Archer reflected that so little had changed. It all came down to flesh and steel, to men screaming at each other as they tore one another open.

The Blackcoats didn't stand against such medieval battery, falling back in dribs and drabs, some running with wounds, some from communal panic at being smashed bloody. Archer gave no quarter, levelling the weapon and working the action, shooting each fleeing man he could see. They tumbled and rolled over, the life gone from them as the cloying blood, propellant and tobacco mixed into a heady recipe which threatened to make him retch.

It wasn't over. At the end of the street, two blocky vehicles pulled into the road. The menacing, angular shapes made him pull the two men down with him as he dived, rifle out ahead of him, breath driven from his chest where he slammed into the floor. A hair later, machineguns opened fire, spraying bullets at the doorway, rounds pinging from the armoured plating behind the windowsills. These must have been the reinforcements the Blackcoats anticipated, and although a little late, they were formidable support.

Whilst the shop was being rent asunder, Archer focused. He reloaded as he checked for casualties. Eisner, Nunzia and Marek were fine, but the youth was lying in a bloody smear. Caught at the back of the room when Archer had cleared the door, he'd been riddled with bullets from the Maxim 08/15's the armoured cars carried, and he lay in a congealing mess, eyes open and glassy, shotgun still clasped in his hand.

Eisner noticed. '*Verdammt!* Idiot boy!'

'Get his shotgun!' Archer shouted above the death rattle of belt-fed weapons.

Eisner flopped on his belly, snaking across the debris choked floor until he got the weapon, pulling it free of the youth's tight grip. He slipped his knife out and cut the pouch with the shells, working his way backwards to Archer, who was busy trying to find the Mills bombs in his satchel. He weighed the bombs, gauged he wouldn't have the time or distance for a safe throw, and even if he did get the bombs out, would they even destroy the cars?

'Can't you do a magic shot, like back at the armoury?' the German bellowed.

It sounded like an entire brass band was ringing the percussion bells on the other side of them. 'Takes too long! If I stick my head up, I get it blown off!'

'It would be an improvement!'

The slander sliding past him, Archer's fingers abandoned the grenades, dabbling in the ammunition pouch carrying the Arcanist bullets, but decided on giving another reason. 'I only have five rounds left!'

'Then use two! *Mein Gott!*' Eisner ducked as shots cleaved a hole through brick and killed another of the defenders. 'Use two, Daniel! Or we are all dead men!'

The German was right. They could hear the engines, the rumbling of the armoured cars as they manoeuvred closer, trying to reach a spot that would give them elevation and traverse over the store. The angle to get back down to the cellar and the underground lair was already covered by those formidable guns, a merciless defilade offering no retreat. The Blackcoats would keep shooting until they razed the building or a canny crewman tossed a grenade in, and finished them.

'Kurt, I need a distraction.'

'Are you joking? You want me to get up and flap my arms? *Coo! Coo!*'

'No, idiot, a decoy! Put your hat up or something – anything head shaped!'

'Have you got any matches?'

'What? No.'

Eisner just looked at him with a pitying stare.

'Wait...here!' Archer pulled his rucksack to one side, delved. He retrieved one of the flare cartridges Nunzia had given him, and tossed it into Eisner's waiting hands.

'You *are* a magician! Get into position, my friend! We shall give them hellfire!'

Marek watched and listened, saw Archer get to his knees and waved to him. 'Quickly! They do not point this way!'

Good enough. Archer pelted for the other side of the room. For several heartbeats, he wasn't shot at, but the bullets soon slapped about him, trying to keep his head down, by which time he was safe. In the short space of the dash, he saw the armoured cars gaining ground. In a minute or less, those machineguns would be peeking over the wall and able to depress far enough to rake the whole shop.

Eisner broke the flare open. He poured out the components, especially the phosphorous powder and magnesium strips. He snatched an entrenching shovel from the dead man nearby and face coated in soot and grime, peered up at Archer, nodding once.

A special round was fed into the *Runebolt's* breech, the blue glint from the bullet flashed odd reflection into Archer's hand before it went into the hungry barrel and the bolt closed up behind it. He adopted a kneeling position, ready to stand up, placing a second round on the floor between his feet, not daring to clamp it between his teeth, else it go off. He met Eisner's stare. They were ready.

The German took the shovel, and handled his axe in the other hand. He stood, placing the pan blade on the top of the window ledge. In the moments before Archer thought he'd be blown to hell, he'd reversed the axe-head, slamming it down. A spark flared in golden brilliance, power illuminating the room with a warming flash. Archer watched, almost forgetting his part, when a monstrous jet of red-hued flame billowed out – and a dragon joined the battle.

Any cries of alarm or wonder were obliterated in the expulsion of flame, a roar consuming air to feed the billowing torrent pouring from the axe. The crucible the German had furnished was mesmerising, and the fire danced to his will. Tearing his eyes from the sight, Archer slithered a hand over the *Runebolt*'s inlaid metals, building up force quickly, the mechanism drinking it to saturation. His stress brought it on faster than he liked, preferring the slow build of a controlled shot. Another bullet impact nearby forced the issue; he snatched the trigger, a blue lance chopping through the fire and choking miasma.

The energy bolt smacked the armoured plate with a tinny echo, followed a second later by the thump of ozone-rich air. Snaps and cracks came from within the armoured car as the ammunition cooked off. He could imagine what hell was unleashed on anyone inside. Blinded by the jet of flame still erupting from Eisner's axe, the second armoured car was firing wild, panicking. Archer loaded again, driving a second energy bolt through the metal beast, putting it out of action completely, with a clean kill.

A harsh cry of surprise and agony came from his left. Archer was just in time to see the axe haft split in Eisner's hand, like a bomb or burst rifle barrel. Still clutching the wooden handle, his fingers were blasted bloody, impaled with dozens of long splinters. Burned wood and pine resin smashed into Eisner's face, and he fell back. Nunzia was fast, breaking the German's fall, but his weight bore both of them to the ground.

Threat extinguished, Marek slid across, face framed in wonder. 'Two magic men!'

'One and a bit now,' Eisner groaned through his teeth, eyes squeezed tight.

The hand was a ruin, charred and blackened. The German had sacrificed more than his Focus Wand; his left arm below the elbow was done for, given to save the rest of them. The smell of burned bacon rind added to the horror.

'We go down,' The Polish soldier insisted. 'Father Ruslan.'

The other defenders picked up bags Archer hadn't noticed, supposing they carried rations or valuable supplies. He hoped it was worth it, but the thing that struck him the most was the damning silence, as though the city was appalled by another atrocity. The people watched them, looking away swiftly whenever Archer or Eisner tried to meet their gaze, a deference and awe shrouded them all as they descended into the tunnels, pulling the trapdoor shut behind them. With the safehouse now beyond use, the bloodied refugee militia took sledgehammers to old wooden props, smashing them down. A cave-in filled the tunnel as they retreated, sealing it with tonnes of debris.

Across town, Preston listened to a battle being fought. It sounded closer to the Citadel than he was, and ferocious – the stutter of machineguns and some kind of cannon. He was too far away to do anything about it now, besides, he and his men were hip deep in bodies. The cannibals were easily dealt with; one of his troops flung a couple of Model 1915 stick grenades, blasting a knot of the flesh-scavengers to pieces in their act of sawing limbs off for later consumption in whatever hole they crawled into. Even he drew his weapons to fire at the scrabbling noises in front of him, blazing away with a Mauser pistol in each hand, accuracy sacrificed in favour of shock and awe.

It didn't matter – once the *Kampfgruppe* left, the savages would return and even if the dead could be buried, the scroungers would dig them up. It wasn't the first time he hoped to die outside the city. Being shot by the British authorities as a traitor would at least buy him a grave. Discarded brass at the Manse gave him more puzzle pieces. Unfamiliar weapon magazines steered him across the Atlantic, and feeling the uniforms with their odd rank badges brought a bitter smile to his face.

They Americans must have come in on the zeppelin, because nobody knew anything about them breaching the perimeter. When Preston investigated the armoury attack, he'd telegraphed the quayside authorities, but they reported no ships docking at port, no Royal Marine raiding parties

– nothing. Who would be escorted by American soldiers? Someone valuable, surely. Perhaps a diplomat, a senior officer, or maybe a special advisor. Preston let out a low whistle, and heard his five-strong team crunching over the rubble to group with him.

'Someone go back to my car. Tell Ilsa to bring Max.'

'*Jawohl, Herr Hauptmann.*'

Thankfully the rain had been light, the wind steady, and his men knew how to behave around the dog. They would protect him whilst he and Max worked together across the blasted cityscape, sniffing out a needle in a haystack.

17:

Morphine let the German relax, Sam administering the dose. Eisner closed his eyes as the relief hit him, the lines of trauma on his face slackening, even as Sam began to gently cut the shredded and partly burned sleeve away from the wound. The German hissed as his arm was bathed in water to soften the fibres heat-welded to his skin so it could be tended properly. If the fibres weren't cleared, it would result in gangrene, and amputation – if it was caught in time.

Father Ruslan waited for a few minutes, moving in with long medical tweezers, deftly pulling fibres away with flesh, paring with a scalpel where they refused him. The operation was done with the quiet competence of a man who knew his business, and when he pulled the splinters from the German's hand, Eisner was staring at the ceiling, his mind elsewhere. Curious children and adults alike poked their heads into the infirmary to watch, the room almost full to capacity with the wounded defenders.

Letting Eisner rest, Ruslan moved among them, assessing the damage, superficial cuts and burns treated with bandages and iodine, before allowing the men to rest. Collecting a bottle and some rolled bandages, he returned to Eisner.

'For you, *Mein Herr* the war is over. A Fire Mage, of all things,' Ruslan said, impressed. He shook his head, an apologetic smile almost concealed by his moustache and beard. He washed his hands in a bowl and then began to dress Eisner's hand, first by holding it over the bowl and pouring the contents of a glass jar over it. Alchemical smell erupted as the liquid effervesced.

'I'm glad I can't feel that.' Eisner grimaced.

'It is not as bad it looks,' Ruslan reassured him, 'the Dakin Solution will keep infection away, for when I treat it again later.'

'We use medical ozone.'

'It is in short supply here, my son, but this is better. Rest now.'

The German lay back and allowed the priest to continue.

'And what kind of warlock are you?' Ruslan threw the query over his shoulder, working with the ease and gentleness of a professional.

Archer made a face, disliking the term, but lacked argument against it. 'I make things die, Father.'

The priest chuckled as he tied the bandage around Eisner's burned hand, making sure he didn't snag any of the wounded flesh. He helped his patient to relax on the cot, placing his palm on Eisner's pale forehead. He muttered something Archer didn't fully catch, but he suspected it was ecumenical in nature and didn't pry. Once it was clear that his patient was asleep, Ruslan indicated Sam should take the opportunity to sleep. The giant stooped, disappearing with a grace belying his size.

'Daughter, will you watch over them?'

'Of course, Father,' Nunzia replied, grasping the Priest's hand.

Ruslan beckoned to Archer and the two men left the infirmary, without speaking. The priest led through the underground vaults until Archer recognised the cellar he'd first entered as the Eastern safehouse. At Ruslan's approach, the sentries opened the door for him to visit the surface.

Dusk was striking, the glow of the sunset matched by the hot embers of war on the opposite horizon, as three armies pummelled and tore at each other for ruined land, trying desperately to prise their opponent from it, but it was obvious the Central Powers were punch drunk, reeling from blows which would soon force their capitulation. Or at least that's what everyone *should* think, he reflected. The war had been going for so long he wondered if peace would be a reality everyone recognised.

'It has a rugged beauty, does it not?'

'Hmm?' Archer was wrong footed.

'The city.'

'Yes, Father. I suppose so.'

'You're not a romantic then,' he laughed, shoulders and chest heaving.

'I get misty about sleeping without being shot at. Does that count?'

He didn't elaborate that all he saw when he looked out on the devastation were ideal sniping positions, routes to reach them, and potential avenues of escape if he had to dismount. He smiled at himself. Would *he* understand peace? Or would he forever be scanning the ground ahead for an enemy helmet to put a bullet through?

A scuff of boots behind disturbed him, and both men turned to see a heavily bandaged man climb up the steps with the help of a crutch. Even in the half-dark, Archer recognised Sergeant Miller, his uniform still distinctive despite the staining of blood, sweat and dirt.

'Corporal,' he forced the word of greeting through bandages around his head, pinned under his chin. He'd certainly been in the wars.

Archer felt for the stock of the *Runebolt* slung on his shoulder. 'I think you owe me an explanation, Sergeant.'

Ruslan frowned, as though the demand was unnecessary, but Archer wasn't feeling terribly courteous. He was tired, and this conference was abrading his thinning nerves.

In contrast, Miller sighed, although it seemed done in relief. 'Sam was in our embassy in Switzerland. We were moving him, but he…escaped.'

'Escaped? What do you mean? Is he a criminal?'

'No.' Father Ruslan held his hands up. 'He's a Mage – rare, like you.'

Not wanting to tip his hand, already stung by the Americans once, silence was the best answer, so that's what Archer gave.

'He was in protective custody,' Miller explained.

Archer made a face this time, having heard that before, once too often. Incarceration in Rannoch Moor was supposedly for his protection, too. 'How rare?'

'Unique,' Ruslan said.

That gave him pause enough to take a different tack. 'So how is he here?'

'Like I said, people choose to come here.' Ruslan shrugged.

'It would never land here,' Archer protested.

'Why do you think he set the fire?' Miller replied quietly.

Implication struck with a slap, but Archer recovered. 'Then he needs to be hanged for murder.'

'Like you?' Ruslan asked.

'What the hell does that mean?'

'You play God, my son. You pick who lives or dies from afar. How many people really have a chance against you?'

'Don't push me, Priest.'

Father Ruslan stepped close, gently gripped him by both shoulders. 'My son, he is desperate. Half the world wants him a prisoner; the other half wants him a corpse!'

'That goes for us all, Father!' It was out of his mouth before he thought it. Taking a quick breath, Archer stepped back, considered the position. The communication from Garfield weighed heavily on one shoulder, his need to fulfil the mission on the other. If he could get Sam out alive, it would snub the Intelligence Major, and would honour General Byng's agreement. Sam supposedly being unique made it all the worse. 'What can Sam do?'

The men exchanged glances, but said nothing more.

'Fine,' Archer shrugged the priest off, turned to go

down the stairs. 'My friend is dead, another one is badly hurt, and I saw what they did to the prisoners from the airship.'

'Daniel, please just listen—'

'Those bastards took a bloke's balls off with a bolt cutter!' he punched the words at them, until they were forced to look away. 'The Kaiser must know Sam is here by now, or someone just as important – the bloody Yanks, he pointed up at Miller, 'know you *failed.*'

'How do you know that?' Miller fired back.

'If what you say is true, it's obvious to your superiors by now!' Archer covered the slip with anger. 'I've got a way out. I'm taking him.'

'With lanterns, torches and weapons?'

Archer looked narrowly at the clergyman, tracked his eyes up and down the burly priest. 'How dangerously biblical, Father.'

'Find your heart, Daniel. Are you just following orders? Is that it?'

He wanted to tell them about whitewashed walls, and doctors without sympathy. Of men in khaki carrying the signature of the King, of Garfield and his threats and warnings, of a family waiting for amnesty – but they were not friends, nowhere near. The accusation of dumb obedience drew Archer's anger, pulled the bowstring taut.

'Render unto *Kaiser*,' he loosed, 'besides, has anyone asked Sam?'

He went back inside to do just that.

Sam wrung his hands, looked past them from where he sat on a log bench. He listened to Father Ruslan and Archer carefully, the Sniper amazed he was allowed to speak his case. Miller remained silent, letting the big man think. The massive shoulders heaved when he heard how the airship crew had been treated – although Archer spared much of the detail, not for Sam's benefit, but the dignity of the dead. The big man shook his head at it all.

'I'm real sorry Mr Daniel; I didn't mean to hurt anybody.'

'My orders were to get you out of here.' It wasn't a lie, not completely.

'Then I'd go home?'

'I don't know.'

'Sarge?'

Miller looked at the ground; his good eye lacked the firm glare from before, filled instead with gentle sadness, perhaps for Sam's predicament. 'Archer's got the best route out. I can't take you,' he said, lifting his crutch to emphasise his point.

'I'm going to stay.'

Archer looked at Sam. 'You still need to answer for the trouble you caused.'

'I'll make up for it here, I promise.'

With that, Archer was defeated. Part of him wanted to believe Sam, but truly it was because he wasn't going to do Garfield's dirty work. Besides, the big man was popular enough that the women and children could stand in opposition, and there was no way he was going to gun them down. Therese and Marie were friends and they'd been through a lot. Murder was his trade, but everyone he killed was a threat to him, someone else, or the mission. Somehow, he doubted Garfield would see it that way.

His concern about the others remained. He'd never been satisfied by either Eisner or Nunzia's responses to his questions, and the good Major hadn't specified what agreements he'd entertained. Even if the German was wounded, he was still capable of wielding a weapon. He was going to have to draw them out, confront it, but he would need a decoy.

'What do we do now, Curtains?' Nunzia muttered, making a face, perhaps reading his mind. She'd been lurking throughout the conversation, merely listening.

Archer thought about it. 'Father, when can Kurt travel?'

'Give me an hour, I'll arrange something.' The priest

groaned to his feet, left.

Resisting the urge to make further comment, Archer turned from the room, but his wrist was clamped in a huge fist, and he was arrested in his flight. He followed the hand to meet Sam's face.

'I'll make it right.'

'I believe you,' he replied, 'I understand. I might have done the same thing.'

Without anything else to do, Archer strode back outside; staring over the city, into the ether. He could feel an itch between his shoulders, the kind when another sniper was looking for him. He couldn't spot anything in particular, nor put his finger on it, but he knew he was right. Someone would be dogging their steps, looking for Sam.

He needed a diversion, and answers.

Panting and snuffling filled Preston's ears as Max shoved his long snout into everything. He knew that Bloodhounds had the best tracking nose, but tired quickly, where Spaniels had plenty of energy to follow up every scent they caught, but this was Antwerp, and Max was a trained guard dog. Fortunately, Max had plenty of brains as well as strength, speed, and a good nose. He was lucky in his loyal hound.

Preston grasped the rope harness around Max's shoulders, the dog steering gently by leading and pushing against Preston's legs. Better than a lead, the harness was a vicarious sensory medium. He could feel the hound pause, step around obstacles, and he followed. He relied on Max completely, understanding that most of the time when tracking, the quarry was lost because the trust between handler and dog was broken.

Max made low noises in his throat, which if they occurred in a human, would be the humming of decision making. Despite the mess and treacherous footing, Preston insisted nothing should be disturbed, that no-one should come near the dog, or attempt to clear a path. Max indicated a tin can in the corner, pushing it around noisily.

'What is it boy? Anything good?' He encouraged Max, tone was everything.

A whine, then the dog came upright, onto his haunches, sniffing and panting excitedly. Dropping back down, Max began urgently tugging. Then Preston could smell it too, as the bouncing and capering canine disturbed the old smell, wafting it up to his nose. Some kind of medicinal alcohol. 'Tell the truck to follow us!'

He turned back to Max, doing his best to keep up as the dog launched off, every step and slope taken at a hunting pace.

18:

Leaving most of their food with the refugees, and an hour's rest under their belts, Archer, Nunzia, and Eisner set off. The German's hand was bandaged with a clean dressing, and he could just about handle his machine pistol in his right fist, cradling the barrel in his left elbow. His other borrowed weapons were all available to his right hand regardless. The trio stalked through the early night, clouds light and moon high, hovering over the city, picking out the tiled roofs still intact nearer the walls.

The others questioned why they were wandering around in the ruins, but Archer spun the lie they were scouting, making the way safe for Sam to follow them with some of the Russians and citizens of Antwerp. He allowed both Eisner and Nunzia to go in front of him, watching them both carefully. This would get settled now. They clambered into an old house, the roof beams and tiles blasted away, perfect for what he intended.

'Alright, this is it. We'll hold here until Sam and the others come.'

'Then we push on again?' Nunzia asked, settling down to watch the road, peering into the darkness. She kept her voice as low as his.

'Right. Like an accordion,' Archer said, hands mimicking playing the instrument.

'Ah,' she beamed at him. 'You have funny ideas, English.'

He pretended to look down the street, the way they came, and chambered a round in his rifle, peeking over the open sights. He glanced around at them before pulling out the flare gun from his belt and shooting the cartridge directly above them. A *snap-pop* and the whole street lit with arterial red.

'What are you doing, *Kartoffelkopf*?' Eisner was agape.

'Don't move, either of you,' Archer said quietly, ignoring the fact Eisner called him cabbage-head, or potato-something. Irritation at the insult swept his rifle around the room, but at no-one specifically. He deliberately thumbed off the safety catch. 'We don't have much time.'

'Everyone will know where we are!' Nunzia hissed. 'Are you mad?'

'There is no rendezvous,' he carried on, flat. 'Sam is staying in Antwerp.'

They were silent, their gazes shifting from each other to him.

'One, or maybe both of you, plotted to snatch him on the way out.'

'I didn't—' Eisner started.

'Shut up. You're *Abwehr*,' Archer damned him. 'There's no time. Any minute now and Blackcoats or cannibals are going to be on us. We can't survive alone.'

Nunzia's eyes were hooded, the red light casting weird shadows across all three of them. His own vision was protected by the darkness of his sniper robes, so he knew they couldn't see which one of them he was looking at. They both remained immobile. No naked flames licked, and it wasn't raining, so their magic was worthless. He'd only be able to shoot one of them before the other charged, but they had seen what the *Runebolt* could do, how fatal it was.

How he never missed.

'We can make it to the submarine,' Archer said, 'but all cards on the table – now.'

Silence. Then Nunzia began clapping, a slow, ironic applause that set Archers teeth on edge, and the rifle slowly lifted.

'Alright. What gave it away?'

'What you said on the boat, things you've said since. Too flirty, distracting me. When I told you I didn't hate Germans, you changed tack. I'm not an idiot. Why would your government just say yes to us?'

'Mr Garfield is convincing.'

There was the sound of feet on rubble, and Archer smiled. A little more pressure wasn't too bad a thing. In the distance he could hear a dog barking, and could imagine the handlers scrambling to ready positions. 'We're out of time. Make your choice.'

'Alright!' she pushed her palms out, showing both hands were empty. 'I was supposed to get rid of you all on the submarine, except for the diplomat.'

'Ha, I knew it!' Eisner beamed in triumph.

'But?' Archer waved the nose cap of the rifle to encourage her.

She cast around, trying to find the words. 'I decided not to.'

'I'm supposed to believe that?'

'*Madre di Dio* - Mother of God, why would I lie when we're about to be eaten by maniacs?'

He didn't want to point out the flaw in the logic, but the way she said it convinced him. He took it at face value. 'What about you, Kurt?'

'I am here for a man named Hiedler,' his voice was solid, lacking any pretence. 'He's better known to Antwerp as the Kaiser. I am a prisoner of war. He dies, I am exchanged.'

'And what about you, English? What was your deal with Garfield?'

'I don't have a deal – I'm on the payroll,' he growled. He stared at them, defying any challenge, but wondered if Ross was promised a pardon.

'Fine,' Nunzia continued. 'How do we know you will not shoot us in the back?'

He answered with a smile. 'It had occurred to me, but no. Sam wants to stay, and Antwerp can bloody have him.'

'So what now?' she asked.

'We go to the submarine. Get the hell out.'

'Alright,' Nunzia let out a sigh. 'We go.'

The sounds of people searching the ruins reached them. Bare feet slapped on concrete and cobbles. Creaking timbers announced the awakening of a slumbering giant. All Archer could think of were beanstalks and huge feet, thundering. *I smell the blood of an Englishman...*

It was almost too late. The horde came down into the ruins and Archer turned, shooting one through the chest, his rifle fired from the hip. Nunzia and Eisner broke and ran, getting distance to put their guns to use. The machine pistol chattered and bowled over men and women armed with poles and cudgels. Clad in nothing but rags, they were a sorry mess, but they hissed and jabbered in a strange mix of French and German cant, an eerie determination not open to reason.

He fell back to the others and they began a mad dash of running, followed by one of them stopping to fire. Eisner tossed the long barrelled shotgun to Nunzia, knowing the value of a scattering shot in the frantic pursuit. Only weight of fire would drive them off. The brutes were almost on them, when Nunzia fell over, tripping on rubble spoil.

'*Tommy*! Do something!'

Dropping to one knee, Archer tripped the magazine release from the *Runebolt*, and the box magazine dropped, a couple of the fulminate rounds falling from the feeding ramp. It sparked a mental note to police them up after. He worked the action, and the chamber cleared, before he pushed in one of the newly issued twenty-round magazines. The Lee-Enfield receiver accepted it greedily, a monster looking to feed.

'Down!' he bellowed.

Eisner spared one quick look behind him, before dropping to the ground in a voluntary, controlled tumble, hurriedly pulling himself on top of the Sea Witch, shielding her body with his own.

The Sniper's hands moved of their own volition. His

mind cleared, without the need to channel energy into his Focus, the magic wand in his hands was just a modified rifle. This was no time for the magic bullets anyway – it was aimed, rapid fire, at one-hundred yards. His body started the motion, finding the rhythm quickly along with the odd breathing cadence.

Ready, Aim, Fire.

The rifle reports were just part of his world; background to the mantra, the cadence of recoil slamming his shoulder was the signal to shoot again. He ignored the ache in his arms and wrists.

Ready, Aim, Fire.

Above the din, he could feel his breathing as the city condensed to a square inch hovering above his sights, the massed bodies were just targets. When the shot screamed down the barrel, he saw them flop and fall, replaced by others.

Ready, Aim, Fire.

Hours of drill, of mindless repetition, training for moments like this, took over. In his mind the number of shots dwindled, and when he counted twenty and could see his magazine follower, he snatched a charger clip from his pocket and fed the weapon, keeping his fingers clear of the hot metal breech. Time and even thought slid away, he couldn't remember where he was.

'They're running! That is enough!'

Eisner's words broke the spell. Archer ceased, and cleared the weapon to prevent an accident. Blue smoky wisps streamed from beneath the wooden stock, so he lowered it, letting it cool on the ground. It was only then he realised what carnage he wrought, when he saw all the spent brass, discarded charging clips, and dropped magazines. He counted the latter as he picked them up. He'd fired three dozen rounds, the skirmish lasting only a minute or so, with no stoppages or mechanism breaks.

The flutter of pride in his chest was smothered when the sound of the wounded and frightened survivors began.

He felt guilty as he watched Eisner and Nunzia pull upright, dusting off before walking towards where he still knelt. Nunzia cast cold eyes over the scene, taking in the wholesale slaughter, wrought without a machinegun.

'There is nothing pretty here,' she said, stared at him.

'Would you rather be on the menu?'

'We had better go,' Eisner said, turning away. He stopped and nodded to the rifle. 'Make sure to bring your magic wand.'

His men reacted to the sudden sizzling hiss and snap, hurrying to cover Preston without needing the order. Max whined, twisting to face it, barking at the distant intruder.

'Flare, *Herr Hauptmann*. To the south.'

Preston was familiar with the sound. 'Colour?'

'Red, sir.'

He didn't reply immediately, thinking about how exposed they were. The flare would draw out the lurking savages, moths to a flame. Whoever sent the emergency signal up had endangered the search party, true, but they were in the greater danger. He pondered that it could be a distraction, but banished that – although to dismiss the risk it presented was foolhardy.

'We continue, keep alert and together. Shoot first, questions later. Understood?'

'*Jawohl*,' one of the soldiers replied.

'Max, find them, boy. Let's go.'

The dog returned to the trail, pulling him along. Preston stumbled and staggered as rubble slid out under his weight, but remained upright until Max guided him onto the flat. They carried on, crossing a road or plaza, weeds springing up from cracks in the ground, his feet snagging on the ankle-high greenery.

His hound kept pulling, until he stopped, barking up at something. Preston clucked his tongue, and immediately discovered the object rearing up right in front of him. He drew a pistol, the barrel bumping against the object, so pushed his knuckles against it instead, and discerned the smoothness of worked stone. He continued to feel it, ran his hand down into the concave slope of a bowl or basin. He brushed against moss and sediment.

A statue?

He placed his pistol in the bowl as an offering, his palm searching the body, finding the face, half smooth, half ravaged. A water carrier, once beautiful, but suffering in the war. Max pulled again, and Preston found his gun, hefting it. He whistled and his men closed in about him.

'Combat wheel!'

They shuffled into formation, to cover every angle of attack. He let Max lead him on, sniffing, indicating something. He knelt down, tugging on the rope harness, telling Max to sit. The dog obeyed.

Preston's questing fingers went forward again, found discarded cigarette butts. He pulled them to his nose. Many things in Antwerp were old, sealed in when the last innocents escaped or moved out, but these were freshly hand-rolled, not manufactured. He listened carefully, heard the creak of chairs and tables being used. Someone was nearby, inside whatever building was in front of them. He detected the sound of weapons being readied.

Perhaps wondering about why a dog was barking so close by.

At that thought he knew he must move quickly. 'Get word to the Citadel. Send a capture force immediately. We'll hold this position.'

His hope was they could wait, but hinges creaked, followed by an alarmed shout in Russian. The voice was to his right, and brandishing his Mauser pistol, he fired in that direction, heard his bullets strike wooden rifle stock and flesh. A sharp cry, and then Max was barking as men hurried up steps.

'Go Max! Attack! Get them boy!'

The animal snarled forward, grappling and lunging, and then his men were right there, the sub machineguns stuttering. Fresh blood stained the air, along with yelping and cries of pain. The torrent of gunfire ceased, and Max returned, his fur wet with thick clots. Preston took a few steps forwards, but a voice stopped him.

'Careful, sir! There is a cellar there, with narrow steps.'

He grunted thanks. 'Well, after that reception, grenades first, then down.'

'With pleasure.' The bombs were readied, pulled from boots or unclipped from belts. '*Achtung!*'

Explosions rumbled in the narrow space below Preston's feet, tearing the air with force, stirring up dust. Powerful arms carried the officer down the steps, machine pistols barking furiously, driving back any defenders waiting for them, but with the speed and violence of their assault, there were none.

The entrance above secured, Preston could hear his soldiers moving into a tunnel beyond. Ricochets and gunfire gave him an understanding of the immediate area. The cellar was broad, but low-ceiling, with a single tunnel leading out. Hollow echoes told him of rooms or tunnels branching off beyond.

They had to be under the old fortress fortifications.

The buzzing of electric bulbs signified there was power down here too, likely siphoned off the main systems used by the Citadel and the defences. He knew that any real resistance here could wipe him out, but surprise was his, and he'd sent word for reinforcements. Hope was dashed when a bang sounded, and hot blood struck Preston's cheek. One of his men swore savagely.

'Spread out as much as you can. Keep firing!'

Women and children began to shout and scream in abject panic, and as Preston passed a doorway, he was assaulted from the side by something huge, something powerful. Tossed sideways by a buffet to his shoulder, he was disarmed completely, his whole side numb from the blow of a meaty fist.

He rebounded from the wall, his troops ceasing fire to try and prevent him from being shot by accident, but steely hands clamped onto his hip and thigh, biting into the flesh there before being violently slammed into the roof, and then discarded. His men suffered the same fate, being battered and tossed. He reached for his other gun, winded, firing rapidly at close range, the cries telling him he'd hit a man.

Everything was chaos as the *force* met them, stopped them in their tracks with bare hands alone. Preston had never met such elemental force. It was like being hit by boulders.

'*Max, defend!*'

The Alsatian barked, growling malevolently, and suddenly his hand was met by fur, and the terrible punishment ceased. Preston grabbed for the rope harness, the dog let him, the pair regrouping, with Max gnashing and straining under Preston's reeling weight.

'Don't let him bite me!'

The accent was American, from the south, and from the direction it was uttered, Preston could tell the man must have been tall. Heavy footsteps came out of a room to Preston's left.

'*Mein Gott!*' one of his men gasped, 'a giant!'

Preston grinned, feeling his split lips and the bruises on his face. His left nostril was blocked by blood. He also likely had a concussion – but he'd won. He was right. An American had made it into Antwerp.

'Airship?' he asked the huge man in English.

'Yes! Don't let him bite me, mister!'

Preston pulled Max in. 'Heel, boy! Sit! Well done, boy,' he said, petting his faithful companion. He straightened up, everything hurting like a bastard. 'Big man, what's your name?'

'Sam! Don't hurt anyone anymore, please!'

'Like Uncle Sam? That's what they call America, isn't

it?' Preston grinned. 'Do you work for the Government?'

'I don't know. Sometimes, I think.'

'You don't fool me, big man. I can tell you're no dunce,' Preston breathed. He leaned against the wall, stroking Max, now the dog had settled a bit. They were all panting as hard as he was. Despite the pummelling, Preston was elated. Hiedler would have to listen now. They might have a bargaining chip in the bigger picture.

The Americans, whether they liked it or not, had just joined the war.

Good old Uncle Sam.

19:

The submarine lurked in the waterways and canals of Antwerp, waiting for the right moment to surface. Between them, Archer and his team-mates selected a spot to shelter. The rain began, pattering down on the remains of the roof of the two storey building. Archer led up the stairs, sweeping the floors with the *Runebolt* to ensure there were no guests, and there was room at the inn. Once Nunzia and Eisner climbed the rickety steps, he signalled to the German.

He tapped his rifle butt on the top of a sideboard cabinet. It had a cracked top, and leaned over at an angle where two legs were broken. 'Give me a hand with this.'

Eisner grinned, held up his bandaged arm. 'You add insult to injury?'

'I didn't mean—'

'*Ja, ja,*' he chuckled. 'I forgive you, Daniel.'

'You'd be the first.'

Eisner clucked his tongue.

Together they heaved the cabinet to the top of the stairs, easing it down several steps to make sure anyone blundering in gave them a moment of warning, and lodged the remaining legs firmly over the stumps of banister spindles. The house was good, with solid walls on three sides, one half-wall overlooking the river below, complete with lit jetties and the glint of steel on sentry bayonets. Harm's way was a stone's throw, the safety of the submarine somewhere beyond.

Nunzia explained in the darkness, waiting for the tide to be right. Out there in the cold shallows, an iron beast hid in plain sight, a giant fish waiting to be tickled to the surface.

'That is what fishing with bare hands is called in

England, yes?' she whispered.

'I don't know,' Archer replied. 'Do you know where it will be?'

'As soon as I hit the water, I will.'

He looked across to where Eisner sat braced against a wall; they doped his ruined hand with Dakin Solution, a parting gift from Father Ruslan, before dressing it in fresh bandages and administering morphine. Archer hid his surprise at how well the arm was mending, putting it down to the bottled salve. The German was intermittently snoring, but the sounds from the distant quay, of dogs barking and boat bells chiming, all rendered Eisner's nasal guttering safe.

If a tad obnoxious.

Unfortunately, they were unable to make a fire, being so close to the wall, and patrolling guards. It reminded him of the shop they hid in with the girls, the near miss with the Blackcoats in the midst of a stuffy shop on a summer day, where he remembered the sweat starting readily. Here, the clouds gathered to pelt down, and the breeze from the water snaked through the gaps in the brickwork with a chilly draft. Nunzia shivered next to him.

Instinctively, he rolled up behind her, the way he would close up to a freezing comrade in an exposed trench. He wrapped his arms to try and pass on his warmth, dropping over her lower torso. Nunzia wrenched away from his clinch, sharply forcing her back to him.

'*No!*' she gasped.

Stunned, Archer froze as she recovered and wriggled around to face him. She rubbed sleep from her eyes, indignation mellowing as she read his genuine shock at her rebuff. She quickly clasped his right hand in both of hers. He could feel the roughness on them, hard work somewhere in her life.

'I wasn't going to hurt you,' he explained. 'I'm used to sleeping close with other soldiers. Sorry.'

'It is alright.' She breathed deeply. 'You just surprised

me.'

'You were cold; I was just trying to help.' He started turning away.

'Daniel, please! I...I want you to hold me, more than you could think. Just...be careful *here*. It is ugly.'

Her discomfort was understandable given the ups and downs of the mission, despite all the flirting. The honesty between them was sudden, fragile. He didn't try to wrest free of her grip, where she clasped his hand against her midriff.

Archer kept his voice soft, and low. 'What happened?'

'My husband and I were on a ship sunk by a U-Boat. I woke up on a rescue vessel, badly hurt. I could do nothing. You know how it feels?'

He did, after a fashion. 'Your husband...was killed?'

'Marco, yes.' Her expression said the rest. She killed the Germans the way they hurt her. He wondered if the submarine was her idea. 'I'm scared.'

'Of what?'

'If you see, you will not woo me anymore,' she said through a sad smile and wet eyes, 'and I don't want you to stop.'

The root of her fear revealed, he tried to be gentle, the soft approach to cooing a shy horse into arm's reach to settle it. He was thrown by this side of her, the confidence so usually brazen and bold reduced to coyness, vulnerability.

'I have seen you already, remember?'

'No, is ugly,' she repeated.

'Nunzia. Show me.'

Her head cocked in confusion, but understanding dawned on her face. After a moment of silence, she relented, pulling her clothes open to lie on her back, stomach bare, under his close scrutiny.

The scar across her body was a long, swooping gouge running from her left, lower rib, to the top of her right hip. It was jagged, not the precise, necessary caress of a surgeon's blade, but a butcher's cleaver. The skin was puckered and pulled, a belligerent disfigurement worthy of hiding.

When Archer placed his fingers on the scar, Nunzia trembled at his touch, an almost animal convulsion to escape, but she held herself down as he traced the wound, gently stroking it, following the curve, understanding.

'They took something special.'

'Yes. They took my husband, stole my child, robbed me of more,' her voice was tiny, but it was heavy with resignation and long years of pain.

'I see.' He stared at the scar, stroking it to try and soothe the wound, rub it away.

'How? How could you?' her fire returned, but when she saw he was sincere, the anger vanished. 'I am expected to fight for my country, kill for *Vendetta*. Can the Sea Witch not be a woman as well? Sometimes?'

'I think so. Do you miss Marco?'

'I mourned him, wore black. I said goodbye.'

'Until we met? Was that why you changed your mind about drowning us?'

He felt her shrug. 'Yes.'

Simple truth suited the occasion. Archer's hand moved from the wound to gently smoothing his whole palm over her taut stomach, feeling the cables of sailor's muscle beneath. Without thinking, he changed the motion from simple gentleness to something else, a touch of pressure and surety, almost intimate.

'Oh, *Mio Dio*,' she gasped.

He stopped, suddenly worried. 'Did I hurt you?'

'No,' she said, but nothing more.

Uncertain, he withdrew anyway.

'What happens now?' Nunzia was exceptionally close, her cheek caught in the moonlight as her head tilted.

'We go back, mission failed. Maybe we say everyone was dead,' Archer supposed. He heard her shuffling again, the rustle of clothes being rearranged. He continued to stare up at the ceiling.

'That is not what I meant – but do you believe Kurt?'

'Yes.'

'And me?'

He didn't look at her, despite her proximity. 'Everything you said.'

'Why?' Her voice was urgent. 'Tell me, Daniel.'

'I want to be the reason you changed your mind.'

Without further comment she rolled over, pulling herself on top of him and putting the moon to her back, her hands pressing on his chest. His breath stopped in his throat, but his heart thundered.

She was nude.

Eager, but clumsy hands explored his body, searching for the buttons and cinches keeping her out, yanking them loose. His shaggy coat and camouflage suit dropped away, forming a rough bed for them, his modesty vanishing with his undergarments as she tugged both away.

Eisner chose to let out a dopey snort, rolling over with his back to them. Nunzia stifled a giggle, banishing the cold as her flesh met his. She lowered onto him, the moon bright above, her mane a shadow where it fell loose, released from the tight plait.

Her lips kissed in invitation to continue, her hot breath sudden in his throat. Archer was stunned, forgot what to do, but only for a moment. The shock relented as Nunzia took her time, his instinct taking over as he moved with her, soft human warmth pushing against him something amazing, and a far cry from the precious clutch of the earth as bullets and whizz-bangs flew over his head.

Questing hands moved over her stomach, feeling the rugged lesion of the old scar again. She didn't interrupt him roaming her body as he pleased, until she wrapped her arms around him. Like the sea, Nunzia rushed onto him, over the shore, pulling and rocking, until the swell finally ebbed. She clung to him in the moonlight, resting against his chest, where his arms circled and held her safe, drawing the robes about them, keeping the cold at bay.

Journeying to the dock they met no-one else, although each of them was tense and ready. Antwerp had proven to be dangerous and full of surprises, so they took no chances, weapons loaded to capacity. They approached the quay from a different direction from the one they took to get in, seeking to dodging the myriad booby-traps and easy ambush by the insane cannibals.

Instead Archer indicated a section of the dock wall which stood taller. Green plant growth indicated no-one had disturbed the foot of it, but he wasn't taking chances. He slung the *Runebolt* and, armed with his bayonet, carefully went forward, testing for wires. He pushed the nose of the blade into the soil to clear a path, focused on the feel of soil parting, waiting for the jarring nudge of a mine or buried bomb. He wished Ross was there, with a palm buried in the earth, he could have told Archer what lay ahead.

The point of the bayonet scraped something. Carefully, and as gently possible, he pressed the bayonet around the site of contact, gauging the size and depth of the object, before waving the others back. The moon and torchlight were enough for them to catch the warning, and they stepped away, but knelt, watching him and the road behind them at the same time.

Teasing out the shape in his mind, it didn't fit any of the mines he'd dealt with before, possibly something home-made. Pulling a long stick from the grass, Archer planted it by the object to mark it. He repeated the process, probing around him, finding a path to his right which twisted and turned in the grass and growth. Checking his watch proved only forty minutes had passed, but his knees and elbows were protesting, and felt like he'd been at it all night.

Archer produced his trench torch, showing each marker in sequence to his comrades before snapping it to his webbing harness. The sounds of the docks drifted over the wall whilst they approached, the slop of water against sturdy piles and beams, and the bump of moored boats. Men called to each other in German, sometimes laughing. Tobacco smoke wafted over the wall in the breeze, contaminating the fresh air breathed into a noisome city.

The grapnel in his hands, Archer played out a foot of rope and began to swing it round, gathering momentum as the heavy hooks bit the air. He locked his gaze to the top of the wall and when he felt the moment come, released the rope and let it play out through his hands. He was rewarded by the sound of metal hitting stone, and he yanked hard, three times. The grapnel was lodged fast, some thirty feet above them. He put all his weight on it, but it was fine, he hadn't missed. It wasn't a surprise to him.

Eisner sighed. 'Daniel, I cannot make that climb.'

'The rope is knotted, take your time.'

'No, that is not what I mean.'

'Hiedler?' he guessed.

'Yes. He was transferred here, from Landsburg prison,' Eisner spoke bitterly. 'He tried to seize power, but failed. Unfortunately, he has powerful friends. He must be removed.'

'You can't do that alone,' Archer told him. 'He's training an army.'

Eisner regarded his injured hand. 'I will not ask. We have respect, even if it is not complete trust.'

Archer shifted away from sudden embarrassment, made his decision. 'Nunzia, start climbing. I'll help you over the top.'

'Then what?'

He patted his pockets, retrieved his compass and map of Antwerp. There would be time…he hoped. If they moved fast, and got lucky, they could make it curtains for this cardboard *'Kaiser'*, and get Eisner what he needed to get home before the Royal Navy pounded everything.

Garfield needed to be told about the situation in Antwerp. Nunzia could help.

Shining the torch onto his map, Archer pushed a dirty

thumbnail into the paper, then again, making a cross two miles upriver from Antwerp.

'X marks the spot. Can you get your boat there, and maybe some help?'

She looked up at him, grinning. 'I can.'

'*Tommy*,' Eisner said, 'that is over ten miles away.'

'That's the point. It will be less when we leave the city.'

'I hoped for a trip to the beach, English.'

Archer grinned at Nunzia. 'Will a river cruise do?'

'*Si*, why not?'

Folding the map, Archer stashed it away inside his jacket, gripping the rope. Testing it briefly, he started the long haul up the knots, hand over hand, trying to keep his eyes on the rope and the wall. His gut protested as he left the safety of the earth, but he fought the urge to look down, grateful the darkness lingered, swallowing the distance to the ground. He kept going, until his hand could grip the top of the wall. With his free hand, he snapped off the torch.

Pinching the rope with his feet, he steadied himself with his other hand and peered over. The dock didn't extend this far, and below him was a forty foot drop, right into the Scheldt. He smiled – it was perfect, the Sea Witch would make a splash. He pulled himself up and straddled the wall, readied the *Runebolt*. A quick glance below revealed Nunzia was climbing up. Below her, he could make out Eisner's bandage, his arms steadying the line. Voices carried up to him.

'Did you want an excuse to watch my bottom, Kurt?'

Her bravado was covering her nerves, the sway and pull of the rope convinced Archer of nothing less.

'Saw it last night,' Eisner replied.

'I thought you were asleep.'

'With all the noise?'

She chuckled briefly, saving the rest of her breath for the climb, and Archer reached down and gripped her hand, Nunzia gained the top with a short puff of exertion to sit opposite him. She looked below and patted a quick tattoo on her thighs in triumph. Her attitude changed suddenly, became serious as she reached across and stroked his face.

'Good luck, Daniel.'

'I'll see you soon, Annunziata,' he fought to dredge up the words. '*Ciao, bella.*'

Pleasant surprise lit her face. 'You wait until now for romance?'

'Is it working?'

'I will tell you when we meet again.'

She kissed him, breaking after precious seconds to pitch her long legs over the wall, pushed off to hurl away and down into the darkness, accompanied by a painful moment of silence. Archer was relieved to hear the loud splash of a safe welcome into her element. The sound of water spattering the wooden dock was met by a shout.

'*Achtung!*'

'*Alarm! Alarm!*'

There was a pregnant pause before the howl of a klaxon seared the night, and a flare scored the sky with white brilliance. The light burned away the darkness for precious moments, a mad scramble of boots and voices calling out, rallying the sentinels of the dock to come and repel a potential breakout.

The response erupted from Archer's left. He swivelled round on the wall to cover Nunzia, hearing her arms slapping the water as she swam, moving faster than anyone had a right to against the tides lapping the base of Antwerp's curtain wall. A machine pistol was brought to bear, and Archer fired, his shot dropping the man into the drink, blood already coating his shoulder. He racked another round, taking a second man in the leg, then a third in the hand.

She dived, disappearing from view as bullets spanked the water around her.

With their target gone from sight, and realising they were under fire from above, the others turned their fury on him. Panic fire raked the wall top. Clods of brick and cement spalled around his legs, bullets plucking at his left arm and shoulder. He toppled, gripping the weapon and wall both, kicking wildly to find a foothold. Boots tangled in the rope as his fingers slipped from the parapet, a human plumb-line dropping head first.

He slammed into the wall, arrested at the knees and ankles. The impact almost driving the *Runebolt* from his hands, but he clung to it fervently. Rounds continued to clip the top of the wall, trying to dislodge the grapnel. The sentries obviously guessed the peril he was in. Angry shouting and orders in German slid over the thick wall, followed by the *chink* of metal on metal, the bowlike *twang* of a taut rope splitting, and all he could think of was the ground below, waiting to receive him head first.

Expectation of being blown to pieces robbed his mind of the drop.

He closed his eyes.

The bushes and shrubs he'd robbed to mark the mines broke his fall sooner than he expected, and he realised he wasn't that high up when the grapnel was shot away. He did find himself staring at one of the strange booby-traps he'd only felt below the surface. His hands reached for it slowly, fingers finding edges, and a texture he was familiar with.

It was a brick.

Archer tried to laugh, but winded from the fall, he gasped and wheezed a moment, before it came out properly. He let it. Relief blended into concern over Nunzia, hoping she was safe. He'd only find out when – *if* – he made the rendezvous upriver. The shadows danced at awkward angles, and a shape erupted from the darkness as his eyes actually managed to focus.

'Potato-head *Engländer!* Are you *trying* to die?'

'Had you worried, then?'

'Hmpf. How many did you kill this time?'

'None,' Archer managed. 'You said no-one outside the wall.'

Eisner studied him carefully. '*Ach so*, you are human.'

'Don't push it. Help me up.'

Everything ached, but Archer got to his knees and Eisner hauled him up. Together the two battered and bruised men fled from the flare above them, hoping they weren't shot in the back or blown to pieces.

20:

The water was a dark, an almost silent tomb, as she plunged under it. The silver shafts from the moon were odd, distorted bars as they punched down, giving her illumination when Nunzia popped her eyes open. There was the stinging sensation of impurities from the city polluting the river, but she kicked out, driving herself up to the surface where she could put speed on. The water yielded to her will, carrying her along on a reverse tide, breaking the surface, noises from the shore altered by water filling her ears.

Nunzia splashed forward in a front crawl, the twisting stroke complemented by shots cutting around her. Turning her head, she got the impression of Archer raining bullets to cover her escape, a tattered grey-black bundle toppling from the wall when the sentries fired on him. Nunzia echoed the idea, gulping a huge lungful of precious air, before bending her torso into a dive, dropping into the belly of the river.

The undercurrent snagged her, until she focused her power harder, pushing back against the fluid, as she expelled some of her breath to counter buoyancy. The trick wouldn't last long; she only had the air in her lungs, her heavy clothes and equipment making it hard work, despite the river's grudging help. She thrashed, tearing off her bulky outfit, shedding weapons and the camouflaged city trappings, retaining only that which protected her modesty.

Unwilling to abandon their duty, the guards kept shooting. This close to the dock; she could see the bullets *plip* and *plop*, hailstones striking the surface above. The projectiles quickly twisted or bent, travelling only a few feet, energy spent. If she could have spared the effort, she would have smiled. She was in her element.

Even so, it was a fickle ally. She needed more air.

A wounded man thrashed in front of her, trying to gain the surface, cheeks bulging to hold in his vital breath. She swam to him, cutting through the bloody slick coming from his shoulder and pressed her mouth over his, striking him. His gasp became hers, the theft completed, she considered holding him under, but there wasn't the luxury. She pushed her victim up to the light and safety of the surface.

So replenished, Nunzia reached out to find *Orca*, the tremble of submerged metal an oddity against the banks, mud and log piles of the docks. An electrical current pulsed from her right, unlike a fleshy denizen of the waterways; it was a regular, mechanical heartbeat. She drove towards it, churning the river around her as she picked up speed, concentrating.

Arcane power blossomed, lighting the aerated bubbles and foam. Champagne glimmer rushed in her torpedo-like wake as her breath got shorter, burning air with the exertion. The chilly water brought her thoughts to Archer. The English Lion was a tricky one, with a mind as fast and sure as his bolt action rifle.

How her uncle would love him if she ever took him home!

Despite being a little stung by the barbed exchanges and dismissive flirting, she'd surprised herself by coming back at him harder, not realising she *meant* it, at least not immediately. Nunzia had been looking for a reason to rebel, and here it was, this Englishman who gave as good as he got, who wasn't repelled by her torn body. He hadn't despised or pitied her...inability. Archer reignited the fire in her, fanning the weary embers into something warm again, something alive.

So distracted, she didn't notice the sheer side of the submarine loom out of the murk until she bumped into it, water giving way to iron. Nunzia made her way towards the bow, thumped on the hull in a specific pattern, the tattoo a signal the beast recognised, for it trembled into motion shuddering on its silt bed. A bulbous glass eye rotated, peering at her, and without any reply, the metal fish flushed water from its finned carapace, the jet stream pushing it up through the watery dark, taking her to the surface, where the upper deck broke the silver sheen of the moonlit river.

Nunzia clung to an outboard rail as the boat floated, catching her breath, before finally dragging her shivering body onto the upper deck. The conning tower hatch popped with a hiss, the sound of boots on metal deck a welcome one.

'Captain! Are you alright?'

She spotted her First Mate. 'I am fine, but quickly, we must get below.'

'Of course, Ma'am.' He signalled to two other hands, and they got Nunzia upright and wrapped her shoulders in a blanket.

'Bring everything to full function,' she ordered, 'remain on the surface until we telegraph our contact. We must alert the British we are underway.'

'Shall we send a full report?'

She stared across the river, found the dark curtain wall that separated her from Archer, some four-hundred yards away. The siren carried across the water, but the lights were sweeping the docks only, the German soldiers and sailors of the security force pulling their comrades from the Scheldt.

'No – I will tell Garfield in person.'

'By your order, Captain.'

'And get me some clothes, if you wouldn't mind?'

Dropping through the hatch still dripping wet, she barged through the narrow spaces of the submarine's gut, until she dropped into the control chair, exhausted. Seizing the control Focus Wand, the urge to keep her promise to Archer was a burr under the saddle, and *Orca* lanced forward at her direction keener than ever. She nervously awaited the telegraph operator in the back, hurriedly signalling the Royal Navy observers blockading Antwerp. The last thing she wanted was to be depth-charged by her allies.

When permission came back, Nunzia pressed her thoughts outside, even though she listed in the chair, hardly able to keep upright. The freedom of the current carried through the control stick, the rush of seas, deep draughts of the ocean ready to welcome her. *Orca* vaulted the obstacles in the Scheldt at her will, an iron thoroughbred loosed to the course, before diving into the deep.

Once more, the War Mages made their way back through Antwerp. The city largely ignored them, yet fleeting gaunt faces haunted the shadows, proving the beast watched them with dozens of eyes. Archer was no fool; this was no show of curiosity, civility or mutual respect, but fearful patience. He hadn't tamed Antwerp, he was simply too big a monster to kill, and they would wait until he was weak, tired, and then finish him off. For now at least, as he and Eisner stalked the broken roads and brick scarps of fallen houses, they went unmolested.

Two hours marching brought both men close to the concealed cellar entrance for the tunnels, and Ruslan's flock sheltering therein. It was a sensible point to begin hunting the Kaiser, but as Archer lay on his belly, he watched the plan scuppered. Peering through the spotter glass, Eisner grunted beside him, playing the telescope back and forth. Archer let him observe, fishing in his pouch for the Hensoldt rifle sight, which he affixed to the top of the *Runebolt* so he could shoot what he could see.

The broken fountain was smashed from the pedestal, razed flat by the front of an armoured car which sat idling outside the refugee tunnels. Timber frames of the ruined houses around and above the barricaded entrance were ablaze. Eisner groaned as he looked, and Archer got a nudge in the ribs.

'Prisoners, to the left of the lead car.'

Archer saw them, a string of large and small figures shackled or tied together. He scanned for Marek, or other familiar faces, but couldn't find them in the press. Blackcoats surrounded them, jabbing at them with bayonets, shoving with rifle butts. Thankfully, Sam was unmistakeable, a giant amongst them, flat cap still on his head. The firelight caught the front of his frame as he stumbled over a body on the ground, pausing to help the fallen prisoner to their feet. Sam's face was bloody and his utilitarian clothes were scored with cuts, soot and red stains where he'd no doubt fought.

'Bastards,' Archer whispered. He sensed Eisner's agreement. He tried to ignore the ache setting in from the bullet grazes to his left shoulder, grateful it wasn't his shooting arm, and that the slugs had scored his flesh, not buried in it.

Thinking of bullets brought him back to the sorry procession. He toyed with the idea of opening fire at three-hundred yards, but the thugs were mingling with the captives, and he couldn't be sure that his rounds would stop inside the bodies of the enemy. Having seen .303 British do amazing and abhorrent things, the Sniper School reinforced the importance of watching the background of what he was shooting at.

'How did they find them? I deployed the flare away from the hideout.'

'It was only a matter of time. *Kriegsglück.*'

Admiring the succinct German for 'Fortunes of War', Archer admitted the point, the refugees had pushed their luck, with the three battles at the town hall, armoury and northern quarter hideout doing them no favours. 'Maybe there's a traitor?'

'I think you are paranoid,' Eisner replied, then grunted. He rolled away into cover to see to his hand, using more morphine and Dakin's Solution.

'This, from a German spy?'

'That is charming, from a British assassin.'

Unable to rejoin with a witty comeback, Archer turned back to the figures being pushed onto the trucks arrayed along the road leading to the fountain. The troops committed to the raid walked alongside the vehicles, as the wagons turned their lights and engines on. Archer shifted his body slightly, lifting on elbows and feet, instantly regretting the pressure on his arm, but grateful for so many push-ups.

When he settled, he pushed with his toes – no more – and the column of misery swung into his crosshair again. The Blackcoats didn't march lazily, like before; they patrolled properly, cagily watching the windows and rooftops for ambush. *Or maybe British Arcanist snipers.*

Flames good enough to see by, he checked his map, carefully plotting the route of the convoy. There was a road running parallel, not too far from the position he currently occupied. He didn't have a plan yet, would have to play along with the enemy for now. If Sam was treated to a spell in the Kaiser's hands, he doubted the big man would want to stay here. At the ugly prospect of Sam joining the Kaiser, Archer vowed he'd find a way to kill two birds with one .303 inch stone.

Eisner rolled back into place, peered at the map. 'We're going to need more than your special bullets if they're going where I suspect.'

'And where's that?'

'They call it the Citadel. It's the old fortress, keystone to the Antwerp defences.' Tracing a finger all the way along the road, Eisner tapped a large castle-like diagram where the road terminated. There was a bridge over the diverted river, broad and long, leading into the fort. 'The German Army doesn't occupy it – officially.'

'So Hiedler and his pals are likely there?'

'Maybe. I hoped the attack on the Armoury would draw him out.'

'It got his attention,' Archer said, shrugging. Nothing was simple. 'Shall we go?'

'Daniel? Why does your rifle muzzle never flash?'

He grinned, ready to repay the earlier poke. 'It's not loaded. I just shout 'bang'.'

Eisner groaned, made a face. He shrugged on his pack, trying to hide the pain from his own debilitating wound and

led off, keeping low.
It was going to be a long night.

21:

Heading to the Citadel ahead of the convoy allowed Preston to weigh his options. He'd interrogated some of the prisoners, including a blonde Englishwoman called Kate. Preston hadn't needed force; the woman was suffering from nerves, continually pulling at her hair.

Instead of harshness he applied kindness, playing his part as a British officer imprisoned in Antwerp, but one who had an understanding with the authorities, while Max behaved himself, even let the woman fuss him. Ilsa too, had played her part, her presence reassuring the stewardess nothing untoward would occur.

As a result, Kate had been forthcoming. There were two teams active, as Preston had known from the battle sites, one British, one American. Yet the British team was odd as two left feet: a female Italian Naval Captain, a German Stormtrooper, some big Canadian with a shovel, and Corporal Daniel Archer – 'a bloke in rags, with a magic rifle'.

Preston burst out laughing, startling Max.

He soothed the dog, scratching behind his ears. In truth, though, he was concerned. Dealing with Antwerp rabble was one thing, but a British sniper was another. Not only an Arcanist, the man would be trained in camouflage, survival and tracking techniques. Beyond that, he'd be an intelligence agent – which likely meant Charles bloody Garfield, and his bag of stupid, dirty tricks.

Memory drew him in. He thought back to the Battle of Loos, four years before. He recalled the dawn assault with absolute clarity. Battalions of British infantry waiting in the trenches, rickety ladders propped against parapets. Lee-Enfield rifles by the dozen, all fixed with gleaming bayonets.

'On the whistle, Company will advance!'

Nervous waiting, checking his watch, he licked his lips as the hands closed on six *Ac.Emma* – or six a.m. Three seconds beforehand, the whistle was by his mouth, two seconds, he gently took a breath in, held for a beat, then whistle in and...*now*. He blew, the sound a rather mournful *fwoot*. That's when hell was loosed.

The idea then was to charge in an oblique, cutting left through shallow craters to assault a machinegun nest. He never got that far. A bullet zapped across his thighs, dropping him to smash his head on an old, unexploded mortar, enough time to recognise the finned pipe as he fell. He thought he'd dashed his brains out. Preston lay on the slopes in the horrid, cloying mud, until he heard the German voices in the darkness, resolving into dark shapes against the skyline. They captured him, dragging him back into their own trenches – which were hardly better than the British ones.

Then, in the prison camp, he met Captain Garfield.

The plan was boneheaded. It called on ten officers to break out of the camp in pairs, some of them supposed to raise hell so they were recaptured, and the Germans would think they'd got everyone. Meanwhile, in the confusion, the real escapees could slip away.

It was so stupid it just could have worked, except Preston fell over in a sewer drain, and chemicals in the effluent got into his eyes, burning them with liquid fire, drowning him in total darkness. Garfield carried him then, for three hours in the darkness and mire, before collapsing from straining his back. *We won't make it like this*, Garfield said. Like a moron, Preston volunteered to stay behind and delay the pursuit force.

Now, with bitter hindsight, he realised he'd been sacrificed like everyone else.

Seething with bitterness, Preston dreamed of returning the favour – of dumping the bloody Intelligence Officer in the same stink. His plans began to coalesce, bits and pieces of a jigsaw he would assemble, using the American and other prisoners to foil his old friend. He just needed to stop Archer and his little band of bastards from doing any more damage.

As the Mercedes pulled up at the Citadel, he got out quickly; Max and Ilsa beside to help, but he knew the place down to the inch. He hurried upstairs, the need burning to present his idea to the Kaiser of Antwerp. They had to airlift the American, maybe with the wayward Russian priest. Kate told him the British team had fled to the docks, seeking to leave the city, and he believed her, but the *Kampfgruppe* couldn't gamble on that. Preston knew Garfield wouldn't let it go, and if this man Archer was as blinkered, neither would he. They would have to assume the British were still here, and if so, needed to draw them out.

Barking a challenge, sentries barred his progress. Pleased they were alert, he fumbled for his credentials, the raised paper along the top signifying his warrant card. A snap of attention rewarded him with admission.

'Ah, Preston, I hope you bring good news?' Hiedler sounded energetic.

He caught a mild floral smell, sweet and pleasant. The clink of a small, hollow glass object into metal, or possibly an enamel dish suggested a syringe. Preston snapped to attention anyway. 'We have an American prisoner, Kaiser.'

'An American?' Richthofen asked. Preston didn't realise he was there, the man hadn't moved, made a squeak. He realised the Baron had held his breath, or at least when Preston entered. A nice trick, the Baron had a presence of mind worth remembering.

'You were right, my loyal *Hauptmann*! I knew I could trust you!' Hiedler gushed.

'Thank you, sir. He came in on the airship with a group of United States Marines.'

'Is it an invasion?' Hiedler turned on his heel, polished wooden boards squealing. 'The Americans have joined the war?'

'No, sir. I believe they were a bodyguard for our prisoner. They have been mostly eliminated.'

'The prisoner is of value then?'

'I suspect him to be an Arcanist, sir. I don't know his Discipline.'

'What makes you believe this?'

'There is a special force here, sent by British intelligence. The American must be the target. I can see no other reason.'

'Except for me,' Heidler said, quietly.

Preston licked his lips, sensed a sudden landmine under his over-extended foot.

'My friend, they would not dare. Our allies would never allow it,' Richthofen cut in, smooth as glass. His words were warm, confident. 'Besides, they would have attacked here first – and died in the attempt!'

'You are right, Manfred. My loyal men would die to protect me.'

'Exactly. Now, there is a prison supply airship coming tonight,' Richthofen added. 'We can fly the captive to Berlin. My squadron can escort them. We can set a trap!'

'I'd rather not do it with real bait, sir,' Preston warned, feeling safe to contribute.

'It's that or wait another week,' the Baron said, 'more Americans, more time for this…special force to seize him. This could change the war. For the Fatherland, we *must* move him.'

'They force our hand, we have no alternative.' Heidler sobered. 'Preston, move quickly. Take your men to the landing site in the Northern zone; prepare to airlift the American.'

'*Jawohl, Kaiser.*'

Archer opened his ears, straining. Eisner, crouching opposite, nodded. They could both hear the convoy trundling along the dilapidated boulevard, the loud engines of the trucks and armoured car labouring as they carried the troops and whatever prisoners they rounded up. It was a demonstration, parading through the streets at marching pace, strong enough to repel the horrors of Antwerp, to cow refugees, cannibals and desperate Arcanists alike.

When the convoy moved, they kept up with it, albeit at a safe distance. It was a devil's bargain. There were shuffling figures huddling in the shadow-shrouded buildings either side, but the proximity of the Blackcoats was keeping them in check. Archer winced at every scrabbling shift of grit under his boots, wondering when need or desperation would overcome caution and end in a shootout, with he and Eisner caught in its jaws, Antwerp ridding itself of the thorn it couldn't swallow.

In the sparse few moments the convoy rested, Archer would shuffle into a good spot where he could watch the street, Eisner taking the other direction, both grateful for a short reprieve from the stalk. The ragged remains of a girl's doll loitered in the corner of a window Archer peered through. It was missing a leg, and some hair, but the moonlight betrayed the doll's stitched smile and button eyes. He got close to it, the dark woollen braids reminding him of Nunzia. A stab of unwelcome superstition struck; that the doll's fate was linked to the Italian Captain. If it survived, so would she.

There weren't any wires leading to any booby trap he could see, so after a quick peek to see if Eisner was looking, he picked it up, shook it to dislodge anything unpleasant, and with nothing other than a wad of stuffing coming out, shoved it inside his battledress blouse. Sometimes soldiers had to make their own luck. Rubble shifted to his left, announcing the *Sturmpioneer*.

'We have a problem. Where is your map?'

Archer reached around and pulled it from his pocket, taking the opportunity to grab his canteen, sipping from it slowly, whilst the German produced a compass, and got orientated.

'We have been heading northwest,' he warned.

Archer got his torch out, hid the light spilling from the small bulb by smocking it with a sleeve of his sniper robe. 'I know. I was wondering when we would turn for the Citadel.'

Archer had checked against his own marching compass for the direction of travel for the past four miles, during which, the convoy never deviated, only stopped for rest. The vehicles had to negotiate uneven streets, occasionally clogged with the remains of the city's buildings. It slowed the convoy down, but conversely made the Blackcoats wary of ambush. The prisoners were forced to shovel the cobbles clear, whilst the soldiers covered any angles of attack. It didn't matter – by their delay Archer was keeping pace, and where they went, he would follow.

'I've been wondering about something.'

'Why we said yes to this crazy plan?' Eisner flashed a grin.

'Apart from that,' he chuckled, 'what happened to your Focus, Kurt?'

'Too much power. It is common in Fire Mages.'

That was a risk Archer understood. Even using his own Focus Wand – the temptation to give everything to the shot was almost overwhelming, as though the elemental force was using him to manifest, a lightning rod for the raw power. It was a terrifying thought. He could only wonder how hot that urge must burn for a Flame Arcanist.

He switched track. 'You certainly know how to wield an axe.'

'I was a *Feuerwehrmann*, a fire fighter.'

'Was the axe your only Focus?'

'No,' the grin widened. 'When I joined the storm troops, I had a *flammenwerfer*.'

Archer put it together. 'A flame-thrower? I should have known. Where is it now?'

'I don't need it.'

'Because you can already *werf flammen*?'

Eisner looked at him with naked despair. 'Against such wit, it is no wonder we are losing the war.'

'Honestly Kurt, why don't you have it?' Archer pressed,

knew something lingered behind the humour and the deflections, the decoy mask hiding something sinister and painful beneath.

Eisner's face clouded a moment, his eyes searching the face of his companion, wondering perhaps if it was safe to expose the truth beneath. 'Let us just say this: Fire is not friendly when it is your own men.'

Archer understood. 'Maybe that's another reason you're here?'

'Maybe,' the German added a shrug to his thin smile, a hopeless offering against the conflict. 'Maybe it is just war.'

'Is it over for you?' Archer gestured to Eisner's bandaged hand, looking to move away from the topic and threatening desolation.

'Possibly, but it is a strange thing—'

'Shh!' Archer held up a finger in the warning.

The truck engines stopped, falling to silence. In their wake, he could hear something else. It came from a distance, a small thing, almost a gnat buzzing in his ear, growing infinitely louder and more bellicose, into a swarm of angry bees. Shapes cut the sky, blocky cruciform silhouettes against the silver threaded clouds.

'Don't move!' he hissed.

Half a dozen hornets skimmed overhead, in formation. Archer couldn't make out which unit they were, too dark for that, but behind them came a much bigger shadow, blotting out the light completely. A leviathan of pale grey and white, running on the wind and heavy propellers, fleeing Captain Ahab's hunting party. Tendrils of thick cable dropped from the nose, dangling jellyfish tendrils ready to snare anything smaller in the air stream.

The huge zeppelin cruised over them, long moments of droning engines drowning out any noise, but in its wake, there was only a wall of silence. The bloated blimp continued to waddle across the cityscape, so large it was unable to disappear, but Archer couldn't hear the Blackcoat trucks any more. He gestured to Eisner, and after the muscle-cramp of forced immobility eased, they made their way down into the street, slinking along a wall until they could get a direct view of the wagons.

They had moved on, swallowed by the darkness whilst he and the German cowered beneath the zeppelin's passing. Archer cursed, but the airship was dawdling northwest with its escort. Eisner pointed, indicating the long gondola rib underneath the vessel, now visible as the squat cigar shape was more discernible with distance.

'It is one of our armed supply zeppelins.'

'Well at least we weren't seen.' Archer grimaced at the thought of the bombs, not dissimilar to a whizz-bang, but with an additional eerie whistle. He wondered about the fighter escort. 'Could the Kaiser have built an airstrip in Antwerp?'

Eisner pulled off his hat, scratched his head. 'No, but a landing station wouldn't be hard. Useful in fact.'

Thinking back to the briefing, Archer tied threads together, the Imperial German Air Service dropped supplies every five days. This must be one of the ships. If it docked with a grounding station, it would ensure the Blackcoats got all the supplies, doling them out to whomever they wished. It explained the cannibals, and all the willing recruits.

Another idea surfaced, and Archer consulted the map. 'What's in the Northeast?'

'Nothing. A country park, open spaces...' Eisner caught himself. 'Sounds perfect.'

'Would they fly Sam out of Antwerp?'

'That's the best idea you've had in a while.'

'I aim to please,' Archer replied, unthinking.

'True,' the German chuckled, 'No-one you shoot ever complains.'

Sudden pain staunched his humour with a wracking shudder through his body. Archer's hand shot out to support him, and Eisner steadied. The experience forced sobriety. '*Danke, Kamerad.*'

Archer merely nodded, waiting for the tremor to pass, steered the conversation away to take both their minds off it. 'What was that odd thing you mentioned earlier?'

Eisner looked at his clean bandages, smelled them and shook his head before moving on, a frown etched onto his brow. 'Nothing.'

Powerful lights stabbed up into the darkness, picking out the airship tethered to the tall gantry. Blackcoats pushed or jabbed prisoners with bayonets, who in turn swept or shovelled. It was obvious that the Kaiser – or Hiedler, was putting the old tradesmen and dockworkers to good use, welders and builders by profession replacing the POWs who used to do the menial work in the Reprisal camp.

Squads of the black coated soldiers trooped around, but there was a difference in them, Archer could see through his telescopic sight. Some were more precise than others, and he realised the big huts built around the landing site must be barracks. Machinegun nests dotted the grounds. There were also light cannon he supposed were *Archie*, but he now understood why Sam managed to get so far, the crews and Blackcoat infantry wouldn't have fired on pain of death.

Sam wouldn't know the landing station existed, it was impossible. He must have been utterly desperate to take matters into his own hands, hoping to make landfall without being incinerated. It spoke to utter terror, that he would risk such a death to be free. Archer sympathised, but Sam had also risked the entire crew, many of whom died on impact, others tortured to death. Maybe they weren't all innocent.

Some of the crew must have known about Antwerp landing station, otherwise why would the airship even come here? It was the AEZ after all. He wondered if the pilot was made a better offer than their American charter fee, and the thought made him scan the ground the Kaiser's men had cleared.

A substantial area, it remained free of any landing strip,

nowhere near big enough for a Fokker or Albatross. He couldn't hear aircraft landing, idling or see anyone in flying leathers either, which meant the planes must have fled to another airfield, yet close enough to support the military bombing craft tethered here.

A hazy picture filled Archer's mind. He could see prisoners from different camps, detention centres across Germany and Austro-Hungary, loading prisoners onto trucks or airships, sending them to Antwerp, a location they completely controlled within and without. They needed trained soldiers for the war, why not recycle those willing? Don't want to fight? Stay in the AEZ, and take your chances.

This lunacy had to be stopped. Archer spilled his thoughts aloud, before watching the coming and going of guards and prisoners alike. The silence between the two men lasted for most of the hour they kept the ramshackle airfield under observation. They could see prisoners being dragged in and out of huts, tents, but still no Sam, or anyone they recognised from the tunnels below Antwerp.

'I do not like this, Daniel.'

'Nor do I,' Archer replied, sharing his friend's unease. There were sentries and patrols here, but far less than expected. Where were the soldiers from the convoy? There were barracks at the back of the zone, perhaps there? He couldn't tell, couldn't see the decoy. Maybe they weren't flying Sam out of Antwerp, maybe he'd just jumped to a conclusion. Why would the convoy deviate, though?

'So what do we do?' Eisner frowned.

'Can you see Sam?' he scanned the glass back and forth, and whilst he was certain the three trucks parked on the western approach road were the vehicles they'd been following, there was no sign of the distinctive American.

'Maybe they took him elsewhere?' the German supposed.

'For an audience with Hiedler?' Archer half-smiled.

'You do not want one. He is very convincing.'

Not sure he wanted to understand any more, Archer let that thought wither. Turning his attention to the landing station, he worried that Sam was already loaded onto the zeppelin for transport. He would have to go into the airship to make sure. He ground his elbows into the soil, keeping low thanks to cover he could use to approach having been cleared, but then again that was the point – a good clean killing field. The only things missing were the tangled thickets of barbed wire.

It was still dark enough to sneak up, but imitating a work gang was a risky business, thankfully, Eisner's knife hand was working fine. Archer swivelled the glass to the right, where two Blackcoats were haranguing a group of three ragged wretches to hurry clearing a ditch of some kind, perhaps a water runoff.

'Let's say hello, shall we,' he said, slithering closer, stopping every few feet to lie still and check they weren't spotted. He could hear Eisner rustling up behind him, but as the wind changed, he saw the orange flare of a lighter flame flickering, and cigarettes being lit. One day, it would get them killed.

Maybe today.

22:

With their attention wavering and immediate night vision destroyed, Archer risked an advance on the work party. Sniper robes dirtying up with earth, his elbows and knees worked hard to prevent him scoring the ground and leaving traces. The guards spoke in low voices, trying to duck under the sharp ears of any Sergeants lurking nearby. He wasn't that surprised to hear some English, but couldn't place the accent. They were in no hurry, enjoying the chance to get away from drill – just like soldiers everywhere.

Tobacco smoke carried on the stale air, the unwashed stench from the prisoners covered his own with the faintly sweet smell of decaying wounds. He knew they weren't from the tunnels, where the altogether different scent of carbolic soap and iodine floated in cool, clean air, and Ruslan practiced his brand of medicine.

Eisner was right there at Archer's elbow, the knife lowered, but a sliver of steel moonlight pointing needle-thin at the enemy. He carefully got to his knees, moving round to keep behind his victim. Archer mirrored the stealthy movements, his own chosen victim helmetless, within arm's reach now, and Archer was just about to grab when the man Eisner was covering stepped forward.

'Get on with it!' The Blackcoat barked. 'That ditch isn't going to dig itself!'

He gave the man he was chastising a poke with his mounted bayonet. His head half-turned, face lit by a subsequent puff on his cigarette, and it was frozen in horror as his gaze met Archer's, over the shoulder of his comrade. 'Jesus!'

There was no time. Archer's arm went round his

victim's throat, locking up in a tight jiu-jitsu choke hold. The man flapped and struggled, but in precious seconds he was near unconscious, whilst his opposite number got Eisner's knife in the lungs. There was a sharp gasp, a look of horror suddenly displaced by surprise pain. Wordless desperation ensued, the sentry trying to get a warning to the landing station as his body failed. The German eased him to the ground with unexpected gentleness.

Archer displayed no such sentiment, kicking his target behind the knee so the trembling legs gave way, but keeping the hold tight, he used the deadweight to break the neck of the Blackcoat with a savage twist. The body crumpled, head bent at a grotesque angle, lolling and rolling as the legs jerked. Once, twice, still. The corpse glared up at him with glassy, damning stare.

'Why not stab him?' Eisner grimaced.

'And get blood on the jacket?'

'You are a hard soul, Daniel.'

'Just keep your pack on to hide it,' he warned the German. 'English?' he asked the prisoners, hurriedly doffing his sniper robes.

The miserable company was stunned, they peered with blank looks.

'French? German?' he tried again.

'*M'sieu*?'

Broken French was all they could manage, Archer hoping that between himself and Eisner, he'd explained what was needed. When the prisoners realised they weren't going to be executed, but asked to fight the Blackcoats, one or two came alive. They were the only ones willing to help.

'Bury the bodies,' Archer told them, kicking one of the dead guards into the ditch that was deep enough a temporary grave. He started shovelling dirt over them and the work party got the idea. Those that didn't want to help staggered off into the darkness, and he let them.

He looked up at the blimp and swallowed. 'Kurt.'

'*Ja?*'

'You will have to go up there.'

'It will be enclosed – and I will be right behind you.'

Archer blew out a hard sigh, before shrugging on the black jacket. It was tight, but what choice was there? He wondered if he was just thinking of the coat. He smocked the *Runebolt* in his sniper robes and picked up one of the fallen Mausers. The few willing workers came with them, trying to hide their excitement, keeping their heads bowed.

Wandering across the flattened, scorched earth of old gardens constituting the landing station apron, Archer had never felt so exposed. Every instinct was screaming at him to throw himself onto the ground before bullets turned him into a sieve. He forced his wandering pace, denying the primal need to run. A distraction presented itself in the balloon above. Moored onto the landing gantry, the craft creaked and groaned, caught in the cool gusts that pulled at it from the river, and the heat draughts from the city.

Perfect conditions for a storm.

As the group closed with the gantry base, the security detail assumed some semblance of alertness, watching them approach with slung rifles, but ready to pull them. Archer thought it was more for the prisoners than he and Eisner. They were accosted in Russian, or at least Archer thought so. He shrugged, assuming the character of an Englishman abroad.

'Eh?' Archer bellowed.

In reply, the sentries rolled their eyes at the attempt to conquer the language barrier through volume alone, and switched into English. 'What is going on?' one asked.

'Polish?'

'Russian.'

'Saint Petersburg?' Besides Moscow, it was the only place he knew, thanks to Father Ruslan.

'Petrograd? No. Vladivostok.'

'Is that close to Petrograd?'

The sentries looked at one another, laughing at him. It

was fine, Archer was old enough to let mockery slide, besides; the joke was on them. They were relaxing.

'Stop,' another man called. 'Where you go?'

'They want weight offloading. Ballast?' He pointed up.

'Weights? *Da*, you go up. You leave equipment here.'

Eisner twisted away as he dumped his pack, keeping the back of his jacket hidden. Archer followed suit, but carefully exchanged the Mauser for his own rifle, passing the German gun to a prisoner. The Russians weren't looking at him. In fact they were doing their damndest not to, which was just what he wanted. They began to climb, the wrought iron lattice around him feeling very unstable.

Rusted plating bolted or welded to the tower formed the steps, groaning in the wind, just like the dirigible above. Archer daren't look up at it, just put one foot in front of the other. He recalled a lecture given at the Sniping and Observation School by one of the men who'd served out in the desert, around Sinai. 'Keep your world small', he'd said.

Archer's view shrank to the toes of his boots, despite being able to see through the slats to the very inconveniently well lit ground below, which got further and further away with each *plonk* and *plunk* of his boots on the corroded metal. There was a squeal and the panel beneath gave way, his weight suddenly shifting sideways. Panic rammed his hands out, the *Runebolt* slamming into the tower spine with a bell-ringing clap. The gantry swayed in the wind, and laughter carried up to him.

'Watch that step!' A Russian bellowed, laughing loudly in the aftermath.

He cursed as his stomach did somersaults. He reckoned they'd managed a stair climb of thirty feet, with more to go. Archer steadied himself, gripping a girder supporting the tower and carried on, turning right onto a short landing, concentrating on his toecaps, trying to count the pinkies hidden beneath the rugged leather.

Without further incident, he managed the climb to the

top. A small shelter covered the stairwell, allowing him to see out, over the curtain wall and the redoubts built into them. Beyond were the dark fields of Flanders and Germany in one direction, the Western Front of France in the other. Flares of firelight erupted, silenced by distance, the guns and whizz-bangs thumped and crashed so far away. He still heard them in the back of his mind, felt the pressure of a near miss buffeting him, almost as much as the wind was doing now.

Another sentry stood at the then end of the gantry; sheltered by the docking sleeve of the zeppelin, where it met the thin plank Archer was going to have to walk. A large man, broad in the shoulder, he was square and stony-faced, a golem barring a secret vault, whilst armed with a machine pistol.

'Ballast and cargo,' Archer bawled over the wind.

The guard un-dogged the latch to the docking sleeve, pinning the door open, while Archer stepped out onto the bridge. His attention was fixed on the door, the airship blotting out everything on this side of the city. It was so huge he was getting vertigo, but he kept upright, despite the flimsy guide ropes whipping and wobbling about like snakes.

He passed the soldier, beckoned to the others. Wisely, the Frenchman had abandoned his rifle before coming up, and Eisner had two weapons over his shoulder, as well as the machine pistol slung across his chest for instant action. He guided the French prisoners, but as Eisner turned his back to keep his balance, the guard stared hard at what his tired eyes were telling him was real, and he opened his mouth to shout.

Archer was beside the man in the cramped arch of the docking sleeve, saw the danger and pivoted, bringing the butt of his rifle up to smack the big man in the face. The warning of alarm was stolen by the wind, but the blow meant to smash his jaw, bounced from the sentry's shoulder and rang from the landing scaffold.

'*Alarm! Alarm!*'

Outweighed by the large oaf, Archer used leverage. He put his left foot behind the man's right heel, driving him back by pressing the rifle against the broad chest, hoping to topple him or force him over the side. Sensing his peril, the sentry abandoned his attempts to warn his comrades, instead fighting for immediate survival. By sheer power, the man regained his feet, and grappled Archer with a meaty paw.

Not built for wrestling, Archer was slammed up against the aluminium portico, crunching his wounded arm into the locking mechanism of the door. The Frenchmen were nearby, but the big sentry seized the machine pistol he carried and menaced them, struggling to remove the safety catch. In a push fuelled by the pain from his arm, Archer stamped down into the man's instep, which earned him an elbow in riposte, casting him to the slender deck below.

Falling sideways, he reeled at the long drop, his brain immediately gauging the distance at fifty yards! He flailed for the guide ropes and got a kick from a burly foot. The others couldn't help, just trying to stay upright, but Archer kicked back in reflex, felt it connect with something soft, and saw the large man's eyes roll as he doubled over. He grabbed the belt of the sentry, pulling hard, and catapulted him over the side.

The scream was curtailed by a solid thump of hitting a hard surface, and Archer looked down to see the red mushroom fanning out from the corpse. Blackcoats rushed to the body, checking him, before looking up. Pale faces reddened with rage and one man threw up his arm to shoot, but a soldier in a peaked cap slammed into him and the rifle failed to go off. For a moment Archer couldn't understand why, but when Eisner helped him up, common sense returned from his height-addled brain. They didn't want to hit the airship.

Wasting no time, he pointed his rifle down and fired, killing the man who'd tried to shoot at him, dropped another one nearby, the .303 brass tumbling down as the targets scattered for cover. *Too slow.* A third life was extinguished, and a fourth before Eisner shoved him.

'*Mein Gott! Curtains!*'

The shout broke his grim rhythm. 'What?'

'Come on! We must get inside!'

The five of them tumbled through the hatch, closing it behind them.

'J'attends ici!' one of them called. The French prisoner peered through the window of the door, knuckles white where he gripped the rifle and held the locking bar fast. He wasn't going anywhere.

Within, the gondola was smaller than it appeared from without; to Archer's mind the deck stretching fore and aft resembled the *Orca*. With the engines off it was just as silent and foreign an environment, the electric bulbs likely running from batteries while moored. The bounce and sway was surprisingly less than expected, and although it felt like he was walking across a firm trampoline, the enclosed space meant he could handle it. He hurried to the forward compartment to confront the pilot, ignoring the portholes, thankful the night rendered them into nothing more than a dark looking-glass, hiding the altitude.

Stooping through the arched ribs of the gondola, Archer tested the door handle to the next compartment. He entered a scene of chaos – several people were in a state of half-dress, others just gawped at him, and he realised these must be the crew quarters. They froze in place, exchanging glares with him and each other.

He slowly levelled the *Runebolt*, the threat of violence transcending language. None of them were armed. He gestured they should move away and they stepped back to his left, to give him enough room to pass. One of them looked like he was about to try and grapple, so Archer slammed the butt of his rifle into the man's stomach, dropping him to the deck where he spilled his guts in a sour stench of wetness slapping onto the metal. Example delivered, they avoided his gaze. He would have no more trouble.

Behind him, one of the Frenchmen came in, and Archer indicated to keep the crew covered as he went forward again, past the radio room, filled with blocky wireless equipment;

until he came to the cockpit. Four men stood or sat inside, two pilot controllers, a deck officer and a Captain, all uniformed Imperial German Air Service.

Archer menaced them all with his rifle, jerking the muzzle cap to instruct them to get up. He herded them towards the front of the cabin. They eyed his black jacket warily.

'*Kampfgruppe?*' the Captain wore several ribbons on his breast, his uniform immaculate. Even without his peaked cap, the uniform and air of authority picked the man out of the herd.

'No. British Army.'

'*Himmel!*' the deck officer cursed, hand slapping the leather holster at his waist, but the Captain struck his arm down and rattled off some angry German.

Archer jabbed the muzzle forward and down. 'Pistols.'

Nodding, the Captain and staff got the message, slowly drawing their guns, bending at the waist to drop them on the deck with a gentle tap.

'Good.'

The tension in the room relaxed slightly now things were under control. He heard the thump of boots behind him on the steel plate, and was joined by Eisner, who burst into the cabin. He took in the situation with a glance, licking his lips.

'There is a locked gate to the bomb bay.'

'Cells?'

'I think so. I could hear people back there.'

'Well done, Kurt.' His attention focused on the Captain. 'Surrender.'

The *Sturmpioneer* translated and the Captain swallowed, drew himself up to full height, speaking in a measured voice, never taking his eyes from Archer's. The defiant posture hinted at what was coming.

'He refuses.'

'Really?' Archer did his best to sound bored, the way British Army officers did before they got their own way anyway. The *Runebolt* came up. The Captain struggled valiantly to ignore the huge bore almost pushed under his nose. 'Tell him, he is a brave man. I salute him – but if he does not surrender, I am going to blow his bloody head off.'

Eisner and the Captain traded words, Archer picked up a few of them, certain he heard the words for 'Englishman', 'crazy' and 'devil' with lots of colourful language in between. Sweat beaded on the faces of the German Airmen, but eventually the Captain broke the stare, face sagging, beaten. He nodded.

'Now, where are the keys for the aft compartments?'

The Captain waited for the translation, before he slowly reached into his left tunic pocket and extracted a ring with five keys, which he held out. Archer took them, thrusting them into his hip pocket, lowering his gun. He quickly stooped and snatched up the pistol from the deck, stuffing it into his belt. He jerked his head to Eisner, and the two of them left the cabin.

'If Sam isn't here, we've wasted our time,' Archer talked, ducking and clambering over joists as they walked down the lattice framework passage forming the ventral support, connecting the different cars of the gondola.

'I am certain he did not go to the Citadel.'

'You know that?'

'I feel it,' Eisner said, tapped his sternum, 'here.'

Archer poked his friend in the chest. 'So do I.'

They fumbled through the keys, testing them in the first door – a solid gate, as Eisner described; leading deeper, into a dark part of the airship. Above them, Archer could make out fixtures and fittings for some kind of mechanism, heavy gauge plating reinforcing the deck. He supposed it made it ideal for a prison transport.

'We are in the bomb bay,' Eisner played tour guide, 'there should be tubes leading to ports on the sides which would drop the munitions.'

Instead there were metal boxes, tall and broad enough to keep a person inside, either seated or standing, with a barred gate for access. It reminded him of the police station, but he cut the memory off. He didn't want to think about Ross, his anger and frustration would only cloud his mind. He focused, passing the empty cell to his right, but he found the others occupied.

'Mister Daniel?' Sam's deep voice rumbled in the dimness.

'Archer? Daniel? My son, are you there?' Father Ruslan.

'*Herr* Eisner is here too. Just hold on,' he told them. He tried the other keys, freeing Sam first, who gripped his shoulder with a massive paw, Father Ruslan a moment later. 'Are there any more?'

'No,' Ruslan shook his head. 'They...killed a lot of our people when they breached the tunnels.'

'What about Sergeant Miller, Marie and Therese?'

'I don't know. Where's Nunzia?'

Archer took a deep breath. 'I'm hoping she's safe.'

Ruslan looked at him, not understanding, but the joy at being freed from the cages was short lived as a voice cut through the ship, echoing from speaker horns in steady German.

'It's the Captain,' Eisner said, 'they want you on the radio.'

'Me?' Archer suddenly knew. The decoy he'd been seeking was the airship – the blimp so big a trap a blind man could have seen it, and he'd blundered right in.

'They asked for *Der Scharfschütze.*'

The Sharpshooter.

23:

Surrounded by the radio set, the zeppelin deck officer tweaked and turned the dials, adjusting the frequency, lowering the scratching noise caused by interference. Wordlessly, he handed up a headset with attached speaking trumpet Archer fitted around his head.

'Hello?'

'You've led me a merry dance, Mr Archer.'

'Who is this?'

'*Kampfgruppe Hauptmann* Robert Preston.'

'Shove it up your arse.'

'Charming. I suggest you surrender.'

'Shove that up your arse too.'

'Vulgar, but to the point, I admire that. I shall reciprocate. Look out of the window, Starboard side.'

Archer did so, peering out into the early morning murk. He could see underneath the airship that trucks with winches were being driven into position beneath the zeppelin, with teams of men running the grounding cables to the back of the vehicles. They were going to pull him down, and once on the ground the gondola would likely be stormed.

'I have a *Flammenwerfer* up here,' he replied at length, glancing at Eisner, 'and I know we're a hydrogen balloon.'

'Oh? How is that?' Preston's voice broke in a crackle of static.

'Your men didn't shoot at us.'

There was a pause. 'Do not do anything stupid. Be sensible.'

'On one condition,' Archer's lips pursed.

'I'm listening.'

'You will safely escort me from the AEZ with my colleagues.'

'I will guarantee your lives, but no more,' Preston replied. 'You are my prisoners.'

He spoke firmly, but without malice, simply placing how far he was willing to bargain. Archer wondered if it was because of his limited authority or that he was just strict. Knowing the Imperial German Army disciplinary practices, he suspected it was a mixture of both.

The promise Preston made wasn't terrible or empty – with Archer being a War Mage, he had value to both sides, and could be exchanged for a German prisoner. It depended on how much the British wanted him back if he failed, perhaps Garfield would leave him in Antwerp. The cannibals would love that.

Putting his future aside a moment, how the hell did they know who he was? He tested the idea Sam talked, but gut instinct rebelled. A nagging suspicion that they knew Sam's value to the Americans gnawed at him. All the rats in a convenient trap he was forced to tempt, the lump of cheese was too valuable to leave. Preston knew that, they were both playing the same game.

A sudden lurch of the gondola and the sounds of engines grunting told him he didn't have much time to reply. 'Preston, go boil your head.'

'You're the lobster in the pot, old man. You've got until the gondola touches the ground to change your mind.'

The radio cut out, ultimatum delivered.

Still tipping, the zeppelin made its stately way to the ground some hundred feet below. Archer saw the smug looks on the faces of the zeppelin crew as the translation was whispered around, if they couldn't tell by the reaction of their blimp. They looked at him, the Captain with a mix of triumph and respect. He left them be, running to find Eisner.

Sam, Father Ruslan, and a handful of other captives were being protected by the *Sturmpioneer* and the Frenchmen.

None of them looked terribly happy, but with the German it was harder to tell, thanks to the mask that hid his humour and sharp mind. Archer found he was staring at the man.

'Are my trousers open?' Eisner demanded.

It took a moment. Archer laughed. 'No, I am just glad you're on my side.'

'Who says?'

'I say.'

'Took you long enough.' Eisner theatrically rolled his eyes.

They all managed a chuckle at the weak joke, but Archer could see how it picked them up, if but a fraction. He explained the situation, the demands and his reply. Father Ruslan frowned, but remained silent as Archer explained what he wanted to do, poking the big American's considerable biceps.

'Ballast?' Sam asked, puzzled.

'Ballast,' Archer agreed.

'What are you going to do, Daniel?' Ruslan asked.

'Something stupid.'

At twenty yards, they could see a large group of men across the landing apron. Each carried a trench club, or truncheon, and weighed down with full trench armour. The heavy plates across their chest, abdomen and groin made them look partly mechanical in nature. Sturdy, reinforced M18 steel helmets topped them off, the Blackcoats faceless behind gas masks. They looked fierce, intimidating.

Their ploy was evident. Not able to risk shooting, they were going to come in with gas, except mustard or chlorine would be hard to control, and they would risk killing everyone aboard. Large canisters strapped to them would likely be loaded with Lachrymal Gas, meant to overpower the defenders for a good old fashioned beating. They'd used it on Sam before, no reason to expect anything less now.

Archer continued to drain the pipes of their precious

liquid, decanting the stuff into barrels. Ruslan and the Frenchmen heaved these across to where Sam stood waiting. Eisner was ready behind the lever which was designed to open the bomb ports.

'Alright Sam! Let them have it!'

Grinning like a child with license to misbehave, the huge man picked up the first metal barrel, nodded to the German, and with a rust-crunching clank, the hatches creaked open. A mighty whoop escaped the American, the first barrel of diesel hurled out to collide with the apron below them, in a jarring wrench of splitting, shearing metal. The slosh of the diesel fuel slapping men and concrete was followed by curses and the stink of fuel-oil evaporating.

Sam didn't stop. Encouraged by Eisner's excited shouts, he grabbed barrel after barrel, the tanks meant to drain excess water and fuel ballast making exceptional missiles which the big man handled like toys. His stockpile was almost gone, six barrels thrown as though they were nothing. A seventh, then eighth followed. Archer had no doubt the munitions would exhaust before Sam did.

Each one elicited more excitement, and Sam threw the cans further and further, sending the black jacketed boarding party scattering, covered in the gloop of diesel thickened with oil to keep the engines of the zeppelin turning. When the barrels had been thrown, Sam erupted in a great cheer as the enemy began to flee.

'Cease bombardment!' Archer yelled, ignoring Sam's disappointment. 'Kurt! *Werf Flammen!*'

Grinning like a fiend, the German storm trooper sat astride the nearest bomb hatch, his back against the apron shell. He took the flare pistol from his belt and shot downwards, quickly slamming the hatches shut. It was at Archer's insistence the fire mage used the gun, unwilling to risk his other hand.

Outside they could hear the fuel as it went up in a tremendous thud of ignition. Screams and yelling were almost drowned out, and the gondola rocked in the sudden up draught, nearly taking Archer off his feet. He tore off the Black jacket, discarding it with violent disgust, just glad to be free of what it represented.

Now, for the next part of his plan...

'Everyone out before we go up!'

The crew had been instructed to help, and seeing their only way out, they popped open the hatch at the rear of the cabin, allowing access to the landing ropes. Archer went first, a Mauser rifle sling saving his hands from the rope as he slid down it, landing on the back of one of the winch trucks. The others were behind him, Eisner holding on through the pain of gripping his own sling, but Archer caught him on the final yard and helped him down.

The two soldiers took position, Eisner firing bursts from his machine pistol, driving the men in the open to seek shelter. Archer used the *Runebolt*, the shattering of toughened glass added to the riot of noise as he shot a man through the lens of his gas mask. Crimson slick slashed into the pre-dawn light from a throat.

Before he knew it, everyone was out and clambering over the truck. The crew took their chances and ran full pelt away from the mad Englishman and his troop of maniacs, whilst Father Ruslan tried to unhitch the winch, to play it out, but it was jammed. He kicked and punched at it, but it wouldn't move. Bullets began to come back, spanking off the metalwork of the vehicle.

'I'll do it,' Sam said, with no hint of breathlessness.

He seized the release handle, but in spite, it broke off in his hands. He looked at it disapprovingly, before leaping up onto the truck bed, trying to stay behind the sides of the wagon and use the large winch windlass as cover. There was the creak of timber, a gut-churning rip of boards and metal and the whole contraption flew up as though moored to the airship by elastic. The large object struck the airship envelope with a wallop, tearing a huge hole in the side.

'Uh-oh.'

Archer looked up agape, just glad everyone else had tumbled out.

'I'm sorry Mister Daniel...'

'Never mind! Kurt! Drive!' Archer didn't bother to look to see if he was obeyed. They had to leave. *Now.*

He leapt into the passenger seat, slamming the door shut.

The truck jumped forward, released from its restraint and under Eisner's heavy boot. Almost beyond his control, it bounced and weaved to avoid the bullets now chewing the ground around the apron, trying desperately to get out from under the zeppelin, which Archer could see in the wing mirrors.

It was alight.

'Faster...faster!' Eisner urged the truck, the solid shadow of the blimp now surrounded by a ghostly haze of escaping gas and smoke.

A checkpoint loomed into view in the windscreen, barred by metal gates. There were two men hurrying to set something up. It was a huge rifle, with a mammoth barrel and bore. They dropped the bipod down and hurriedly threw sandbags on it before an officer of some kind took over, charging an oversized bolt handle. Oddly he wore black sunglasses and an Imperial German Air Service flying jacket. The combination was quite distinctive.

'What is that?' Ruslan shouted from the bed of the truck.

'It appears to be an anti-tank rifle, Father,' Archer replied, oddly matter-of-fact.

'Oh. Well...shit.'

The Blackcoat commander offered a cold, knowing smirk and Archer knew, just knew without doubt, it was Preston – and that he wasn't going to miss.

A blind man could have seen it.

Eisner swerved, but the world just seemed to stop with

a crack of thunder, the force of a giant fist hitting Archer in the chest, followed by something wet and sticky sluicing across his face. It smelled sickly and distinctive. He knew it, just couldn't place it, but that was no matter, because he was flying.

Strange, that he didn't find it upsetting even though it should be, because he was afraid of heights. He could feel himself being lifted, turned, just like when his father used to pick him up and throw him into the air, and he would float back down for his father to catch him. A little feather, he said. He heard his own giggle and his mother's voice warning 'Da' to be careful.

He remembered then, the time when he was thrown from his swing. He went so high! Higher than ever! He tried to float, but couldn't. He was so heavy, and his father wasn't there to catch him. He broke his right leg, three ribs and fractured his left arm landing on a pile of broken masonry. He was sick too. He felt guilty about that, because his mother had made the dinner specially. Now he was sad, and it stank.

There was another sound, a terrible crunch of metal into metal, the snap of chain links and the scuff of bricks being smashed by something big and heavy. Everything was so slow! He'd been rushing to go somewhere, but he was upside down now, falling over. He tried to flap his arms, right himself, but he couldn't move.

Then everything sped up.

He was in the truck, spinning end over end, walls on either side of the lorry as it smashed through the checkpoint gates. It was a cacophony of tearing metal and broken glass, the sound of a machine dying, crunching onto cobbles, kicking dust in his face. He couldn't breathe and his chest hurt; his arms were on fire, but there were no flames, and he couldn't feel his legs at all.

He cast around for his rifle, needing it, but the *Runebolt* was gone, nowhere to be seen. A strong breeze rushed in, the cab of the truck torn open and now hurtling at a brick wall. Eisner's stone cold, utterly calm face bounced into his line of sight, blue eyes open and clear. His right arm was gone at the shoulder, a ragged red stump replacing the limb. Shrapnel decorated his breast with ragged medals.

'Do you regret anything, Daniel?' Eisner managed.

'Nothing, *Kamerad*,' Archer offered an idiot grin, as he remembered a walled garden filled with booby traps.

Another wall loomed.

Thunder far away, but stupidly, near.

The curtains closed.

Tugging on his legs and under his arms, roused him from his unpleasant slumber. He'd dreamt of being crushed into pulp, among other strange things; a metal man, a talking boulder, and some seahorses. Archer's world swam, flames made silhouettes of the shapes clutching his limbs. Heat from the fire only warmed the terrible pain just beginning to swell in his entire body, the imps dragging him convinced him he'd died and gone to hell. Hobnail boots crunching masonry spoil, the awful smell of crisping flesh, and horrid singed hair stink only served to add certainty.

'Daniel? Can you hear me?'

He tried to speak, but his lips were shut, mouth clenched against waves of agony. He felt a hand in his, a pressure on his chest. He could hear Latin, the language of Heaven. He took a breath, and then wished he hadn't as his whole body convulsed in coughing.

'Oh God,' he managed.

His reward was a chuckle. 'No, my son.'

'I'm dying?'

'Not if I can help it. Hold on.'

Blinding white streaks fired across his vision but he bore down, forced the hurt into the grip he exerted, driving the pain into one point, focusing, dearly wishing he had the *Runebolt* to pour the agony into, to blast it at the enemy like an arrow of raw power. Burning rushed from him, to be replaced by coolness and ease. He relaxed; a deep sigh that seemed to come up from beyond his boots, and soothing black came with it.

When Archer woke, it was to claustrophobic darkness. For a moment, terror gripped him – that he'd been buried alive. He could hear his rapid breathing, feel his heart pounding and the dull ache of broken bones set. Lashing out, he met nothing but air, and his panicked twists and turns made whatever he was stretched out on, creak and sway. Light filtered from a doorway to his right, before filling the room with golden light.

'Father Ruslan,' Archer breathed, glad to see him alive.

Yet the priest was haggard, with deep hollows under his eyes, reeling not from drink, but from fatigue. He reached out and gripped Archer's flailing wrist. Injuries flared at the contact, the flex of muscle and sinew still traumatised. He could smell fresh blood welling up, and the tincture of iodine.

'Peace my son, rest,' Ruslan began speaking in Latin, and Archer felt a familiar coolness in his body, to match the stone walls of his crypt. Fatigue stole his consciousness, and yet he saw the room light with brilliant radiance before fading back into oblivion.

Opening his eyes again, Archer remained silent. He was still in the stone-walled room, perhaps another cellar. It was brighter down here now, several oil lamps shedding a warm, cosy glow onto a dirt floor. He was propped up, trussed by thick bandages, nose assaulted by the tang of Dakin's solution.

His left arm and both legs were completely covered, his chest was wrapped and so were his feet. Archer could see his toes poking out. He wiggled them to make sure they worked, prompting a smile. Pain flared, stretching his parched lips only served to crack them open. He breathed heavily, sucking in air to drive off the lethargy. He cleared his throat, sensing movement behind and to his right he moaned. It was all he could manage.

'Shh, *ne parlez pas.*'

Universal understanding in gestures told him to keep his trap shut. His eyes swivelled round and she came into focus. When a damp cloth mopped his forehead, the relief was almost overwhelming. 'Therese.'

'*Oui, c'est moi.*' She smiled, pleased at being recognised, although it was uncertain. The teenager looked older. Worry would do that to a person, he thought.

'Marie?'

She pointed above her head, put her hands together and rested her head on them.

'Upstairs, asleep,' he mumbled. 'Doormouse?'

'*Dormir?*' She nodded firmly, adding a smile because he tried. She took the towel from his brow, wrung it out over a bowl and replaced it. The sweat wicked away, cooling him. Such simple bliss when his body was on fire was a huge blessing.

'Where is Kurt?'

Therese shook her head, Archer unable to tell if it was response or she didn't comprehend. Strange how he couldn't remember what the French called the Germans, five years into the war and it remained elusive. '*Ami*, Kurt?'

'*Désolé,*' she looked helpless, trying to find the words, but just settled for sorry.

Father Ruslan entered, answered. 'He died in the crash.'

'He was...a good man.'

'Yes, he was.'

Archer examined the priest's face. It was terribly pale and his black beard was now decorated with bands of grey. He looked as though he'd been awake for days, and under terrible strain. At first, Archer thought he was leaning on a stick, but it turned out to be a rifle stock with the barrel blown out and useless. It made for a handy crutch.

'Swords into ploughshares.'

Following the glance, Ruslan chuckled.

Therese looked at Archer, but the priest waved her to leave, pulling a heavy wooden chair closer to Archer's hammock by leveraging his bulk to shift it. Archer noticed the metal rings in the ceiling he was suspended from. There was an array of them, and vicious, sharp hooks on the wall.

Noticing, Ruslan gave a weary smile. 'You're in a butcher's cellar.'

'Apt. How bad am I?'

'By all rights, you should be dead in a wreck.'

'How did I survive?'

'Providence, my son.'

'I deserved that.' Archer groaned. 'You pulled me out?'

'Not quite.'

Ruslan adjusted his cassock before he sat to talk. He told him of the frantic escape, how the priest had rolled one way, Sam the other. In the confusion and the flames, they pulled Archer from the cab, then when the Blackcoats came, Sam fought them off in hand-to-hand, drawing them away whilst the priest and patient lurked in the house.

'I know there were more of you,' Archer thought of the shadowed imp-like figures.

'Some of our street orphan friends. Sergeant Miller helped too.'

'We came looking,' Miller's voice betrayed where he lurked at the cellar door, 'especially with the ruckus you made.'

'Thank you,' Archer told them, meant it.

'I owed you. Look, I'm sorry about Eisner,' the US Marine continued. 'We couldn't get to him. The flames...' he waved his hands in the air, mimicking the size of the fireball. 'I'm amazed you aren't charcoal. Everything else was.'

Archer allowed a grim smile, 'He was a *Feuerwehrmann*, a fire fighter.'

'Joe, could you leave us?' Ruslan inclined his head, and the American obliged.

It wasn't until then, Archer realised the Marine only wore an eye bandage. The rest of him was whole. No battle-dressings, no crutches, just a subtle limp. Thoughts racing, Archer forced up memories of the tunnels under the city, the clean smell with a hint of damp. Eisner's hand. 'I couldn't smell gangrene, sickness.'

Ruslan eyed him sternly, took Archer's wrist. 'Do not concern yourself. Rest.'

'How long have I been here?'

'Nearly a day. Sleep now.'

'No...you don't understand...with our shield...or...' he tried to protest, but his eyes were so tired and his body so heavy, that he was asleep in moments, bathed in warm glow again, enough that the dank cellar melted away, and all he felt was the impossible, gentle heat of winter sunlight on his skin.

24:

Flares cut the night, throwing jagged shadows the length of the trench Garfield stood in. He was grateful for his riding boots, legs caked in mud to mid-calf. He'd dropped in on the 8th Battalion of the South Staffordshire Regiment, the first unit who'd managed to respond to the attack on the British Army's extreme right flank. Their tenacity attracted Garfield, knowing that he had a better chance of accomplishing his mission with a solid wall of bayonets to fall back to.

It was a necessary consideration. They were well into the second day of a massive German assault, designed to split the Allies apart. The tactics were blunt and brutal on the face of it, but they were working. British Fifth Army reported scattered units all over, and none of the Intelligence Officers he'd sent messages to the day before had responded. The telephone wire was cut and he didn't want to risk sending runners into the arms of the Germans. They needed intelligence, and he was responsible for getting it.

He ignored the tired stares of the men around him, some of them looking at him strangely, never having seen an officer armed with a rifle. Others wore vacant expressions due to the mind-numbing barrage on the first day, when the Germans dropped a ribbon of red fire, a hundred miles wide, with the sound and fury of a war in heaven – with all the terror such a notion brought. He smiled grimly, feeling the powder burns and scratches on his face pull unevenly where it scabbed. Maybe, after the war, he would write poetry.

Garfield peered from an observation loophole hurriedly installed into his section of the line, trying to discern what lingered out in no-man's-land, under the spill of artificial white light. Ahead, the Scouting Zone was in ruins, torn to shreds first by artillery, then skilful Stormtroopers. Whoever was left was either dead or captured.

The soldiers alongside him hadn't slept for three days, low on rations, nerves and ammunition. Handfuls of stale bread and broken biscuits were jealously hoarded. Some men smoked, but even those too tired to worry about German snipers were careful not to illuminate their fellows, and lit up under gas capes. Garfield was one of the few officers with them. A Lieutenant tried his best, but the bone-weariness robbed the enthusiasm.

'Any time now lads, reinforcements will arrive and it'll be over.'

Handling his rifle, Garfield doubted that. If he wasn't mistaken, somewhere over in the distance, well off to his right, the Germans were punching the Fifth Army hard. The night before, as he'd gathered his equipment, Haig told Byng over dinner that he had to stay in contact with them, *hold out to the last*. Looking at the South Staffs beside him on the fire step, he hoped they wouldn't have to.

He cleared his throat. 'Lieutenant?'

'Sir?'

'We need prisoners. Six volunteers for a raid.'

'Baskeyfield, you lazy sod! Where are you?'

Groans greeted the demand, but a single man stood up. He booted the crossed feet of his comrade lazing on a pile of pile of sandbags, propped well up out of the mud. Grinning, the layabout dropped his pretence of sleeping, in turn shaking the shoulder of a third man, then a fourth, until a clutch of six weary men – *of trusted old pals*, Garfield thought – pulled to their feet, using their rifles as crutches. They shambled into a loose line for his inspection or orders, and not one of them would have passed parade. One stretched, caught Garfield's eye and offered him a resigned shrug.

'Thank you, lads,' he offered, although stiffly. He looked them up and down. 'We're going to bash a few heads in, and come back with guests. Any questions?'

The chance of doing anything other than being shot at and shelled seemed to draw them from the lethargy. They looked at him earnestly, seeing him properly perhaps for the first time, not just an eccentric officer. That he carried a rifle, like them, bought him a hint of amused respect. Their unspoken reply was good enough.

He patted his letter pocket for luck, chambered a round. 'Alright, let's go.'

Flares lingered in the air, lighting faces peering through red-rimmed eyes. His volunteers wearily picked up their rifles, trench clubs and sharp-edged shovels, quietly following him to the trench-sap, where he paused, grasping a very rough hewn ladder, intent on going first. He took long slow breaths, and pushed up, feet clogged up with enough clay-mud to feel like he was carrying several pounds of chain around his ankles. He looked down and realised he'd cleared only three rungs. His back chose to spasm then, but he bit his lip, hard. The distraction and the blood in his mouth brought him relief from the white needles in his vision, and he felt a hand on his back.

'You alright, sir?' a Staffordshire accent whispered.

'Just a nasty splinter.'

A gentle murmur of amusement accepted his lie, but he sensed it wasn't malicious. The man spoke again. 'You want me to take over, sir?'

In reply Garfield fought his way up the ladder, slithering out into the gap in British defences. A pummelled ruin of earth, with barely a lump of soil above head height, he felt terribly exposed and alone. He supposed Archer felt that way sometimes. At that moment, he detected a man nearby, then another, until all seven of them were up together.

A lucky number.

Lifting to his knees in the near pitch-black now the flares stopped, the Major licked his lips, considering his options. Trying to avoid any tell-tale sounds of his boots sucking in deep mud, he assumed a crouch, his rifle out ahead of him. Desperate to ignore the pain in his back, he forced his mind to work, plotting out the route, mentally mapping the shell holes, deep craters and laces of razor-wire against a rough sketch drawn by one of the Sniper Observers roaming the sector.

'Right,' he whispered. 'Forward. Keep close.'

Moving painfully slowly, the group kept together as they crossed no-man's-land, guided by Garfield's hushed whisper turning them left or right as they stalked onward. The section of enemy trench Garfield chose was well-chosen, as the sounds of equipment being readied escaped the deep cuts in the earth, covering the movements of the British stealing upon them in the night.

A small stove was carefully hidden, but not enough to prevent the gentle, warming glow illuminating a short section of trench. Garfield's eyes, desperately trawling the inky murk ahead for a light source, latched onto it as they got closer. He kept going until he could hear them, a hushed whisper. He caught a few of the words, certain they were French.

What were their allies doing beyond the British line? He tucked his rifle stock into his shoulder and stood up fully, the meagre light enough now for hand signals. He spread out his volunteers, and then as one, they approached the lip of the trench. Difficult to make out any Regiment or even army affiliation, the men below wore dark clothes, with strange armbands carrying a design Garfield hadn't seen before.

He spoke firmly. 'Do not move. Hands up, or we shoot!'

Taking no chances, Garfield repeated it in French.

It must have seemed like the British soldiers just erupted from the ground – the spectral light enough to render them hazy shapes, restless ghosts of the battlefield. A moment of tense silence followed, the men around the stove looking up at them. He couldn't read their faces, but they suddenly exploded into action, one leaned to spill the stove, to kill the light before they themselves were killed. The other two men below broke apart for nearby weapons, and although it happened all at once, the experienced British raiders beside him didn't falter, dropping down into the trench and brawling.

Frustration proved the deciding power as the South Staffs swarmed the trio, taking it out on their targets. Garfield could hear boots and steel meeting flesh. The sickening sound of a rifle butt finding a weak bone in a victim.

'Good God, leave off!' Garfield snarled. 'Enough!'

The bashing abruptly stopped, and someone voided their innards in a choking retch. The stench of stale food and acid-soured wine added the final touch to a pleasant evening. 'We need to return to Army HQ.'

'All of us, sir?'

They'd earned a break, and he appreciated they'd volunteered for an awful, bloody job. Garfield flashed a smile at the shadows. 'Why not?'

He wasn't worried about the sound of half-senseless, punch-drunk men being cajoled out of the trench. Any reinforcements would be slow in coming, wary of what would happen to them if they chose to investigate in the dark. No shots had been fired; no-one had managed a proper cry of alarm. An effective, if violent little bit of work. The subtle pleasure of it bled out of him in a slow sigh. His night was just beginning. These strange prisoners had some questions to answer.

Evening stormy skies prevented any positional navigation, but Nunzia knew where she was anyway as *Orca* weighed anchor in the deep channel, keeping her keel away from the shallow drafts and sandbanks of the berth reserved by Major Garfield. The squall tossed around the launch sent for her, but she guided it to dock, gritting her teeth. The sea was a proud mare not even the Sea Witch could corral into complete obedience.

The Royal Navy crew of the launch pulled oars alongside her, the Captain not afraid to bend her back to the task, until finally the prow bumped the concrete quayside. Nunzia was up and moving in her heavy raincoat and all-weather boots, the sloshing spray threatening to soak her. She leapt ashore, closely followed by her First Mate, who lashed the rope to a capstan, the white paint chipped and flecked where larger boats moored.

A small shoal of British Sailors awaited her under shelter; among them an officer in a peaked cap, obviously in charge of the detail. When one of his men pointed her out, he hurriedly dropped his cigarette, extinguishing it with a swift grind of his heel and marched out to greet her in the rain. Nunzia vowed to keep her temper, it wasn't his fault a detour around German warships had resulted in two days lost. Archer could be sitting waiting for her at the rendezvous, fighting for his life against half a German Siege Division.

Or those bastard Blackcoats.

'Captain Corvalho?'

'*Si*! Who are you?' she shouted over the howling, coastal gale.

'Lieutenant Matthew Wells, ma'am. Royal Navy.'

Nunzia had to close in, near enough to catch the nicotine stink of his breath. He was just a young man, handsome enough, with dark hair under his hat and a good strong chin. She absorbed his rank and ribbons, but her impatience got the better of her. She tossed her head in frustration.

'I see that,' she whinnied, 'where is Major Garfield?'

Wells was taken aback. 'He's at HQ. He asked us to deliver instruc—'

'Nonsense! You will take me to him,' she demanded. A short stamp of her foot added more petulance than she felt.

'The car is right this way.'

'This must be fast. Do you drive fast, Lieutenant?'

Wells grinned.

As the car drew up at the steps of the Town Hall where Garfield was billeted, Nunzia cracked the door open before Wells had a chance to fully brake. She thanked him with a quick press of lips to his cheek, pulled her bag from the passenger footwell, and marched into the Hall.

She took a deep breath. 'Major Garfield! Where are you? Must I shout the house down?'

The duty officer stumbled down the broad wooden staircase, pulling his braces over his shoulders as he moved. 'What's going on here? Who are you?'

Nunzia swept on, pulled off her coat, bundled it and shoved it at him. He groped at it as she advanced, trying not to drop it. She went right past him, headed for the stairs he came down. 'Major Garfield!'

Her boots rapped on the boards not covered by thick carpet, her pace not slowing. More officers and even soldiers, half-dressed and wearing red-topped hats came out, brandishing batons and revolvers, but when they saw an unarmed woman, the redcaps moved to simply block her, lowering their guns.

'Major –'

'What is it, Sea Witch?' Garfield's voice was flat, unperturbed despite havoc being raised at midnight.

'Finally! Antwerp is hell, worse than anyone could have guessed! Archer is in trouble. He needs help.'

'Couldn't you have radioed or telegraphed that?'

'With German ships hounding me, *buffoni*? I lost hours dodging them!'

Garfield didn't flinch from her, instead tapping the military policemen on the shoulder to allow her to come past, and ushered her into his study. Once they were alone and the door was closed, he chose to confront her in icy chill.

'He'll have to fend for himself, we're tied up. There's a new division in action, multi-national. Fanatical. No-one knows where they're coming from.'

Nunzia froze, her temper ebbing away. 'They wear black coats.'

Garfield sobered, eyes narrowed. 'How did you know that?'

'Antwerp is full of them.'

'My God, of course. Reprisal camps. They're ex-POW's.'

'There is a man called Heidler in charge. Archer and Eisner have gone after him.'

'Where's Ross?'

She sighed, pressed a palm to her forehead. 'He's...dead. He gave his life for us.'

'I can't spare anyone,' he replied, stiffly.

Nunzia's face hardened. 'They're fighting a city! Those bastards were all over us!'

After long moments staring into space, marshalling his thoughts, Garfield sighed, shoulders stooping. 'It doesn't matter. The Americans have told us there is no diplomat, it's all about some bloody rogue Arcanist.'

'I know that! Give me some Royal Marines! I can get Daniel out—'

'*Daniel*?' He cut across her bows, with a half-smile. '*Corporal Archer* has uncovered something inconvenient, and the Americans want it buried.'

She looked him up and down, ignored the cuts and powder scorches on his cheeks that showed he'd seen fighting. Dismissing it, she lifted her nose above the smell she perceived. 'You told Daniel to kill Sam. *Mio Dio*,' she felt her mouth drop open. 'It is 'curtains' for the American, no? Then for Daniel, after he does your dirty work!'

Garfield's face was suddenly dark. 'I suggest you forget it. It was a fool's errand, and we overplayed our hand. We all have our orders – *don't you?*'

The old, familiar anger came on then, a rush of boiling water above a magma vent deep under the ocean. Garfield somehow knew about her dishonourable instructions to dispose of everyone but the American. Rallying, she considered what she'd given up to become the *Sea Witch*. The war had taken and taken from her, but now she had a chance to return the courtesy. She pulled to a proud, defiant height.

'I will not let Daniel be a name on a memorial

somewhere,' she simmered, bolstered by the rightness of it in her chest. 'To hell with you, my uncle, and this war!'

'Captain Corvalho! Control yourse—'

'*No!*' Nunzia harpooned him with a look, jabbed an accusing finger at his face. 'If anything happens to him, I will blame you! *Asini!*'

Nunzia turned on her heel, calling for Lieutenant Wells once more, hoping he was still outside. She cantered away to get her Lion from his den.

Garfield watched her go, and retired to his office, neither blaming her, nor sharing the sentiment. Archer's fate was out of his hands, or even Byng's. There were bigger games at play here, indeed, his thoughts drifted to an army, which shuddered and clung to the sodden earth as the rain turned everything into a quagmire. The weather was slowing the German Offensive, but the fanatical Blackcoats arriving day after day were making it up for it. Worse, their existence drove a political and physical wedge between the Allies, who saw a demoralising effect in being attacked by their own soldiers.

British lines were not nearly as complete as command preferred to admit. The scouting zone was already in enemy hands, and even if he could send some men to Antwerp to stem the tide, what good would it do? Every rifle counted now, even his own. It sat in the corner, newly cleaned and wrapped in the canvas shipping bag to keep the dirt off it. He sought it out in the gloom.

The weapon made his thoughts circular. He didn't hate the Sharpshooter, he just wanted the potential in him realised, albeit now futile. Such was war. He allowed a small snort in self-mockery, he was jealous of course, just a little. As a member of the King's One-Hundred, Garfield was one of the best shots in the army, but the Sniper School had never been in his sights, the higher-ups having earmarked him for Intelligence work. His fondness for the unconventional found a home.

He dwelled on the last, urgently seeking his tunic, the one holding the letter. Archer wasn't the only one who wanted the war over. Dirty tricks would just see it finished *faster*. Haig didn't believe in the operation, claiming it was just a lot of nonsense and 'Music Hall Theatre'. Who could blame him after this fiasco? They couldn't send Archer more orders now anyway, not after the weather machine was smashed up in another forced landing. The gambit was turning from tragedy into farce.

Still, lessons were learned, even if he had to write this one off. Haig was an echo of many without the mind to see what difference strategic, small-scale operations could make. With the American admission about the identity of their man in Antwerp, as an intelligence officer, he was in the doghouse, true, but at least Byng trusted him and…it wasn't over yet.

The phone rang. He resented the disturbance, so let it chime, before snatching up the handset anyway. 'Garfield.'

'Charles, Douglas Haig. What was all the humbug down there?'

'I apologise if you were woken, sir.'

'Was it for anything interesting?'

Garfield told him the story, leaving nothing out.

'Why didn't you tell me sooner?'

'I wasn't sure, sir. Not of everything.'

Haig allowed that. 'Can we get a battleship or two up that bloody river?'

'I'd have to check, sir,' Garfield stalled. He'd already investigated the Scheldt's depth and tide, knew that both *HMS Warspite* and *HMS Revenge* could make the trip. He carefully lifted the technical reports off his desk, dropping them into a drawer he slowly closed so Haig couldn't hear. 'It could take a while.'

'Fine. Get onto the Navy, with my compliments. I want Antwerp blown to pieces. That'll stop those black-coated bastards.'

'Sir, my team is dealing with it, I'm confident –'

'Major, *I'm* confident we're about to lose France to the bloody Huns! Blast that city to gravel, that's an order!'

There was no room to be had. He tried anyway. 'With respect, sir, the Admiralty will want it in writing. So would I.'

The Field Marshal shouted for his aide, slammed the phone down.

Garfield had to believe Archer was good enough, had to *hope* that the others were. He felt fate laughing at him for his temptation, the empty threat of naval artillery now a very real one.

A knock at the door preceded ADC Schofield's entrance. 'Are you alright, Major? Hell of a racket.'

'I'm tolerable, William. Has Captain Corvalho left?'

'In a right tear, too. I heard her yelling in foreign.'

'She called me a donkey.' Garfield chuckled. 'Is she heading for the docks?'

'I believe so.'

The Major pursed his lips, thinking. 'Tea, William, I must have tea. And get the emergency telegraph ready. I have a message to go the naval station.'

He had to get back to the real war, and any minute the Field Marshal's order would come to raze the Belgian city, but he could at least give Nunzia a head start, waste the Navy's time a bit for a fighting chance. There was room, he just had to find it, use all the dirty tricks he could think of.

'Anything else, sir?'

'No. Yes. Haig's ADC, Astor, is it?'

'Yes, sir. Makes a bloody awful brew by all accounts.'

'He'll be carrying orders. Find him,' Garfield said, looking up from the desk. 'Trip him up; knock his papers over, dunk his letters in tea, anything. Buy me time.'

'Leave it with me, sir.' Schofield smiled and nodded, withdrawing to let the Major get on, door closed behind him firmly.

25:

Crashing to the ground was almost progress. Archer tipped out of the hammock, spilling onto the earth floor, glad it wasn't tightly packed soil. He dragged the blanket over his nudity, hiding the huge purple bruises and fresh, angry red scars. Burn scars dotted his arms and legs, and he suspected there was a severe wound still under the bandages around his chest.

He crawled on hands and knees, bones creaking in protest, until he got to the chair and, with awkward balance, heaved his tormented bulk into it, to take stock. He wiggled his fingers and toes, and although it hurt, they all worked fine. He was going to live.

But that only meant more people would die.

Footsteps sounded on the steps leading to freedom above, and steam wafted down in the gentle breeze. Therese stood there, hair tied up and covered by a scarf, an apron too big for her keeping her safe from the tray and steaming bowl. She braced the tray with one arm, her palm out to stop him. He acquiesced as his stomach growled. Therese smiled, put the tray across his lap, holding out a wooden spoon, and it didn't matter that the bowl was chipped, or that it was obviously for feeding children.

'Thank you – *Merci*.'

She blushed, quickly fleeing upstairs and leaving him to his meal. He tried it, uncertain of both heat and taste, but the hearty soup was delicious, with vegetables and finely chopped bully beef. Maybe she was an Arcanist? His ribs still hurt when he chuckled.

More footsteps sounded and Father Ruslan came down with Miller in tow.

'I hope the condemned man is enjoying his meal?' Miller grinned, his uniform scraped free of crusted bloodstains.

'It's lovely, tell Therese I said so. Condemned?'

In reply, Miller merely pushed a scrap of folded paper at Archer, who flicked it open, to reveal a reasonable likeness of his face. The warning was in German, French and strange letters that looked a cross between hieroglyphics and blocky handwriting. He said as much.

'It's Russian Cyrillic,' Ruslan said, testily.

'Saying..?' Archer prompted.

'Wanted: Dead, corpse as proof.'

'What am I worth? Francs? Marks?'

'Neither,' Ruslan replied heavily, stroking his now gaunt face and grey beard, 'a Pardon, provisions, and safe passage for up to five people.'

Archer dropped his spoon into the empty bowl. 'They didn't appreciate us blowing up their balloon? Shame.'

'There's more,' Miller added.

'There always is.'

'Our people are being held in the Citadel. Kate and Sam have both been taken there as well, I'm told.'

Archer smiled and shook his head. The morning, if he allowed for grim British understatement, was getting better and better. Miller whistled and another person came down into the cellar, a young man carrying a bundle under one arm and a long, hessian wrapped pole in the other. He had an automatic pistol tucked into his belt, which fell out onto the floor when the lad halted abruptly.

It was Archer's Webley-Scott.

He frowned at the two men, took the bundle from the boy. Leaving the pistol on the ground, he untied the string and shook the clothes loose before shrugging them on. He retrieved the gun, now feeling altogether more human and strong enough to wield it. German webbing, complete with a full canteen, went round his waist, and an attached Luger holster accommodated the Webley. They had even recovered a Mills bomb, which Archer placed in one of the pouches.

'And the Kaiser? Is he at the Citadel?'

'We believe so,' Miller met his stare.

'Any word from Nunzia?' he thought to the plane and his tingling teeth. 'Odd flashes of lightning?'

Miller made a face, thrown. 'Nothing like that.'

'No flares or anything from outside the North wall?'

The men shared a glance, Miller shook his head.

Archer closed his eyes tight, fought the tide of anger and sorrow threatening to drown him. He felt stupid for letting her go, for saying goodbye. He crushed it, ruthlessly forcing memories of her long hair and sharp smile out of his mind. It had to wait. He had to put it off, hope she made it. She was a sailor and she'd gone to the sea. He took a deep breath, blew it out, changing tack.

'What do we know about Preston?'

Ruslan shrugged. 'English, very clever. Uses a dog, two pistols.'

'And anti-tank rifles. Thank you, by the way.'

'For what?' the priest was nonplussed.

'For not saying he was like me.'

A knowing smile twisted the thick facial hair.

Moving to take the lead Archer made for the stairs, but Ruslan laid a hand on his arm, pushing the long pole at him. His hands grasped it, knowing the feel even as they pinched through the cloth. He tore the wrap free, the wood battered, but sanded and stained black to keep it smooth. One of the front sight protectors was bent to the right, but everything else, apart from a few new dents was present and correct.

His fingers took up familiar positions, cycled the bolt. Fresh oil greeted his nose. The rifle had been cared for as much as his body. He felt infinitely better; the *Runebolt* completing him, his Magic Wand put both of them back into the fight.

'Shall we go?' he said, but wasn't sure if he was talking to the gun or the room. When he looked up, he could see the same thought playing across both faces.

'Just be careful, my son.' Exhausted, the priest sank slowly into the chair Archer just vacated, slouching forward.

'Physician, heal thyself?'

Father Ruslan grunted, choking a laugh. 'Miracles we can do, Daniel. Leave the impossible to God.'

Archer walked up the steps, Miller falling in behind him to give the priest privacy and peace. His feet got lighter as he rose, climbing the flight of stairs up into the kitchen of the old butcher's shop. He spied Marie in a corner, near the stove, keeping warm. With her on the cot was a button-eye dolly with one leg. Soldiers made their own luck. He smiled, ruffled the doll's nearly threadbare scalp, before marching outside, into glorious daylight.

Miller went first, just the two of them against an army. He was festooned with ammunition pouches, American grenades, and Archer was no different. He carried his rifle and pistol, with as many rounds as his allies could salvage from the crash. Only one of the special Spitzer-Brice bullets was recovered. He put it away, a candle to blow out on a special occasion.

The spot Eisner died was a few miles north of their location. Patrolling with Miller gave him time to think about that now, understanding why Ruslan chose to come to the AEZ, why he got special dispensation from his Bishop to go with the Russian soldiers into battle. Archer would wager the Prelate didn't know one of his priests was a Healing Mage.

Being one himself, he was aware of sub-divisions of the Arcane Colleges, how it was recognised even as far back as the Ancient Sumerians where a Physician was known as a 'Master of the Oils and Waters'. The history classes were always fascinating.

'Do you want to stop by the truck?' Miller asked.

'No, we push on.'

Parts of the nightmare were coming back to him anyway. Given a chance to rest, his brain made sense of them, but they were photographic, just plates frozen in time and space. There was nothing he could do for Eisner, his resting place a crumpled truck cab inside a smashed house. He would be nothing but ashes and dust, adding to soot-smeared Antwerp. He thought of Ross, his resting place marked by a ton of rubble, a grave of sorts. How many others on the Western Front didn't even have that?

Dodging heavy Blackcoat patrols, the two men wended through shell holes from when Antwerp was first bombed in 1914, to houses that still reeked of propellant and gelignite. Archer placed his feet carefully in the piles of rubble, looking for solid beams to step on, reducing the chance of falling or springing booby-traps.

They cut through a factory, ladders and gantries cut away or sheared at the bolts from the wall, to prevent use. Old workbenches, naked of tools, now mouldered where once men had toiled. Two-storey walls, scarred and pocked from bomb splinters, sported greenery in the gaps, plants tenaciously clinging to the bricks and mortar, pulling it further apart.

Light came through broken windows, not a pane of frosted glass intact. The shafts fell with enough brightness to dispel the murk of the interior, showing the path which led through the shell, past beams and stanchions once painted in a pale blue colour, now given over to flaking undercoat and rust. Loops of chain lay piled as though ready to be collected, maybe to be melted down for war materiel.

Progress was barred by a chasm in the shop floor, running from one end to the other. Archer looked down, peering into a canyon six yards across, pitching down into the bowels of the complex. He fancied he could see the ground, perhaps twenty or so feet under his boots, but the light failed to penetrate the gloom, so he couldn't be sure.

The concrete floor had given way to fall into the hollow cellar beneath. He pulled back from the precipice and closed his eyes. Miller's hand on his belt brought him back to his senses, and he looked around with a grateful nod. The Marine peered over, rummaging in his pockets. He produced a match and struck it, letting the flame take hold before dropping it. It floated down, illuminating a small patch.

'Jesus.'

The match didn't last long, but what light it shed was powerful enough to catch on the pale white of desiccated bone. A leg, and what Archer thought was a hand, poked out from beneath a pile of wreckage. Scouring the sides of the building, he desperately searched for any kind of bridge or stairs he could get to. A gantry ran across the gap, but the ladder on their side was gone, and he didn't have the grapnel anymore.

Old metal sprockets and gears at one edge of the pit suggested there was an old lift built into the factory, but curiosity aside; he didn't feel like cranking the handle to bring it up. Near to the lift mechanism he found the way across. Mostly hidden by weeds, he spied three girders, placed in close order to form a bridge. He nudged Miller and they began to make their way over to them. After looking at their only method of progress, Archer held the Marine's gaze, and pointed at his eye patch.

'We'll have to go around.'

'Why? We'll lose time.'

'You can't judge distances. You could fall. We need a safer route.'

'Horse hockey. If Death is down there, I spit in his eye!'

The American hacked up a gobbet of phlegm and proved his disdain, by blasting it over the side of the trench and mounting the girders. Archer shrugged, and mounted the bridge, treading steadily, spreading his weight, moving six paces before the metal gave out an ominous creak. Miller followed onto the makeshift metal bridge, a lonely span with nothing but empty space either side of it, arms out for balance as he defiantly strode on.

He was halfway across when Archer felt the tremor and creaking in the steel as it bowed and flexed. He remembered something. 'Don't walk, shuffle.'

'What?'

'Cadence will make the girders vibrate.'

Bridges were the only time a soldier never marched. When advancing over one, the Sergeants would give the command to break step, which inevitably led to the soldier's second favourite pastime of dawdling.

Miller's face betrayed he wasn't convinced. 'It'll be—'

Crunch.

A plume of dust spat up, then with a sickening tumble, the other end of the concrete parapet began to slough away. Both men reacted at once, racing for the end of the bridge, Archer stretching, leaping up even as the girders began to fall. His speed made the beams bang up and down harder, further damaging where they met the floor, churning up old and new grit together as he launched up and long over the chasm below.

Following him by mere feet, Miller's leap was painfully short, and Archer watched him vault into nothingness, the girders gone, clanging and tumbling with a shocking peal that rattled his teeth and echoed through the factory in a damning ring. No-one could have failed to hear it, and the dust obscured what happened to the American. The noise continued for several painful seconds, after which the silence was stirred by the drop and slap of lumps of concrete into the chasm.

Archer swiped his arm, trying to cuff away the cloud, stumbling forward he clutched the nearest upright column, a rock in a fast-flowing river of blinding dirt. He could hear coughing coming from behind, and dropped to his hands and knees, seeking the edge of the precipice.

'Miller! Are you there?' He could picture the marine lying broken atop a pile of rubble, a girder for his tombstone.

'Need a hand here!'

The haze cleared and Archer caught sight of scuffed and bloody knuckles gripping wrought iron spars jutting from the smashed escarpment. 'Hold on, Yank!'

'I didn't plan on anything else, Limey!'

He grinned at the American's sentiment as he lay down,

placing his *Runebolt* safely out of the way before slithering forward. He peered over to see Miller's pale face, his body poised over the depths. Archer thrust his arms out, gripped the man, anchoring him. He hooked his toes under the bottom of a workbench, hoping it would do.

'Climb up me for God's sake, you're heavier than I am.'

'Must be all that fine Antwerp cuisine.'

'Move!'

Miller grunted, grasping handfuls of Archer's jacket, pinching the healing flesh below, tugging on the webbing. Archer formed his hands into a stirrup, heaving as soon as Miller got a knee into it, and was subject to the mad scrabble as he was used as a ladder. Archer rolled over, and both men lay on their backs panting, staring up at the cracked and patchy ceiling several yards above. Miller coughed, cleared his throat. His breathing began to slow enough to talk, but even then, the words tumbled out in a rush.

'How the hell did you make that jump?'

'What do you mean?' Archer was suddenly guarded.

'You just took off.'

'I weigh less than you,' Archer grinned, 'must be all that healthy living.'

They shared a gentle chuckle at their brush with death.

'Alright! Don't move!'

The demand fell from above, the voice certainly English. Archer could see figures standing on the gantries. How they got up there, he didn't know, but as his eyes adjusted, he could make out bows and slingshots being directed at him. One of the people stepped into the light, and shock must have registered on Archer's face, because the young lad who confronted them must have been all of sixteen.

And he wore a bowler hat.

'That's right!' he put his hands on his hips. 'You're in Rooks territory now!'

'What?'

'You deaf or sommat?'

Archer ignored him, counted the figures above quickly. They shifted about on the gantries, twelve of them in all. Children and youths armed with only low powered weapons, but whilst a volley of arrows would prove a nuisance, stones would be biblically ferocious. 'I heard you.'

'Good. You scared then, eh?'

'No.'

Such a robust reply led to confusion. The lad licked his lips, puffed himself up a bit more. 'It don't matter. Hand over all your loot and we'll let you off.'

'Look, I'm with the British Army,' Archer tried. 'I'm trying to get into the Citadel.'

The lad looked sceptical. 'The big fort? What for?'

'I'm going to blow the Kaiser's head off.'

'Why didn't you say so? We'll be right down.'

26:

Miller and Archer got a suspicious look from the boy, who was easily the oldest of the motley crew. He wore hard-wearing dungarees which were worn at the knees and roughly cut off at the ankles, a pair of German Army boots tied around his feet with string to make them fit. The bowler hat on his head was battered, but still retained both brim and distinctive shape, and he had a large mechanic's spanner as his primary cudgel. A quiver of arrows and a bow were strapped over his shoulder.

He had a sly glint in his eye as he appraised the two men, obviously one of the sharper ragged children, wise to the streets. Archer didn't need to ask how any of these foundlings came to be in Antwerp – enough merchantmen, soldiers, sailors and their families ended up on the wrong side of the wall. Some for no fault of their own, others refusing to believe the Germans would actually do what they said, and close the city.

He listened to the melange of different accents and words, blending into a cohesive street slang. Verbs and tenses were confused, or missing, but they understood each other perfectly well. They all had English to some degree, flavoured by their origins. He could discern German, possibly Flemish, and even the sing-song lilt of the orient.

One of the grubby-faced scamps had a brace of large rats on his belt, which prompted Miller to slowly pull a ration tin from a pouch. Their eyes latched onto it.

'You guys eat those things?' Miller pointed to the rodents.

'Better than eating *people*,' one of the girls said, making a face.

Miller just grunted, but Archer nodded sagely, and indicated everyone should congregate in a corner, where a stout tree was branching out into the factory. He noticed each child carried a pocket of black feathers, but from Crow, Jackdaw or Raven, he couldn't tell. He reasoned they supplemented their...ground diet...with birds, which was clever.

The thought gave him pause, transporting him to Rannoch Moor, and exercises at the Sanatorium. He relived flights of birds pulled to the ground by air mages. The shocked twittering given to silence as the creatures were grounded, but confused. After a while they regained their bearings and launched into the sky, jabbering and calling in their own tongues, not unlike the Rooks surrounding him now.

Shaking his head to dislodge the memory, he pulled some older, dead branches from the floor and with Miller's help and a bit of water from a canteen, they prepared a small fire and stout branches to hang canteens over the flames for cooking.

'Why under the tree?' one boy asked.

'It will take the smoke up.' Archer pointed. 'Spread it out so no-one can see.'

This brought a few conspiratorial whispers, which the bowler-hat youth stilled with a hand. He beckoned to the boy with the rats, who placed the offering by the fire. The other children came to sit too – all but three, who kept watch.

'Wise.' Miller nodded.

'We ain't stupid,' the lad replied gravely. 'Anyway, I'm Derrick – like the cranes on a ship.'

The girl sat adjacent gave him a look. 'We have not been introduced,' she huffed.

'This is Maisie.' Derrick jabbed a thumb at her.

'Such mannerly folk,' the American observed.

Archer let Miller cook and serve out some fried concoction he had made, using all four of their mess tins, and a handful of canned food to feed the children. When the rats were offered up for dressing, Miller quickly dropped them behind the tree when no-one was looking. For his part, Archer grasped the *Runebolt*, and began the process of stripping it for cleaning. It didn't really need doing, but the simple solace of the familiar, which was second only to the stillness when he concentrated, helped to settle him.

'You're one of them arsonists,' Derrick supposed with a snort, putting a bit too much sneer on it.

'*Arcanist*,' Archer corrected, stopping short. He spotted the trap late.

Derrick grinned. 'Same difference though.'

Archer conceded with a shrug. The boy was right.

'What's your game then, eh? Make puddles, set fires, dig tunnels?'

Nunzia. Kurt. Hal. He recognised the thoughts as decoys. 'Many tunnels around here?' he asked instead.

'Oh aye,' replied a Scottish boy, spooning from one of the mess tins. He froze when he realised his mistake, yelped when an elbow caught him in the ribs.

'These tunnels,' Archer continued, 'do any go under the fort?'

Silence greeted that, not one of the children looked up at him, suddenly very interested in the food and watching the smoke rise. 'Are they sewers?'

'Ugh, no,' Maisie protested. 'They have water that stinks sometimes. Got to be careful.'

'The water is there all the time?' Archer continued to talk to Maisie; her long chestnut ponytail reminded him of his sister. He half wondered what she was doing whilst he spent his days being shot at, but ruthlessly crushed the thought. There was a time and a place, and Antwerp afforded neither.

'No. It goes up and down. Tidal.'

'I'll show you,' Derrick said, his eyes straying to the holster. 'In trade for the handgun.'

Archer tapped the pistol butt. 'Not a chance.'

'I can help.' Miller offered his canteen around. 'Do you

want to leave the AEZ?'

'What's the Ay-Easy?' one girl asked.

'He means Antwerp,' Archer drily corrected.

The youths looked at each other.

'How?' Maisie barked, but blushed, perhaps expecting an elbow from somewhere. Still, she didn't take it back.

'If we get out of here, I can sponsor you as refugees. American families can see what's happening, they want to help.' He shrugged.

Derrick looked around, stood up. 'Alright,' he proclaimed, 'we'll show you. Um, you got any fags? For my old man, like.'

Archer groaned, knowing the orphan boy would likely use them, but he needed the advantage of surprise the tunnels offered, so he gave in. He fished into his pocket and took out his packet of German cigarettes recovered from the man whose neck he'd broken, tossing it to the lad. He gave him a long, lingering stare.

The boy shrugged.

'One last thing,' Archer warned as they cleaned the mess tins and began packing up, 'you try to prank us, I'll break your head, Derrick, and if you try to lose us, I'll come back and pull everyone else's bloody ears off.'

They grinned at him.

Hands gripping one half of the hatch, Archer let Derrick and Maisie go down first. It was mostly dark, the tunnels worming away in darkness and damp, the occasional storm grate in the street cutting through in strange, broken interludes. He looked down, could see the running water was only a trickle, but the tidemark was high, above his head. He didn't like the idea of being in here too long.

'Tide's still out,' Derrick said, leading down the artery, 'won't come back for hours. Plenty of time.'

Archer was uneasy, but had to trust the boy's word. They children were down here with him after all. The strange tidal ebb would naturally correspond with the waxing and waning river Scheldt, according to his map, the tunnels helping to prevent flooding of the city. Now they were a trap for fools attacking an enemy stronghold.

The group moved on in relative silence, their only companion the gentle trickle of water, with the youngsters venturing confidently onwards. Archer tried to remember the turns taken, first right, then left, straight on for a hundred yards, then left again in this awful maze. He couldn't fix any landmarks in his head either – everywhere was the same darkness and algae smeared dank.

They were forced to stop, twice. The light from above was cut out by the passing of men and materiel. Judging by the direction and pace, they were moving towards the Citadel. The troops above laughed and joked, diesel fumes and the stale smell of tobacco tumbling down into the storm drain in their wake.

'Something big is happening,' Miller whispered. It was as loud as they dared, having made most of the journey in silence, they had quickly discovered that their voices carried, echoing with surprising force.

'Doesn't change anything,' Archer replied. 'We get inside and get everyone out.'

That seemed to settle any discussion, and the group pressed on for the best part of a third hour, until they arrived at a short passage leading to a large chamber with a broad ramp. The area glowed with light from humming bulbs. Derrick pointed.

'That's it.'

'What's up there?' Miller whispered.

'Dunno. Never been up there. Now, what about us?'

Archer produced his map so the boy could see, tapped a finger to a small church in the northernmost apex of the curtain wall. 'Can you get there?'

'No problem, Maisie knows the way. What time?'

'When the tide comes in,' Archer suggested.

'Roughly sunset? Alright.'

'Be careful,' Archer said.

The lad turned and Maisie wordlessly followed, their boots telling the story of their mad run, banging and splashing on the tunnel floor. One look at the US Marine was enough and Miller started to carefully make his way up the slope.

The chamber opened up as they stepped from the tunnel, a large, square formation of bricks and buttresses, with large pipes running down to point broad-mouthed funnels towards the slope, and Archer realised it was a cistern, with a platform that circumnavigated the room. They climbed up to stand on the brick parapet, a single metal gate separating them from a lit passage going deeper into whatever building lurked above.

'I hope you can pick locks,' Miller grunted.

'A door is only as good as the wall it's in.' Archer ran a finger along the mortar, and it came back with grey crumble. 'This brickwork has been exposed to damp, it's a century old. Can that heavy popgun of yours take any abuse?'

'Limey, this here is one of John Moses Browning's God-given instruments.'

'Then start praying, Yank.' Archer smirked, clearing the breech of his rifle for safety, and slamming the butt of the *Runebolt* into the edge of the wall holding in the hinge brackets. A few moments later, Miller's cleared gun also struck, and the two of them attacked with steady rhythm, emulating the navvies who likely quarried and laid the tunnels. Archer just hoped the noise reverberating in the cistern wasn't going any further, whilst cursing he didn't have Hal Ross there to cleave the door free with his uncanny power.

Anger at the Canadian's death fuelled the five minutes of exertion before he stopped, indicating both men should pull, and their work was rewarded as the brackets tore from the surface, and the gate came off at the hinges. They set it upright against the wall.

Miller grinned across at him.

In reply, Archer drew his pistol, menacing the passageway beyond. He hugged the left side, allowing Miller room for his own handgun as they negotiated the tight space, heading swiftly towards a solid steel door at the end of the tunnel. Archer could only feel a sinking in his gut that they might be thwarted. Maybe it was unlocked? He reached out to try the handle.

Within touching distance, the handle turned. Hinges squealing, it opened to reveal a man carrying a holdall. He was older than the others Archer had fought so far, a flat cap adorned his head, sheltering two shaggy grey eyebrows, and his face had ingrained dirt and creases, which twisted in shock as he was confronted by the two soldiers.

Archer pressed the pistol muzzle to the man's forehead. 'Shh.'

It was enough. Thick woolly brows arching, the man dropped the bag, the tools inside rattling, and slowly lifted his hands. His lip trembled, but it was just shock. The old man shuffled backwards, and Archer pushed, forcing his prisoner to the wall, pinning him like a butterfly to a board. Miller came in close, pistol changed for bayonet, but Archer shook his head and the American grunted, patting the prisoner down instead, checking his waist and ankles for weapons. It gave Archer a chance to examine the room he'd erupted into.

There was a high-backed chair, the seat very well worn green leather, splitting at the sides, and discoloured by oil and grime. A pair of tall gumboots waited under a peg holding a weather-beaten donkey jacket, next to a table with an ancient wireless, a stack of old newspapers and books with threadbare covers. A pipe lay half packed, with a tobacco pouch close at hand.

'Nothing on him,' Miller reported, satisfied.

'Blackcoat? Kaiser?' Archer demanded of the man.

'Me name's Alf,' he replied, hands shaking.

Archer overcame the temporary dislocation of Alf's accent, slowly stepping back half a pace, lowering the gun.

'What are you doing here?'

'I came on a boat.'

It took every ounce of willpower not to grin. 'No, what are you doing *down here*?'

'Thought a pipe burst in't cistern. There were a terrible bangin'.'

'That was us, sorry.'

'You 'aven't broke sommat, 'ave you?' Alf moaned. 'Please tell me you 'aven't...'

'Just a door. I need to find the Kaiser. Do you know where he is?'

Alf lowered his hands. 'That moody bugger? Upstairs, rantin' like usual. If you want 'im, you'd better hurry. Someone said 'e's leaving soon.'

'Why?'

'Dunno. Lot 'o folk up there comin' and goin'. Load 'o marchin' and bugles. I don't ask. I just work the pipes, listen to the wireless.'

'Mind your own business?'

'Aye.'

Any warmth Alf's honest nature provoked was doused with cold concern. The troop build-up, the convoys of weapons, munitions. With the amount of people available in Antwerp, the German Army looked like it was about to get sizeable reinforcements. If Eisner had been telling the truth, someone in the *Abwehr* wanted to prevent that. Now Archer had the chance. He wouldn't discount that was Garfield's plan all along.

'Where are the prisoners kept?'

'Sorry, I can't 'elp yer there.' Alf shrugged. 'If you're wantin' out, top of the stairs, third door on your left.'

'Going to give us trouble when we're gone, old timer?' Miller demanded.

'Me? Nah. I'm too old fer messin' about.'

Archer patted him on the shoulder. 'You might want to leave, Alf.'

'You makin' mischief?' The old man found the nerve to give a sly smile.

'Just a little.'

Archer drew some fresh cartridges and topped off his rifle. He winked back at the old plumber, heading for the steps.

27:

The rooms directly above the cistern were deep cellars. Crates and boxes of non-perishables were gathered in the middle of the arched vaults. Save for pipes dripping and the scurry of tiny, rodent feet, they were alone. A serried row of lamps illuminated Alf's route down to the tunnels below, a long straight pull following the adjacent wall, keeping the older man clear of tripping over loosely stacked stores or ploughing through rat droppings.

Archer led, rifle at low ready now he had the space to use it. Light spilled across the flush cobbles of the cellar floor, revealing a corner turning right. More lamps hung from this wall and he sensed they must be at the back of the Citadel – the side facing Antwerp. He understood why Alf took so long to get down to the cistern, and why he'd made a den.

There was a bright arch where the lanterns ended, another flight of stone steps leading up, but here the lamps gave way to bulbs set into cages, to prevent them being smashed by unwieldy crates. Carefully covering the landing, Miller went ahead, up the first flight, to where the stairs turned back on themselves. He carefully nudged out to peer around the corner, before waving Archer to follow.

The British sniper took over, climbing the last few stairs on elbows and knees, staying low. He poked his head above the level of the top step. He nodded down and they went up, going into a passageway which branched off left and right. Without speaking, they both took the shorter right-hand corridor, electric bulbs keeping an otherwise gloomy place well lit. It wasn't as damp here, and Archer wondered if they were above ground yet.

A door opened almost immediately into what Archer thought was another cellar, but this room was vastly different from the one below. A cross between a training and punishment room, tall wooden poles ran from ceiling to floor, with manacles and anchor points for ropes. Archer had heard about the discipline for infractions in the Imperial German Army being strict. It was a deterrent against desertion in the same way the death penalty was meant to deter suicide.

Moaning and coughing came from the back of the large, connected rooms, echoes magnified by the vaulted arches above. The design of the place suggested that they were old powder and shell magazines for the fortification batteries, or storage for provisions. Loud ringing of metal on metal drew Archer's attention, and, as he and Miller came through the iron-barred wooden door, they went past the corner of a rudimentary sparring ring. Negotiating it revealed the back half of the training barracks were caged off, with a dozen people either sitting or lying down, being yelled at.

The voice, working in both German and French, came from a tall, wiry individual wielding a metal club. He was beating this onto the cage bars after each sentence. Due to echo and noise, Archer hadn't got a clue what he was saying, but the language of violence was apparent. The bully reached for a man wearing a grubby vest, daubed with blue paint. He could see others, women amongst them, wearing similar clothes, except with red splotches. Their bare arms and faces were bruised and reddened, making the game obvious. Despite the swelling and puffiness in their jowls, he thought he recognised a few of Father Ruslan's flock. There was no sign of Kate.

Finally, limited, broken German transposed the nature of the argument. No fighting, no food. No fighting, no sleep. No comfort or peace besides the oblivion of exhaustion. Archer noticed several pock marks on the walls, and a pistol was harnessed at the instructor's hip. It looked like the occasional motivational shooting occurred down here.

He cocked the *Runebolt*, such a distinctive sound drew

the Physical Training Instructor's attention at once. The man had a thick moustache, which bristled as his lip curled. He regarded the soldiers with open contempt, and stomped closer to the upstarts interrupting his drill, carrying him clear of the prisoners. He drew a breath to shout, gesturing with his bludgeon.

Archer shot him in the face.

The crash of .303 in such a confined space hid the sound of the body falling to the floor, metal pole clanging down with him. He called to the American. 'Take these people below. Get out via the tunnels.'

'Where will you be?'

'Sam is in here somewhere, I'll get him. One way or the other.'

Voices shouting questions could be heard in the corridors outside.

'Magic Man! Over here!'

At the voice, Archer turned to see the Polish solider, Marek. He was beaten black and blue, but looked pleased to see a friendly face. Miller got the keys to the cages and freed those who could get to their feet. Archer hefted the metal pole and instructor's pistol, offering both weapons to Marek as the soldier emerged. He readily accepted them.

'Follow the Sergeant,' Archer said, 'but split up when you get into the tunnels, yes?'

Marek nodded. 'Father Ruslan?'

'Alive and well, waiting at a safe house. A butcher's shop?'

The Pole thought a moment, smiled. 'Yes, I know it.'

'Any sign of Sam?' Archer tried.

'I am sorry. I do not know.'

Archer shrugged. What else could he expect?

Between the three of them, they helped to get the prisoners to their feet, and through cajoling, gestures and shouting, Miller and Marek finally got them going, pushing them out into the passage leading to the cistern.

'Good luck, Magic Man.'

'*Hallo?*' someone called from a door on the opposite wall.

Several pairs of heavy boots hammered in the corridors. How he missed Kurt. One quick blurt of German and the problem of breaching the fortress would be averted, or they could have played some pantomime trick to get past the guards. Archer assessed the situation, would have to make do with what he had. With the refugees out of the way, Archer fished for a Mills bomb, made it ready and hurled it through the door in reply before dropping flat. A gasp was all he heard before the grenade went off, shaking everything with the explosion, shrapnel careening around the room.

Miller and the others had already vanished, leaving Archer to duck back out of the training room, taking the other passageway, leaving confusion and panicked calls behind him. He moved at a brisk jog for fifty yards, before slowing and resuming a stealthy pace. He rolled his feet heel-toe on the outside edges of his boots, forcing the pace as much as he dared. More stairs offered him the option of escape, and Archer went up them, out of the immediate search zone around the training room. The explosion would draw the enemy to the place he'd been, not where he was going.

He emerged to a tiled floor, black and white chequered tiles in another long corridor, but this one was furnished with wooden carvings, framed paintings. Windows looked out onto a courtyard, a pretty quadrangle with pink flowers in pots and planted borders with blue and violet blooms stirred by the breeze. Shrubs and bushes with a riot of colour in the castle grounds were a welcome, wholesome sight after so long in the grey-brown vistas of Antwerp. Nature always somehow went on.

The practical voice nagged him about decent hiding places.

More voices, this time laughing and joking outside his own head, made him hurry into an alcove. Hugging the wall, he could hear the stomp of booted feet approach, and a group of Blackcoats passed his hiding spot without noticing him. He waited until they'd gone, before he slipped further along the hall, finding more stairs, going up. The enemy wouldn't expect him to go deeper into the lair.

A balcony led from the first landing, this floor even more opulent than that below, thick pile carpets, plaster and marble busts of great leaders, or perhaps men of political significance, but he kept away from the plinths, not wanting to knock them over. He stepped into the sunlight, keeping close to the arch admitting him, and what he saw stopped him dead.

It was a big wasp's nest they'd kicked. He saw a knot of black-coated men, recognising them as having passed him a minute ago. They tugged on peaked caps and hastily buttoned up their tunics, hurrying across gravel to meet a comrade carrying a sword and pennon bearing the crest of the Imperial German Army.

There was a lot of shouting, followed by boots thumping together in formation, and Archer understood the quiet before, as a parade marched at standard speed into the courtyard. He knew they would have been there, awaiting the command to move. Rank upon rank of Blackcoats trooped in, wheeling and following the commands barked at them.

A Company entered, over three-hundred men, but he could see women too, all hands turned to the desperate fight on the Western Front. It didn't stop there. Another Company filed in, all armed with Mauser rifles, all sporting German equipment and insignia. He quickly assessed the room in the courtyard, and as the parade dressed off, aligning themselves and moving in tight order, he watched as the square below him was filled with more of Antwerp's bully militia.

A Battalion of Blackcoats. A foreign legion with a thousand rifles.

How many of these bastards had Antwerp exported?

Archer's attention was drawn to a pair of large shutters being flung open, high on the side of the castle proper. A broad balcony fitted with finely wrought black iron railings was disturbed by two men bringing armfuls of cloth, which they unfurled, long red banners dropped to the ground below, carrying the marks of the Imperial German Eagle and some symbols Archer didn't know.

The parade was ordered to ground arms, and the crash of brass rifle butts bounced from the walls, amplifying the noise. They all looked up as a small man appeared at the balcony, his uniform exceptionally well tailored. Bareheaded, his jet black hair was trimmed at the sides, swept over on the scalp. A tight moustache framed his top lip, and he began to speak. Archer looked from him, watching the faces of those below, rapt, half-smiling as they listened to him. Somewhere in the back of head, he knew this was the Kaiser.

The words came in German, and they were wasted on Archer, but they tugged at him until he was forced to step back, massaging his temples at the sudden migraine. He bumped into one of the plinths and heard the rocking of something beginning to topple. Desperately turning, he caught it, but the heavy bust bore him to the ground, winding him. He shuffled over and put it safely on the floor, before clambering to his knees with the help of the banister, and headed further into the Citadel.

The sirens began.

Lurking in the crevices of huge flying buttresses, Archer watched through tall windows, as men ran to wall-mounted machineguns, whilst others scrambled to man observation posts, emplaced mortars and cannon to repel an air attack. He retreated from the windows, hugging wooden panelling on the other side of the corridor, trying to gauge the best route across the maze of passages and stairs of the fortress. Feet pounded up the stairs he'd recently vacated, and frantic shouting ensued. The Citadel was finally responding to the danger. He just hoped Miller, the children or the refugees weren't killed or captured.

He waited a handful of heartbeats and then rounded

the corner; quickly entering a room dominated by maps on the wall, and a model of the Citadel at the centre. Connected fortifications and defences were matched to scale. Every map was exceptionally detailed, lines drawn in red ink with dispositions of the forces available. A lot of strongholds across the city corresponded with his memory of the map in his pocket: the destroyed arsenal, the ravaged zeppelin grounding station, the network of tunnels hiding Father Ruslan's refugees – which the Blackcoats were attacking from all sides in order to purge it from the city. More worrying was a map of Germany with other camps marked with a *Kampfgruppe* flag. Prison camps all across Germany were being turned into recruiting stations. Perhaps the AEZ was the final stop – or the template.

Field telephones were bolted to tables with more rolled up maps, the communication cables running through walls in bundles. Some phones were splicing into extensions, resulting in a tangle of wire across the floor, trodden flat under a thick rug. A trio of hot water urns stood on a bench at the back, and the smell of hastily brewed coffee stung Archer's nose.

One of the junior officers, turned, a steaming enamel mug in each hand. He kept his head down to avoid spilling the brew, stepping smartly over loose cables. He looked up at Archer; smiled in greeting, until his brain caught up with his eyes. The officer froze, the noise of the room hiding any gasp of surprise, drowning in the rattle of crank handles to put charges into field phones, and barking demands for reports.

Archer shifted left, just out of the doorway, keeping the wall to his back. This gave a good angle, putting everyone in the room under control of the gun. There was no way they could get to the door without entering the line of fire. Even so, it was seven against one, and the distance wasn't enough to kill them all. He gestured with the muzzle cap, and the startled officer obeyed, moving so no-one was obscured. Hefting the rifle in one hand, Archer drew the Webley Self-loading pistol, thumbing the hammer back until he felt it seat at full draw. Not even this disturbed the scene. Satisfied with his preparations, he kicked the door shut with as much force as he could.

The solid bang of oak and iron meeting brickwork sill was almost as good as a gunshot. The assembled staff looked up at the door first, and then simultaneously noticed him. Phones rang, but no-one moved to answer them. All talk ceased and Archer gestured for the officers to put the phones down. These men ran the base. They should know where Sam was, he would just have to persuade them to tell him. At least with the door shut, the air raid siren was suppressed enough to allow normal speech. It would also muffle gunfire.

'The American. Where?'

A Captain smiled, examined the *Runebolt*, offered a polite bow. 'You are the Sharpshooter,' he replied, his English coloured by a French twang. 'A brave man, but even you must know you can't fight the central garrison.'

Archer nodded. 'I only have to fight you at the moment.'

'A fair point, but—'

'Where is the American? I won't ask again. Answer or die.'

The Captain looked at him for long moments, searching his face, turning over the threat in his head. He nodded. 'He was taken to the stateroom, for an audience with the Kaiser.'

'Who has the key to this room?'

Another officer raised his hand and then slowly dipped into his pocket with the other, drawing a set of three keys on a ring. He tossed them to land at Archer's feet, which caused the sniper to groan internally.

'Now what?' the Captain asked, with a knowing smirk.

That was clever, Archer allowed. Picking up the keys meant putting down a gun. He carefully handled the rifle, slowly and deliberately slinging it onto his shoulder, left hand threatening with the boxy pistol. He wished Eisner or Ross were there.

'Keep your bloody hands up.'

The Captain complied; the others caught on and

followed the example, lifting flat palms, although not very high above holstered guns. He didn't bend over, but slowly lowered himself into a crouch. When disaster came, it was from an unexpected quarter. The door barged open, a young boy wearing a black jacket three sizes too big for him dashed inside, colliding with Archer, threatening to topple him, knocking the pistol harmlessly aside.

Time slowed to a smooth pour of treacle, everyone but the coffee-carrying officer moving, snatching for handguns. Archer abandoned trying to remain upright, his martial arts training letting gravity take hold and roll him to the side. He kicked out, catching the youth at the knee, sending him back to slam the door shut once more.

Archer fired twice from prone, his shots hammering the Captain in the chest, but as he fired again, the recoil from the automatic pistol took the bullet wide, merely injuring the second target, plucking at his shoulder. The casualties bought him room, the number of the Blackcoat officers working against them, their comrades falling, dragging at them for help. In the gap, he fought to a kneeling stance.

Taking a weapon designed for one-handed shooting awkwardly in both fists, he continued firing. A bullet buried itself in brickwork, a freak occurrence, as the intended target slipped on blood and smashed down onto a table with a hollow thud. The fall saved his life, but the man was out cold. His body lay sprawled across a map, and as he slid to the ground, the map fell like a blanket over his insensate body, small figurines tumbling with it.

Hot coffee slashed through the air at him, followed by the enamel cups, forcing him to turn and fire quickly, catching another man in the hand, driving the Luger from his fist. Abandoning close range fire, Archer lashed out with his right boot, catching the junior officer who'd tried to scald him behind the left knee, and with a yelp the young man fell over, dashing his head against the table leg. The remaining two opponents, one to his left hand side, and another opposite, fired fast – trying to murder him with a desperate fusillade, but the prone youth flailed at Archer's ankles, grabbing his belt, pulling him over, and unintentionally saving him.

Hitting the floor, the impact drove the breath from his lungs, even as the dust drove into his face. Two hard kicks met his left leg, one in the calf, the other in the thigh, followed by a red hot lash snapping across his back. Stone chips tore at him as 9mm bullets ricocheted and struck close. His left palm met a fallen Luger and he grabbed it up.

Thrusting his arm up and out, Archer let fly, both pistols erupting at almost point blank range, tearing open the groin of the man to his left side, eliciting a howl of agony, before Archer rolled over onto his back, just in time to deflect a descending boot from his face with an elbow.

Abandoning the empty German gun, he grabbed the ankle with his left hand, yanking hard, a cry of alarm as the man was pulled off balance and forced to perform a gymnastic split of his legs. Archer finished him off with a chop of the Webley, the heel of the pistol striking the man down and out.

'God almighty,' Archer said to the room.

He rubbed his face down with his left hand before reloading the gun. Scrabbling behind announced someone still lived and he span, his left leg protesting where it supported his weight, his gun searching for something to kill.

'*Non, non!*' The boy's hands were outstretched, shaking to ward off death.

Chest heaving, Archer held his fire. He stood gasping, recovering his breath. He kept his aim, the seconds stretching out before he could even speak, let alone try to plan. 'Take off your trousers and jacket.'

'*M'sieu?*'

A groan escaped one of the wounded men. Archer fired down, the sound of the fatal shot huge in the eerie silence. If anyone else was alive they were likely biting their tongue in half. The room reeked of blood and nitrocellulose. The youth flinched, terrified at the display of casual murder, but his togs were clean, unsullied by the fight, and Archer could use the uniform. It would be a pinch under the arms, but he'd made do with worse.

'Coat, trousers,' he demanded. The ache came, the shock wearing off from where he'd been shot. Archer pulled at his jacket and his trousers, pointing at the lad.

The younger man nodded anxiously, throwing his uniform at the murderous maniac threatening him, and sat unmoving. Archer tore cable from one of the field telephones and mimed the man should cross his wrists. He obeyed, only for Archer to truss him up to prevent mischief, hurriedly changing his torn, bloody clothes and retrieving whatever weapons he could scrounge. He took two pistols, shoved them into his belt at the back. He recovered the Captain's peaked cap from where it lay discarded on a map table, tugging it into position to hide his brow and eyes.

'Stay here,' he told the survivor, closing the door and locking it.

Now to find the staterooms, he thought, before remembering his leg and shoulder. Pain was flaring on and off as adrenaline ebbed. Maybe visiting a dressing station along the way would be a good idea. He backtracked, desperately searching, until he found the red crosses on small boards. He just had to follow the signs.

28:

A nurse was inside, counting bandages and ampoules. It wasn't a surprise, since the Citadel was under attack, and everyone had reported to their assigned station. A male counterpart was with her, but by the armband snagged and twisted around his left bicep, he was a stretcher bearer only. Archer shouldered the rifle, just another soldier carrying a gun – he hoped. His injuries could be explained, and he didn't have to feign the limp.

He rounded the corner, made his presence obvious with a groan. 'Help me, please.'

'*Vite*,' the nurse called to her colleague.

They both reached out to catch Archer under the arms, and he got a close look at them. She was the same height as the man, also of slighter build. Auburn hair was trapped under a medical cap, keeping it mostly out of the way. Tired brown eyes looked him over, assessing. The man was unarmed, short-cropped dark hair and a clutch of scars on his cheeks and chin, perhaps a childhood injury or illness.

The other occupant of the aid station was a body on the only treatment table, a sheet covering it for dignity. They sat him on a bench, directing each other in French, her hands fluttering over his injuries, peeling back clothing. She studied him, but instead of bewildering him with her own language, she addressed him in slightly confused English. He couldn't take umbrage, his French was horrific.

'It look much bad than is,' she reassured, fetching scissors and bandages.

The Stretcher-bearer prepared bottles of iodine and a morphine syringe. He mumbled something, as Archer stared at tumbling locks of blond hair dropping from beneath the bloodstained sheet at the back of the infirmary.

'*Pardon*, he ask what happened?' She broke him from his reverie, started making his short trousers even shorter. At this rate he could give them to Derrick.

Archer kept it simple. 'Angry man, with a gun and bombs.'

'We have danger?'

'*Non*. He ran away. The alarm is...for caution.'

'Ah.' The man relaxed a little, jabbing the needle into Archer's thigh.

'You help the Kaiser?' Archer asked of them.

An uncertain look graced the Stretcher-bearer's face, like he wanted to spit, but realised it might not be a good idea in the presence of a Blackcoat officer. He gave a Gallic shrug and the nurse gave him a few words in a strict tone.

'It is war?' Archer tried instead.

'*Oui*,' she replied, daubing iodine.

White strapping went around Archer's leg in two places, like odd, mismatched puttees. A long strip was tied around his chest, the nurse forced to move his ID discs out of the way. 'No bullet,' the nurse said, catching the tags between thumb and forefinger. She frowned, eyes going wide in understanding. '*Mon Dieu, l'Armée Britannique!*'

Archer cursed. None of the Blackcoats wore tags that he'd noticed, and the British Army discs were circular, unlike French, German or even American ones. He hadn't even thought to discard them. 'Do not shout,' he warned, 'it is a secret.'

She swallowed, shaking. The man clutched her by the shoulders, in more than a comradely embrace.

'Wife?' Archer saw a pale band of flesh on her finger.

The Stretcher-bearer nodded.

'Where are the big rooms? Officer rooms?' he kept his voice low, but held the firmness in it from before. He had to exploit their fear. The connotations of having a British soldier as witness to the war crimes going on in the citadel wasn't lost on any of them, nor was having treated an enemy of the 'Kaiser'.

'*Regarde*,' the man stepped across, past the medical cabinet to a map of the Citadel. He pointed, finger tapping the dressing station. He traced a route up two floors, to a suite of rooms in the upper fort.

'*Merci*,' Archer thanked them, standing.

Instinct drew him to the body he noticed earlier, and he limped across to the sheet, his fingers dabbling in the tumbling golden hair. He carefully peeled back the covering and breathed out in deep sigh. He found Kate. She'd survived the airship and the torturers, only to lie here. A single crimson circle congealed on her upper torso. He pulled her eyelids down with some effort. She looked peaceful now.

'I'm sorry, love.'

'*Monsieur?*' The question came from leagues away.

'Nothing,' he muttered.

Withdrawing from the body, he covered her back up, and then was gone, hurrying out of the small place, one of the few points of hope spoiled by Antwerp's despair. He was a hundred yards on before he realised he'd never asked their names. Maybe it was better he didn't know. Everyone he got close to seemed to die.

Marching onward, trying to leave those thoughts behind him, he reached the first flight of steps, and was met by a party of soldiers led by a Corporal. When they saw the state of him, the Non-commissioned Officer held out his palm. Archer was ready to take his brewing ire out on them, so intercepted the question.

'I must report to the Kaiser! The prisoners have escaped!'

This caused some exchanged glances, but the alarm, even though it had now stopped, had everyone on alert and scepticism was to be expected. They looked at him narrowly, but Archer had a trick up his sleeve, having served with enough bumptious officers before. He visualised Major Garfield, tried to pinch his accent with an Old Etonian sneer.

'For God's sake man, I was just there! Move! Otherwise you're for the high jump!' he jabbed a finger into the Corporal's chest, volume increasing an octave. 'You! Big trouble!'

'This way, sir?' the Corporal replied in accented English.

They broke into a small jog, Archer haranguing them at every step, shouting irrelevant orders in the loudest voice he could muster. One soldier interrupted, asking something in French, but Archer rounded on him immediately, pointing at the headdress and jacket of the poor individual. The man was taken aback by the barrage, but tried to smarten himself up as he grasped the nature of Archer's complaint. Other guards broke their vigil with a sidelong glance, hurriedly shying away as they pretended not to see him. It was working; he was hiding in plain sight.

Oh the wonders of a peaked cap.

He was taken to the stateroom, to stop outside simply carved, but exceptionally sturdy oak doors. The dark wood was crossed and inlaid with cast iron reinforcement, thick bolts no doubt carrying through to both sides. A sentry banged on one of the doors, and after a moment a creak and clank of a bolt being drawn opened a crack.

The scent assailed the corridor, of pungent coffee and burnt timber from a fireplace. It caught and lingered in Archer's nostrils, but he forced his face to remain rigid, ignored the desire to cough the noisome perfume away. Angry German flew back and forth, until the voice inside stepped out, to reveal a full Major sporting the dress uniform of the Imperial German Air Service. He left breast was decorated with a myriad of crosses and ribbons, and as Archer looked up, he knew his gambit was lost.

'I know you from somewhere...ah! *Herr Kriegsmagier* - War Mage!' Manfred von Richthofen beamed, gripping his shoulder in delight, 'better luck next time!'

Archer slowly raised his hands as his weapons were

taken.

'Come in, won't you? I've been looking for you everywhere.'

'Do forgive me, I'm not properly dressed.'

'Yet I insist!' Richthofen continued, enjoying it all.

Speed, surprise and violence of action – the jiu-jitsu instructor's voice rang in his ears. The antithesis of his sniping trade, where the maxims revolved around patience, observation and the considered restraint of discipline, yet all funnelled the killer instinct. With nothing to lose, Archer exploded into combat. Four Blackcoats surrounded him.

It didn't matter. They were close enough.

Smashing one in the face with an elbow, the dull splat and shock of a nose pasted flat registered his first blood. He clocked someone in the groin, but their yelp turned into pain erupting along his legs where someone batted him with a truncheon. He flew forwards, rebounding off the door, desperately defending against a kick aimed at his own crotch.

Another fist cracked him on his right arm, numbing the bicep, and as he went forward under the assault, someone grabbed at his face, fingers searching for his eye sockets. In reflex, Archer bit, sawing his teeth together on the hapless digits. A scream followed, and the pressure released, leaving his mouth clotted with someone else's blood. He spat it out at one of his attackers, but didn't see it land, thanks to a rifle butt driving into his kidneys.

A boot connected with his right knee, and before he knew it, they had his rifle trained on him, and he was staring up into the muzzle cap. He fancied he could see past the crowned edge of the barrel, and could make out the lands and grooves of the rifling. Grasping it was the Corporal he'd shouted at, his face suffused with beetroot anger and blood from a smashed nose.

He fumbled the safety catch, yanked the trigger.

Click.

The man cycled the bolt, confused and frustrated,

shucking the unfired cartridge before roughly ramming the barrel into contact with Archer's brow. The force was enough to send a white flash across his vision.

Click.

'*Teufel!*' Another unspent round tumbled free as the German reloaded.

'*Halt!*' Richthofen barked.

Archer puffed and panted through his pain and humiliation, the temptation to try again written large on his face, but he thought better of disobeying a real superior, reversed the rifle and brought the battered brass butt down.

Water sloshed onto his face, choking him, and he fought against drowning. Archer gasped and coughed as he came to, strong hands holding him down. He stopped to breathe, tried to fight off the pinning fists, but his wrists were tied together at the front, where they could be seen. No chance of carefully wiggling out of the ropes.

Everything ached, and even his eyeballs felt too large for his head. The Blackcoats holding him made sure he wasn't going to fight, and stepped away, boots slamming into parade attention. Archer gingerly touched his forehead, felt the lump. He winced, and the act drew a chuckle from his right.

Naked of its magazine and ammunition, the *Runebolt* turned over in Richthofen's hands, the inlays of gold and silver catching the firelight from the large hearth. Looking at it, Archer imagined a hunting lodge in Bavaria, deep in the Black Forest. Wooden shields hung above the fireplace, some with military devices depicting the colours and symbols of regiments, larger ones with mounted animal heads. A large clock on the wall ticked with a solid step, marking time that Archer didn't have, if he was ever going to meet with Miller, or Nunzia, although the latter was a hope too far yet.

His eyes were drawn to one of the men behind Richthofen. Immobile, and ramrod straight he was a caricature of a Prussian Officer and probably an ideal Blackcoat as well.

There was something oddly familiar about him, his eyes hidden behind black, circular glasses, shoulders swathed in a flying jacket. He clicked. The man at the zeppelin grounding station…what was his name?

'Exquisite,' the Baron said, examining the rifle closely. 'Making Focus Wands is an art, don't you think?'

Not answering immediately, Archer considered the different focus wands, they held many names, but they all did the same thing in connecting an Arcanist to the element they commanded. Some simple in form, like axes or entrenching shovels, all were as complicated as a rifle or steering column. Each amplified the power of the War Mage, directing it depending on the discipline and ability of the wielder.

'I suppose,' Archer replied, but he was watching another occupant of the room, tucked into a high-backed chair, a replica of Archer's wanted poster lying crumpled on a side table, along with a bottle of Cognac and a large glass.

'Holland and Holland, of London,' Richthofen continued. 'Magnificent!'

'It does the job.'

'Hmm.' Richthofen looked up, dissatisfied with the answer, but when he followed Archer's gaze, he smiled in understanding.

Opposite, was a slight man huddled under a red and green chequered blanket, face was drawn and sallow, eyes transfixed by the glowing logs. A curl of his lip twisted the tightly cropped and shortened moustache under his nose. It would have been comical, had it not added to the intensity with which he stared into the flames.

Richthofen propped up the *Runebolt* against a cabinet, the rifle's odd, unevenly stained wood fitting with the dark, forest oak. He took another chair, this one with a winged back and furnished with deep crimson cushions. The Baron folded one knee over another, fishing a cartridge from his pocket. Archer spotted the .303 Spitzer-Brice round, the distinctive rimmed cylinder and tapered body showing its British origin, the sparkling blued bullet betraying something else altogether.

The moustachioed man said nothing, offering only a cursory glance before returning to the dancing flames in the fireplace, face taut, hard.

'It is odd, don't you think?' Richthofen mused, pinching the round between the thumb and forefinger of his left hand, spinning it around with casual flicks of his right index finger.

Archer licked his lips, tasted the blood and salt dried on them.

'Why would the British issue ammunition with no primer, or powder?' He showed Archer the back of the hollow cartridge. The light shone down the tube, glinting on the back of the bullet buried at the neck. 'Unless the gun is actually an air rifle? In the hands of an Air Wizard?'

Archer stared.

'Do not feel bad!' Richthofen grinned, mightily pleased at his sally. He patted Archer's knee in a comradely manner. 'It takes one to know one, as they say!'

The admission dropped everything into place. No wonder he'd dodged the magic bullet, soared on thermals like a vulture. He was an Air Mage too – and maybe a way out, a fellow Arcanist who might be appealed to. 'You control the bullet yes? You feel the air current; it goes where you will?'

'Not quite,' Archer demurred. It was bloody close though. A charged air cylinder inside the rifle needed his skills to make it work, releasing the pressure with enough strength to blow the bullet down the barrel at two-thousand seven-hundred pounds of force. He looked up to find them smiling at him.

'We know everything,' the officer with two pistols and dark glasses stated. 'Prisoners talk. Priests tell me things to stop their friends being hurt. I know you are Garfield's man.'

'Remind me, who are you?'

'Hauptmann Preston–'

'Ah, yes. Did you kill Kate?' Archer slurred, head still fuzzy at the edges.

'No. Regrettably, she was shot whilst attempting escape,' Preston replied heavily. 'I had no hand in it.'

'But you killed Kurt Eisner, didn't you?'

'Who?'

'A friend.'

'I did something right then,' Preston sneered.

Archer fell into sullen glowering.

'Come now, gentlemen,' Richthofen smoothed. He sniffed at the bullet before holding it up to light. 'Impressive. Mercury fulminate, silver nitrate and magnesium, I wonder what the core is?'

'*Was ist das?*' the small man demanded, his trance broken. He became animated, holding his free hand out for the special round, grasping until it was dropped into his palm. He stared at it as much as he had the flames.

'It's the one chance I need to blow your head off,' Archer muttered.

'*Blitzschlag, Herr Hiedler,*' the Red Baron smiled, ignoring the impotent threat from their unruly guest. His gaze fixed Archer's. It contained more professional admiration than amusement now. 'A lightning bullet.'

The Baron took the cartridge back, toying with it.

Archer shook off his lethargy. He looked at the small man; indeed to be confronted with the Kaiser of Antwerp was a touch disarming. They had spared him and brought him inside. He wondered what the game was.

Hiedler looked up, studied his prisoner with an eerie, silent stare.

'You will give me the American,' Archer began. 'There is a treaty between our countries.' A half-truth bled from Garfield's orders.

'It does not concern us,' Richthofen replied. 'The American will be a hostage for Antwerp, then Germany.'

'Not if he's dead.'

'Explain,' Preston demanded.

'If he is not released into my custody, and a signal given

to that effect, this place will be destroyed by our warships.'

'Nonsense,' Richthofen barked.

Preston's face didn't look so certain. Archer directed his reply to the traitorous Captain. 'Two days ago, I sent word to Major Garfield,' Archer did his best to sound confident, tried to summon Byng's bluff nature. 'You will have a report of a breakout at the south containment wall, and a flare.'

Looks were exchanged, and Preston unbent. 'Go on.'

Archer knew he didn't have them, not completely. The enemy had looked over the parapet, he just had to make the shot, get the kill. 'The Royal Navy will be in range soon. Major Garfield told me that if I was unsuccessful, the big guns would do the job.'

Knowing it and saying it were two very different things. The words were real enough, so he doubted Garfield was bluffing; the Major seemed to enjoy offering an open hand whilst his other fist held a grenade. With what was on the line, Archer wouldn't put it past anyone. He cursed inwardly at not invoking Paragraph Ten of the Dispensation when he'd got the chance, refusing the suicidal order. He began to laugh, a bitter choking sound that filled the room.

Hiedler looked like he'd just found out Archer had urinated in his morning coffee, his whole body vibrated and his sallow face went white. He rammed the poker into the fire with a bayonet lunge, coming erect to his feet, the blanket tumbling off him.

Launching into a rant; he beat the air, then his chest with both hands, twisting his head and biting off words. Even Archer couldn't fail to at least be moved by the strength of feeling, the depth of emotion in the man's oratory. He could see the Blackcoats from the corner of his eye, faces rapt, listening – no, *experiencing* the great moment of performance, of perseverance in the face of the indignities heaped on them.

Despite the sophisticated German being used, Archer felt he understood. What did the Allies know of the starving Fatherland? What did any one man expect to do against a unified Germany? How could anyone refuse the call? Discipline! Work! Strength! Belief! One people, one nation, one leader!

With monumental effort, he struggled to pull free of a sucking, treacherous crater, tearing himself from the sight and feeling. Looking now, the subtle glow of power playing around the man was obvious, and he realised the utter danger of such an aura and why Eisner was dispatched to eliminate him. Hiedler was an Arcanist, of a type never encountered before, and a bloody dangerous one. *It's a prison for wayward Arcanists...a deserter's paradise.* Garfield's words, mixed with his own.

He wondered where Hiedler plotted in the hated Manville Codex.

Watching the little man blowing himself up like a bantam at a cockfight, and with the others entranced, Archer stamped hard on Richthofen's foot. With a howl, the Baron dropped the Spitzer-Brice round by reflex. Archer lunged from his seat, grasping for the cartridge, shuffling his boots on the carpet pile to build up the static rapidly. A fleeting memory of performing for men in white coats fluttered into his head. Then, it was a light bulb he held, grinning at his trick, proud of himself. He couldn't understand his mother's worried frown.

The Blackcoat guards frowned, Preston was flummoxed. With all of them several precious seconds behind, he threw himself to the right, rolling onto his side, pressing the round up to his lips. It was difficult without his Focus Wand, but he had air and the punch of electricity, so he blew into the tube, playing a penny whistle. The crack of the gunshot was instantly drowned by a barrage of kettle drums, choking seaside-air was thick in his throat, mouth filled with blood from the percussive discharge. Blinded briefly by the blast of the concentrated lightning bolt, it took him a moment to see what the result was.

The magical bullet had torn Hiedler's head. The intended killing shot scooped a large chunk of flesh from his right temple, maiming him, and tossing brain matter over the Bavarian-style room. His wound flash cauterised as the bolt continued, smashing out through the brickwork, sublimating old stone into a fine cloud of dust. Archer had moments to leverage his advantage, the shock and awe stunning the Blackcoats.

Lunging through the miasma, he grabbed Richthofen, using the man's weight to pull himself to his feet, even as they grappled. Forcing a jiu-jitsu hold, he managed to loop his tied hands around the Red Baron's neck. He kept the man between him and the guards, giving them plenty of room to run and protect their injured Kaiser.

It wasn't an accident – the Baron could speak English, answer questions. He jerked the pilot backwards, heading for the window as the guards in the room coughed and spluttered, doing their best to take control of the situation, make weapons ready in this sudden chaos.

Archer scanned the city through the smashed tower, the wind whipping up to stir the thick sediment in the room. He was facing north, and he had a rendezvous, with or without Sam. He pulled the Baron towards the gap as the figure of the Kaiser was hurriedly borne away, his head being compressed by a coat and three pairs of hands.

Gunfire slashed the smog, spanked off the wall. Archer recognised the snap and report of pistol shots, but ignored them, dragging a choking Richthofen with him, a knee or boot handy to encourage compliance. He felt the cold, empty air behind his back, and in contrast, wet warmth seeping through the bandages.

'You...fool,' the Red Baron gasped. 'You have no idea what you're doing!'

'Flap your wings, play pigeon.'

'Have you lost your wits?'

'Time yet.'

Archer heaved through the broken window, Richthofen in his arms, the two men tumbling headlong through free air, locked in a death grip, the cobbled streets of Antwerp three storeys below.

Two.

One.

29:

There were three of them, their hulls a domineering presence in the swell and toss. Other steel fish lurked in their wake, swimming below the surface. The tremble through the Focus Wand mounted in *Orca* gave Nunzia the tale. She was supposedly in the British naval patrol zone, according to the charts Lieutenant Wells provided at Garfield's order.

She shook her head at the madness of mounting a naval bombardment of Antwerp. There were innocent folk as well as the deserving inside, certainly, but the British command wouldn't see it. Nunzia pored over the coastal map, reading the markings and notes as though she'd made them in her own hand. With one palm on the column, and the maps across her knees, she steered every change of course, plotting it all up in her head.

Confusion pulled at her, an underlying current whisking her thoughts and concentration into deep-running waters. The ships above were just *wrong*. Everything told her instincts of their purpose; the small shoal was likely a resupply convoy, but they were outside the new British cordon. The other vessels were boats like hers, albeit sharks, not killer whales. With pursed lips she considered the warships could be strays, the last, lingering naval pickets before their attack. She had to be sure of their origin.

'Periscope,' she called over her shoulder.

Valves opened while she gently steered the boat to the appropriate depth and pulled the device down from above her seat, scanning. It wasn't long before she caught the ensign of the Imperial German Navy in the glass. She blew out a sigh, pushing the periscope up out of the way. Moments later, *Orca* hugged the seabed.

She shook her head sadly. A Wolfpack.

A worthy effort, but the Allies had five thousand tonnes of supplies for each thousand the Central Powers sank or intercepted. She let her consciousness drift in the current, hand clasped tightly around the control stick. The sympathetic tremble of *Orca*'s hull betrayed her nerves. Nunzia dared not exert herself too much; the resulting illumination from the use of her powers would be visible to whoever was looking over the rail of the surface ships – and they *would* be looking.

The Germans had obviously exploited a gap in the blockade between the Scheldt estuary and the North Sea. Nunzia imagined the worried sailors above, scanning with strong binoculars and powerful naval glasses, trying to spot danger in all its forms, ready for trouble since they were running several gauntlets; from a deadly torpedo bombing to British surface attack.

She was going to have to be careful, and use the skills taught to her by her Uncle, hoping they would be enough. If not, well, they were all sailors, and this was the sea. The ocean tugged at her, the tide slipping down and away. There was no time to circumnavigate the flotilla, and attacking them was suicide.

Decision made, she let the flow take her, the metal shell allowing the push of the current. Deceptively strong, it wrapped around them, slowly twisting the propeller in a tighter and faster spin. The screw rotated freely, a slow metal-on-metal grind increasing as they carried towards the patrolling ships, drifting into a den of killers.

Around her, the air became stained with sweat, humid breath and fear. One destroyer was prey; this was trouble not even *Orca* could bite off and chew. She frowned, needing to get past them, make rendezvous.

Above, the dark shapes circled, then multiplied, the strange fizzing barrels tumbling down. She smiled, though her thoughts were bitter. Someone up there must have been a Water Mage, or was using the new microphone systems lowered into the water. She suspected the latter, the signaller in the ship having heard the difference in Orca's engines to the German keels. Her only advantage was that she could see in the depths, allowing precision steering. Nunzia felt the attention of her crew, and once more the terrible burden the Captain's chair carried. What was it Daniel said? *For what we are about to receive...*

A prayer and a curse.

The first three barrels exploded so close, the ribs of the submarine protested, the pressure around them shaking the entire world. Nunzia urged *Orca* forward, more depth charges raining down, the glass canopy creaking under the man-made riptide. Behind her, rivets holding the boat together began to pop like champagne corks, sheared metal bolts heads zapping and pinging around, crewmen crying out in pain where the impromptu bullets found flesh. Shouts of alarm went up as seawater began to spurt into the hull, drizzling sparking electric panels, threatening the ultimate danger of fire. She wrestled a sluggish control stick, pointed the nose up.

Nunzia had only one chance as the water poured in, drenched her to the knees – blast a hole and punch through.

'Launch!'

Having bravely – or stupidly – launched from the tower, he was now unwilling to see if he was going to be dashed, along with any hope, Archer closed his eyes for the inevitable. There was an odd sensation, and he wondered if the weightlessness was his soul abandoning his body for the trip up to judgement and a harp. The feeling of falling continued, but he cracked his eyes open a fraction, just in time to see both of them settle down onto the ground.

Like little feathers.

When they finally came to rest, he could feel the hard resistance of sharp stones under his body, but they were both alive and unharmed. Quickly, he slipped his hands from around Richthofen's neck, and the man lay on his back rubbing his throat.

'The answer is no.'

'Sorry, sir?'

'You should be, I do not...'flap'.'

'My apologies, sir.' Archer groaned, stood, and offered his hand to the German pilot.

Richthofen grinned as he was helped to his feet. 'You cannot fall?'

'No, sir. My father could,' the cat was out of the bag, talking about it now was simple. 'I can glide a little.'

'Ah, so not the high jumps.'

'Only when I do something wrong.'

Richthofen absorbed the words, laughed when got the joke.

On the face of it, bantering with the Red Baron was ludicrous, yet it was merely the refreshingly honest talk of one professional to another. Shouts from above drew Archer's attention to the faces of guards looking out of the smashed window, pointing rifles down at them. He grabbed the Red Baron, pulled him close to prevent any trigger-happy types getting too keen.

'Clever,' Richthofen said through his discomfort. 'But futile.'

'Where is the big American?'

'Your guess is better than mine. He's loose in Antwerp somewhere, after bribing a guard. The man told us this to lessen his punishment, but he was shot. Speaking of which, may I suggest taking us under the window here? Their aim is obscured.'

Archer obliged, releasing him so they could both stand under a window box full of yellow flowers. 'Why help me now?'

'Just listen,' he admonished, fingers working at Archer's bonds, freeing his hands. 'Get the American out of here, do what you must. It is vital, do you understand?'

'But you're—'

'*Kartoffelkopf!* Just go!'

'You know what Sam does, don't you?'

A rifle shot cracked overhead, smashing the window box and dumping plaster dust, soil and foliage over him. Archer twisted to see where the shot came from, finding a party of three Blackcoats coming from his left. A quick check of his escape routes showed him a small wall to the right, leading behind some ruined houses.

Sharp shouts came from above, in English. 'Archer! You're a dead man!'

Preston.

'He makes big rocks into little rocks!' Richthofen shoved him. 'Now move!'

Feet thankfully working faster than his brain, Archer went, pelting forward as bullets scored the earth and walls around him. He plunged back into a devastated city, heading north, to get to Church on time.

Alarm bells continued to ring as Preston hurried, leaping down stairs, running along passages. He knew every inch of the Citadel by sound, by feel, and the only problem was when he'd nearly gone flying headlong over a bust someone had left lying on the carpet.

Once outside, he could pick up the trail – he had to. It was now just a matter of survival.

If Archer told the British about the traitor in Antwerp, they would burn down the city looking for him when the war ended, if of course the Royal Navy hadn't blasted everything to smithereens. He believed Archer completely. Even if the Sharpshooter was lying, he wouldn't put it past Haig, or even Garfield to do that out of spite.

It was in Preston's hands now to prevent that – somehow. What would the Allies do to Ilsa if he failed? He hadn't even said goodbye, told her how he truly felt. Gritting his teeth, willing his body to hurry on, fretful hands found door handles, and ripped them open. He charged out into the courtyard, heard someone desecrating a flowerbed, trampling stalks as they moved.

'Halt! Who's there?' He tore at his pistol holster.

'It's Richthofen! Hold your fire! Archer went north.'

'Are you harmed, sir?'

'I am well, just go – go!'

Preston turned, knew the direction was to his immediate right, he barrelled on, calling for reinforcements, but only his voice echoed from the walls. It was enough to go on, placing the broken barriers and clods of gravel he avoided with only a small stumble. He suddenly met a pothole and went over, cursing. He needed help, the only help he trusted.

'Max! Here boy! Max, I need you!'

There was an answering bark in the distance.

Exhaustion, like the Blackcoats, dogged his steps. They weren't going to forgive him for near-murdering their so-called leader, nor for all the damage he'd caused, but he had to keep going. He was in barely held together rags, but at least his boots were hanging on. He probably looked like almost any other denizen of the accursed place now. He winced as he hobbled down a rubble slope that was once a cafeteria front. Scraps of the faded awnings poked up through the rubble like bones. Archer felt some sympathy, Antwerp had ground him down to nothing, to match all the destitute creatures that crawled and scraped a living.

Early morning sun stung his eyes as he continued north, stamping one foot in front of the other by force of will and need. He could hear shooting behind and to his left, perhaps half a mile away, the sound a crackle of burning wood in a fireplace, snapping and popping. He idly wondered who they were firing at, but he forced the idea aside, letting the sound spur him on.

Another hour of this staggering gait, and he could see the spire of the church he was looking for. It wasn't hard, since it was one of the few buildings completely intact in the quarter, standing head and shoulders above the rest. He made for it, approaching the grounds with hands raised, to show he was unarmed.

'Good grief, what happened to you?' Maisie popped up from behind the remains of a cherub atop a gravestone, its head and wings shot off. The odd shape hid her perfectly.

He reckoned she'd seen him a good way off, because her bow had an arrow nocked. 'Long story. Is everyone inside?'

'Sort of. I'm really glad to see you.' She hopped over the ruined graves and patches of grass to stop short beside him and grab him in a hug. He froze, unsure of what to do, and then settled for patting her gently on the head, the way he used to treat his sister. They went inside together.

Miller was propped up on a pew, in fact the only pew remaining before the altar. His right arm was in a crude sling, the remains of an automatic rifle by his feet, bent into a horseshoe. Archer approached him, ignoring the aches and pains. The American's head lolled, obviously dealing with his own share of discomfort.

'What did I miss?' Archer asked, hushed. This wasn't consecrated ground anymore, but shouting and bawling still felt sacrilegious.

'Sam. We met him in the tunnels, carrying a sack of coal, of all things.'

'Going to visit the naughty girls and boys?'

Miller chuckled, but it was bitter. 'I tried to force him to come with us, but he grabbed the gun and my arm with it. Turned both into pretzels.'

Archer wasn't sure what a pretzel was, certain they didn't exist in Rannoch Moor or British Army rations, but the evidence more than made up for his ignorance. He could easily believe Sam was the culprit.

'Which way did he go?'

'West, I think. To hell with him.'

'How long?'

'Ten minutes.'

'Get these kids moving. We're heading for the river.'

'What for?'

'If Nunzia made it, she'll meet us there.'

Miller grunted, tried to stand, and Archer helped him up. The American pressed a Colt automatic pistol into his hands. 'It's fully loaded, but all I've got. I'll get the kids to the drain outlet. Be there?'

Archer remembered a thumbnail in a map. His brain finished Miller's thought. If he didn't make good time, the tunnels would fill, and he would drown. He nodded, checked the weapon, pleased at how intuitive it was, and set off in the general direction the US Marine indicated. It wasn't long until he discovered the opened storm drain, and just like rain, splashed down inside.

Water sloshed about at mid-calf level, not stagnant, but certainly not fresh. Archer's skin tingled where the salt and stirred-up sediment soaked him, flooding over his boots and lapping near the wound on his left leg. He halted every now and again in the gloom, listening for a deep rumbling voice, but when he approached a junction in the pipe network, he couldn't be sure if the sound came from left or right. He stopped, let everything go silent, holding his breath.

A pale glow trickled down the right and the sound was louder, not just a blunt humming, he could make out half sung words.

'Down by the riverside...down by the riverside...'

The voice carried a hint of urgency, and Archer moved slowly, striding into the water now rippling around his upper calf, following a bend around a corner, the tunnel ceiling partially cracked and broken, a reminder of the punishment dealt to everything above ground. The glow was stronger now, in accompaniment to the voice. He was close.

He rounded the corner to find Sam sitting in the water, hands locked together.

'Ain't gonna study war...no more,' he finished, opening

his eyes. The light faded, but he saw Archer on the bend. His eyes flicked to the pistol, and back up. 'Please don't shoot me, Mister Daniel.'

Archer licked his lips; tasting thinly mixed sea and river water that now swelled around him. He thought carefully, didn't raise his voice, keeping it matter-of-fact. 'It isn't safe here. The Kaiser won't stop chasing you. You have to come with me.'

He knew Sam was no fool, but he had a job and a reward waiting, and he wasn't about to give it away so easily, nor did he want to provide Sam with any comfort. He kept the borrowed pistol levelled, wishing for the *Runebolt*. He'd seen what happened to Miller, remembered Sam set fire to the airship he'd tried to escape on, dooming everyone aboard. The big American let a small stone fall out of his hands and onto his lap, rummaging in the sodden sack beside him, retrieving what looked to be a lump of coal. His pale palms were thick with soot.

'I can't,' the deep bass of Sam's voice made the sewer walls reverberate. 'They keep me in chains. Locked up, when I didn't do anything wrong.'

'What happened, Sam?'

'I worked in the mines, they were good folk. We'd carry lamps and cut rock until the sweat was boiling off us. That was real honest work.'

Archer took a very slow step forward.

'I used to find big lumps of coal, big rocks. I crushed one, made it small, pretty. Then I did it again and again, just with my hands.'

Slowly, slowly, the British sniper crept forward, as he had a thousand times before, an incremental pace to reach the best position for the killing shot. He would have to choose, here and now, and damned either way.

'I showed the men from Washington. Showed them my pretty stones, but they said I had to leave, go someplace safe.' Sam wasn't looking at Archer now.

He focused on something far away and began to sing again, tears rolling down his cheeks. Light erupted around them as he forced his hands together, and Archer could hear the crack of rock, the grind of gravel against stone. Something about the big American's quiet sorrow found a home in his chest.

'I know,' Archer replied.

Sam studied him, his head cocked to one side. 'You do, don't you? Sergeant Miller couldn't understand being kept behind walls, just because God gave you something special.'

'I wouldn't know about God, Sam,' he didn't lie, but neither would he mock the man for it, 'or having anything special. It's a curse. We're kept locked up to keep others safe.'

'You don't believe that. I know you don't. Why else you here?'

Archer said nothing.

'I want to be free. To go where I want, meet people I choose.'

Sam threw Archer one of the pebbles, which he caught left-handed. It was beautifully clear, and he held it up to the light, where it threw sparkles of almost every colour across his face. For a crazy moment, he supposed it was glass, then his brain caught up, and he could sense the terrible weight bearing on Sam's shoulders, remembered Father Ruslan's words.

Half the world wants him a prisoner; the other half wants him dead.

He had to decide which half he was in, now the truth of it lay bare. On one side the Kaiser and the Germans were hell-bent on capture, on the other the Americans preferred him dead to losing him – and why he'd been sent to Switzerland.

'What if someone kills the goose that laid the golden egg?' Archer spoke to himself.

Sam smiled at that. 'I'll die on my own terms.'

'You proved that with the airship.'

'I'm sorry about that, but I couldn't see a way out. You could let me go. Nobody has to know, Mister Daniel.'

'Right, because a huge black bloke wandering across Europe is hard to spot.'

'Problems go away when you throw pebbles at them,' Sam continued, 'a poor man helps me, gets rich. A guard ignores me; he buys the castle he's watching.'

'What about that guard in the Citadel? What can he buy after they shot him?'

'He made the choice.' Sam tossed another jewel at Archer's feet; it went into the murk above his knees with a lazy *splosh*. Three more followed it. The surreal insanity of a man throwing diamonds away like spent cartridge brass was staggering. 'Take the bag,' he offered, 'for your folks.'

'I'm many things, Sam, but I'm not for sale.'

'I ain't buying nothin'. I'm giving you the chance to live.'

Archer felt the water on his thighs, the weight in his chest. His heart was a knot.

'I heard Miss Nunzia call you Curtains. It because you're fast on the draw, or kill folks. You cut everyone off, to save the pain of losing them.'

'That's enough.' Too close, too near the bone. Archer raised the gun to ward the suggestion off.

'You don't have to hide in the darkness. You got a pretty lady, shiny pebbles; don't have to study war no more.'

'Nothing is that simple, Sam.'

'Then make it simple...Daniel,' Sam replied, looking up with tears in his eyes.

Archer aimed, re-gripped the pistol. He fired until his magazine was empty. He threw the empty weapon down the tunnel with all his might, anger boiling in his veins. He snatched up the bag and stormed from the drain, fighting the current now soaking his groin, threatening to tear him from his feet, to drown him in darkness.

30:

Max led Preston through a cemetery. He knew that because of the strange stillness and the numerous objects laid out in front of him in serried ranks. The dog pushed through the gates, old ironwork squealing on rusted hinges. Preston threw them open, and almost immediately collided with a headstone – a long, arched top of slippery marble. The edges were cracked and worn, unattended by gardeners or relatives for many years, probably even before the war. He briefly brushed fingertips over the name ground into the marble, patting it to apologise for any intrusion. A sniper could be hidden and waiting behind any one of the headstones, but Max kept pulling without any warning barks, so he followed.

Crossing the threshold of what he perceived to be the church, the Alsatian drew him to bloody bandages and a broken weapon. Beyond use, the hardened steel was twisted, vexed by a pair of mighty hands. The buffeting Preston took in the tunnels left him in no doubt Sam, the big American had been here, and yet the sharpness of ozone remained. It followed Archer, clung to him as though the man was the element. A whiff of coal dust mingled with it, an earthier contrast, and rather out of place.

He worried so many scents would confuse the dog, and sensing his concern, Max offered a strange moan of frustration. He sneezed, again, but then a low whine announced he'd got something. Resuming the hunt, Max led out of the church, down the gravel path, taking a sudden lurch to the right. Preston was drawn onto a small trail which split off from the main track; gravel changed to springy loam underfoot, and long grass snatched at his boots. Low branches from shrubs and thinned trees whipped his face, but then he heard the rushing water.

Only dampness and mould assailed his senses, No effluent or offal stench. It had to be the flood-mitigation tunnels. Max lay down, indicating the quarry was close, *very* close. Preston knelt and fumbled, found the open grate and carefully dipped his hand down, brought the resulting slime from under the heavy iron manhole cover to his nose.

'Brine. Definitely coming in from the river,' he told Max. He took off his tunic, made sure his pistols were on tight. 'Go home, boy! Defend Ilsa!'

The dog warbled and whined in reply, pacing in the grass, pawing at it.

Preston lowered himself down the hole, could immediately feel the water under his feet. As he went down, Max licked his forehead, a broad wet wipe across his brow. He had to laugh, but he almost lost his grip. 'I worry about me too, boy. Find Ilsa!'

With a final bark, the Alsatian's solid, reassuring presence was gone, a rustle of leaves marking his passing presence as he raced away, leaping through bushes.

The tunnels were grim, dark, and oppressive. All this Preston knew from the ebb and flow of the noise; the press of air in the confined space; the riot of smells that told him of mosses, lichen, brine salt and seaweed; and the rusted iron bars, flaking paint and gouged, wet concrete – the kind of information most people just ignored

Up ahead, a long way distant, maybe five – no six-hundred yards, a splashing sound, a man wading through water, voices, and a deep timbre carrying the words of a mournful song. If it was open terrain, he would have missed it, yet here, in the confined tunnel, his senses favoured him, focusing the noise. He just had to strain out the echo. It was as if he was behind his quarry, could hear the harsh panting erupting from tired lungs, from exertion. Gunfire crashed out.

It had to be Archer.

Launching into the water, Preston had to risk the tide, couldn't leave the chance Archer might escape. Hiedler was a Bedlamite, but he was still nominally in charge, and the figurehead of the *Kampfgruppe*. Besides, a debt was a debt, and he was well aware of what would happen to Ilsa if he failed, and the Kaiser lived. If the man was replaced, Preston wanted to be the next in line for the sake of mere survival, so Archer had to die, and whatever plan he was working to, stopped.

The old hatred stirred in his chest, the thought of how it would hurt Garfield, how it would spite the British who abandoned him. Above all things this spurred him, put fire into his limbs, and he charged onward into the rushing water, tall cavalry boots keeping the chill Atlantic swell at bay for now. The noise was horrendous, but he forged ahead, stopping every few feet, to re-orientate.

Pistols holstered to keep his hands free; his touch was a prize commodity here. Even a sighted man would lose his way if careless. He wanted to seize the guns now, have their certainty, but his nerves held. Preston would draw them when he was ready. The thrill of the hunt pulled at him, and he let it, pushing off, keeping the walls of the tunnel as a constant guide under the fingertips of each hand, carefully stepping and listening where there was a gap leading down a bend or section of the huge drainage system.

The splashing ahead became more pronounced as the water continued to rise, and even though he was gaining as he coursed the maze, time was against them both. Preston may be able to end Archer with a bullet, but the British Sniper could still have the last laugh as they both choked to death on the mix of bitter sea and river water. Besides, the bastard could be toting a shotgun, and in these confined quarters, no weapon was deadlier, except maybe a *flammenwerfer*. At least with that he could duck under the water.

He almost laughed, thinking of the last time he'd gulped effluent, but captured the anger, let it drive him on and force the cold from his aching bones. He had no idea what

Archer looked like, instead summoning the spectre of Charles Bloody Garfield looking *down* at him, thinking of the cold and austere face of the Intelligence Officer, lit by distant firelight and flares in a desperate escape doomed to fail.

Preston would wipe that look off Garfield's face by slaughtering Archer.

Which was easier said than done now his senses were inundated with information. The North Sea was thirty miles away, but close enough that the odours obliterated the Sniper's distinctive scent, the rumble of river traffic, and the city living astride it destroying Preston's advantage of sound. The noise came from two directions, which meant the tunnel had branched. He carefully patted the brickwork, mapping out a fork in the passageway. Instinct drove him to the right, where something rolled under his foot, and nearly spilled him into the drink.

Preston stopped, water soaking his knees, suddenly filling his boots in a rush to remind him that he didn't have much time. He reached down, groping silt and slime. The floor was scraped and scuffed, clods of moss dislodged. He gripped it, ignoring the congealed algae mess, realising it had been recently disturbed. Archer must have fallen over here. His hand discovered something cold, smooth. Smiling, he knew he'd found treasure in this hunt, so rubbed the little brass tube clean, and blew gently.

A muted penny whistle.

The noise flushed the fox, stirring panicked sloshing from up ahead, accompanied by a customarily British curse as someone lost their footing. Relief flooded Preston's veins, even as the Scheldt flooded the tunnel, driving him forward, both guns blazing.

The heat and blast were fierce in the close arena, powder striking his face, burning. The darkness he'd lived with for so long illuminated by the terrible brilliance of imagined muzzle flash, and Garfield's face beyond – stuck in that look of mocking concern as he left Preston to die. He didn't know how many times he pulled the trigger, each shot driven by years of resentment. He filled the tunnel with bullets, a fusillade to the Mars and Minerva he once served.

When the weapons clicked dry, the sound of empty guns was a sharp echo in the aftermath. Strange battlefield silence descended, spoiled only by the slop and slap of water against the tunnel walls. Preston licked his lips, tasted the salt on them. He felt nothing from his victory, no elation, no catharsis.

Sound and fury, signifying nothing – except the acrid fug of propellant.

'Garfield?' Preston whispered. Cursing his folly, he tried again. 'Archer?'

His mind determined absence, the words bouncing only from the hard tunnel brick, almost mocking in echo. No wounded man staggering, no body floating. Something was wrong. Did he take the wrong turn? He took a few tentative steps forward, feet given only a meagre purchase in the moss and slime accumulated on the tunnel floor. *He should have felt the body hit him by now; the tide would have carried it* – a creak of steel, the smell of old rust and brickwork. He instinctively looked up.

So simple a trap, a blind man should have seen it.

Archer dropped down from the perch above, the metal grate squealing under his weight, bricks dislodged from where he'd wedged his feet. The water rushed over Preston's head as the British Sniper took him under, senses entombed, breath driven from his body by sudden, sharp blows to his ribs. He desperately tried to defend against the jabs, but was well and truly out of his depth in more ways than one.

Preston thrashed blindly, as he had for so many years, but when Archer's arm locked across his neck, he knew the game was up. He felt cold, detached, until he could hold out no longer, and he began choking on the brine through a constricted throat. Drowning was supposed to be peaceful, but the reality was nothing so comforting. Panic chewed his breast, clogged his mind, until he was clawing and scraping to fight free with powerless fingers. All sensation fled, carried by the tide in a tunnel.

Archer launched up from the water, breathed hard, gulping air. He dragged Preston up with him, punching his back until he choked and coughed up some of the river bile he'd swallowed. With difficulty, he eased the man into the water, let him float. He twisted his hand into the collar of his jacket, fighting the inexorable tide. The power of the water was formidable, but even though his bones ached from cold, and his burden threatened to drag him back, he put one foot in front of the other, the way an infantryman did.

Only a fair swimmer, Archer was soon up to his elbows, forced to hook his fingers into crevices, dragging his body forward almost by his nails. He backtracked to the left-hand branch of the forked tunnel, where he'd noticed the string with three black feathers dangling from one of the fixed storm drain grates. Determination renewed in his breast, and he frantically fought on against the rushing tide, only the merest purchase for security. Preston bobbed and bounced in the foamy surface, half sensate, spluttering. He seemed to grasp the situation and thrust his hands out, latching onto low-hanging bricks in the roof of the tunnel.

The chill was getting to him, making each movement sluggish. His wounds didn't hurt anymore, the dressings long gone. Dim light surrendered to daylight proper, the passageway opening out. Salt and ozone odour beckoned, and with a smile, he launched forward, groping for the mouth of the tunnel, he gripped it with all he had.

'Hello? Anyone there?'

No response for tense moments before he tried again, until a small head dropped down, under the lip of the outflow pipe.

'He's here!' Maisie cried.

A dozen pairs of small hands gripped his wrists, pulling with surprising effort. The Scheldt yielded him up onto the riverbank, where he collapsed to get his breath. Looking over his shoulder, he looked up at the broad, tall tower of the Citadel, dominating the skyline. Gaze falling back down the monstrous building, he caught the sight of the band of misfits hauling the foundering Preston onto the riverbank, although the US Marine was doing most of the mauling.

When finished, Miller was above him in an instant, checking his wounds.

'Sam wouldn't come,' Archer said. 'I did what I had to.'

'I understand,' Miller said, tone and face at odds with it.

The half-drowned Blackcoat officer swung his arms about wildly. 'Hello?'

'Who the hell is he?' Miller nodded at Preston, who rolled onto his side and was promptly sick.

The retching was obviously painful, and the waft of bile carried. Preston gripped Archer hard, but was calmer now, albeit still dripping wet and gasping. 'You knew didn't you?'

'I don't know what you mean,' Archer lied. He'd seen how Preston worked during the interview with Hiedler, how he'd turned his head to find the speaker, how his nose wrinkled at Archer's unwashed smell.

'Why? Why didn't you kill me?'

Archer tried to find a glib witticism, failed.

The American shrugged. 'Can you walk, Daniel?'

'I'll crawl if not, Joe.'

'What about this other Limey?'

'Leave the ungrateful bastard here. Let's go.'

They got up to do that, abandoning Preston to try and void his guts again.

An hour trudging across the riverbank was far from idyllic, the cawing of gulls spoiled by a flight of aircraft droning overhead in an arrow formation. Archer spotted the markings of the Imperial German Air Service, but none carried the various crazy lozenges of red or pink of Richthofen's squadron. Some of the aircraft were large, sturdy birds, carrying bulbous cargo. It was not a good sign.

'We'd better shift,' Archer muttered.

Dropping flat was useless, since there was no cover to speak of. From memory, the Fort where Nunzia would pick them up was a good six miles away. He led off, breaking into a march to force feeling back into all the bits of him he hoped were still attached. The planes didn't leave them, following and swooping, declining the opportunity to strafe.

'What are they doing?' Miller asked.

'Following us. They'll probably guide ground units to intercept.'

'They don't have radios, surely?'

'Do vultures?'

A flare burst over the group.

Miller frowned. 'We'd better shift!'

Not even close to the drop point, Archer heard what he feared the worst, engines pumping up the road running parallel to their planned escape route. He was almost amused; wondering what took the Imperial German Army so long. His mood was short-lived when he realised the pursuers were Blackcoats, so he began haranguing the fugitives along the waterline as a score of riflemen dismounted in a slew of barked orders and banging tailgates.

Desperately scanning the water, Archer could see no ships, chimney smoke or silhouettes dotting the surface. Hopes of any rescue ship died at the lack of even a tug boat plying the waterway. A long white breaker trailed a thin object he mistook for a shark's fin, and he began to laugh at how appropriate *that* was, as a glint of glass cut the river surface. He dismissed it at first, thinking it just reflection of sunlight on water, but no, he could see it again.

Desperation lit a fire in him. 'Everyone get into the water, now!'

'What? Why?' Derrick protested.

'You need a bath!'

'Eh? I washed last month.'

'Do as you're told!'

The small group obediently hurried to stand in the water, all of them up to their knees. It was a far cry from paddling at Great Yarmouth, but it was the only thing he could think of. Archer could hear rifles cocking, as he staggered down, splashing into freezing water, struck by a cold wind hinting at a storm brewing, far out to sea.

'*Hande hoch*!' The command bawled flatly across the water, repeated in French.

'Alright!' Archer turned, faced the Blackcoats as they pounded down the banks, holding his hands up. 'I surrender.'

Miller and the children copied him, seeing the soldiers grinning as they marched forward, bayonets fixed. His old friend the Corporal was there.

'You have big trouble!' The man grinned.

A gust pushed at all of them with ozone breath, and the smile faded from the German's face as it went dark, a cloud falling, axe-like to turn everything into twilight. His eyes travelled up, and up, kept going until they fixed at a point twenty feet above Archer's head. A giant's throaty rumble rushed around their ears, the tide sucked away from the land as though afraid of it, and he heard the wonder in the Corporal's reaction.

'*Mein Gott...*'

Archer risked a glance behind, and saw the cavalry had arrived.

31:

Tumbling white manes a yard long tossed and thrashed in a wall of water, a mighty herd of ponies storming up the river swell with inexorable force. As they came nearer, the Blackcoats tossed their guns away and ran for their lives. Stallions gave voice in roaring water, chomping at the bit to finish their drive, heedless of Archer and the children in their path. He gathered the children to him, feeling their fists grab around his back, arms. He drove the small bodies into his chest. Miller followed suit, gripping chicks in mother-hen clutch.

'Hold on tight!' Archer pleaded.

The wave reared, horses gathering to leap a fence, and the briny apparitions nosedived over the fugitives, clearing them completely save for a light shower in passing. Obscured by the torrent, Archer could only just make out the point it slammed into the black jacketed thugs, flattening some as though smashed with a shovel, throwing others into the air in a churning mass of thrashing hooves and gnashing teeth.

Another wave thundered in, the water so dark it matched the stormy sky, and the power of the ocean beyond battered the men in black coats, robbing them of any force or threat, sucking them into the churning depths only to spit them back out onto land. Archer's group was untouched, trapped in the eye of a freak typhoon. Before he knew it, Poseidon's rage abated, and the enemy lay helpless, coughing up water. Their trucks were mangled, crushed into unrecognisable scrap. Beaten into submission, they were alive, but were finished. The waves subsided into calm glass.

'What are you waiting for, English?'

'I'm a little busy! You cut that fine!'

'You should be wooing me, yes? Or saying thank you?'

'Thank you!'

Nunzia laughed, a wholesome sound across the calm tide, dangling her legs in the water, over the side of her small boat, bobbing in the middle of the broad river. She splashed in a playful paddle. Even at this distance, Archer reckoned she looked done-in by the effort of kicking half the sea into a weapon of war.

'You missed me, no?'

'Yes. Yes I did.'

'Good, it is nice to be the first person you missed.'

He chuckled, treading water, because the Sea Witch and her submarine floated closer, and Archer went towards it, the swell suddenly helpful, carrying him. He tossed a glance over his shoulder and saw the same rocking movement bringing in the little brood, until the strong hands of Italian sailors pulled children and adults alike onto the deck, heaving and spitting water.

'Couldn't you just let us walk across?' Archer grinned.

'Only one man could do that,' she replied, hitting him with a warning scowl.

The planes ceased circling, peeling off one by one into dives, engine noise increasing in pitch as they attacked. Nunzia cursed as bullets spattered her deck. 'Get the *bambini* below!'

Miller shepherded them, along with her sailors, pushing the children in front of them, warding them with their own bodies. More rounds clipped the iron-wrought hull of *Orca*, eliciting further bad Italian words. A scream of air, a splash, and a column of water erupted as a bomb went off, rocking *Orca* with a solid hit.

'Quickly, we must go down!' She pushed at Archer.

Smoke began to billow from the back of the boat, and another rip of machineguns came close, and Archer threw himself on top of Nunzia to shield her. She went deathly still beneath him as the pings and clatter of bullets sang around them, close enough that he could feel their breeze. A brief silence was shattered by the clank of metal on metal, before heat and fire savaged the upper deck towards the rear, tearing open plating.

The boat rocked violently as another bomb blew thirty yards away, thrashing and pitching the deck, the explosion nearly overturning the steel killer whale. The aircraft buzzed and whirled away, but another lined up, looking to make another run. To sink a submarine was a fair prize, and one on the surface was the dream of such dive-bombers.

'Nunzia?' he shook her, but when he took his hand away there was a lot of blood. She didn't move. 'Help me! Help!'

A sailor popped his head up, understood immediately, and took Nunzia's legs as they desperately tried to get her below. Archer dropped her deadweight as another volley came in. *Pap-pap-pap-pap.* A bullet grazed his right hand. It was getting far too close.

'Can we dive?'

'No, *signor*! Broken inside! Smoke! Water!'

Pointing to the burgeoning squall over the estuary, Archer barked. 'Go there!'

'Are mad? Storm! If much waves, we sink!'

'Go there, or we are dead men!'

'The planes come! More bombs!'

'Do it! Trust me!'

The sailor crossed himself thrice, and vanished below. It would take at least ten minutes to get into open water, but for good or ill, the storm wasn't waiting. With the *Runebolt* gone and no firearms to rebuff the aircraft, they could strafe and bomb the submarine with impunity. 'Close the hatch!'

They did.

There was one, insane idea – Archer had to let the elemental power take over. He felt calmness steal over him, the certainty and control that occurred before he killed. The boat turned sluggishly, heading right into the teeth of the squall. He grasped loops of rope along the deck, used for mooring the boat when near to a quay, trussed them about his waist, fixing him in place as the submarine charged through the water. The wash leapt up to soak him.

The planes followed relentlessly, vicious mosquitoes, looking to draw more blood. Lining up perfectly on the submarine's hind quarters, they fell into a formation to unleash machineguns and bombs in a single punishing run. Above, thunder cracked hollow and the clouds lit with blinding flashes. A quick glance to check proved the radio antenna was extended to full length, so he gripped the steel spar as the rain began to pelt down. This downpour would kill him if the enemy didn't.

Now all he had to do was wait, even though he didn't like it.

It was going to be a near-run thing.

'For what we are about to receive...' he growled between clenched teeth, focusing all he had left into the air around him, the static making his hair lift, harsh light pulsed a second golden sunrise over the water. Everything burned with painful, snapping sparks, his teeth felt about to explode. He had one shot, couldn't afford to miss.

Not now, of all times, not now.

The lightning struck.

Cleaving through tortured air as the heavens rumbled, the bolt earthed into the submarine, power coruscating across the deck in arcs, cracking and sparking from the plating, blistering paint marks from the metal. The passengers inside were safe, the steel hull a lightning shell. Unbidden, Archer remembered a man with a stained white coat, and glasses thick as jam jars explaining it. He crushed the stupid thought.

The moment froze, and he could see for miles upon miles, travelling the single thread of electricity as it laced the clouds above land and oceans. He perceived the power from a trawler's diesel generators, the light bulbs of a cruise-liner, even the friction stirred by sails and tiny specks of electricity in the flesh of crewmen.

Refocusing on the aeroplane threat, he struggled to ignore the numerous distractions – even from his own flesh, as every single nerve ending began to burn, liquid fire racing up and down his limbs. At least it warmed them from the dull ache of an ocean's caress. He'd never felt power like it. Raw charge was barely under his command, but he braced his mind against the agony, ramming his thoughts elsewhere, ignoring the rank odour of singed hair and burning bacon rind from his crisping flesh.

Sinews boiling, he drew back his fist, imagining a giant bow, pulling the string until the arrow nocked tight against his ear. He concentrated, loosed the bolt and rode the lightning, directing it as he would a Spitzer-Brice bullet, snaking and streaking to hit the aircraft – so small, so tiny. He could hear the scream in his ears, not realising it was from his own throat as he struck. The canvas kites burst into vibrant flame, ammunition and bombs cooking off, fireworks tumbling from the heavens, trailing smoke.

Carrion birds with broken backs.

Everything faded as quickly as it came; the energy, his anger. Reeling, the front of his thighs struck the metal cage of the railings directly ahead of him, keeping him upright as he stared at the falling lights. He was dimly aware of the rain pounding his burned body. Hands pinched his flesh where they gripped him, bearing him up with a sensation of falling like a feather, as the thunder died. Bright sun spilled down onto his face, the storm spent, and darkness fell as he dropped into blissful oblivion.

The fortified manor house had long been repurposed into a college and hospital, sporting several other attached buildings, thanks mainly to the necessary study of Arcanist Disciplines, although Archer discovered the Europeans handled things differently. There was no Manville Codex here, and the whole place felt different to Rannoch Moor Sanatorium, despite being a prison of sorts.

With a ceasefire holding, the War Mage detainees who once filled the halls had all moved on, yielding the walled grounds to Third Army Headquarters Staff, a perfect billet tucked in a fold between rolling green hills of the Somme, nice and quiet for months after the British beat back the final assault of the last German offensive.

After recoiling from the onslaught, the Allies regrouped, advancing rapidly with infantry, artillery and tanks. Archer hoped that this time they'd hold the ground won with tears and blood. Pivoting on crutches, he turned from the window framing the pastoral scene outside, waiting to be called into the briefing room.

Dressed in a freshly issued uniform, pressed into regulation folds and fit, the battledress was a little tight after the days in loose clothes and sniper robes. He'd opted to wear one of the newly approved and issued Austrian style side caps, as opposed to the peaked one, since it was more comfortable on his head. At least until his hair grew longer. He was about to sit down, when the large doors to the study opened, and an officer appeared.

A silver *Légion d'honneur* gleamed in the light. Introduced only briefly, Archer recognised Commandant Delacroix, the former head of the military hospital, and once-mayor of Dunkirk. His staff had repaired much of the damage inflicted to the British soldier by Antwerp. Straight backed, his impeccable uniform was resplendent with gold braid looped over his campaign ribbons.

'Corporal Archer? Please come in,' the Colonel said, his face open and warm. He held the door open.

'*Merci, mon Colonel.*'

Delacroix beamed, closed the door from without.

Trapped within, Archer tap-marched his crutches over the wooden block floor, and manoeuvred across the plush carpet to come to a stop in front of the huge desk dominating the room. It was filled with maps, letters and ledgers, a writing slope and assorted ink wells and pots. It even sported half a mug of ADC Astor's infamously awful congealed tea.

A large Grandfather clock struck one 'o clock with a repeating bong. Archer waited, anchoring his right crutch before saluting. 'Corporal Archer, reporting as ordered, sir!'

Field Marshal Sir Douglas Haig nodded, his fingers laced, immobile on the desk. He looked Archer up and down with a stern glare. Flanking the British Commander-in-Chief were Sir Julian Byng and Major Charles Garfield.

Only Byng showed any hint of pleasure at seeing him again, a light sparkle in his eye. Byng smirked, nodding to the corner. 'I take it you remember Captain Corvalho.'

A pair of long legs unfolded from a deep-backed seat, and Nunzia moved to stand beside Archer in a few sinuous strides. Only a little worse for wear, having been shot twice in the back, she offered him a polite bow in a tightly tailored Royal Italian Naval summer uniform of white blouse and trousers. Gold lace looped at the shoulder and brocade at the collar matched the service medals pinned to her chest. A short-peaked dress cap was tightly trapped in the crook of her left arm, her raven black hair pinned up in a magnificent French braid.

Archer tried to remain focused, but the memory of when she'd found his room the night before was freshly vivid, both of them testing the limits of French healing Arcanistry and British Army surgical stitching. He could still feel her against his skin.

'A pleasure,' Nunzia said, giving Archer a nod.

Haig huffed through his exceptionally bushy moustache. 'Quite.'

'You failed, Corporal,' Garfield cut in coldly. 'No VIP, half your team dead, one wounded US Marine, a damaged submersible, your weapon abandoned, Captain Corvalho injured, and a boatload of feral children!'

Admiration sprung unwilling into Archer's chest. The fact the Major only used one breath in his litany of condemnation was impressive.

'The loss of our comrades breaks my heart, but we rescued the *bambini*. That is what good soldiers do.'

'Even so, Captain, you will agree the performance overall—'

'I was *very* satisfied with Corporal Archer's performance,' Nunzia advised haughtily, cutting Garfield off with a wicked grin. 'Several times, in fact.'

Her rank as a naval Captain in command of her own ship gave her a standing of Colonel in the current assembly, while her position as a foreign Officer made her fireproof. She could say what she wanted. Archer couldn't have wished for a better advocate, but blushed when he realised what she'd said. Haig repeated his huffing objection to draw a line under her contribution.

'What happened in Antwerp? In your own words, lad,' Byng interposed himself as the voice of moderation, eyes twinkling. He'd appreciated the joke.

Taking a deep breath, Archer told them about Sam, Miller and the mission to the AEZ. He steadily reported his conflicting orders, his decision, and reasons. They listened carefully, without interruption. He found a great sadness stir when he spoke about Ross and Eisner, but carefully left Preston out of it.

'They were honourable men,' Archer finished.

'We'll make sure both are commended.' Byng said, solemn.

'A bad business,' Haig opined. 'The Americans got what they wanted for little investment.' He paused to stare at Archer. 'You were damned lucky. If there hadn't been delays to their orders, the Royal Navy would have blasted you sky-high.'

That was partially true. After some frantic explanations, the crew of *Orca* sent the all-clear to the British warships lurking in the North Sea. Would that the Navy had been on time, maybe Nunzia wouldn't have been hurt, or the submarine wouldn't have been dive-bombed in the first place. On the other hand, Archer allowed, they'd have killed him.

There was no winning, sometimes.

'Yes, sir,' Archer replied, doing his best to stare one inch up and to the right of Haig's head. He found conversations with bumptious officers went better that way.

'An opportunity for leverage you squandered, Corporal,' Haig continued. 'You'll have to serve your Dispensation term.'

'Indeed, sir.'

Haig looked at him, sceptical of his remorse, trying to find the sarcasm. Only Byng smirked. Garfield produced a folded paper, that Archer couldn't get an angle to read, but it looked like orders, signed by Haig. The document had seen better days, stained with tea and torn at the corner. Archer wondered what had happened to it.

The Field Marshal huffed, tore it up, handing it to an aide to put into the fireplace. He watched what had to be the Amnesty going up in a flare, feeling brutally guilty for it, hoping there would be other opportunities which weren't such a gamble, and his crushing disappointment wasn't showing. He subtly searched the faces of the officers for some denial of his fears, some sign of another chance.

Did Byng wink?

Impossible, Archer thought. Morphine must be wearing off.

Saying nothing, Haig reluctantly reached under a newspaper and drew a broad envelope. It was thick creamy paper; a type rarely gracing the trenches. He turned it over to reveal a crimson wax seal, proffering it to Archer.

Byng was grinning openly, Garfield scowling, and Haig was blank, unreadable. Archer took the envelope carefully, read his own name on the front when he turned it over. He swallowed, breaking the broad, flamboyant seal with his thumb, working at it gently to keep it as intact as possible. Extracting the letter within, grains of blotting sand fell to the floor. He opened this fragile thing, expansive scents of furniture polish and fine powders wafting from it.

The swirling hand of His Most Britannic Majesty, by

the grace of God, King George V, greeted him. He agreed that his most loyal subject, Corporal Daniel Archer, had volunteered much to the war effort and the security of these British Isles. In recognition for the courage and patriotism displayed in his most recent military undertaking, it pleases His Majesty to confer the favour of the Crown upon his household, hereby granting leave to reside indefinitely within the Commonwealth realm of Canada. This grace of release is entrusted to, and dispensed with our permission by, His Majesty's most honourable representative and appointed special advisor in Crown Service, General Sir Julian Byng.

Archer slowly looked up, stunned, gawping.

'And bloody well deserved too,' Byng said, chest puffed to bursting.

'Hmm.' Haig drummed a brief tattoo on the table. 'Perhaps a small promotion is in order – to keep our Royal friends happy.'

'Capital idea, it'll look good in Dispatches, too. Sergeant Archer?' Byng suggested. 'Sound good, Daniel?'

'I..I..' An Italian elbow found his British ribs. 'Yes, sir. Thank you, sir.'

'And two weeks leave,' Byng added swiftly, rocking on his heels, enjoying himself. 'To foster Anglo-Italian relations.'

Haig twisted around sharply, moustache bristling, but relented. 'Very good, have the orders drawn up. Dismissed, *Sergeant*.'

With that, it was obvious the interview was concluded. The Field Marshal took up a fresh sheaf of papers, his mind moving to other matters. Dazed, Archer saluted without thinking, unbalanced on his crutches, but Nunzia was right there, helping him along, pride blushing out at him. They got outside the room and Delacroix duly reappeared to slam the broad oak doors shut.

The unlikely pair continued down tiled corridors, the sharp tap of crutches marking the cadence down the halls and passageways until they came to Archer's room. Furnished with white-painted cheap wooden cabinets and wardrobe, he could smell the mothballs in the corners, keeping his clothes free of pests and holes. Nunzia's scent was a pretty flower mask to the medical alcohol and Dakin's Solution. It reminded him of absent friends.

'How are the children?' he asked quietly, still shell-shocked.

Nunzia looked at him earnestly, searching his face. 'I will take them to Italy, to my uncle. He has a mansion with a lot of empty rooms. The laughter of children will be welcome there.'

'They can fix your boat too.'

She chuckled. 'I think Derrick might pawn all the golden rivets.'

'And you'll be mother to an odd family?'

Unlike the previous silences, this one was stilted, awkward. He was almost amused at it, having shared danger, inhumanity, and concocting mad schemes to thwart both. Now, neither of them knew what to say. The words, so safe, so easy before, would not come in the pointed quiet. Taking his hand she stepped close to him, pulled it up to her cheek and pressed his scarred knuckles against her soft face.

'When the war is over, you can come too. Now your family is taken care of.'

'I must introduce you. When your boat is fixed, shall we honeymoon in Canada?'

'Daniel!' Nunzia gasped, recovering quickly. 'Now *that* is how to woo me.'

'Is that a yes?'

EPILOGUE:

TUESDAY, 19th AUGUST, 1919. 0455Hrs

Garfield stared into the fire without seeing it. The flames shuffled and snapped in time with things lighting his mind. He stretched, pressing his ankles together. Doctors told him to alter his posture as much as possible to keep his spine from seizing. Not even the healers could repair the damage, and he didn't want them to. Let it remind him of failure, of an old friend, and of a vow that drove him ever forward.

He picked up the letter from the desk, neither his name nor rank on the envelope, just a title, but one which was the most precious on Earth. It still contained orders, after a fashion – the only ones that mattered, even though men should die and the heavens fall. Garfield already knew what it said, but forced himself to open it slowly, the delicate writing paper inside scrawled with pretty curves. He read the final line again.

Father, please come home soon. Mother and I miss you so much.

Sighing, he held the flimsy letter against his chest. 'Soon, Dotty. I promise.'

'Morning *Herr Hauptmann*, how is everything?'

The Captain, once of the Kampfgruppe now wore the proper uniform of the Imperial German Army. Licking his chops beside the man, an Alsatian sat upright on his haunches, both in good Prussian style. The plumber and general handyman tidying the garden didn't even break from what he was doing, simply rearranged his battered old flat cap and carried on snipping the cotoneaster, mumbling under his breath.

'Well, sir.' Addressed in English, Preston replied in the same language, leaning in conspiratorially. 'The patient is at his oils again.'

'And how is Ilsa?'

'Blooming, sir.' Preston looked a tad pink of cheek.

Manfred von Richthofen grinned, tapped the book he clutched with a pleased knock, and strode into the small house converted into a sanatorium. He followed the halls through to the sunroom, greeted the French nurse who was coming out. The Baron reflected the staffers were quite an eclectic mix. As soon as he closed the door behind him, the wheelchair squeaked around to face him.

'Manfred! How are you?'

'I'm fine Adolf. How is your head?'

The Kaiser of Antwerp looked up; touching his face and temple, a huge trough carved though his skull, a large mass of seared and fused flesh on the right side of his face, where he'd been lobotomised by a magic bullet. According to the doctors he had no memory of any of it – even back to the Berlin Beer Hall Putsch.

'I'm...I don't know. They say I'm better.'

'Good, good!' Richthofen smiled, handing the book across. 'Is this your recent canvas?'

'Indeed! Aren't the lines of the column lovely?'

'They are,' Richthofen replied honestly, suitably impressed.

'I worked hard on them,' Hiedler said, enthusiastically leafing through the tome.

The Baron folded into a comfortable chair, listening with half an ear, brain working on the wheels within wheels. He'd already made arrangements with his opposite number in the British Army. The Americans were chairing talks, a ceasefire was in place, and hopefully the end of the Great War was in sight. Yet stirrings in the East bothered everyone, word had reached the Abwehr that the Tsar's daughter was still alive, trying to flee the country ahead of the Bolshevik uprising, which was threatening to spill to into Poland.

He wondered if Garfield would be open to another joint endeavour.

A train thundered into the night, heading south, down towards Italy. He'd always wanted to see the place, remembering the paintings and frescoes hanging in the embassy in Geneva. He slotted the shovel into the coal bunker, hefting a huge load of the precious fuel and tossing it into the fire of the engine boiler with a knowing grin.

They were burning an absolute fortune.

It was a good job he'd already filled everyone's pockets.

'Can I pull the whistle?' he asked the driver.

The driver's face was thick with soot, just like the engineer beside him. They shared a glance, before the driver grinned. 'Why not? Give it a good old tug, Sam!'

The whistle blew long and loud.

THE END.

AFTERWORD

Thank you for reading War Mages: Sharpshooter!

Aside from the elemental magic and some other oddities, a substantial amount of what you just read was rooted in fact. As usual, truth is stranger than fiction, and in war, there are a lot of things that could be called weird, or even 'before their time'. I have drawn information from many sources – any mistakes I make are mine.

The Sniping, Observation and Scouting School (SOS) did exist, and was established in 1915 in response to the escalating toll the German snipers took on the Allied Powers. They had huntsmen, telescopic sights made by the finest companies in the world, and the command structure who knew how to use it all. The figures estimated by Archer are not fiction. A single German sniper in 1915 was taking (killing) somewhere in the region of eighteen men a day across his sector of the Western Front, and multiply that by the sectors covered and you easily hit three digits in an afternoon.

Until the SOS was formed, the British response was laughable. It was down to a few low and middle-ranking officers, mostly with hunting or 'big-game' experience, who never gave up, that the School was formed at all. They continued to push and develop the techniques of the nascent training regime despite War Ministry short-sightedness and some misunderstanding from army command. In the early days, the bulk of competent snipers came from the Highlands of Scotland, or the Commonwealth countries, where tracking, fieldcraft and marksmanship were a way of life, but the pool of recruits massively expanded over time, in no small part to the simple morale boosts friendly snipers provided to beleaguered sectors.

The School trained their students in map-reading, ranging, compass work, personal camouflage, weapons training and familiarisation, and jiu-jitsu. They tested new trench armour models, evaluated enemy countermeasures, the list goes on. The scout-snipers produced could, by today's standards, be referred to as Special Forces; (enjoying the same love/hate prejudice they still do today), and such renowned Regiments like the Lovat Scouts paved the way to lead British snipers well into the future – and forefront – of sniping warfare.

I owe a great deal to Major H Hesketh-Pritchard and his book, *Sniping in France*, and it is well worth a look at for some of the terrible blockheadedness that came to characterise the public's perception of the First World War. It would be unfair of me not to say some of this was due to the changing nature of the war, and the hard lessons that brought with it. The British came out of a lot of backwards-thinking over the course of the First World War, and some of the Generals were actually competent as well as lucky.

General (later Field Marshal) Sir Julian Hedworth George 'Bungo' Byng, 1st Viscount Byng of Vimy, GCB, GCMG, MVO) was a British Army officer who proved his worth to the men he led, and his strategy was cited as the reason for the success during the battle of Vimy Ridge. As in the book, he had a love of Music Hall Theatre, and played the banjo. He was well regarded by his soldiers, and enjoyed a popular reputation with the Canadians as Governor General. A man of innovation and reform to the Metropolitan Police, I could think of no better patron for Garfield's crazy schemes, or Archer's benefactor – and yes, he had a mighty moustache.

Whilst not a true 'midget' submarine, Nunzia's boat is heavily (and loosely) based on the *Galileo Ferraris*, a Pullino

Class Submarine built by the Italian Navy. With a crew of nine, she could make only seven knots surfaced and was capable of carrying two torpedoes or mines. Her intended purpose was to act as an underwater delivery vehicle for diver-saboteurs, to enter into harbours and carry out raids on enemy ships.

These tactics, described as innovative at the outbreak of World War Two, began nearly thirty years earlier in 1915. Nunzia's encounters with the German Imperial Navy are reasonably accurate as well, with Depth Charges being invented in 1915 by the British Royal Navy in order to combat the U-Boat threat. A copy of them in German service is not outrageous by the time of the book. It all just shows how some things have been around longer than we might think.

On that note, going back to the sniping school for a moment, there are several instances of 'sniping robes' being mentioned. These robes were canvas over-garments which came in a uniform, pale colour. The snipers would dye-stain or paint them themselves, adding any sacking or loops for foliage they preferred to break up their outline, and Archer apes this process, albeit for an urban environment. Sniper robes can rightly be thought of as precursors to the specialised 'ghillie' suits we see today.

Leaving the innovation behind, we turn our attention and sympathies towards Antwerp. Of all the victims in this book, the city is certainly the biggest, and whilst a lot of things have been exaggerated, the suffering of Antwerp and her citizens isn't lost in them. The city was bombed by zeppelins and shelled by German heavy siege guns for months, before the Imperial German Army invaded. There were forts, towers and flood plains, but although it slowed the Germans, they weren't to be stopped, and despite the Allied Powers fighting within and without, Antwerp was occupied.

We should also mention Dunkirk, since that is our jumping off spot for Archer and his band of mystical madmen. The punishment meted out to that city is not exaggerated. It was relentlessly devastated during the First World War, but the citizens never gave in – it was awarded the British Distinguished Service Cross, the Belgian *Croix de Guerre* and the French *Légion d'honneur* for their courage. In 1940 during World War 2, there was a mass evacuation from the port by the British Expeditionary Force, and the French who fought alongside them acquitted themselves well. In British parlance, when the country faced one of her darkest hours, it gave rise to the so-called 'Dunkirk Spirit'.

The British and Dunkirk have a long, shared, and strange history.

Speaking of which, unlike the town represented in the book, Dunkirk was never a Hanseatic Port, (and neither was Antwerp – per se, but there *was* a Hanseatic *Kommandantur* there, a warehouse for goods) but I felt it fitting that should be dropped in to add a touch of 'olde worlde' to the story. It felt appropriate, since there was a Hanseatic League Medal kicking around during the Great War.

Reprisal camps, sadly, are not an invention. They were one of three distinct tiers of prison camp established, and the most brutal. They were intended to put pressure on the Allied Powers to improve POW camps in which German and Austro-Hungarians were incarcerated. The conditions in these reprisal camps were awful, poor food and hard labour sprinkled with harsh punishments – the German Army practice of 'poling', by which an offender was chained by the wrists to an upright telegraph pole, found its way into these camps as well, but was discontinued in early 1918.

Mentioning the Germans...the man named as Hiedler is the person you expect, just before he changed his name. I didn't want to use his actual name, as this is alternative history. In truth, he was incarcerated in Landsdorf Prison in 1921 after the failed Munich Beer Hall Putsch, and albeit a failed takeover, his influence grew from there. He did indeed fight in WW1, although he never actually enlisted, he just 'turned up' and served as a runner, awarded a gallantry medal for carrying messages under fire, although this is viewed with a little scepticism even by German officers of the time. I moved him about a bit and gave him a different ending.

How that will pan out in this universe remains to be seen.

Manfred von Richthofen, the Red Baron, was a real pilot and is still well known for his legacy of innovation to aerial combat and sense of honour (even if romanticised). He was a pilot of such renown, albeit not as flamboyant as portrayed within these pages, it was apparent to me he must be a winged wizard! Richthofen was one of the participants in the lethal air war over the trenches, and forced the Allies to design new concepts for formations just to deal with him and his own squadron. In this book he flies the Fokker D.VII biplane, a late-war model, not the usual triplane he is associated with. I didn't specify that clearly, since that would delve too deep into historical minutiae.

Coming down to earth, a lot of attention focuses on the ground combat, especially the trenches. It should be noted that a lot of Sappers ended up buried or fighting for their lives in the deep darkness, very much like Hal Ross. They were men from all over the country, miners and labourers who knew how to work clay, chalk and rock, pressed into service in a war of nerves in the claustrophobic black of a tunnel. Indeed, Intelligence Officers employed geologists who matched the ground of Flanders to the miners used to working in the same material. You can't beat experience.

Similarly, there was indeed a Meteorological Service provided to, and by, the army. At the outbreak of the war, the Met Office offered their expertise to the British, who declined with a line I paraphrase in the book: 'The army does not go to war with umbrellas.' When the unusual weather bogged down efforts during the Somme offensives in 1916, the Army changed their tune, and brought the Weathermen into the war. The Met Office has supported the armed forces ever since, providing integral intelligence for operational briefings.

The combat with the South Staffs Regiment is based

on actual events in 1918, and is part of the Hundred Days Offensive, Ludendorff Offensive, or *Kaiserschlact*, where Germany mounted their last huge push of the war. Attacking across hundreds of miles of lines, the elite Stormtroopers used the morning mist of the first few days for cover, and infiltrated the British and French positions quietly, erupting violently to almost batter the two armies apart. Haig did indeed tell General Byng to hold the line to the last man and the last round, and that is what the Staffordshire Regiment did, not giving an inch despite an almighty pummelling.

Among other skilled people who kept the troops ready to fight, were the manufacturing companies on the civilian front, who late in the war, were staffed mainly by women (apart from reserved posts). Again, the home fires were burning well before 1939. A lot of women even decided to sign up with the auxiliary army services, or as nurses. Several of them were killed on the front line, or in accidents in ordnance factories, and they deserve to have a voice in the book too. The most prominent of these is Nunzia, supporting a long line of so-called military maids (even as far back as the Crimean War) going into service for their nations.

Speaking of keeping the troops supplied, one provider of arms was indeed Holland & Holland, who sold a clutch of armour-piercing, high-calibre rifles to Major Hesketh-Pritchard, mentioned above. I brought the gunsmiths in to do a little James Bond style armoury work for Archer's deadly companion, the *Runebolt*. Firearm enthusiasts will be scratching their heads over this one – it's a mash-up between a Pattern 14 Enfield, and No.1 Mk III, Short, Magazine Lee-Enfield. A special rifle for a special man, you'll have to forgive a few alternative history design liberties. Archer also has some twenty-round magazines, which were manufactured in 1918 by Linley & Co, and yes, those types of magazines (if not exact model) appeared on both rifles, sometimes referred to as trench magazines. Officially they were prototypes and are now exceptionally rare, with only 200,000 being fabricated.

The American weapons are referred to as Machine Carbines and Machine Rifles. That's British terminology for submachine guns and what we now call assault rifles. The Thompson submachine gun was introduced in 1921, and was designed for trench fighting, much like the German MP-18, which is described as a Machine Pistol, a German term. Effectively these names are all interchangeable for a modern audience, but the definitive nomenclature remains at least in technical circles. As an extended note, there are a few instances of Archer 'shooting from the hip' which is not the correct term for British manuals of arms at that time. Whilst correctly referred to as the 'assault position', and generally applied to the Lewis and later Bren gun, I chose to keep it simple.

I did plan on giving the US Marines the Lewis Assault Phase Rifle, (based on the Lewis LMG action and design), which was massively ahead of its time, and looks remarkably similar to the FN FAL/L1A1 SLR, but they ended up with 1918 Browning Automatic Rifles (BARs) to avoid confusion and having to explain the concept. There were even more esoteric weapons that could have been folded in, like a semi-automatic Russian rifle, (the Fedorov Avtomat) and numerous attempts at 'steampunk' style conversions of bolt actions (the Canadian Huot Automatic Rifle, for example).

Contrary to a lot of misconception, semi-automatic handguns were fairly available in WWI beyond the Luger and Colt 1911. The French, Belgians, Germans and Americans all made them, as did the British, who had one made by Webley-Scott as a Royal Navy service weapon, (also used by Archer) and was available for private purchase in 1913. Again, I didn't stray too far from simplicity and familiarity.

Other equipment or devices featured in the novel are also examples of real world machines, prototypes or also-rans. The weather machine/lightning engine is a real item, developed by Mr James Wimhurst: the machine generates electrostatic energy, using spinning glass discs and metal brushes to capture the static charge, which then is discharged through bars and bells made of brass. Upon transfer, the resulting energy looks like lightning bolts. Given Archer is a Lightning/Air Mage, what better way to drop him a voicemail? Maybe it will catch on.

The blimps, airships or zeppelins were either helium or hydrogen cell dirigibles in common use with airlines and air forces alike. Military craft existed for the purposes of bombing, as propeller-flight bombers were still in infancy, yet therefore short-ranged, with the fighters taking much of the priority in flight engineering. On that subject, the Germans were well advanced of the British again, as already mentioned. The blimp ballast tanks were drained in a similar way to that described in the book; and the fuel tanks were accessible (with a bit of artistic license) for improvised caber tossing by Sam via the installed bomb-channels.

The truth is often stranger than fiction.

And on that note, this adventure draws to a close, with Archer resting his weary (or lazy) bones, but the continent is still in the grip of war, and bloody revolution – so we'll see where his adventures take him next. Until then, thank you for reading and I hope you enjoyed this book. Even though it is fiction, please don't ever forget it is firmly based on fact – and no matter who fought, survived or died, no matter which flag they lie buried under, may they always be remembered, and live/lie in peace amongst their comrades.

Lest We Forget.

ACKNOWLEDGEMENTS

The Dauntless Few:
My dearest family and friends who said I can, and should do it.

My Very Important Test Crew:
Pauline, Steph, Bob, Ian, Chris & Lydia (Germany), Simon, Dan.

The Production Crew:
Sarah Dronfield for editing and guidance, Magic Pencil for proofing, copyedit and support, Ken Dawson at Creative Covers for all his wizardry.

Special Thanks:
Maj. Hesketh-Pritchard, Imperial War Museum Records, *Historica Regia Marina* (Italian Royal Navy Archives), The Antwerp Tourist Information Bureau, The Meteorological Office (Archives).

And most important of all:

You, dear reader!

ABOUT THE AUTHOR

Arron Owen

Arron is an avid fan of Science Fiction and Fantasy, having been captivated at a young age by gritty adventures in the far-future, and ensorcelled enough by the stories of sword and sandal heroes enough to delve in underground dungeons for treasure.

He's been writing and sharing stories with friends for over 20 years and has turned his hand to writing professionally. He hopes he's good at it.

Arron has a legal background and an army upbringing, has worked for Executive Government Agencies and has an enthusiasm for arms, armour and the associated military history of many periods.

With his head in the stars and feet annoyingly on the ground, he currently lives and works in England and hopes one day to grow up enough to enlist as a space cadet, or a barbarian adventurer. (No sandals).

BOOKS BY THIS AUTHOR

The Ares Gambit

It is 3025, and the Protectorate holds the Solar System in an unsteady grip.

In this fractious time, Sean Egan is a disgraced soldier, chasing pirates in the darkness, forgotten and ignored by the organisation he swore his life to.

But when Mars declares secession, the Regent of Terra sees an opportunity to cement his position, making an example of the rebels in a daring raid, led by someone expendable.

Promised redemption, Egan volunteers; yet he discovers that someone else is playing another game, one that will determine the future of the Nine Worlds.

Haunted by his past, and surrounded by enemies, Egan must cross a lethal chessboard, in order to force a checkmate – before he is sacrificed.

Children Of The Glyph

VICTORY AND DEATH: Ben Mason, a victim of war, now commands the deadliest force on Mars. A law unto themselves, they reap a terrible vengeance, fighting to win and seeking death in battle.

ON A MISSION: When a ship from Earth crashes onto the Red Planet, spilling twisted horrors onto his home, Mason is manoeuvred into leading a joint team of friends and foes to Earth in a bid to prevent living nightmares overrunning Mars.

AGAINST EVIL: Beset by difficulties, they must overcome mutual distrust and work together when the true threat is revealed: A malevolent being known as Mother, with the power to corrupt even the strongest through her Song.

FOR THE SOUL OF HUMANITY: Racing against time, helped by unexpected allies, Mason battles treachery and chaos, fighting monsters within and without to silence the Song, before mankind suffers annihilation by a menace who has stalked it for millennia.

The Knitted Knomes (As Arran Cable)

Old toy soldiers never die. They're simply frayed away.

1940. World War Two is in full swing, and bombs are falling on Britain. When his evacuee granddaughter goes into hospital, James Phillips has to keep busy. Without money or coupons, he makes do and mends, knitting four toys – which secretly come to life!

As they begin their adventures, the 'Knomes' realise that James can't win the war alone. They learn the terror of conflict, and the depths of human spirit, making every effort to do their bit through ingenious schemes and a dash of stern fibre.

Will Tom and his woolly friends hang together, or will it all unravel?

Printed in Great Britain
by Amazon

34161213R00198